POST TRUTH WORLD

Published by Sherlock Press

Printed in the United Kingdom

Paperback ISBN: 978-1-7390881-2-5
eBook ISBN: 978-1-7390881-3-2

Cover design and layout by www.spiffingcovers.com

POST TRUTH WORLD

DOUGLAS BLACKBURN

BOOK 2 FROM THE *UNCTC* FILES

This book is dedicated in loving memory to Marco Antonio.
The world is a much poorer place without him.

Acknowledgements

To my wife Cristina for her unceasing energy, patience, advice, encouragement, and love.

Preface

This story is the second in a series following the exploits of a currently fictional, yet highly plausible team of gifted international engineers, scientists and agents that form the United Nations Centre for Technology and Culture (UNCTC).

It is set very firmly in our current world. A world of fake news, newly emerging empires and rapid global change. The story explores how events could unfold and how the world could be ordered if we continue to act as we have in the past.

Today's battlefields have many domains, ranging from sodden fields and arid deserts right into our very own living rooms and workplaces. Kinetic warfare now sits alongside economic & political sanctions, and Deep Fakes.

With nowhere else to turn, the Secretary-General of the United Nations has given a Cambridge-educated former Chinese diplomat an almost impossible challenge: to lead a team of experts, brilliant enough to detect, and intervene in, the most urgent and destructive problem facing the world as we know it.

A global strategic game with seismic outcomes is afoot. A newly confident and seemingly unstoppable Eastern Alliance is gaining strength daily and is ready not only to wrest power from America and her Western allies but to utterly subjugate them.

The recently established UNCTC, who were formed, as with all things at the UN, through compromise, Is represented by some of the world's most, brilliant, and capable people. It was originally established to provide energy and technological stability for the increasing areas of the world that have fractured into small independent states.

Now, fresh from preventing a global oil shock and descent into intercontinental nuclear war, the team find themselves reluctantly pushed into a worldwide hunt to understand and get ahead of China's all-consuming strategy to reorder the world. and in an even more sinister twist, to uncover who is manipulating and killing Europe's and Africa's political leadership and preparing to unleash a devastating biological terror attack.

Prologue

nationalism [noun]

Definition of nationalism

Loyalty and devotion to a nation

Especially: a sense of national consciousness, exalting one nation above all others

- *Intense nationalism was one of the causes of war.*

Vilnius

"Hey Herkas, Careful! this bag's bloody heavy you know." Domas, the slighter of the two young Lithuanian youths, was sat on the pillion of the stolen 400cc Honda motorbike. Herkas, a bulky 20-something year old with a shaven head and a dislike for authority, had recently borrowed the bike from its owner. Borrowed, thought Herkas, whose wiry arms strained as he clung precariously to the back, was being generous, as far as he knew, the bike's owner was still blissfully unaware of this one-sided transaction.

Unusually for the pair of Lithuanian ultranationalists, whose features were masked by their helmets and visors, today's ride wouldn't be their typical after-hours' city joy ride. No, today, the bike they had 'borrowed' from its owner was to be put to more serious and determined use. "It's not me, it's you and that bloody heavy backpack of yours, I can barely keep the front wheel on the floor" replied Herkas as, slowing slightly, he not so carefully crashed down through the gears. The underpowered motorbike wobbled and skidded under the weight of the two youths and the heavy bag.

Recovering the bike's balance, the two skinheads now began to turn and head over the small waterway that frames eastern Vilnius and eventually flows into the larger Neris river bordering the north of the Lithuanian capital. They were drawing close to their destination and the thrill and tension was building inexorably in the two young nationalists.

Turning right, Herkas slowed the bike a fraction as the regal Cathedral of the Holy Mother of God came into view in front of them. Domas unconsciously shifted the weight of the cumbersome pack on his back and prepared to dismount. Clad in the typical nationalist's uniform of jeans, combat boots and a long dark grey trench coat, Domas slid off the back of the motorbike before it had even ceased moving. He ran past the long line of trees which framed the edge of the cathedral's grounds, simultaneously releasing the straps on the heavy pack and fingering for his mobile phone in his pocket.

The youths had timed their attack to achieve maximum effect. The date was the 8th of September 2018 and Vilnius' principle Russian Orthodox Cathedral was celebrating the Nativity of the Mother of God. It was 0930 in the morning, and not uncommonly for this Orthodox Church, many of the worshipers from the morning Matins service were still in the church even though the following Eucharist service had already begun.

Bursting through the heavy oak doors, Domas released the draw cord surrounding the neck of the backpack and summoning all of his considerable strength, he hurled the backpack high into the air above the heads of the assembled mass of mainly Russian worshipers. As the dirty olive-green backpack struck the ground, dozens of pairs of eyes turned and stared in stunned disbelief. Six large metal cylinders burst from the pack and skittled and hissed menacingly along the hard stone floor. The cylinders swirled and danced their way amongst the petrified congregation.

Unlike many western churches, this orthodox cathedral had no chairs. It was just as their mystery benefactor had informed them. Today's special service had meant that the church would be full to capacity. Jammed together in holy communion the congregation stood as one in a tightly-packed assembly, seemingly riveted to the cold stone floor like giant uncomprehending neolithic icons. Nearly 400 pairs of eyes, young and old alike now stared back towards the entrance as the spinning metal cylinders, whirled and clanked their way across the hard smooth church floor.

Domas stood defiantly in front of the petrified congregation, arms raised, framed by the clear blue sky streaming in from the large doorway behind him. "Lietuva Lietuviams" Lithuania for Lithuanians, he bellowed victoriously. Stepping backwards he strained to close the heavy oaken doors then keyed the send button on his mobile phone. Domas was already straddling the back of the Honda as the first of the canisters detonated.

The canisters were crude but effective devices. The outer casings had been hand-machined with a series of grooves spread barely 1cm apart running around their circumference. These grooves were designed to subtly weaken the structural integrity of the canisters, which served to endow the homemade devices with the same devastating killing effect as a fragmentation grenade.

The outer shell casing would shatter into tiny splinters of coarse white-hot metal as the tightly-packed explosive inside detonated. The interior of the canisters held only a relatively small amount of plastic explosive. The rest of the canister's interior cavity had been filled with gasoline and polystyrene.

The random distribution of the scattered devices coupled with the Cathedral's hard stone floor would only serve to magnify the effect of the bombs. The initial blast released a thick cloud of fuel vapour and thousands of tiny vicious steel fleshettes, which ricocheted off the heavy stone pillars and floor tearing deep lacerations into the exposed innocent flesh of the uncomprehending worshipers.

The heavy sticky gasoline mixture quickly coalesced to form a napalm-like coating on the clothes and skin of the congregation, as well as creating a slick slippery surface on the smooth stone floor. Before their brains had time to register the intense pain caused by the tiny steel fragments, a brilliant flash ignited the gasoline and polystyrene mixture, temporarily blinding the worshipers as, in their attempt to escape the inferno, they blindly slid and slipped over each other on the slick hard Cathedral floor.

"Ride Herkas, Ride" The Honda, skidding to gain traction in the damp autumn weather, raced away north and then west through the town towards the university campus. Their mysterious contact and benefactor had told them to ditch the bike at the university campus where a small blue sedan would be waiting for them to drive out of town. Herkas, drove carefully sticking to the speed limit. Sat behind Herkas, adrenalin coursing through his veins, Domas did all that was humanly possible not to keep looking back over his shoulder every time he heard a police siren.

It was Sunday and the university car park was almost empty as they entered. Herkas brought the old Honda to a stop by the side of the only other vehicle, a blue VW sedan. Both boys climbed off the bike and no longer able to supress their elation, turned to hug each other. The two ultranationalist skinheads had done it. They had struck a real blow for Lithuania. Not the usual banal petrol bomb through the letter box of an asylum seeker's door, no, this was a strike at the true threat to Lithuanian independence.

"That was fucking awesome, did you hear that shit explode man?" Domas, was jumping up and down in the car park, screaming at the top of his lungs. Having already spent considerable time as a guest of the Lithuanian Government inside one of Lithuania's correctional facilities for aggravated assault, Herkas, the older and bulkier of the two youths had been more suspicious than the younger Domas, when they had first been contacted by their anonymous patron, who claimed he could help the Ultranationalist cause to 'strike a real blow against the Russians'. "Hey Domas, shut the fuck up right. Are you trying to get us caught?" "I told you he would come through, didn't I?"

They had never actually met their benefactor, all communication had been through an online chat forum, but he'd certainly delivered the goods thought Herkas. "We need to keep moving, we will not be safe until we are out of Vilnius" Herkas said as he released Domas. Climbing into the small blue VW, Domas, with a huge grin on his face, looked over at his friend as he placed his thumb and index finger onto the worn plastic end of the car's ignition key and twisted it.

The car erupted into a fireball, lifting several feet off the ground before crashing back down to the car park floor. The blast caused by the tightly packed ball bearings embedded in the military plastic explosive, shredded the car's interior, slicing through the boys' clothes and flesh, finally blowing out the car's windows.

The subsequent medical examiner's report would be a brief one, describing two adult males, probably, between 20 and 30 years old. - Cause of death, well what could one say, was it the dismembering shock of the initial explosion that had killed them first, or was it the flash-burning caused by some petrol-based accelerant?

The few unburnt patches of skin that remained, showed signs of tattooing. A fragment of what looked like a swastika was found on the severed hand of one of the corpses and 'Lietuva Lietuviams' was partially visible on the sleeve of the lower arm of one of the victims. The Examiner knew that given this amount of trauma, it was highly unlikely that the corpses would ever be identified.

outgun [verb]

Definition of outgun

To surpass in firepower

broadly: outdo

- *First airborne division was heavily outgunned by German forces.*

Lithuanian - Belarussian Border

Consisting of just three fighting Brigades, the Lithuanian Defence Forces were, by any measure small. Despite being fiercely proud of their relatively recent independence from the now defunct USSR, the Lithuanian government, like so many European governments, knew that if it were ever seriously threatened, it would be completely reliant on their western neighbours' commitment to Article 5 of NATO's Collective Defence Treaty.

Recent provocative behaviour by Russia had led to a strained relationship between Vilnius and NATO. This relationship had only improved marginally by a distinctly reluctant token support package being offered by NATO. A small under-strength German – led Battle Group had been based in the country to counter the Russian aggression. An increasingly nervous Lithuania dissatisfied by this pitiful show of force had deliberately stoked nationalist anti-Russian sentiments amongst its youth as it was forced to begin to rely more heavily on its own National Defence Volunteer Forces. The most elite element of these rapidly growing Volunteer Forces were the reconnaissance troops of the Aukštaitija Light Infantry Brigade.

For three weeks now, Matis and his best friend Lukas had been entrenched on the side of a shallow forward-facing slope along the border of a pine forest less than 500m from the Belorussian border. Matis and Lukas' unit had been on high alert for the entire period of the Russian and Belorussian annual joint exercises.

As Elite Brigade Reconnaissance troops, the two young men specialised in the art of infiltrating, unseen into a position close to the enemy and observing them for weeks, if necessary, whilst remaining undetected. This often involved the painfully slow ingress of a small heavily-laden 4-man team by foot into an area, followed by many hours of back-breaking trench digging and camouflaging at night until the hide was set up and the small team were in a position to observe and report back on enemy troop movements.

Matis, was a ruddy faced and fiery tempered 24-year-old who had just gained his corporal stripes. Unfortunately, Lukas, one-year junior to him, was once again back in the rank of Private, having recently had a fight in the Company bar with his platoon Sergeant. Lukas was by far the better soldier, a farmer's son, from the east of Kaunas, he was a tall rangy lad with broad shoulders and huge shovel-like hands. His best friend Matis was a short powerfully built city boy from Kaunas, and as with nearly all of the young men and women who had volunteered for the reserve forces, was fervently patriotic and despised the increasing Russian interference and influence in his country.

This particular exercise had demanded far more from the youths' patience than usual. Normally they worked with another two corporals from their platoon in a four-man cell, but because of the increased Russian posturing and the threat posed by the new Russian next-generation main battle tank, the Armata, it had been decided by those higher up the food chain, that the two young recce troops should be joined in their hide by two German soldiers from the 1,000 strong NATO reinforcement unit recently based in Lithuania.

The German soldiers were not recce troops, they were infantry anti-tank troops, who specialised in using the new Javelin anti-tank missile. For Matis and Lukas the two-week long exercise, buried away in the tiny 4-man trench had been all but unbearable. The two Germans were clumsy and noisy in the hide, but it was their arrogance that really annoyed Matis and Lukas.

They simply refused to be told what to do by the Lithuanians. Being professional soldiers, they looked down on the Lithuanian reservists, and this had nearly caused the four men to come to blows several times in the last few days. The atmosphere in the trench was growing worse by the day, the only consolation being that the exercise was due to finish in two days' time.

The exercise was due to end straight after the joint annual Russian / Belarussian exercise concluded and Matis and Lukas couldn't wait. The task they had been given was to all intents and purposes a simple one, observe and report on the Russian troop movements, calculate enemy strengths and build up a battle plan of their intentions and capabilities.

Although it was only an exercise, the Lithuanians took it very seriously, recording every detail of what they saw through their high-powered scopes and thermal imaging equipment. Meanwhile, their German counterparts seemed happy to sit at the back of their trench stuck in a repetitive cycle of eating, sleeping, playing cards and complaining.

It was 2pm and Matis had just taken over watch from Lukas. Rubbing his eyes to clear the sleep from them he tried once more to focus through his periscopic binoculars. He thought he had noticed small, seemingly random smoke plumes in the distance, but he could have been mistaken. Checking the graticules on the lens of his binoculars he estimated the smoke to be about 1km south of the border.

Until now the large Russian combat formations over the border hadn't ventured too close to their observation area and Matis' heart skipped a beat. Would he be the first to catch a glimpse of the new Russian super tank? Excitedly, he scribbled his observations in his report book and turned briefly to the back of the trench to get Lukas' attention. "Lukas" he whispered. "Come back here and have a look". Lukas who had been crawling into his sleeping bag, groaned audibly and reluctantly complied, unzipping his sleeping bag and crawling back over the two sleeping Germans to the front of the trench.

Matis looked once more into the binoculars before handing them to Lukas. This time he noticed that the small random smoke plumes had organised themselves into a neat line and seemed to be rolling closer to the Lithuanian border. Moving to allow Lukas to see, with a broad grin on his face he said. "I think its them. The new Russian tanks" Both boys were excited, they would be the first in their unit, indeed, the first in the entire Lithuanian Land Forces probably, to have seen the tank in action. When Lukas removed his face from the binoculars, he had stopped smiling.

"Wake the Germans, now!" he urged "I want them to set up their anti-tank missile, we need to measure the distance accurately and report this back to HQ." "We can't" replied Matis. "The Major will kill us. We are not supposed to break radio silence and give away our position. This is only an exercise Lukas." Lukas, the larger of the two youths, seized Matis by the collar with his huge hands and forced the other boy's head back into the eye pieces of the binoculars.

"What do you see?" he whispered, his mouth only inches from Matis' ear. "We have a Regiment of next generation Russian main battle tanks in column formation heading towards the Lithuanian border at nearly 50km per hour. Doesn't that strike you as strange? Do you want to be the one to explain to the Major? how we laid here and idly watched as Russia invaded Lithuania?"

Still unable to believe what he was seeing and reluctant to give the order to break radio silence he wavered. "Maybe… they are just lost?" "Impossible!" hissed Lukas, "they are heading in column formation, at speed, down a public road towards a well sign-posted border crossing!"

Just as Matis was diving towards the back of the trench rousing the German anti-tank soldiers on his way to the radio set, a shrill screeching noise filled their ears followed by an ear-splitting explosion. It seemed to Lukas that the earth itself was going to swallow him up.

The entire rear of the carefully camouflaged trench wall collapsed in on top of one of the Germans who was unlucky enough to still be in his sleeping bag. The reinforced steel picquets, that had been supporting the back of the trench, now sat like deformed and twisted stumps, pointing uselessly up into the forest above.

Lukas, sat frozen in horror, looking out of the now open back of his trench as the creeping Russian heavy artillery barrage worked its devastating way up the forward slope behind his position. "No this can't be happening. Matis, Matis!" Matis did not reply. Looking back, Lukas saw his friend's silent body laying lifeless at the back of the trench.

Matis' skull, pinned down by the weight of the heavy earthen trench roof had been squeezed against the hard steel casing of the radio set. Lukas' normally ruddy complexion turned a deep crimson with rage. He reached behind him and with the help of the one remaining German soldier, he dragged the large and unwieldy Javelin anti-tank weapon to the forward edge of the trench.

Although much lighter and more compact than its predecessor, the MILAN missile system, the Command Launch Unit and missile of the new Javelin system still weighed nearly 25kg, Lukas' breathing was hard and laboured, not only with the exertion of dragging the heavy missile over the trench debris but also due to the massive adrenalin dump that had begun coursing through his veins after the shock of the artillery bombardment and after seeing his best friend Matis die.

"Jürgen!" Lukas was speaking only inches away from Jürgen's face, trying to shout over the noise of the deafening heavy artillery barrage. "How do we fire this thing?" Jürgen, stared back at Lukas, his eyes wide and unblinking. He seemed unable to speak. His senses slowly stirring, he began to speak. "We need two people to fire," he stammered, "I have only practiced on the simulator. I have never fired a real missile before."

The sound of small arms fire interrupted Lukas' thoughts, the Russian tank column had just breached the Lithuanian Police Border Check point. Raking gunfire from the heavy calibre remote controlled machine guns mounted on the turrets of the Armata tank had made short work of the lightly armed checkpoint.

"Look at me Jürgen." demanded Lukas, both men knew they could not stop the column of armour and supporting artillery from overwhelming their position, but they were not going down without making the Russians pay for their arrogance. Breathing heavily, Lukas asked Jürgen once more what they needed to do.

"OK, OK," replied Jürgen, he had now just about recovered his senses from the initial attack and was starting to organise his thoughts. "Once we fire the missile it is self-guiding, I will load the missile and select the top-down attack mode, but then you will have to fire the missile, because I need to use the target locating equipment to acquire the target lock before sending the information to the firing unit." "Get on with it man!" was all Lukas could say as the earth around them began to tremble with the deafening rumble and clatter from the approaching tanks.

Jurgen loaded the missile and dialled-in the top-down attack mode, this mode was unique to the Javelin missile, it meant that instead of trying to penetrate the thicker armour on the front or sides of the tank, the missile would fly first vertically up above the target, then screech down and impact with its 8.4kg armour defeating charged warhead onto the weaker top side of the tank.

"Here," Jürgen said. "keep the firing unit aimed at the column, once I have locked onto a tank I will tell you to fire, lift up that cap and squeeze the trigger then prepare to reload." Lukas nodded and squeezed the firing unit tightly into his shoulder whilst pushing his eye tightly into the viewfinders rubber surround.

Clutching the two black handgrips and placing his eyes to the optical sight, Lukas immediately noticed how well balanced the launcher was. "OK Lukas, relax a little and keep the launcher on the target." It felt surreal to Lukas, it was like operating a video game. It was only the increasing rumble and intense vibrations being caused by the Russian armour churning up the earth in the flat ground in front of them, coupled with the rolling heavy artillery barrage that dragged Lukas back to the present.

"Lukas, lead tank, fire!" Jürgen screamed into his ear. This was it, thought Lukas, lifting the hard plastic protective cap and depressing the trigger Lukas felt a surge of power through his right shoulder as the pre-booster rocket ignited.

Initially Lukas thought the weapon had misfired. The warhead seemed to creep out of the launch tube, then hung, almost suspended in the air, before the main rocket booster ignited. Lukas still clung tightly to the plastic handgrips squeezing the rubber eyepiece tight against his eye.

Jürgen was shaking Lukas and shouting at him, but Lukas, still dazed from the launch, couldn't comprehend what the German wanted. "We need to reload, give me the launcher." Ignoring the German, Lukas remained transfixed on the missile's sighting system, his eyes tracked the missile as it arced gracefully into the air above the lead Armata tank which had just left the road and begun to speed up the hill towards what was left of their now visibly vulnerable position.

He watched the warhead reach the apogee of its parabolic arc and begin its falcon-like fall onto its prey. Slowly at first, then with increasing speed and menace towards the Russian tank. Just before the warhead struck the tank, the huge Russian beast seemed to spit a white-hot shower of tiny particles high into the surrounding air above its turret. The anti-tank missile exploded creating a red-hot blast searing an indelible image into Lukas' retinas as he sat still staring at the explosion through the Javelin's x4 sight system.

Jürgen had stopped shaking Lukas and sat quietly surveying the scene in front of them. Something was wrong with the picture in front of him. Jürgen's mind was racing through a checklist of the missile launch procedure that had been drilled into him by his instructors. – Missile fitted, Top-down attack mode selected, Target acquired, Coordinates sent to firing unit, Successful launch, Detonation – Check, Check, Check. Then why the hell was this terrifying Russian monster still thrashing and crawling relentlessly up the hill towards their trench?

No time to reload. The tank was now only 50 metres from their trench when the turret-mounted remotely operated chain gun began to fire. The heavy 50 calibre rounds began striking the hard-packed earthen mound in front of the trench. Turning in unison, Lukas and

Jurgen both stared in fear and desperation at the open back of the trench which had already taken a hit from a Russian artillery shell and collapsed on top of their two colleagues.

Trapped inside this earthen coffin, was his best friend Matis, laying lifeless on top of the crushed radio set, Lukas felt the desperation and fear take over his body. Barely had this emotion registered in his brain than the Russian gunner found his mark and the dense uranium-tipped rounds tore through the light metal trench supports and filled the inside of the trench with lethal lumps of highly-dense metal, that ripped through everything they came into contact with, including the two young men.

contingency [noun]

Definition of contingency

An event, such as an emergency, that may but is not certain to occur

- *We have to have a contingency plan and be ready for the next emergency.*

Cabinet Office Briefing Room Alpha (COBRA) Meeting, Downing Street, London

"It's a bloody mess that's what it is." reiterated the British Foreign Secretary to the Prime Minister and the Heads of the British Ministry of Defence. His heavily jowled face quivered as he spoke. The Foreign Secretary, a product of Eton and Oxford, had spent his twenties as a subaltern in the Scots Guards, and had seen action in many of the bitter little wars of Independence which had marked Britain's gradual decline from a pre-war global power to a nation of far lesser ambition and standing.

The Prime Minister, some fifteen years younger than his Foreign Secretary, appeared far more composed than the Foreign Secretary, he was a more progressive politician, and a strong advocate of a more connected and globalised world. He had been a mere schoolboy during the dying days of the Cold War and as such, he lacked such first-hand memories and experiences of the realities of Russian belligerence.

Turning to the defence minister, calmly he said "Toby, please give us the latest update." The defence minister nervously licked his lips and with one eye on the Chief of MI6, who sat owl-like in one corner, he briefed the assembled heads. "At 2pm today in Vilnius, a bomber claiming to be a Lithuanian Ultranationalist entered a Cathedral packed with ethnic Russians and detonated a series of incendiary bombs filled with shrapnel. At last count the death toll was 165, with dozens more severely wounded." The Minister noted the look of disgust curl around the edge of the Prime minister's lips as he recounted the gruesome details.

"The reaction by the Russian Government was swift, they immediately mobilised their exercising troops in neighbouring Belorussia and invaded Lithuania. They quickly and convincingly overwhelmed the Lithuanian Forces and as at midnight GMT they have taken and still hold a land corridor connecting Belorussia with the Russian-owned enclave in Kaliningrad. A state of curfew has been declared in the Russian controlled territory and all ethnic Russian citizens are being 'asked' to move immediately into the Russian protected area." The irony of his words was not lost on anyone around the table. After Ukraine, everybody was fully aware of what it meant to be 'asked' by the Russian military to leave your home.

Putting down his briefing paper, and glad to be out of the intense gaze of the MI6 Chief, the defence minister turned to the Chief of the Defence Staff, General Sir Rupert Heeringly. "Gentlemen, the NATO units stationed in Lithuania, were taken completely by surprise and surrendered after being surrounded by vastly superior Russian forces."

Barely able to disguise his disdain, at the mention of superior forces, the Foreign Secretary, guffawed and mumbled something unintelligible, yet loud enough to make his feelings known, under his breath. Fixing his Foreign Secretary with a withering stare, the Prime Minister interrupted.

"Please continue Sir Rupert." "The situation is, err, challenging to say the least Sir, enemy forces occupying Lithuanian territory are at least three full armoured divisions in strength and NATO satellite imagery shows that they appear to be equipped with the latest Russian main battle tanks. Of course, that doesn't include the considerable Russian land, sea, air and missile forces that have been mobilised from their garrisons in the Kaliningrad enclave. Our latest intelligence reports their ground troops being mobilised along the Lithuanian and Polish border with increased air and sea patrols."

The General flicked briskly through a series of situational maps as he spoke. "We have mobilised our Rapid Reaction Brigade and they are sat, as we speak, at RAF Brize Norton awaiting orders. I feel I must add a codicil Prime Minister." The General looked questioningly at his boss, the Defence Secretary, and received a barely perceptible nod as approval to continue.

"The past several consecutive years of swingeing defence cuts has left us in a rather parlous state I am afraid. Our Rapid Reaction Brigade is, in reality 1 Parachute Battalion, 1 Battery of light Guns, a Squadron of Engineers and a troop of light tanks. I think you will all agree that this force may well not send the correct signal of intent to the Russians." The General left this final phrase hanging as he peered over his glasses at the assembled group.

The PM's demeanour had changed somewhat, his skin had developed a distinct ashen grey pallor as the true scale of the problem finally struck him. Uninvited, the MI6 Chief rose and addressed the room. C, as he was known, very rarely spoke at these meetings. "Prime Minister, Gentlemen. In my organisation, we simply do not believe in coincidence. As such we have very strong doubts about who was behind the attack on the cathedral."

Noticing he had their full attention he paused to take a sip of water, then continued. "As you know, under the UN Right to Protect, a sovereign state has the power to intervene in the affairs of another state if it can be proved that its citizens are in danger. This is clearly what the Russians would like us to believe. However, my sources indicate to me that although the attack was indeed carried out by ultra-nationals, we believe they were stooges, unwittingly manipulated by the Russian FSB as a ruse to be able to create their long sought-after land corridor between Kaliningrad and Russian-friendly territory."

C's raptor-like eyes raked the room as he spoke.

"GCHQ, our gleaming silver doughnut-shaped government listening station in Cheltenham, picked up and managed to decipher segments of significant coded radio transmissions between the Russian Embassy in Vilnius and Moscow. I am sure you understand that I can't go into sources and methods in this forum, but suffice it to say, we believe we have sufficient intelligence to support the theory that it was Russian agents who had infiltrated the ultra-nationalist network in Lithuania, who were the ones who supplied the explosives and the ones behind the planning of this operation."

Unable to hold his temper any longer, the Foreign Secretary banged the table again and shouted "We need a full mobilisation now. We need to take the fight to the Russians!" Sir Rupert, who had spent his formative military years as a Battalion commander as part of the 1st UK Armoured Division in Germany turned to the Foreign Secretary.

"Foreign Secretary, I fully concur with your desire, but the reality is that the cupboard is bare. The best we can possibly hope for is to scratch around and mobilise sufficient troops to put 1 Division into Germany. My Staff Officers reliably inform me that this would mean the compulsory activation of nearly 7,500 reservists and would also mean stripping equipment and troops from several other high priority tasks."

"Thank you General." cut in the Prime Minister. "We get the point." Keen to bring the meeting to a close, the PM continued with his summary. "I have, of course discussed this with the US President and we have formally requested a UN Security Council meeting for tomorrow morning. NATO is, as we speak, holding a crisis meeting and deciding on its options regarding its obligations to defend another NATO member. We will of course be demanding the immediate withdrawal of Russian Forces occupying Lithuanian territory and reparations for the deaths and damages caused."

With this the PM stood up and declared the meeting closed. As he left, he caught Sir Rupert by the jacket sleeve and quietly whispered into his ear. "General, you have my full support, I want you to begin mobilisation plans at once, and that includes the compulsory mobilisation of our reserve forces."

bargain [noun]

Definition of bargain

An agreement between parties settling what each gives or receives in a transaction between them or what course of action or policy each pursues in respect to each other

- *They struck a bargain to sell only to each other.*

Vladivostok

For a man who was making one of the biggest strategic gambles since the Cuban Missile Crisis, President Mikhail Mikhailovich Voronin of the Russian Federation seemed remarkably calm, thought Zhang Wu. Zhang, a diminutive figure in his late 70s, cut an unassuming pose, a trait which he had often used to his advantage. Long ago, he had learned the value of being underestimated.

He was a thin reedy man with a stooped back, arms that somehow seemed too long for his body and a creased and weather-beaten face. His physical stature had been the product of ten years spent in a Chinese Communist Party forced Labour and Re-education Camp after he fell out of favour with the Party's leadership. However, despite his tired-looking physical appearance, one only needed to peer into his steely grey eyes once, to realise that Zhang was, in reality, a cold, calculating reptilian predator.

As a member of the 7-strong Politburo Standing Committee of the People's Republic of China, he was now one of the country's most influential men. Indeed, thought the ambitious bureaucrat from Shanghai, if the final phases of the Politburo's 15-year plan went as expected, then he, Zhang Wu, would be one of the most powerful men in the world, with power and influence that stretched far beyond the borders of his own country. China's age really had come, he mused silently to himself.

Greeting President Voronin, Zhang bowed deeply and then straightened to shake the hand of the Russian President. "Thank you for meeting with me at this time Mr President." said Zhang, in the most subservient tone he could muster. Still gripping Zhang's hand tightly, Voronin eyed the elder Chinese man and replied in English. "It is my pleasure, Minister Zhang. Although…. I was expecting to meet with the Premier himself."

Unruffled by the obvious rebuke, Zhang replied. "The Premier sends his most humble apologies Mr President. Unfortunately, urgent matters in Beijing have kept the Premier from coming to this most important of meetings."

The diplomatic snub hadn't gone unnoticed. Inwardly Voronin was seething. – Who does that little yellow insect think he is? - thought Voronin of the Chinese Premier. He knew it was just their Chinese way of playing diplomatic chess. Trying to show who the senior partner was in the relationship. The problem was that Voronin knew that after many years of western sanctions against his country as well as his own personal assets, he and his country desperately needed the hard currency that the Chinese were offering.

"My Premier is keen to learn how the plan went. Do the Europeans or Americans suspect anything?" President Voronin had his back to Zhang. Dressed in an immaculate dark blue suit he was staring fixedly out of the large penthouse windows of the Hyundai Hotel. It was Vladivostok's only 5-star hotel and the Russian Security Services had emptied it completely for today's meeting. In the reflection of the window, he caught sight of a few new grey hairs. Vain to the point of being obsessional, he immediately made a note to get them dyed to match the rest of his light brown hair.

The ironically named Vladivostok, which in English translates as 'Ruler of the East', lay in the extreme southeast of Russia. A small peninsular jutting out into the Sea of Japan. The distinctly Asian city was surrounded by China to the west, North Korea to the south and the northern islands of Japan which lay less than 500km to the east across the Sea of Japan.

Despite being Russian territory and being home to the greater part of Russia's newly remodelled navy, Voronin knew that every year the ethnic mix of the population was tilting more and more in favour of the Chinese.

The President also knew that Russia in its present state couldn't hope to stop China's inexorable rise, not in the short term at least. But he could certainly capitalise on it. If it was the Rodina's land and resources the Chinese wanted, they could have it, at a price of course. Better to cut a deal with the Chinese and sell them land and resources than to watch it slowly being taken from the Russian Motherland.

Anyhow, thought the President, as he slowly turned from the window to face the stooped and gnarly old Chinese emissary, Russia's dwindling population could live quite comfortably in about a third of the country's current size. So what, if he used a small slice of the barren tundra of Siberia as a bargaining chip, especially if it helped Russia gain back some of its territories in the west, lost to the Europeans after the fall of communism.

"The plan worked perfectly. Thanks to the work of both our and your cyber warfare units, social media sites, news outlets and selected journalists, all believe that the attack on the church was inspired by Lithuanian Ultra-Nationalists in a campaign of violence against ethnic Russians living in Lithuania." A thin predatory smile passed briefly over the President's mouth as he spoke of the deception.

"The few western news reports suggesting that Moscow was behind the attack were quickly dismissed as being anti-Russia propaganda and as being unreliable. Once our technicians mocked up a Deepfake of the two youths who carried out the attack, discussing their plan in a bar full of skinheads. Don't worry, these stories were quickly discredited."

Zhang listened patiently to the Russian President. He was very proud of China's own cyber warfare abilities. As the minister for electronic security, some five years ago he had personally overseen the expansion of the then couple of thousand strong team of young hackers who were paid to monitor the billions of Chinese internet users.

Under his guidance he had realised the futility of trying to work defensively in monitoring his citizens access to information. Instead, he had augmented the force to over ten thousand strong and created a small city of hackers, whose sole objective was to work offensively, creating the news that the state wanted its citizens to receive. This had worked so well that the scheme had been adapted by Zhang's successor to work offensively by generating story content that was able to both subtly affect and infect the minds of millions of internet users worldwide.

It wasn't even that all the stories pushed out into the World Wide Web were necessarily false. All the legion of hackers had to do, in order to slowly change people's perceptions, was to ensure that positive stories about China's successes on the environment, civil affairs, technology developments and foreign aid etc were pushed to the front of the electronic queue on people's search engines and news feeds, whilst at the same time ensuring that the same methods were used to highlight, western corruption scandals, unpopular and ineffective military interventions and environmental disasters.

"And what is the reaction to the invasion of Lithuania?" Zhang asked conversationally, staring directly at the Russian President. "The invasion was, as we calculated, quick and decisive. With weak inexperienced commanders and no firm rules of engagement, the few NATO troops in the country lacked the will and intent to fight." There it was again thought Zhang as the barest flicker of a smile passed over the President's face.

"Once our lead tank and artillery formations were within firing range of their barracks they quickly surrendered. The few Lithuanians that we did encounter around the Border, were mostly reservists, they were brave and fought hard, but ultimately, they were no match for the speed and firepower of our superior forces."

Zhang could now hear the pride rippling through the Russian President's voice as he outlined his army's successes and strategies. "We currently have three full armoured divisions supporting the occupation of our 'safe haven' in Lithuania. As we speak other forces are digging-in to defensive positions along the borders with Baltic states, Poland and Western Ukraine. With our new financial resources, we have managed to mobilise 7 full divisions and we have increased production of the new Armata battle tank to an output of 50 per week."

The bull-headed Russian President was becoming animated as he strode around the penthouse. He was clearly proud of his nation's recent military success and particularly so of its all-new battle winning tank. The tank indeed, was at least a generation in advance of anything the Americans or British had.

Little did the Russian President know, thought Zhang, that the Chinese military already had copies of the tank's blueprints and had begun the painstaking process that the Chinese were so good at, of reverse engineering the production of the vehicle.

Pausing, as if sensing that the older Chinese man had lost interest, the Russian President returned to his seat opposite Zhang. The Russian President crossed his legs, adjusting the crease in his fine wool trousers, however he failed to completely mask his anticipation as his leg began to bounce ever so slightly up and down in expectation of getting the deal signed.

"You have the documents I presume?" "Of course, Mr President," replied Zhang, nodding briefly towards the far end of the table, Zhang summoned an aide who bore a small briefcase. Zhang keyed in the security code and opened the case. From within, he withdrew three single-sheet documents and placed each one in turn onto the table's smooth surface.

He withdrew his hands from the documents like a dealer revealing the house cards, Zhang paused slightly, trying to read the Russian President's expression. Outwardly calm, inwardly President Voronin could barely contain his excitement and frustration at being toyed with by a lowly Chinese functionary.

Mikhail Mikhailovich Voronin knew that once signed, those three documents would represent trade deals worth over 1 trillion US dollars. A hefty portion of which had already been paid by the Chinese as an advance. The first document would effectively secure China's oil supply overland from Russia via the new Russo-Chinese oil pipeline which was nearing completion.

The second, secured China's access to Russia's supply of rare earth minerals, which were critical to the manufacturing of nearly all modern technologies from smart phones to submarine-launched nuclear missiles. More critically though, it confirmed a joint cooperation accord to establish a lunar mining corporation, that would, according to each country's scientists, grant access to an almost unlimited supply of rare earth metals that were found in huge concentrations on the moon and in orbiting asteroids.

The final document, and by far the most lucrative, promised the Russian government sole trading rights on oil, gas and specific advanced rocket and aviation technologies for the principal countries that were currently being connected by the Chinese Silk Road Project.

These countries would stretch from the 'Stans' of Central Asia, northwest through Turkey and Syria then down into Egypt and East Africa, whilst simultaneously extending southwest through Afghanistan, Pakistan and Iran into eastern Iraq and Yemen. The Russian President knew that however poor and impoverished a nation's people were, governments like these governments, never lacked the money or more importantly desire to buy advanced weapons.

Focusing his mind and willing his body to relax, President Mikhail Mikhailovich Voronin carefully withdrew a pen from his pocket and slowly read, then signed the three documents. In turn, and on behalf of his Premier, Zhang also added his mark to the three contracts. $1 trillion is an awful lot of money, thought Zhang to himself as he applied his mark to the final document. Well, it was an awful lot of money to a country like Russia, but not to China.

Zhang knew that the dollar currency reserves that China held as a result of the US / Chinese trade deficit was almost three times the amount his country had just agreed to give to Russia. It was ironic Zhang thought, as he stood to bid farewell to the Russian President, the money being used to settle this deal, was actually US money. Without knowing it, the American debt crisis had effectively bank-rolled the Russian military and with it had unwittingly begun the slow dismantling of their own world hegemony.

Standing reluctantly, to bid a formal farewell to the Chinese emissary, the irony of the situation was not lost on Voronin. - Was it not the Americans that had choked and bled the life out of the Soviet Union with their economically debilitating arms race? Now, nearly thirty years later, in the new Russia, Voronin's Russia, the Americans and their western European lap dogs would watch impotently as slowly and inexorably they sank under an unbearable burden of debt, political indecision and public unrest.

diplomacy [noun]
Definition of diplomacy
The art and practice of conducting negotiations between nations

- *The talks have now gone into a stage of quiet diplomacy.*

United Nations Security Council (UNSC) New York

The UNSC had been meeting daily now for nearly 4 weeks, in a vain attempt to solve the growing military situation in Lithuania. It was no secret that NATO was struggling to find the money and troops to be able to take military action against the Russians. The US had begun deploying thousands of extra troops back into hastily repurposed military camps in Eastern Europe.

As ever, with military campaigns, it was the logistics that were the key. Whilst Russia could resupply and support its forces, on effectively its own territory, indefinitely, and at little cost, the Americans had to fly or ship, huge quantities of heavy and sensitive military equipment thousands of miles by sea, to reinforce the NATO bases in the Baltic states and Poland.

The Chinese and Russian UN envoys were all too aware of the US and NATO predicament and also knew that despite the rhetoric and harsh economic sanctions placed on Russia by the US and EU, that at the moment at least, the US was not in a position either economically, militarily or diplomatically, to seriously consider all-out war with Russia.

The truth was that the US hadn't fought a full-on kinetic war against a near-peer enemy since Korea, and that hadn't exactly gone as planned. Indeed, it was still technically ongoing. mused the Secretary General to himself as he observed the huddled conclaves of like-minded tribes of Ambassadors as they struggled to make their point to their opposite numbers.

After 4 weeks of intense debate and hushed back channel

diplomatic meetings between UN representatives and the major powers, the UN Secretary General was beginning to see, with disheartening certainty, just how polarised the world was becoming, with both Russia and the West becoming ever more entrenched and enmeshed in their diplomatic uncrossable or unacceptable 'red lines'.

Barely able to disguise his growing frustration any longer, the Secretary General called the Security Council meeting once more to order and re-read the proposal to be voted on. How had the situation deteriorated so quickly? the Secretary General thought to himself. The two sides were no longer discussing a complete resolution to the annexation of the southern corridor of Lithuania. No, now the focus of the discussions was on; how many artillery pieces and offensive missile forces each side was allowed to deploy within the conflict area.

Guilherme Oliveira, the UN Secretary General was 60-years old. A tall handsome man with a well-groomed beard and large bushy eyebrows. As a young jeans and T-shirt wearing Brazilian student he had personally experienced the effects of the Cold War in Brazil. No, he hadn't been living in a small town in Western Germany, in constant fear that a 6 million strong Soviet Army massed along the East – West border would one day decide to tear straight through the Iron Curtain and occupy the rest of Western Europe. Instead, he had noticed the subtler, yet in many ways, more brutal effects of the Cold War.

In his country, as in many Central and South American countries, a constant proxy war had been fought between pro-Soviet and pro-Western elements. Factions within these countries from both sides of the political spectrum were being officially and unofficially supported by their respective superpower sponsors.

The net effect of which, was that in countries like Argentina, Chile and Brazil, despotic military dictatorships, whose secret police and intelligence services regularly detained and tortured those dissidents brave enough to stand up to them, were being kept in power, and all because according to western intelligence and security analysts, these countries represented pawns in a global chess match being played out between two superpowers and, as in the game of chess, to protect the king, some pawns would always have to be sacrificed.

Guilherme had been one of the thousands of protesters that had taken to the streets of Sao Paolo in the mid 1980s, whose actions ultimately helped to cause the downfall of the military dictatorship in Brazil.

Dragging his thoughts back to the present, Guilherme counted the votes in favour of the new resolution. Typical, he thought. The Chinese and Russians once again had voted against the proposal to reduce missile defence batteries within Lithuania territory. He sighed audibly. "Gentlemen, thank you for your time. This council will resume session tomorrow at 10am." Guilherme slouched back in his chair with a resigned look on his face as the diplomats and their delegations filed out of the chamber.

High up in the gallery, sat an older Chinese man who had been watching the Security Council proceedings with interest. Li Qiang Wu, a former senior member of the Chinese Politburo, was now technically a stateless person. He now lived and worked, with UN diplomatic credentials in New York.

Over a year ago, his fledgling UN agency had played a pivotal part in preventing a series of coordinated attacks on key global strategic oil storage sites, aimed at destabilizing global security and possibly triggering a nuclear war. Since that event, he had been told in no uncertain terms, that he would never again be allowed to return to the People's Republic of China.

His smart phone buzzed in his pocket and the message on the dim screen read; 'Assemble the team. Meeting, your office, 5pm today.' Li didn't need to look at the sender's ID, he simply stood, nodded politely at the Secretary General, still sat slouched in his chair, far below at the Security Council meeting table and left the gallery.

Chapter One

mission [noun]

Definition of mission

A specific task with which a person or a group is charged

- *Their mission was to help victims of the disaster.*

Bernese Alps, Switzerland

As the first tentative rays of spring sunlight began their daily battle to pierce the mask of twilight, illuminating the thick pine forest floor below, Erik De Vries lay prone and completely still in the chill morning air. Separating him from the clawing damp earth, lay only a thin sheet of foam matting of the type that can be found in any camping and outdoor shop. He had been laying in this exact position, peering intently through the fine morning mist into the small forest clearing below for nearly 2 hours now.

Unlike Erik, his target appeared apparently unaffected by the seeping dampness that pervaded deep into the darkest corners of the forest below. Despite the target being over 500 metres from where he lay, it seemed to Erik that, when viewed through the Accuracy International L115A3 sniper rifle's 12 x 50 magnification sight, his quarry could almost be close enough to touch. Erik observed every movement of every fibre of his target, picking up on the subtle queues that only an expert could divine as to the animal's state of mind and intentions.

Adjusting his position slightly and fixing the target in the centre of the rifle's sight, the coarse fibrous grey and black hairs that lined the distinctive ridge of the creature's back were clearly illuminated by the penetrating rays of the weak morning sun.

A yellow hue reflected from the creature's razor-sharp tusks which jutted skyward at awkward angles from its huge deformed bony head. Stretching languidly, as if oblivious to the hunter's presence that was focused so keenly upon him, the creature snorted loudly, then clawed at the ground, with its powerful hind legs.

For the last three days Erik had lain secreted from view, on the edge of a wooded escarpment, in a hide that he'd skilfully constructed from the surrounding thick pine branches and fine bracken leaves. To ensure that his scent couldn't drift downwind to where, he believed his quarry to be, Erik had used plastic bags and a plastic bottle when eliminating his bodily waste.

Thanks to the years of training from Erik's Uncle Rudy, the former Rhodesian Army Special Forces Operative, the hide's exact position, when viewed both from a topographical as well as tactical position, had been meticulously chosen. The Dutchman had laboured for over six hours, under the leaden skies of the late spring afternoon and near complete darkness of the moonless evening, on its construction.

Being careful not to disturb the natural lay of the existing vegetation, he had painstakingly constructed a low camouflaged hunting hide that afforded him a clear sight line to a very particular clearing in the forest below.

To the East, the sun's rays had begun to trace a silhouette around the jagged contours of the towering Jungfrau Mountain. At an altitude of 4158 metres, this majestic peak, dominated the surrounding landscape. The ever-encroaching ski resorts, guided glacier walks and the Jungfraujoch railway that cuts a scar around and through the mountain, all add a veneer of comfort and domestication to the mountain. However, this grand dame of the Bernese Alps seemingly never tired of reminding, those foolish enough to believe she had been domesticated, of their own mortality.

Despite the relentless damp and cold, which after three days of occupying the hide had permeated into every pore of his body, Erik was happy. He removed the 7.62 copper-tipped round from his inner coat pocket, where it had lain, pressing into the hard muscles of his abdomen, a constant reminder of his purpose on that bleak mountain, for nearly three whole days. First, he scrutinised the round carefully, ensuring that there were no defects, then he wiped its surface clean, to ensure all moisture had been removed.

As he did so, he could vividly recall, as clearly as if it were yesterday, the first time he had felt the electrical pulse of suspense that the thrill of hunting brought with it. It had been in the Drakensberg Mountains in the Kruger National Park in South Africa where Erik's uncle Rudy, a former Rhodesian Army Selous Scout and veteran of many covert and overt military operations, had taught him how to track, kill and butcher wild animals.

Erik had been sent as a young teenage boy to live with, and learn from, his uncle in South Africa. Erik's father, who had been a Minister in the Protestant Gereformeerde Kerk, Dutch Reformed Church, in Holland, had once told his son that the word of God had come to him in the form of a vision one night. And in this vision God had called upon the old Pastor to give his first-born son to the church to become one of Christ's soldiers in the coming battle between good and evil.

That had been 20 years ago thought Erik, as he carefully made the final adjustments to his position and began to slowly regulate his breathing, beginning the process of becoming one with his rifle. Today, right in this moment, only he and the large razorback boar 500m below him, existed.

Over the last 20 years Erik had stalked, cornered and killed both animals and people. For Erik there was little difference in the techniques he employed to kill either. He did, however, make one distinction. When hunting the former, he would never use the rifle's 10-round capacity magazine, choosing instead to manually chamber one 7.62 round directly into the rifle's breach. This was because, killing the former was, as Erik saw it merely practice for terminating the latter.

Finger, curled around the trigger, taking up the 3.3 pounds of pressure, Erik's mind began to work mechanically through the marksmanship principles which had been engrained into him by his Uncle Rudy, as a young boy, high up in the South African mountains. As he lay, peering through the rifle's sight, he could feel his uncle's presence, just behind him, whispering the principles of shooting into his ear.

It was almost hypnotic, thought Erik – *The position and hold must be firm enough to support the weapon.* Check! *The weapon must point naturally at the target without any undue effort.* Check! *Sight alignment, (aiming) must be correct.* Check! *The shot must be released and followed through without any undue disturbance of the position.* Click!

Slowly taking up the remaining ounces of trigger pressure, whilst holding the small amount of air left in his lungs, the round was released from the rifle's muzzle with a thunderous roar that ripped through the cool morning air, towards the boar at nearly 850 metres per second.

The large boar's head had been raised in the air just before the shot had been fired, almost as if the animal's finely tuned and acutely sensitive nose had detected the scent of the hunter, high up there on the escarpment.

For what appeared to be several seconds, the animal's head remained poised in the air as the heavy copper jacketed bullet entered its right eye socket and began tumbling through the beast's small brain cavity, ejecting as it did so, fragments of bone and brain matter in a bloody pulp that spurted from the fist-sized exit wound in the side of the animal's head.

Erik continued to stare through the rifle's 12 x 50 sight, as the powerful front legs and shoulders of the huge boar ceased receiving signals from its brain. He watched with fascination as the majestic creature, began to teeter slightly, slowly at first, then more violently as the chemical-electrical signals that travelled down its spinal cord to its remaining muscles ceased arriving at their desired destinations.

With a shuddering thud the animal toppled to the earth, causing tiny tremors and vibrations, clearly visible as they rippled through the carpet of the forest floor, disturbing leaves and insects and sending a cloud of fine dried leaves and tiny fungal spores high into the surrounding air. Once more Erik heard his Uncle Rudy's voice in his ear. - *The shot must be released and followed through without any undue disturbance of the position.* Check!

Showered and changed, after an exhausting 8-kilometre hike, pulling the dead weight of the lifeless boar on a hastily made sled,

Erik was now sat in simple black trousers and a plain white shirt open at the collar. Perched on a bistro stool at the granite counter of his open plan kitchen he ran through the protocols that would ensure that the voice and video call with his handler would remain secure, even to the prying ears of the US NSA and the UK's Electronic Information gathering service, GCHQ in Cheltenham.

Sipping from his glass of crisp chilled Riesling wine, Erik began the series of protocols required to enable the Quantum Key communication on his laptop. To most people, Quantum Key Encryption was thought to still be a purely theoretical way of exploiting the counterintuitive behaviour of inherent uncertainty in quantum particles such as photons, to be able to send and receive messages securely.

Well, that is how it had been described on numerous websites that Erik had read, when researching the technology. If he was being truthful to himself, he was only half surprised, when he learned that a division within the 'Organisation' had not only proved the concept but had actually developed a working technology.

Maybe, this was the reason why in the 20 years he had been employed by the 'Organisation', he had never seen more than two of them together at one time, and more frustratingly for Erik, why he had never been able to identify his handler.

Erik had lived in the small Swiss village of Lauterbrunnen for nearly three years now. The village was the picture postcard type, that one would see in the movies. Indeed, boasting just 75 inhabitants and located at a natural cul-de-sac within sight of the towering Jungfrau Mountain, Lauterbrunnen was perfect for a man who valued easy access to the wild mountains and his anonymity in equal measure.

As with all things Swiss, it was neat, clean and functional and as such was perfect for Erik's needs. His neighbours, being Swiss were both polite and discreet. Never commenting on the many last minute 'business trips' that took him away from home for days or even weeks at a time. But of course, why would they, after all wouldn't an Insurance Underwriter for a global insurance consultancy often be asked to travel away at short notice?

As usual, the large plasma screen mounted on the kitchen wall was playing silently in the background. The subtitled BBC World Service reporter was stood outside a nondescript Viennese house. "We can confirm that the Austrian Chancellor Kurt Waldinger of the Sozialdemokratische Partei Österreichs, (Social Democratic Party of Austria) has been arrested after weeks of speculation as to his involvement in a child pornography ring."

Her face was difficult to read thought Erik. On one hand she was struggling to disguise the disdain that she felt towards the now ex Chancellor of Austria. Yet on the other, she was doing a very poor job, of masking her delight at breaking the biggest news story of her young career, Erik mused. Slowly releasing the breath, he had unconsciously been holding Erik sighed. How morally corrupt the world had become, he thought.

It was obvious that, consciously at least, the young female reporter was working very hard to express her very real distaste for the alleged actions of the Ex Chancellor, yet there she was, stood in front of a camera in Vienna's twilight, her smart grey business skirt and jacket and her demeanour were oozing professionalism and confidence.

However, for the more observant, and if Erik was anything, he was observant, once you looked through her thin professional veneer and noticed that she had left one button too many, undone on her crisp white blouse, and her crimson lipstick adorning her full lips, just screamed out her willingness to do whatever it took to go the next step up the corporate ladder of journalistic success. She was Lustful, desiring more than she possessed. Yes, he thought, turning his attention to the new speaker, her sin was Lust.

The Chief Commissar of Vienna's Criminal Investigation Division was being interviewed. "I can confirm that our forensic analysis team have recovered several petabytes of data containing child pornography images from Mr Waldinger's personal tablet. In addition, Mr Waldinger's active involvement in an online paedophile chat forum has been verified through the analysis of metadata that linked his IP address to his username on the site."

Erik took another long sip of the cool Riesling. Now, the Commissar's sins thought Erik, where should I start? Looking at the bloated bulk of his frame and the thick jowls that spilled over his tight shirt collar and seemed to fill the camera lens, it was obvious that the policemen was no stranger to the sin of Greed. But then also noting the small inaccuracies in what he had reported to the Press. It appeared that Sloth was also vying for a place at the top of the list of the senior Policeman's vices.

I mean, really, would anyone today actually believe that a tablet could store several hundred petabytes of data? Either this middle aged, overweight idiot had confused a laptop for an external storage device, or he didn't know a petabyte from a gigabyte! No, this bloated buffoon's principal vice was clearly Pride thought Erik, as he typed in the last command prompt into the quantum encryption software. Hadn't he been taught by his father that Pride was the worst of all the seven deadly sins? Wasn't it Pride and the belief in your own superiority that led to your eternal damnation?

The pulsing green light on his laptop indicating that the call had been connected securely, brought Erik quickly back from his musings. "Did he do it?" Asked Erik to the dark ubiquitous silhouette of a man's head that had appeared on his laptop screen. "Doesn't matter, people think he did it. That's what matters." The accent was mid-Atlantic, sometimes he thought he could hear a hint of Scottish brogue when, on rare occasions, his controller seemed to be in a good mood. Most of the time though, Erik only heard an undefinable North American or possibly even Canadian accent.

With no more preamble the control began his briefing. "Ok Erik, you know the score. Big picture first then little picture. The organisation believes that the time is right for us to commit to some more, err, concrete action to advance its aims. The Brothers have been following with interest the seismic upheavals that are taking place within the EU."

Erik knew from several of his previous missions that the Organisation didn't only passively watch from afar. He knew that they had been investing significant time and treasure whispering in the ears of the Mandarins throughout the European Halls of Power.

Normally it was a subtle suggestion to a minister here, some financial support for an election rival there. Sometimes though, the

Organisation's guiding hand was a little firmer, requiring more direct action. Requiring the sort of unique skills that Erik possessed.

The referendum on leaving the EU had been the point that most contemporary commentators had identified as when the British had finally hit the self-destruct button and begun, what appeared to many outsiders, as an act of extreme self-harm, in voting for a Brexit from the EU.

France and Germany, who had sat squarely at the traditional heart of the European Union and had never really understood or particularly liked their closest island neighbour, had watched helplessly as the centre of gravity of the EU had drifted steadily eastwards.

Without Britain's geographical and economic anchor, the older Western Franco / German bloc now found itself pitted against the newer, Eastern, Visigrad bloc in a bitter struggle for control over the EU's future. Knowing that most migrants didn't actually want to settle in Bucharest or Bratislava but were more than happy to spend their self-imposed exile in London or Paris, it had been easy for the Visigrad group to use this desire for Pain au Chocolat and Pasties to leverage their position against the Western Europeans.

Tempers had really flared in the European parliament when a much delayed and hotly contested Europol investigation showed clear evidence of the Polish, Romanian, Bulgarian, Croatian and Hungarian governments' collusion in actively providing a coordinated network of military vehicles and school buses to transport the waves of economic migrants to, and in some cases over, the border into neighbouring Germany, Austria and Italy, from whence many would doubtless find their way onto the streets of Calais or Cardiff.

The exact timing of the beginning of the real problems for the EU though, could more precisely be linked to the collapse of Italy's banking system in the late winter of 2017. The popular nationalist Italian Prime Minister, one of three to hold the post in that year, had declared that his nation could no longer service its debt burden.

As such, the Italian government had defaulted on all loan payments, and government bonds, leaving the EU in general, and the French, German and Dutch taxpayers in particular, with billions of euros of worthless Italian government bonds.

This economic turbulence invoked a Tsunami-like wave of political unrest around Europe. It had triggered the bitter and often violent Catalan referendum and eventual partition from Spain. The result of which was not only a geographical cleaving of territory from the Iberian Peninsula, but also a significant draining of income for the Spanish government in Madrid. The latter factor, if you had asked any Madrid-based politician at the time had raised far more ire and dealt yet another significant blow to Spain's struggling economy.

The path to an unrivalled fourth term in office had not been easy for the veteran German Chancellor. In order to shore up her traditional support base and prevent her from having to seek a coalition with one of the more nationalistic parties she had been forced into committing to a manifesto pledge which all but prevented the German government from providing any further stimulus packages to the weaker European States.

The German voters had long grown weary of giving away their hard-earned wages in loans and grants to countries, from which they knew would never be in a position to repay them. Their reluctance to continue to finance the EU's southern flank had led to the Greek government declaring a Grexit in early February of 2018.

Slowly, it seemed, the soft underbelly of Europe, upon which the northern countries had invested so much time and treasure in creating political alliances was beginning to falter.

Erik had mentally tuned out for a while as Control had held his diatribe on the state of the EU. He had been wondering if the 300 pounds of wild boar that he had butchered and which was now hanging in his cold storage room in an outhouse next to his home, would spoil if he was away for more than 3 days. Yes, this would have to be a quick operation he thought to himself.

Control continued speaking, switching the focus to the mission specifics. "Following the unfortunate fall from grace of the Ex Chancellor, a new Austrian General Election is to be held in three weeks' time. Of course, we have a preferred candidate. His name is Christoph Berger of the Christliche Nationalistische Partei Österreichs (Christian Nationalist Party of Austria).

"You have been assigned to his security detail as part of the pre-election run up. His main election themes will be Austria first, anti-EU and anti-Immigration. Specifically, what the organisation would like you to do is to ensure that Jens Schneider, the proposed candidate running from the disgraced Ex Chancellor's party does not pose a threat to the success of our candidate."

The implied euphemism was clear to Erik, although he always marvelled at the way that those giving such orders were never able to verbalise in clear English exactly what they wanted to be done.

Erik had been 24 when he returned from South Africa. The man that returned was markedly different from the youth that had arrived over 8 years before. The harsh African veldt coupled with the tough routine that Uncle Rudy had set for him, had shaped him, or perhaps sculptured would be a better term. Uncle Rudy had been sad to see the boy go.

Erik had been a good student, he was bright, he never grumbled when things got tough, and he had an almost intuitive ability with a rifle. Rudy knew from his time as a Selous Scout that a man can be trained to be a good shot, but that truly excellent shooters possessed intuition.

For Erik's part, it had been the making of him, a simple disciplined life. Each day his uncle would teach him a different aspect of his selected profession. They would rise at dawn and work outdoors in the veldt or mountains until dusk. Sometimes, they would not return to their village for several days at a time, instead sleeping on simple blankets under the starlit heavens. The only rule that was never broken was that they had to be home each Sunday for Church.

After leaving South Africa, he hadn't flown directly back to Holland, instead, at the insistence of his father who had arranged an introduction for him with some like-minded brethren, he had flown from South Africa to Salem, which lay just north of Boston, USA.

In total he spent 6 months living in the small Puritan community, which still occupied settlements dating back to 1626, having been settled by the hardy Puritans that had survived the harsh Atlantic crossing from England.

The Puritan community lay just outside of the town of Salem, which featured the very first Puritan church in North America and functioned a little like a commune or Jewish Kibbutz. The commune entrance proudly displayed its iconic logo a long thin black cross with its sharpened base above its entrance gates. The position of the cross caused all that entered to peer upwards at the sword-like shape and consider their own mortality before God.

Within the commune people dressed simply, in plain black trousers and simple white shirts which also displayed a smaller version of the elongated cross on the breast pocket. They ate their meals together, and their days were filled with bible study, lectures and discussions on the nature of politics and religion.

Erik had been raised a devout Protestant, he was fiercely proud of this fact and although he didn't understand many of the discussions on politics, he really enjoyed the hours of discussions on the merits of the Protestant work ethic and the shortcomings and misdeeds of the hierarchical Catholic church.

Several months after returning from his time in Massachusetts, Erik received a phone call from a stranger asking if he would be interested in applying his skills to work for a Philanthropic Organisation. At that time, Erik didn't really understand what his particular skill set was, and his interlocutor certainly didn't expand in any detail as to the nature of the Organisation.

Chapter Two

wall [noun]

Definition of wall

A high thick masonry structure forming a long rampart or an enclosure chiefly for defence

- *The enemy threw itself against the city's walls.*

Oval Office White House, Washington DC.

President of the United States, Carlton, P, Simpson, was about as Texan as they came. His two main passions in life were converting shale oil deposits into dollars and flash-searing huge chunks of red meat on a grill before devouring them. The former passion had made him into one of the wealthiest men in the nation. In turn it had also allowed him entry in those rarefied social circles where not running for political office would be perceived at best as weakness of character and at worst as unpatriotic.

The latter passion was probably the principle reason why his lower intestine was now about 17 inches shorter than the average, and why he continued to take tumour supressing medication, even 5 years after the operation.

Despite, or maybe because of his incredible wealth and recent cancer scare, he had, against all predictions of the polling agencies and all the political commentators, won the 2016 US Presidential election.

You see, above all, President Carlton P Simpson was a businessman, and despite retiring from his own Shale Oil company and handing over the reins to his two sons, Carlton Simpson could not resist trying to seal the biggest deal in his life. Running for the office of President of the United States was a challenge he simply could not ignore, because men like Carlton P Simpson, simply didn't retire.

Over the last twenty years Carlton P Simpson had witnessed the slow decline of American international influence and the decay of its industrial heartland. With growing anger, he watched as ever more American jobs had been 'outsourced' to the Chinese and how nowadays, the Russians seemed to be able to get away with anything they darned well liked. In his day they would have sent over a Division of Rangers to kick some Commie butt and show them who the boss was.

As President elect he wasn't alone in these thoughts and it was from his base of popular support which ranged from the northern rust belt, through the rapidly desertifying farmlands of the mid-west all the way down to the southern border towns and cities where Spanish was more widely spoken than English that he had personally managed and funded an election campaign which tore up the conventional playbook and rewrote the rules.

It soon transpired that contesting the election had been by far the more stimulating and straight forward than actually acting as the President. With no real political ideology or affiliation and as an outsider to Washington, it had taken the first two years of his term in office as President to find his feet, understand the game, and learn which palms required greasing.

No different to any other profession, he mused to himself, turning away from the Oval Office window and refocussing on the morning's brief. All the regular attendees were present: The President's Chief of Staff, an old Washington hand called Charles (Chuck) Lewis, The National Security Advisor, Helen Broxton, General Curtis Lee Hayward, the Chief of Defence Staff, John Linton, the Press Secretary and the Vice President, Charles Laurel Henderson.

Charles, L Henderson, who was most definitely Charles and certainly never Chuck, was a quietly spoken Bostonian. A deeply religious and very conservative man, who would never have received his party's nomination for his own ticket to run for the Presidency but having secured the conservative religious right vote for the President, both he and the President had formed an unusual, yet successful alliance.

The VP knew his way around the Washington village circuit and could always be counted upon to secure political support from both sides of the aisle. But most importantly, he wasn't a threat, thought the President. The man had about as much appeal as wet fart in a paper bag.

"Keep it brief today Chuck, I got one of them darned migraines coming on." Helen Broxton, the National Security Advisor risked a sideways glance at General Hayward. The General didn't seem to have noticed her looking at him, until, on closer observation, she could just about discern a slight raise of his left eyebrow.

Everybody in the room understood all too well that the President having one of those darned migraines really meant that his golf clubs were being packed by his Secret Service detail into his limousine, and that this morning's meeting was the only thing between him and the pinging sound of a small white dimpled ball hurtling its way along the 485 yards of the first tee at the Lake Presidential Golf Course in Maryland.

"Mr President," Chuck continued, "Four main items today," It hadn't taken Chuck long to determine the President's attention span. On a good day he might risk 6 items, but on a day like today, even these four points were going to be a challenge, he thought. "Mr President, the Russians are preparing for their annual exercise in their Western sector." "Just remind me where exactly their Western Sector is please, Chuck?"

A fact little known to the country at large was that President Carlton P Simpson had only been issued a passport after being sworn into office and he had only been out of the country once. The occasion was a state visit to Australia, South Korea and Japan to reassure those countries that America was still committed to their collective defence in the face of an increasingly assertive China.

"Their, Western Sector Sir, covers their border with the Baltic states, Belorussia, which is a Russian ally, and then Poland down to Ukraine in the south." "OK, OK I got it thanks Chuck, General, do we need to be alarmed?" "Not really sir, I mean we can monitor the situation with our air assets out of Ramstein in Germany, and the NSA's satellites, but since the withdrawal of most of our heavy fighting forces from Europe and our pivot East to Asia, there isn't a whole lot we could do if they decided to go on the offensive."

"Is that a realistic possibility General?" asked the President, who stole what he thought was an unnoticed peek at his watch. "No, Sir, I don't believe so. Our satellites have picked up a large concentration of heavy armour, including some of their newer stuff as well as mechanised infantry movement into Belorussia, but it is about what we expect for this level of exercise."

The General began to speak, then paused. Looking across at the National Security Advisor, who gave him a consenting nod, he continued. "With their economy the way it is now, those Russians don't have the fuel or resources to keep their forces out in the field for more than a couple of weeks at best. And that's stretching it." "OK General we got the message," the President said, with more than a hint of impatience in his voice. "Chuck, next item please"

Turning to a satellite map image projected onto the wall of the Oval Office, Charles Chuck Lewis, began to trace out a line on the map from Shanghai in the east of China westwards across China to the Pakistan-Kashmir border then northwards to Astana in Kazakhstan.

"Mr President, that line represents the extent of the Chinese Silk Road Project so far. Port facilities are under construction all down the east coast of Africa, from Sudan in the north, Mogadishu in the Horn of Africa, down through Mombasa in Kenya and even as far down as Dar Al Salaam in Tanzania." Red dots lit up on the map as the President's Chief of Staff traced a line down the East coast of Africa with his laser pointer.

The President knew about the Silk Road Project, and he had to admit, the sheer scale and speed of development was awesome. The largest infrastructure project ever undertaken by humankind, would incorporate a transport network by road, rail and ship connecting the globe from eastern China to northern Russia and western Europe, and across Central Asia, through Pakistan and Iran and eventually on to Africa.

It wouldn't impact directly on US areas of influence, the President knew, but it would further embolden the Chinese concept of becoming a regional power or maybe more. But then again mused the President, anyone that thought they could get the Central Asians, Pakistanis, Turks, Iranians, Syrians and Africans to cooperate on a project of this scale was either delusional or demented.

"Helen," the President said, looking over at the National Security Advisor. "What does Langley think about this?" "Well, Sir, as you know we don't have any Human Intelligence assets inside the PRC, but our East Asia analysts tell us not to be concerned. There is too much bad blood throughout the region. The Russians still don't trust the Chinese, even though their last war was over 100 years ago."

"Most of the route passes through Muslim Western China, Iran, Pakistan and the Caucuses and both the Chinese and the Russians have their own issues with the Muslims. And then don't forget that amongst the Muslims there is a considerable concentration of Shia in Iran and Yemen, that hate the Sunni Muslim states surrounding them almost as much as they hate us." The last part drew a wry smile from the Texan President.

Chuck hadn't survived life on Capitol Hill for over twenty years by being stupid. No, Chuck knew how to deliver the news to his boss. What did they call it, yes that was it, the hamburger method. Soften up the boss with some good news, slip in the meat of the bad news then finish on a high.

Of late, the hamburger had been lacking the happier bottom part of its bun, Chuck thought. With little good news on the Foreign Policy front, resulting in no small part from the President's almost complete disinclination to engage in foreign policy in the first half of his term, and a rising speculation in some of the more left-leaning news outlets about Russian cyber involvement in the election campaign.

No, of late, his presentations had become more like a rising stack of beef patties topped off with a thin Communion wafer. Not that the President would know a Communion wafer from a hot dog bun, thought Chuck as he flicked through to his last slide.

Well, thought Chuck, here goes the really bad news. "Mr President, our assets close to the Syrian government, tell us that, as of last night, President Assad and his family have been relocated to Iran." Unsure if the President had heard him, Chuck looked over to the President who by now was quite overtly checking the time on his watch. "Sir" cut in Helen Broxton. "Satellites confirm the President's move by aircraft from Damascus to Tehran, and the NSA have confirmed that a joint Russian, Turkish and Iranian deal has secured a ceasefire in Syria.

The three countries will act as guarantors of security whilst a coalition government is built." She paused at this point to see if the profundity of the message had registered with the President, but more importantly, because she didn't know how to tell the President the next part. With more than a little trepidation, she began.

"We are expecting a communique delivered via the UN tomorrow stating that the newly created Syrian Arab Republic demands the withdrawal of all US troops by the end of the month." "What the!" In a flash the President was on his feet, pacing the room. "Chuck, is this true?" "Err yes sir, Iranian and Turkish social media sites are already awash with stories of the peace deal brokered by the three powers."

The Vice President stole a cautious glance at his boss, trying to discern if the true magnitude of the event had registered with the President. No, he thought, I mean sure he's angry, maybe embarrassed a little, that these three countries would be seen to force US troops out of a combat zone. But the honest truth was that this arrogant swaggering Texan probably couldn't even find Turkey on a map if his life depended on it.

More troubling, thought the Vice President, was the amount of political and military cooperation required by the three states to have achieved this deal. I mean it was only last year that the shooting down of a Russian fighter jet by the Turkish Air Force had nearly led to war between the two countries. He filed the thought away in the back of his mind and continued to sit dispassionately, leafing through the Washington Post.

Knowing the President well, and knowing his focus was on domestic, not foreign policy, Chuck Lewis seized the opportunity. "Sir, John, and his Press team, already have a Press strategy prepared. We are selling the story that in line with your policy of the US no longer being prepared to spend US taxpayer dollars to be the world's policeman. You had decided that after consultation with the three regional stakeholders, which the US has been supporting, through diplomatic back channels, that it was about time that they took on the responsibility for what is happening on essentially their own doorstep and come up with a solution."

The President was sat back in his chair and had calmed considerably. "Good Chuck, good. Anything else, this migraine is really starting to bite." Good, thought Chuck, here comes the bun. "Just one more thing sir. Good news on the wall." The wall was more than just a security project to try to once and for all secure the Mexico / US border. It was the cornerstone of his New American Century project that had won him the election in the first place.

Despite, for the most part, not actually being a physical wall, it had, due to the President's insistence, kept this name. "The contractors have informed Homeland Security that the project is ahead of schedule and should be ready for early November, two months earlier than anticipated."

The President, now animated, and seemingly unhindered by his migraine, jumped to his feet once more, and strode to the Oval Office window. It was really good news indeed thought the Vice President reclining back in his chair and observing the President, who was framed by the light pouring in through the Oval Office window.

There were still some elements of a physical wall that had been kept in the Project plan, mostly close to residential areas. John Linton, the Press Secretary had already had members of his team out scouting for the perfect location and backdrop for the opening, or should that be closing ceremony?

The remainder of the nearly 2000-mile border was actually protected with a sequence of control towers. In the air a fleet of autonomous drone swarms would keep a vigilant eye on anyone attempting to cross by foot or vehicle. A specialized road surface had been prepared along which autonomous self-driving vehicles would drive, equipped with thermal heat sensors and ground penetrating radar, capable of picking up on subterranean movement, the type of which could be made by people burrowing underground.

If any movement was detected by either the drones or the self-driving vehicles, then an automatic signal with GPS coordinates would be sent to the nearest two control towers which would then send out armed patrols to detain the migrants.

The President's Chief of Staff glanced over at the Vice President and noticed that he appeared for the first time to be showing interest in the brief. The Vice President had actually put down the copy of the Washington Post that he had been pretending to read and appeared to be listening with genuine purpose and interest to the discussion about the wall.

Chapter Three

suicide [noun]

Definition of suicide

The act or an instance of taking one's own life voluntarily or intentionally

Other: ruin of one's own interests

- *A case of attempted suicide….*

Vienna

It had been nearly 10 years ago now, mused Erik, as he finished recording the short video. Yes 10 years almost exactly since he had first been asked to supply his very own discrete form of assistance to the Organisation. In that time his very particular skill set had been used on over 30 occasions.

Sometimes, it had involved infiltrating large corporations and gathering industrial intelligence, other times it had been of a more direct nature, rather like today, he thought, as he casually climbed the fire escape towards the balcony door of Jens Schneider's sixth floor apartment.

He was relaxed, confident in the knowledge that no-one was at home. After all, hadn't Jens' wife Hannelore just phoned him asking him to come directly home as their young 10-year-old daughter Dagma was ill and they needed to go to the hospital?

On entering the apartment, Erik paused momentarily to take in his new surroundings. The apartment was both simple and elegant, not ostentatious, but definitely aspirational. The large professional photographic portrait of the family that hung on the wall opposite the balcony doors, showed a happy family unit, mother, in her early 40s, Jens guessed, and father nearly a decade older, who carried that cultivated aura of confidence that he and his party hoped the Austrian voters would consider confident and cultivated enough to elect him as their new Chancellor.

"Hannelore, Dagma mein schatz, wo seid ihr?" Entering the apartment via the main door which led directly through a narrow hallway into the kitchen, Jens called out to his wife and daughter. Unusual, he thought, entering the living room. "Was zum Teufel! …" Jens didn't get to finish his sentence as he was pushed roughly onto the leather sofa by a stranger who was holding a pistol in his face.

"Look at me" said the stranger, tossing a small wooden box towards Jens as he spoke. Erik had always found it preferrable in these situations to rapidly overwhelm and disorient the targets senses with information, before beginning his work in earnest.

"In a minute, I am going to ask you to open that box. From this point forward you will not speak. Do you understand?" "What do you want? Who are you? Where is my family?" stammered the politician. The pistol's butt made a dull crunching sound, rather like a heavy boot crushing a large cockroach on a concrete floor, as Erik drove it into the politician's nose, smashing cartilage and bone as he did so.

"Nod, if you understand." Tears streaming down his face and clutching, the pulpy, bloody mess where his nose had once sat, the politician nodded. "Open the box." Obediently, Jens opened the box, then, as if struck by a huge jolt of electricity, he dropped it into his lap, then began retching violently, emptying his stomach of its contents. Inside the wooden case lay two fingers, one appearing to be a miniature version of the larger one, which sported a platinum diamond wedding band.

Before he had fully recovered his senses, Erik pointed to the mobile phone which he held in his hand. Swiping the screen, he pressed play on an application. It appeared to show a live video feed. Wiping blood, tears and vomit from his face, Jens stared in horror as he watched the images of his wife and daughter play out on the small backlit screen.

They seemed to be in an underground garage. Both had their mouths gagged and were tied to chairs. They were frantically screaming and struggling, and both wore a small blood-soaked bandage on their ring finger, or at least the finger designated for a ring, for those old enough to wear such items of jewellery. "Proof of life." declared Erik. The video showed a clock in the background which displayed the current time. Physically and mentally overwhelmed, the politician slumped back into the sofa and began to sob.

"Here's the bit when I tell you how you can help them." Erik's own face was now just inches from the politician's. Looking into the man's eyes Erik saw nothing. No fight, no anger, not even fear. Just acceptance. It was all about speed on jobs like this thought Erik. He knew that his actions had to be delivered in such a way so that the victim, in this case Jens Schneider, didn't have the time to process the information.

Casually glancing at his own wristwatch, Erik delivered his pre-prepared speech. "You see, in about one hour from now. The police are going to find a rather large quantity of heroin and a briefcase containing 100,000 euros in your apartment. This, they will conclude, is related to why you jumped from your sixth-floor balcony, in an apparent suicide. Of course, if you do this little favour for me, then, I will do something for you. I will set your lovely wife Hannelore and that delightful daughter of yours free."

The politician nodded soberly to Erik and spitting blood and vomit from his mouth, he said. "I will do what you ask, for my family. But first I must see them one last time." Swiping once more on the phone Erik pressed a button and passed the phone to Jens. Half blinded by his crushed nose and the tears that were now flowing freely down his face. Jens stared at the blurry image for a long time.

After several minutes, Erik gently took the phone from the broken man and crossed the polished parquet floor to open the balcony door. Today, thought Erik, this man would die for his sins of Lust and Envy.

Despite his carefully cultivated media image, Jens Schneider, like all politicians, Erik thought, was driven by his lust for power. Barely had his closest colleague, the Ex-Chancellor been laid in his coffin, than Jens had "selflessly offered himself forward", envious for all those years of his friend's position as Chancellor, he hadn't exactly been slow to seize the opportunity to fulfil his lust and satiate his envy.

Sat in the Business Lounge at Vienna's International airport waiting to board the 9pm Swiss Air flight to Bern, Erik, was drawn to the subtitles appearing on the primetime Euro News Show that was silently playing in the background. Deputy leader of the Austrian Social Democratic Party, Jens Schneider, found dead after plunging from his sixth-floor apartment's balcony.

Police have not ruled out suicide. An unconfirmed source claims that a large quantity of drugs and cash were found in Mr Schneider's apartment. His wife and child are not at the apartment and police suspect that they may have fled the country.

This comes only weeks after the Ex-Chancellor, Mr Waldinger was exposed as a paedophile. The reporter thanked the smartly dressed, yet grossly overweight, Chief Commissar of Vienna's Criminal Investigation Division for his time and turned back to the camera. Yes, definitely Pride, thought Erik. Slipping the small wooden box into the trash bin by his side, Erik stood, put on his suit jacket and rolling his carry-on luggage behind him, made his way briskly to the departure gate.

technology [noun]

Definition of technology

The practical application of knowledge especially in a particular area

- *A car's fuel saving technology.*

United Nations Centre for Technology and Culture (UNCTC) HQ Singapore

The United Nation's Centre for Technology and Culture or more simply the UNCTC, had originally been conceived in 2016 as a non-partisan UN sponsored body. Its mandate was to be able to integrate cutting edge power generation, environmental and construction technologies into small autonomous communities, that either existed as independent states, or existed within an existing nation state, but were marginalised by the state's own government.

Well at least that had been the plan. The core team based at their Singapore HQ, led by Li Qiang Wu, a now stateless ex-Chinese diplomat himself, could broadly be split into two halves; The scientists and the analysts, or as Li had come to refer to them, the thinkers and the doers.

The thinkers; included Charu Usmani, an Indian maths and computer prodigy, who specialised in the up and coming science of Complexity. Although relatively young, Charu technically headed up five regional science teams, each working on a different cutting-edge technology and based in different geographical locations around the world.

The other half of the thinking team was headed up by the famous Danish anthropologist Matthias Peterson. Matthias' gift was an unprecedented understanding of the interactions between differing cultures and the ability to transpose the underlying values and thought patterns into expected behaviours. He was, to put it another way, a kind of anthropological equivalent of a criminal investigator, piecing together actions and behaviours to be able to forecast future events.

Despite his professional genius, Matthias lacked even the thinnest veneer of social etiquette. A recovering alcoholic, separated from his wife after a tragic accident which had led to the death of their only child, Matthias had an infuriating habit of 'reading' everyone he encountered, and then much to everyone's annoyance, he would vocalise his 'reading' of that person to their face.

The other half of the team, the Doers; had been drawn from the US Secret Service, British MI6 and Russian Special Forces. Despite all three being excellent operational agents, it had taken some time for them to accept and trust each other and respect the considerable unique individual skills that each one possessed.

The glue which seemed to hold the whole team together was a giant bear of a man, a French-Canadian oil engineer called Philippe Gagnon. Coming from the oil industry Philippe had a first-class engineering mind and being married to a Canadian Inuit he also possessed a first-hand understanding of the issues affecting marginalised ethnic groups, living on the fringes of large modern states.

However, it was Philippe's firm but fair attitude and natural air of confidence in the face of a crisis, that made him more often than not, the one they all turned to for advice or guidance.

It had been just over one year since, unbeknown, and mostly unrecognised by the rest of the world community, the team had discovered a centuries old plot to destabilise and re-shape the current world order. A plot which had brought the world to the brink of nuclear war. It was this extraordinary series of events, which had forged this group of diverse individuals into a tightly knit and truly unique, international team.

The whole team was assembled in the Conference room of their Singapore HQ. Charu was sat patiently explaining to the team's newest member, Walt Sanderson, how to use the interactive conference table. "Simply draw a large square on the table's surface, like this." She described a large rectangular shape like a picture frame with her index fingers on the table's surface. "That's right. Now just hold your thumb in the centre for 3 seconds whilst the table reads your fingerprint." Walt looked at Charu, with a disbelieving look on his face.

Walt, or rather Dr Walter Sanderson, a 50-something, retired Australian Diplomat, who had spent most of his government service working from Beijing, held a Doctorate in macro-economics from the London School of Economics. His PhD thesis had been extremely specialised and focussed specifically on the future of China's 15-year economic plan. Despite being highly intelligent and very good with numbers, it was obvious to Charu that he lacked the millennial's intuitive grasp of technology.

"That's it, she coaxed gently, now look, you see this area of the screen now belongs to you, just tap and swipe like you would on any digital screen to retrieve your own documents, and if you feel like sharing anything in your area, just swipe it in the direction of the person you want to receive it."

"Wow, thanks, that's incredible!! You know I'll probably forget all this by tomorrow morning, don't you?" "Don't worry," Charu said, smiling, and unconsciously pulled back her long black hair to reveal her face, as she looked at the older man. He was tall, broad shouldered, and despite his age, had a hard toned torso. His fair hair, greying around the temples framed a kind face Charu thought.

The other female team members, Penny and Maria had both commented when they had seen his resume photo, that, he looked like one of the attractive mature guys that you see on the front cover of GQ magazine. The one inescapable fact that all who came into contact with Dr Walt Sanderson agreed upon, was that he had the most mesmerising blue eyes that seemed to radiate intelligence with an unbridled intensity. "There you go she said, you're set. I think we are starting in 5."

Looking out of the conference room window across at the ventilated glass-walled smoking cube that Li had insisted be installed, Charu could see Li, Matthias and Philippe, finishing off their smokes. Li and Matthias smoked Marlborough's and Charu watched them as they drew forcefully on the last inch of their cigarettes.

Next to them stood the towering Philippe, who was thoughtfully scraping the bowl of his briar pipe and carefully tapping the charred remains of the tobacco remnants into the metal disposal bin. Every movement of his huge hands was calculated and precise, almost meditative.

To even the most casual of observers it was obvious that all three men smoked for very different reasons. This was evident not only in what they smoked but more importantly in how they smoked. Li had grown up in Communist China where everybody smoked and most cigarettes were cheap copies of the western brands.

Maybe Li had gravitated towards the Marlborough cigarettes with their distinctive red packaging because they were the first real western cigarettes he had ever smoked, or maybe it was because of the image generated by the ad campaigns of the free-riding western cowboy, that had been so attractive to him.

Whatever it was, he was now a confirmed chronic nicotine addict. He had struggled initially moving to New York then Singapore, where most public spaces and buildings are designated smoke-free zones. He once confessed to Penny that he felt anxious when he had to leave the office and did not know when he would next be able to have a smoke. For Li it was simple chemistry, his body needed nicotine to function and going without it was like diving under water into a cave and not knowing when or even if, he would be able to surface for air.

Matthias, on the other hand, was an addict, and as he couldn't consume alcohol, his usual drug of choice anymore, he smoked to try and fill a void. It was, he knew, pointless. Drinking was a social activity done with other people. For Matthias, it reached into and stimulated each and every sense. The comforting reassurance of the thick glass or bottle in your hand, the sounds and gestures of the people around you, then the tingling hoppy scent as the first few gulps of cold beer hit the back of your throat. Finally, that sensation, the one that only alcohol brought. The sensation as the first fractions of a gram of alcohol oozed from the stomach into your blood stream. It was like a creeping euphoria, warming you from within, gradually rising from the depths of your stomach, upwards towards your head. It appeared to cocoon the drinker like a baby in a mother's womb. You were present, you could hear and interact with the outside world, yet at the same time you were on your own, free to think and behave as you liked.

Smoking on the other hand seemed oddly cold and anti-social. Despite the burning tip of the cigarette and the clouds of billowing smoke, the effect was dispossessing, almost binary. But there was still an effect Matthias knew. He inhaled on his cigarette and within seconds the smoke seemed to travel directly to his head, swirling and encircling his brain.

Somewhere near the furthest point at the back of his skull he would experience a lightheaded prick of consciousness, but this was always accompanied by a foggy numb feeling as if his brain had been dampened by cotton wool padding. His senses seemed muted, he imagined this is what it must be like to be one of those patients in a psychiatric ward, permanently kept on high doses of medication to keep them docile. No, it was obvious to any observer that Matthias smoked because he simply needed something to do in between thinking.

Philippe, well, yes, now he was the outlier in the group. Despite being naturally gregarious, Philippe smoked with other smokers to be alone. He knew that inside the cube his two companions would understand and respect this unofficial smoker's code. The tacit understanding and respect for the privacy that can only really be achieved amongst fellow smokers.

Like everything in the mind of this engineer, smoking was a process. He drew in the smooth smoke through the barrel of his briar pipe, watching the faint glow from the bowl of the pipe as the cool outside air was drawn over the tobacco. Then, slowly, he tilted his head a fraction, closed his eyes, and after waiting, for what to the observer, appeared to be several seconds, he could be seen exhaling calmly through his nostrils, eyes opening, a slight sparkle reflecting off his clear grey pupils, sometimes showing that moment of illumination as a small piece of a larger problem was moved neatly into the correct place.

Li stood as he addressed the team in the conference room. Matthias, as ever, was observing him closely. Li's gaunt, almost translucent skin stretched tightly over prominent cheekbones. Perched lightly upon these porcelain-like cheekbones sat half-moon glasses whose thin, slightly tinted lenses seemed to magnify his owlish eyes. The whole effect made Li look more like a sage or wizard than the head of an UN Department.

Matthias was fascinated by Li. He had once commented to his old friend Philippe, that observing Li was like staring at a painting by Rubens or Van Dyck. It was simply impossible to take it all in and understand everything with one reading, you were compelled to keep going back again and again and each time you did, you learned something new. Matthias had spent half his life reading people and never before had he come across anyone as complex as Li.

Despite initially mistrusting the older Chinese man, Matthias along with the rest of the team had grown to respect and admire him for his honesty, intellect and leadership. All of which had been evidenced during the recent world nuclear crisis where the team had been pivotal in uncovering the plot to destroy the world's oil supplies by a fanatical Iraqi scientist.

"I have just finished a meeting with a rather frustrated Secretary General. As you are all aware the situation between Russia and the West over the invasion of Lithuania seems to be getting worse instead of better. The British Ambassador to the UN just announced that the UK would be forward basing a full heavy combat brigade in Poland and rebasing three squadrons of their Eurofighter Typhoons back in their old base near the Ruhr in Germany. The Americans have already begun construction on permanent basing for 3 forward brigades to the west of Lithuania in Poland and to the North in Latvia and one reserve base in Germany, plus, as we speak, they are restocking their Air Base at Ramstein with more combat aircraft than it had at the height of the Cold War. This is serious, really serious!"

Li looked around the room trying to gauge his team's mood. Penny, sat head down, was busy scribbling away with her digital pen on the table's surface, she was writing in Mandarin, Li noted. Andrei, the former Russian Special Forces officer appeared distracted and kept glancing at his phone.

Penny was the first to speak. "I was doing some quick maths and you said the UK has committed a full heavy brigade to Poland. I don't think the MoD has the troops. I know the Foreign Secretary is an old war monger, but the Chief of the General Staff Sir Rupert Heeringly is a cautious man who has been railing against Defence cuts for years now. What I'm trying to say is," Penny, cast her gaze around the assembled group. "I don't think the UK has the troops or the budget to forward base an entire brigade on a permanent footing?"

"Yes, glad you concur Penny. You see that's what we thought as well" said Li, "Penny can you reach out your people at MI6 and see if you can get any clarity on the situation. Is the UK bluffing hoping the Russians will move?" "Certainly Li" replied Penny. "And Maria, could you maybe see if your Secret Service contacts can give you any ideas on the American's thinking?" "Sure boss," replied Maria.

Peering over his half-moon glasses, Li glanced around the table once more, then started to speak again. "Ok back to business. Before I let Matthias give you an update brief, I wanted to focus your thinking a little. You see we have one priority task, which I know you are already deep into the planning for. That is to provide energy and border security capabilities for the newly fractured European States. I want to stress at this point this remains our key focus. However, we have just received a secondary tasking from the Secretary General."

Despite looking tired, Li's eyes flashed mischievously as he spoke.

"We have 30 days to prepare a report for his eyes only, regarding the Lithuanian problem. As you can probably all imagine the resumption of a Cold War in Europe would have severe effects on European geopolitical structures. Energy supplies, raw materials, transport links, flows of capital and investment could all be switched off or moved in a matter of days. Our report is to analyse two things: The possible geopolitical and economic effects of a continued occupation of Lithuania by Russia i.e. the status quo. And what the world may look like if NATO and the Americans feel they want to remove Russia forcibly from Lithuania"

Li dropped his briefing file on the table with a heavy thud, as he finished his final sentence. Looking around at the now silent room. Five very serious pairs of eyes stared back at him. The sixth pair belonged to Andrei the Russian, who appeared not to have noticed that Li had finished speaking and was sat staring fixedly at his mobile phone frantically trying to refresh an app. Li quietly noted this but chose to say nothing.

"Li," "Yes Penny" "Sorry, before we move on to Matthias' brief, I have that information on the UK deployment for you" "My God, that was quick" With a slightly nervous smile, creasing Penny's smooth pale complexion, she replied. "Yes, err, Charu helped me renew my old log on details at Vauxhall Cross."

Staring suspiciously once more over his half-moon glasses, Li said "Do I want to know how she did this for you?" "Err, probably better you don't." replied Penny who's usually pale and blemish free face had become diffused with a blush of pale red. Glancing over at Charu she saw her partner in crime, whose face, in comparison to Penny's appeared to be positively glowing, as she desperately tried to cover her embarrassment by hiding her face behind a sheath of paper notes.

Quickly, recomposing herself, Penny delivered her brief summary. "It's fascinating actually, I got access to a government White Paper from 6's database" Penny usually referred to her old organisation simply as 6 instead of MI6, or as it was actually officially called, the Secret Intelligence Service.

"So, yes, the paper recommends an open-ended commitment. Funding is to come from an emergency funding source for operations, they call it Net Additional Costs to Military Operations. And despite the core of the brigade being Regular Forces, for the first time they have invoked emergency powers and have activated compulsory Reserve call up for the Reserve Forces who don't volunteer. They plan for 60% of the Brigade to be manned by Reserve troops each on one-year tours of duty."

Matthias grasped the meaning immediately and started scribbling furiously on his piece of the table. Penny, a trained Intelligence Officer knew full well that simply reciting facts, could be done by anybody. Synthesizing the data and creating solid analysis was why she had been considered by many of her peer group at MI6 as an outstanding Intelligence Officer.

"My analysis of this." Penny continued "is that this is too much expense and commitment for simply maintaining a long-term defensive force. This to me looks more like Her Majesty's Government is seriously considering military action. Having a reserve Brigade already in situ means they could augment this brigade with another brigade within 48 hours, by mobilising the UK's high readiness rapid reaction brigade, to the area if they decided to attack the Russians."

"Your government and their American friends are either committing to war with Russia, or they are playing a very high stakes poker game. Either way I guess we are about to see how strong that 'Special Relationship' is." said Matthias, standing as he did so to begin his phase of the presentation. Double tapping on his area of the table, Matthias selected an icon then using a five-finger-spreading hand gesture he 'virtually' thrust the icon out of his area of the table.

Instantly the table's surface filled with a high-definition colour map of Europe. In fact, the result was so startling that each of the 7 assembled team members sat around the table physically reacted by pushing themselves and their chairs back from the table. Philippe who had been lounging back in his chair at the time, toppled backwards onto the floor as his chair, overbalanced by his huge frame, caught a strip of carpet beading and tipped over.

Silence filled the room, as the bearded Canadian slowly rose to his feet. As his huge head appeared above the edge of the table a grin splitting his face from ear to ear was the first thing the team saw. They all fell about laughing. "Huhum!" Matthias said. "If we are all sitting comfortably! I will begin." Matthias began his brief.

Walking around the table, Matthias first tapped on the 3D multi-layered satellite map image of Spain, as he did so the country fragmented, in front of their eyes. A pulsing, shaded, upside down triangular section in the northeast of the country stretching from the Pyrenean border with Andorra and France in the north, down to its tip around Valencia in the south vibrated. After the vibrating stopped a new thicker inter-country border line now traced its way from north to south between Spain and the newly formed independent Republic of Catalonia.

This event wasn't news to anyone sat around the table, but seeing it happen in front of you in such a dramatic and visible manner, really hammered home the fact. Reaching further east Matthias next tapped on Italy. This time the graphics on the LED tabletop were even more impressive, Walt, the newest member, flinched and jumped back as a holographic representation of Italy and its islands, seemed to leap up from the surface of the table and then shatter into 6 independent pieces.

As the pieces fell back into the table, five of them began to pulse slowly just like Catalonia. "From this point south until you reach the toe of Italy," Matthias was pointing to a point just north of Rome. "This is all that is left of what you and I remember as the Italian Republic. Formed 157 years ago, and now just like the Roman Empire, merely a chapter in the history of the Mediterranean." Matthias' hands circled like a weatherman around the rump of what was left of the Italian State.

"Currently, it is without a functioning government after the previous government, which had only held power for 6 months, declared bankruptcy and foreclosed on its EU debt obligations. Sardinia, Elba, Capri, Venice and Sicily have all followed Catalonia's move and declared themselves independent of the Italian Republic."

"Most interesting is what has happened in the north. The Lega Nord, which has long sought independence from the Italian Republic, has declared a new state, the State of Padania. The Lega Nord and not the Republic of Italy now had France, Switzerland, Austria and Slovenia on its northern border and stretched down through Florence and Sienna to a line dissected through Perugia and Rimini on the east coast. Finally," said Matthias, reaching further over the table and tapping on Athens, "Finally, we have Greece."

Greece and all of its 6,000 islands large and small, seemed to sink into the table, then slowly resurface to just below the level of the other countries. "As you are all aware, Greece announced its 'Grexit' from the EU last week after the Italians declared insolvency."

To conclude his mesmerising and somewhat unnerving presentation, Mathias clicked his fingers and the hologram of a red bouncing ball popped up out of the table due north of Geneva above the town of Besançon in the east of France. In one arching leap the ball bounced across the table to just northeast of Nuremburg in Germany, and to everyone's amazement the little red hologram appeared to be straining to stop itself being pulled 400km further east to the Czech capital of Prague.

"That little red ball shows us how the geographical centre of the EU has changed over time from the founding of the EU in 1958, until today. With the UK out, Italy and Greece both effectively out, most political analysts will tell you that the real political centre of gravity probably lies around Prague, and is being pulled steadily north eastwards towards Warsaw, as the rising power of the former Eastern European states, now collectively known as the Visegrád States of Czech, Hungary, Poland and Slovakia vie for ever more power from Paris and Berlin."

"So that's the overview," said Matthias, looking from face to face as he returned to his seat after his stunning presentation. Every single person around the room with the exception of Charu, who had helped him make the presentation and Andrei, sat speechless. Andrei, Matthias noted, still seemed more concerned with his mobile phone than interacting with the group. This had been going on for nearly a week now. Matthias made a mental note to speak to Maria, Andrei's girlfriend, about him.

"Oh, I nearly forgot, before I begin the analysis and Charu brings you up to date on the interventions we have planned." Matthias placed three fingers and a thumb in his area of the table and drew them together as if trying to pick a small object off the table. As he did so, the map zoomed out to become a globe, rotated smartly westwards then zoomed back up to scale, to show North and South America.

One final gesture, another click of his fingers, and a holographic wall sprang up along the US/Mexico border. At which point, Walt couldn't help himself anymore and reached forward to a point just below San Diego and tried to touch the holographic wall. "It's incredible, isn't it?" he said looking around at the others. "It is indeed said Li, and its thanks to our resident genius here, Charu." Charu blushed and lowered her head once more. Matthias coughed to regain the focus and began his analysis.

Matthias spoke for nearly an hour explaining the political and economic strain the current situation was having on the EU and on Mexico. "The long and short of it is, whilst the EU is trying to figure out whether to allow these new states to be full members, and whilst Mexico is coming to terms with the social and economic hit it is taking as the US withdraw all factories and industry from Mexico, people are suffering. Essential central government services such as border security and power generation have either stopped working or are being used as political bargaining chips."

Matthias glanced across at Philippe, who took over. "Matthias and I have been working up plans after speaking with the 'de facto' leadership of each of these independent states. Also, Penny, Andrei and Maria have been out on the ground gathering data on sites and locations for us to place our infrastructure. Finally, Charu and her team leaders at the different Tech Transfer Centres around the world have worked up technical plans and costings. Handing over to Charu, Philippe took his seat once more.

Charu, stood, clapped her hands together twice and began to speak. As she clapped, a myriad of small icons flew up and hovered over the newly pulsing states on the digital map. "The icons are of different sizes as they represent the amount of each resource we will be putting into each area." Scooping up a turbine-shaped icon from above Catalonia, she released it and it hovered a foot above the table and slowly rotated.

"As you can see, from this example in Girona, where we were already trialling the reservoir-based hydropower plant and the sea-based wave-energy generators, these two forms of power generation alone will supply over 75% of the energy requirements for Catalonia. And the rest will come as we lay the Piezzo-crystal matting..."

"Sorry," interrupted Walt, waiving his hand in the air. "Yes, Walt, what do you need to know?" Charu asked looking directly through the holographic turbine icon over at him. "Erm, two questions, firstly, I am happy with hydro power generation, but what the hell are piezzo-electric crystals, and most importantly how will this be paid for?" "Both valid questions. I'll answer the first part then pass you over to Philippe to answer the second part."

"Piezo-electric crystals generate a tiny amount of electricity when they are placed under pressure. Basically, our team in Windhoek Namibia have created a durable rubber matting made from recycled tyres and the crystals. We have identified the busiest sections of road and pedestrian areas and these will be covered in this matting. The rest is simple, as people or cars traverse the matting, the force they generate pushing down onto the matting generates electricity for free. This electricity is fed directly into sub stations and distributed locally."

" OK," said Walt "sounds incredible, but say I go along with the idea. I'm an economist and I know nothing comes for free. How is it paid for?" Philippe jumped in at this point. "Unlike typical power generation, there is no base cost for raw fuel such as gas, oil or coal required to generate the electricity, therefore all of the costs are for the initial infrastructure, such as the matting or the sea generators. The payment part is unique but actually quite simple. As no other power generation is available there is no competition. If you want electricity you have to sign up with us."

"Very smart," cut in Walt. Philippe smiled. "People simply pay their fuel bills directly to us. If you like they are making loan repayments on the infrastructure that we are providing. It is actually fascinating, it took us several months of negotiation to get the World Bank to agree to the principle."

"In effect the World Bank put up the capital required based on our estimates and the money is paid back to them via a form of crowdfunding website. Consumers in these areas simply sign up to the crowdfunding site and pay what we consider from our projections at least a monthly bill 30% cheaper than the average."

"Wait, so you are not dealing with a government?"

"That's right" Philippe said. "In many cases legitimate governments are in a kind of legal limbo as arguments over sovereignty and status continue. So, we thought it better to deal directly with the customer." Walt, leaned back in his chair, a broad grin on his face. "Bravo," he said, slowly clapping his hands in admiration. "You know in my field of economics, an idea like that could earn you a Nobel Prize."

Matthias noticed that Charu, seemed almost confused by Walt's statement. Her eyebrows remained flattened, pupils exhibited no change in size and her head and neck muscles remained relaxed. Nothing in her body language or demeanour showed any hint of the type of excitement expected when someone tells you, your ideas could win a Nobel prize. The truth was, Matthias thought, still staring absentmindedly at Charu, that Charu simply could not be classified as usual.

In the time Matthias had been working with her, he had personally experienced six or seven different ideas or inventions from fields as diverse as quantum physics, complex systems, chemistry and computer science that could have earned her a Nobel Prize. Put, quite simply, this rather fragile looking, socially-awkward Indian-born maths prodigy, worked on a different intellectual plain to nearly anyone on the planet. Anyway, mused Matthias silently to himself, at least this new encryption puzzle Charu had been given to investigate might keep her hyper-intelligence occupied for a little longer than usual.

An old friend of Penny's who worked for GCHQ, the UK equivalent of the American NSA, had been in touch to ask a favour from the team. As part of their work in monitoring illicit dark web activities, they had been doing a routine data sweep of encrypted internet traffic and had picked up an infrequent series of satellite-borne messages that were encrypted in a way that no-one working at the UK's highly prestigious listening station had ever seen before.

In essence all they had was a general trace or address-based direction of each message, but nearly all of the message's metadata simply disappeared every time the messages were intercepted and viewed by an analyst. Penny's contact had asked if Charu could make any sense of the random batch of data that had been collected and see if her modelling could draw out any decipherable patterns.

Keen to get her speaking part over with as quickly as possible Charu continued with her briefing. "Finally, we have the border security issue." Placing the palm of one hand flat on the table directly over Rome, she vigorously swiped it side to side as if trying to wipe off a stubborn stain. The movement generated a small cloud of pixels that seemed to rise up above the table and hang suspended in small swarms around the contiguous borders of each of the newly formed independent states of the former Italian Republic.

"Remember the mini-drone swarms our Sao Paulo team developed to monitor the rainforest? Well, we simply deploy these around the borders of these new mini-states. The drones can be cheaply and quickly produced locally through 3d printing and once aloft, they will self-organise and maintain coverage almost indefinitely. The UN and Interpol, plus several of the richer European nations have offered funding for the project. It is in nobody's interest for a break down in law and order to occur in these areas."

As she spoke, she grabbed the edge of a drone swarm and physically pulled it to cover part of Croatia. "You see, they move as swarms and are easily re-deployable. The UN and the richer EU states such as Germany, France and the UK know full well that the cost of this border security is far cheaper in the long term than allowing uncontrolled migration, and criminal activity, which will without doubt affect northern Europe manifesting itself in increased asylum seekers on the streets of Paris or gang wars over drug distribution on the streets of Berlin or London."

"OK I get that we can monitor the borders through these drones." Maria, the former US Secret Service Agent emphasised the word monitor "But how do these small states track down and prosecute the criminals?" "They don't!!" exclaimed Charu. "What I mean is that the vast majority of the type of crimes we are talking about are multi-jurisdictional inter-country crimes, that span continents in some cases. This is work for Europol, Interpol or even UN criminal investigators. What we do, is provide the evidence. Here let me show you."

Turning towards her area of the desk, Charu typed rapidly on a virtual keyboard on the desk's surface. "OK, watch the screen, starting near Paris." Each person in the room began to focus on a small red dot just west of Paris near Calais. Charu gave a commentary as the screen began to bloom thin multi-coloured tendrils of interconnecting nodes.

"Look here, Calais, Paris, Marseille, Barcelona, all the way down the coast of Spain to just east of Gibraltar. Now look." The multitude of coloured tendrils snaked across the Mediterranean Sea, then like a spider's web, they spoked out in a web of connections from Tangier eastwards, all the way back to a point of concentration centred on a small dusty town called Az Zawiyah which lay just an hour and a half west of Tripoli in Libya.

"What you have just witnessed is the effect of 'Digital Exhaust Tracking" Charu held up both hands and gestured with two fingers, the universal sign for quotation marks. "Using ATMs, cell phone data, surveillance cameras, GPS, electronic payment receipts, and a host of other data. It is effectively possible to track a person or group of related people over time."

"Bloody Hell" muttered Penny. "What you have just witnessed are the interactions between a group of migrants from North Africa and their journey to the holding camp at the port of Calais, commonly known as the 'Jungle'."

"The lines represent movement of the migrants themselves, but the nodes, these are the really important part. They represent communication between the refugees and the people responsible for this disgusting trade in human trafficking. The people who pass the migrants from city to city, milking them of their wealth, pride and dignity along the journey. In this case, we managed to trace back the organisation's leader to Az Zawiyah in Tripoli. I believe, the gentlemen in a property we identified using digital exhaust tracking, recently received a surprise night-time visit from a joint Interpol and UN team."

After another half hour of discussions, the meeting broke up and the team members filed out of the conference room and made their way slowly back to their work areas. Maria grabbed Andrei by the wrist and said, "I think we need some fresh air." Moving outside the impressive steel and glass building in the heart of Singapore's tech centre, Andrei and Maria started to walk around the forest-lined series of avenues that made up Singapore's version of Silicon Valley. "OK out with it. What are they saying? Did your friend get back to you?" Maria asked.

Before joining the CTC, Andrei had been part of the highly secretive Project Ultra. As leader of his 24-man team of Russia's FSB Border Guard Service, he and his team had been put through a gruelling 3-year programme of physical development and genetic endurance enhancement. A genetically modified haemoglobin carrying molecule had been grown and harvested to match the DNA of each individual member of the team.

This enhanced oxygen carrying molecule was then reintroduced into the subjects' body. The net result after the 3-year trial was a group of ultra-soldiers known under the code name of волф пакк or Wolf Pack. The Wolf Pack had been originally conceived to chase down terrorists and insurgents in the mountainous terrain of Chechnya and Dagestan.

The results had far exceeded any expectations. In a fully trained and charged state, one of these elite men could run for up to 10 hours over any terrain at altitudes of up to 5,000 metres, without taking on any extra food, at speeds that an Olympic marathon runner would struggle to match. In addition, these men could achieve these feats of endurance whilst carrying a load of up to 10kg. Not a heavy load by military standards, but sufficient to carry, a pistol, sniper rifle and ammunition.

Andrei had been part of the Ultra programme, indeed he had been the Wolf Pack's leader. But, by the time the programme was preparing to be made operational for the first time, Russia had invaded the Ukraine. His Commander, General Korinski, had called him into his office and delivered the crushing news. Due to a relationship that Andrei's sister had once had with a Ukrainian dissident, it had been decided that making Andrei operational and trusting him with top secret operational information would pose too high a security risk. As such Andrei had been de-commissioned from the programme and sent to work for the UNCTC.

Passing his cell phone to Maria, Andrei said, "Look at the levels." Maria opened the app that had been created to record the haemoglobin levels of the ultra-soldiers. Once a month Andrei took a pinprick of blood, rather like a diabetic would for testing. The resulting levels of modified haemoglobin were displayed on the app. Maria, glanced at the data on the app, and read the indicator which looked like a battery icon. Only one bar was visible and it was flashing red.

"What does it mean Andrei?" she said turning to him with a worried look on her face. "Dr Aziminov, the programme's lead doctor, told us that this was the only drawback to the programme. You see, the level of enhanced haemoglobin slowly drops over time as the molecules get corrupted and die off." "But, but, does this mean that you will lose your abilities?" Maria asked. "Not entirely, you see, half of my high endurance levels come from the intense restricted diet training they put us through, but the extra performance relating to my ability to metabolise oxygen, yeh, they, as we can see on the app, they are almost gone."

"So what can we do about it?" "You know I'm persona non grata, at the training facility? Don't you? And you know that they would never willingly give me any more haemoglobin? Do you remember Pyotr, who was on the programme with me?" Yes, isn't that the guy who called you about the Russian bombers, last year?" "Yeh, that's him. I have been in touch with him, and it seems I still have an ally in Dr Aziminov." Maria looked questioningly at Andrei.

"Dr Aziminov was the medical lead for the project. I was one of his first subjects and I think he sees me more like a father does a son. Anyway, long story short, Pyotr texted me this morning. Dr Aziminov is prepared to synthesize some more haemoglobin for me, but it is very risky. If the General or any of the other scientists catch him" Andrei trailed off "Well let's just say Dr Aziminov may become subject to the less-friendly type of people that work in the Lubyanka."

"So what's the plan?" "Pyotr wants us to meet up to exchange the haemoglobin in Helsinki. There are regular flights from Moscow to Helsinki and it shouldn't arouse too much suspicion it's a popular weekend destination for young Russians. There is a catch though." Andrei turned to Maria, "I thought there was something else. Is this why you have been so weird towards me the last few days?" Andrei didn't know how to ask Maria. He had to admit, he had grown very fond of her over the last year and the thought that he might be putting her in danger, was tearing him apart.

"You know I said we would do the exchange in Helsinki, well the fact is that because Pyotr is FSB, he will automatically be followed when he enters Finland, not just by the Finns, but by our guys as well. If he is seen meeting with me then I am afraid, well he might find himself sharing a cell with Dr Aziminov once he gets back to Moscow." Maria, interrupted Andrei, "So you want me to be the one who meets him?" Andrei couldn't hold her gaze any longer and turned away.

"You big dumbass, of course I'll do it. Just promise me one thing. That you never keep anything like this from me again?" Visibly relieved, a tearful Andrei turned to Maria and hugged her. "So, what happens next?" "We fly together to Helsinki. I'll wait in the hotel whilst you go to the meet and pick up the haemoglobin serum. Bring it straight back to the hotel and then I'll sit in the hotel room, hooked up to a saline drip for about 4 hours whilst the haemoglobin is slowly introduced into my body."

"When's the meet?" "Saturday evening" "Saturday!!, that's in two days' time!!!" "I know it's short notice, but Pyotr only has a small window of opportunity, his unit is preparing for a big deployment, he wouldn't tell me where, but he says it's a big deal and very hush hush. I have checked flights, there is one flight a day, Finnair, I think, it leaves daily just before midday, we would need to fly out Friday and return on Sunday. Can you do that?"

"Sure, but you owe me, and by the way, you better tell Li and Matthias about this. They know something is wrong with you." "What, tell them about Project Ultra?" "Li, already suspects, when he was in Moscow recruiting you, he told me that the Colonel who is aide to the General was very chatty about the programme. He doesn't know, or even need to know specifics, but I am sure you will find a sympathetic ear, if you go speak to them. Maybe, don't tell them about the danger involved in the handover, or that Russian intelligence is involved. Just tell them that you are going to Helsinki to get some reboot juice and that you fancied making a weekend of it, so I am going along with you.

Chapter Four

deception [noun]

Definition of deception

The act of causing someone to accept as true or valid what is false or invalid

- *You've been the victim of a rather cruel deception.*

Erik, Bernese Alps

This time the conversation with his handler had been mercifully short. No boring lectures about the new European political landscape. Instead, he had simply told Erik to view the file on the target and then he had gone on to explain who Erik could contact in Berlin for access to resources, once he had decided on how to execute the target.

Erik always appreciated the latitude he was given with his assignments, he considered that he took great care, and if he was honest with himself, great pleasure in devising, planning, and executing each of his assignments.

One night, almost 20 years ago, after spending three days stalking an injured male lion which, in itself was being hunted and harried by a pack of hungry hyenas, high up in the Drakensburg mountains of South Africa, Erik's Uncle Rudy had taught Erik his most important lesson. He taught him that hunting and killing were as much about strategy and art as they were about tactics and techniques.

Laying his wiry frame down onto his bedroll and gazing up at the stars Uncle Rudy asked Erik to think. "So my boy, how do you think we are going to kill that old rogue lion?" Uncle Rudy had asked as the cool night air caused the two men to shiver. They had deliberately not made a fire for fear of scaring off their quarry.

"We are going to shoot it right, then take it back home and skin it?" Rudy looked at Erik and said; "that is what we have to do, I want to know how we are going to do it? Let me explain the problem: We need to get close enough to the lion to get a clean shot, agreed?" Erik nodded, "If the hyena hear us they will alert the lion with their howling and maybe even attack us. If we shoot from too far away, the hyena will get to the beast before we do. So what should we do?"

Rudy peered into the young Erik's eyes and watched him as he pieced together the elements of his hunting strategy. "OK, so there are too many hyena for us to kill, so we distract them by killing an antelope for them to feed on. You taught me that they will always prefer an easy safe meal to running the risk of getting injured by hunting right?" Rudy nodded his encouragement. "Whilst they are eating, we wait for the lion to move on. We know he is moving towards the migrating wildebeest herd in the valley, when he is close, we shoot and use the distraction of the panicked wildebeest herd to get away with the lion's carcass, back to the pick-up truck."

It was now Erik's turn to stare into his Uncle Rudy's eyes. Had he got it right? Did the old soldier approve? Uncle Rudy's muffled yet throaty roar startled Erik, but not as much as his giant calloused hand striking him on the back. "Bloody good plan my boy, we'll make a hunter out of yet. You got it all, we use deception, distraction, and choose the time and ground that best suits us. My boy I have been teaching soldiering skills for the better part of my life, and you know what? Now don't let this go to your head boy, but you are a natural, you understand the subtleties of our art. I think you are nearly ready to go back to your father in Holland, there is not much more that this old soldier can teach you."

Erik lay, slightly stunned by the older man's comments. In the past 8 years that Erik had been living and learning from his Uncle Rudy, he couldn't recall one single instance when the old man had shown his emotions or even uttered any real praise. Of course, Erik hadn't needed the praise, and to be fair he hadn't expected it from the grizzled former Selous Scout, but there had been times, he knew when it would have been nice to hear a few words of encouragement.

Shaking away the memory of his final hunting trip with his Uncle Rudy, Erik returned his thoughts to the present. The file on his latest target had been received through the Organisation's unique quantum internet security protocol. To Erik, the really amazing thing was how this quantum technology worked. The file that he was viewing, quite literally only existed when he viewed it on his specially adapted computer. Just like Schrödinger's cat, it was the very act of observing, or looking at the file, that changed its state.

He couldn't download the file, it didn't sit on his hard drive, in actual fact the particular arrangement of qubits that formed the information and images in the file that Erik had received, would return to their natural resting state, that of a blank screen, as soon as the device's camera recognized that he had looked away from his screen for more than 30 seconds.

Of course, the quantum capability was limited, in that it would only work when he was connected to his Control, which meant he had to memorize the information before he left his smart and ultra-modern Swiss chalet for the short, but enjoyable drive, through the Swiss Alps to Zurich.

With over eight flights per day connecting the two cities, Erik could take his time getting to Zurich, well maybe not take his time, but certainly enjoy the drive. Releasing the parking brake on his cobalt blue BMW i8 Erik eased the hybrid electric supercar out of the underground garage and onto the drive. The 357 horsepower four-wheel drive car could make the journey of a little over 150km in just over an hour.

Running on electric power only he slipped silently out of the village and waited until he was several kilometres outside the village before he thrust his foot down hard on the accelerator and felt the full brutish force of the supercar invade his senses as he was thrust physically back into his seat and the landscape around him accelerated to a blur in seconds.

The drive essentially traversed a meandering valley, heading north, then north-east. The idyllic alpine valley road was punctuated by a series of magnificent lakes, starting with the Brienz See which cupped the southern flank of Interlaken for nearly ten kilometres.

Leaving Interlaken behind, his journey was framed on the left, that is to say, to the north by the Hohgant mountain in the Emmental range, and to his right, to the south, the magnificent Jungfrau mountain which stood nearly twice as tall as the Hohgant. The i8 flowed onwards past the Sarnesee, and onto Lake Lucerne.

It was at this point, with about half the journey remaining that Erik, who had subconsciously been considering his strategy for his latest contract, had his attention spiked temporarily, as he realised that he had become interested in a news report on German radio about the German government's policy on integrating Asylum seekers from North Africa.

The debate was beginning to heat up. The presenter had been pressing, or maybe to Erik's trained ear, provoking the interviewee, the mayor of Berlin. "50% of crimes in Berlin against women were committed by North African immigrants last year Herr Bürgermeister! 5% of hard-working Berliners' taxes this year will go to rehousing, social and education programmes for these people."

The Bürgermeister had been trying to interrupt her diatribe for the last 5 minutes, without result. "Also, we have documentary evidence proving that these immigrants are directly associated with ISIS in North Africa. How long will it be, Herr Bürgermeister, until one of those terrorists detonates a suicide vest killing innocent Berlin residents?"

Finally, a chance to speak, thought the mayor "Ms Loebstein" The Mayor, stressed her name, subtly highlighting the fact that she was from a German Jewish family. "Ms Loebstein, you of all people must realise that the German state has a legal and ethical obligation to protect refugees and minority groups, whatever their religion!!"

He knew that the reporter was part of a significant and ever-increasing minority group that was anti-Islamic. Germany was traditionally a Christian country, predominantly Catholic in the south and Protestant in the North. The legacy of the 1st World War had led to a large influx of Turkish migrants after the collapse of the Ottoman Empire, this alone had led to large scale violence on numerous occasions especially in Kreuzberg, the predominantly Turkish suburb of Berlin.

The Nazi's appalling crimes of Holocaust during the 2nd World War had led it to accept, or maybe tolerate would be a better word,

Jewish settlements in the modern post-war Germany. "Frau Loebstein, the figures you are quoting are..." The Bürgermeister was abruptly cut off, as the young radio presenter, who had timed her segment to perfection, introduced the regional news report. "Thank you Herr Bürgermeister I am sorry we don't have any more time to discuss this important issue...."

Erik smiled to himself, "Deception, distraction, select your killing ground and choose your time." he said to himself under his breath. His strategy was beginning to take shape.

strategy [noun]

Definition of strategy

The science and art of employing political, economic, psychological, and military forces of a nation or group of nations to afford the maximum support to adopted policies in peace and war

- *I've just been explaining the principles of strategy to my Generals.*

Office of the Russian President, Kremlin, Moscow

President Mikhail Mikhailovich Voronin, was in an unusually buoyant mood, thought Grigori Grigorovic Popov. The two men had known each other for nearly 25 years, ever since they were young recruits at the, then KGB's Dzerzhinsky Training Academy. It was 11.30 in the evening and the two men were sat at a casual table in the President's official suite, with a half empty bottle of the President's personal vodka open between them.

"Grisha, tell me what do our comrades in the Cyber Division have to report?" Mikhail Mikhailovich Voronin often used the now defunct term, Comrade. Politically he was as far as it is possible to go along the spectrum from being a Communist. However, he maintained the usage of the term because it served to remind both him and his audience of how powerful Russia, or as it had then been known, the

Soviet Union had once been.

Grigori Popov, architect of the entire Lithuanian occupation strategy and head of the Russian Intelligence Service, the newly named FSB, was himself a former crypto analyst. He knew that he was the more intelligent of the two men sat at the table, however, and rather more importantly, he also knew that his long-time friend and now President of the Russian Federation was by far the more ruthless, ambitious and cunning of the two of them.

"So Misha," He used the diminutive of the President's first name, only when they were in private, reflecting that, with the exception of the President's wife and his various mistresses, he was one of the very few people in the Federation who would dare even consider using this name.

"You know unlike the, now what is it the General's call it. Yes, that's it kinetic military operation to seize the Lithuanian corridor, which by its nature needed to be swift and overt, this war we are waging with our Cyber troops, it, err, needs to be more, subtle and suggestive." The President knew full well that his friend's rapacious brain, didn't falter over small facts such as military terminology. He knew it was just an old spy's affectation, to pretend not to be quite up to speed with a conversation, to downplay your level of knowledge and alertness. Once learned such skills were difficult to switch off.

Grisha, downed another shot of vodka, refilled both of their glasses and continued to talk. "You see, it all needs to be unattributable of course, but more than that, if it is to succeed it cannot be coercive. We are allowing people to believe they are informing themselves, generating their own opinions, discovering hitherto hidden truths."

President Voronin didn't interrupt his old friend, he genuinely enjoyed his friend's company. He knew Grisha was both talented and passionate about his work, and if Voronin's gamble with the West was going to pay off, he desperately needed his old friend Grisha's rapier-like intellect.

"You know Misha, my Head of Psychological Operations told me something very interesting the other day. He told me that humans are fundamentally pattern finding animals. They call it err." There it was once again, the affectation, pretending to search for words, like the absent-minded school professor.

"Yes! Now I recall, it's called Patternality!" A triumphant smile on his face. "Apparently, according to my head Shrink at least, it is hard-wired into our brains. In order to survive you see, we as individuals have to process a bewildering amount of data. Too much data actually. So what we do is simply to aggregate all of the data we have, into groups and fill in the blanks ourselves. In fact, in today's world, luckily for my department, we tend to allow the internet to do a lot of the aggregating for us." Voronin smiled at the comment and raised his vodka glass. "Nasdarovje!" the President said raising his glass.

Downing the shot, Misha continued "Our job at Cyber Security is to ensure that those mindless western Millennials, believe that they themselves have chosen enough data to be able to aggregate it into an opinion about our target person or in this case, country. Because humans are essentially group animals, if they receive the information from a group or website that they trust, then they automatically aggregate that information without suspicion. It kind of slips past the suspicion filter in our brain."

The President had read Popov's report, and the attached target list. Popov's team's targets were the youth of the EU and the USA. Its aims were to discredit political figures and highlight failures by their respective governments. The Chinese he knew were attempting a similar form of manipulation. They were trying to achieve the same aim, but their efforts were aimed not at the West, but at a series of key States such as North Korea, Iran, Turkey, Yemen, Afghanistan and Pakistan.

Obviously with these countries, they had little pushback trying to make people believe that the US were essentially bad. No, instead with these states, they were actively promoting Russia and China as viable allies and even alternatives to the US and the West.

Pouring them both another generous glass of chilled vodka, the President picked up the conversation. "Grisha, let me tell you where we stand. We have three interlinked strategies: Economic, Geographic and Political; Our new agreements with China, creates huge new gas and oil markets which mean we are not obliged to sell to Western Europe anymore. Additionally, we will need to spend very little reforming our armed forces because, as the Americans see it, they effectively have to have a Defence Strategy that can defend against Russia and China."

"But Misha" Grigori Popov cut in, filling the President's and his own vodka glasses once more, as he spoke. "Misha, do you really trust that little Chinese ant, Zhang Wu? Don't you think he and his old cronies in the Politburo won't try to fuck us over as soon as they have what they want?"

Raising his vodka glass, staring fixedly through the clear liquid for several seconds before downing the smooth, ice-cold spirit in one gulp, Mikhail Mikhailovich Voronin, President of the Russian Federation, looked coolly into his old friend's eyes. "You know Grisha, I always thought that you were the smart one between us. But today I think I actually know something that you don't!" His old friend laughed and drained his own vodka glass.

"Grisha, The Chinese economic miracle is also the Chinese curse. You see, they are trapped by their own success. Unlike our poor Mother Russia, they have an enormous population, which is growing exponentially, not just in number, but as they become wealthier, also in expectations. In order to create jobs for all of those people, China needs to continually increase its GDP and grow the markets where it sells its goods and where it can export its people and technologies." A slightly bleary-eyed Popov nodded his acknowledgement.

"If the Communist Party ruling elite cannot achieve this, then it will only be a matter of time before they are replaced. They are betting everything on their One Belt One Road Project. This new Silk Road has the potential to create a single trading bloc, with all of the connecting infrastructure that would be twice the size of the Soviet Union. To achieve this, they need our political support at the UN, they need our strategic support to defeat America and more than ever, they need energy and raw materials." The President, saw the seeds of understanding beginning to germinate in his friend's eyes.

"Thanks to climate change, our Arctic territories and Siberian regions are now more accessible than ever before. The Russian Federation is the single most resource rich entity in the world. Coal, oil, gas, iron, copper, gold, rare earth elements, I could go on." Misha was beginning to get into his stride, back onto a topic of conversation he was passionate about, thought Popov.

"The reason we lost the Cold War wasn't because we didn't have enough gold, it was because world markets wouldn't tolerate us selling enough of it without the price crashing. Now we will be creating our own new market, with the Renminbi and Rouble as the trading currencies."

By now Misha was beginning to feel the effects of the vodka, he felt relaxed, more so than he had since this plan to annex Lithuania had been put into effect. Reaching for his, still smouldering cigar from the gold ashtray embossed with the two-headed Eagle, he slumped back in his chair in astonishment, as the words of his oldest friend sunk in. "Grebany ad, (fucking Hell) Misha, that is brilliant, let us toast to our new, strong Russia!"

"One moment my friend before we open another bottle, I need to be sure that you understand what you need to do. Your job is to make sure that the world's smartphone and internet users understand two things: Firstly, how weak the United State of America is politically, and secondly, how ineffective the Americans are in policing the world. They are a State in decline Grisha." Grisha, drew hard on his cigar, exhaling the blue smoke high into the air, as he considered whether their old enemy America really was as weak as his friend was making out.

"Their corruption, insider dealing, political scandals, failed military interventions, poor trade and environment policies. These are what I want you to implant as thought seeds in the heads of all of those western Millennials. Oh, the last thing. Regarding Carlton P. Simpson, the US President, we need him to stay in power. What I am saying Grisha, is, just be careful how you use the dirt we have on him. Just enough to keep the Democrats and Republicans at each other's throats, but not enough to get him impeached." Popov inclined his head slightly at this last piece of information.

"Carlton P. Simpson is working for us, although he doesn't quite know it yet. He is foolish enough to spend tax dollars building up the US military, but he will never actually use it. He understands our agreement. He can build up their Armed Forces as much as he wants, but if the US ever attacks the Russian Federation, then we finish him."

"But what happens when he leaves office in three years' time?" a slightly confused Grisha asked. "In three years' time, it will not matter who is running America. They will be an insignificant regional power by then." Wrapping his huge fist around the vodka bottle, he placed his other arm around his old friend's shoulders. President Mikhail Mikhailovich Voronin of the Russian Federation stood up.

Nodding his head towards an anteroom, he said, "I think we have talked enough about politics tonight, don't you Misha my old friend? I think now maybe we should see if Katarina, Tatiana and Anastasia can find it in their patriotic duty to soothe the worries of these two old comrades."

Voronin winked at his old friend and pushed the door to the ante-room open. The opened door revealed the President's latest collection of courtesans. The three women were sat immodestly, in lingerie that would make Victoria Secret blush, thought Popov. The gilt-edged glass surfaced table in front of them contained two empty vodka bottles and several thin trails of white powder next to a discarded credit card and a thin gold-plated short straw. With complete composure, Anastasia, the self-appointed leader of the trio, turned to the President of the Russian Federation and coolly purred, "Misha, so glad you could join us. I hope you don't mind that me and the girls started without you?"

Her large green eyes were like deep pools. Pools that the Russian President couldn't wait to dive into. "Oh, and I see you have bought a friend to join our group." As if on cue, Katarina and Tatiana, stood on slightly shaky legs, Grisha couldn't tell, if it was the cocaine, the vodka or the stupendously high heels that was causing the girls to sway. To be fair, he wasn't that concerned, removing his jacket and slapping his old friend Misha hard on the shoulder, he allowed himself to be escorted by Katarina and Tatiana over to a corner sofa.

Chapter Five

remittance [noun]
Definition of remittance
Transmittal of money (as to a distant place)
Alternative: an instrument by which money is remitted

- *Monthly remittances make up one third of the country's GDP.*

Erik, Berlin

Germany's chancellor had been the longest serving German leader in the country's history. Surpassing even the indomitable Helmut Kohl. She had proved herself to be a skilful mediator with her EU counterparts, and prudent manager of the country's fiscal affairs. She had successfully steered the country through the financial crisis of the previous decade and the country had continued to see strong economic growth. As the senior partner of the two-country coalition at the heart of the old European Union, she had expended considerable political and economic capital to try and support the, economically speaking, weaker European states through the banking crisis.

Ten years on, her gamble had failed. With Italy and Greece both effectively reneging on their sovereign debt obligations, the burden would have to be borne by the honest hard-working German taxpayers. It was an open secret in Brussels and Paris that the bulk of the economic bailouts for the Greek and Italian banks had been generated by German Sovereign Debt obligations, and not, as some might want you to believe, from the coffers of France, the other senior coalition partner at the heart of the EU project.

She was now certain that her political career, as the longest serving Chancellor in German history was going to founder. It had become increasingly obvious that the solid, dutiful German taxpayers were never going to see a single Euro paid back to them by the Greeks and Italians.

She had hoped to delay her announcement to call an early election until closer to the end of her natural term in office, but the recent spate of attacks on German women by groups of young male asylum-seeking refugees had been the icing on the political cake. Under pressure from senior figures in her own party, she was under pressure to step down, allowing for her replacement to carve out their credentials with the voters before the next electoral cycle came around.

Erik's short flight to Berlin Tegel airport touched down punctually. It was hardly unexpected, Erik mused to himself. I mean if you leave a country famous for making watches and fly to a country obsessed with punctuality, you are hardly going to arrive late are you? Although he had flown from Zurich to Berlin, his actual destination was Munich. He had flown to Berlin as a diversion, he would spend the day in the city meeting with the Organisation's contact man to collect the military grade plastic explosive, timers and detonators, that he required for his plan.

After a detour to buy a video camera, he would head south, driving the vehicle provided for him by the Organisation, through the night, along the German Autobahnen, until he arrived, sometime around dawn, by his calculations in Munich. The plan was designed to leave minimal traces of his presence in the target city of Munich.

The plan had been calculated to the minute. The one drawback was that he personally wouldn't get to sleep until he was on his flight out of Munich back to his shimmering Cobalt blue BMW which lay parked at Zurich airport.

Erik climbed into the back of the ubiquitous beige Mercedes German taxi. Giving the taxi driver the name of a common chain hotel in Kreuzberg, he sat back in his seat and tried to close his eyes and grab 30 minutes' sleep. It was a matter of personal security that Erik always sat in the seat behind the driver. From this vantage point, it was easier to control the driver as well as being far harder for the driver to point a weapon at you.

Despite this reassurance for his own personal security, Erik was beginning to regret choosing that particular seat in that particular taxi. The driver, who had introduced himself as Klaus, must have weighed over 130kg, most of it fat, Erik thought. In order to cram his huge gut behind the steering wheel, Klaus had forced the driver's seat as far back on the rails as he could manage. To add insult to injury he had adopted the ubiquitous cabbies semi-prone seating position, by reclining the seat back.

The second annoying thing Erik had noticed about Klaus, was that he had talked incessantly ever since Erik had first entered the taxi. In his abrupt Berlin dialect, which still rendered his speech impolite, even when he was speaking English, Klaus gave an ongoing commentary on the football game.

The match was a local derby between two Berlin teams, FC Union Berlin and Hertha BSC. Neither team was ever going to challenge for the German championship, but as with all local derbies the match generated a Marmite mentality. You loved one team passionately and hated the other even more passionately.

The floor of the front passenger side of the vehicle, Erik noticed, was littered with old cigarette packets and polystyrene takeaway food boxes. The resulting fetid odour that permeated throughout the car was rank.

Erik recalled, once, whilst on a hunting trip with his Uncle Rudy, they had come across a half-eaten three-day old zebra corpse. The bloated cadaver lay at an awkward angle, three legs protruding upwards towards the sun, the other leg was missing. The corpse was smeared with congealed blood and covered in flies. Despite his best efforts, the smell was so rancid that Erik had to vomit.

Now, looking from the lank grey hair of the obese driver, down to the yellow imprints of day's old sweat rings under the armpits of his once white shirt, Erik's stomach began to stir once more as he thought of the bloated zebra.

The combination of stale cigarette smoke, day old congealed kebab fat and Klaus' fetid body odour was almost too much to cope with. He was almost relieved then when the driver wound down his window to swear and gesticulate at one of the thousands of tourists on one of the now ubiquitous city rental bikes.

The tourist had foolishly managed to swerve in front of Klaus' taxi, whilst simultaneously trying to steer the bike and navigate using his smartphone which, until Klaus had blown his horn, had been tightly clutched in the unsuspecting tourist's hand. The phone now lay in pieces on the asphalt. It hadn't broken up on impact, but Klaus had taken great delight in driving over it as he pulled away. "Arschloch!!" growled Klaus, closing the window.

For a brief moment, it seemed to Erik that the heavy diesel-filled air that had rushed into the car, through the temporarily opened window, had to some small degree allowed a momentary sensory reprieve for Erik's olfactory system. Erik was just about to ask the driver how much longer the journey would take when a news bulletin interrupted the football commentary.

"After several days of discussion amongst the CDU Party's leadership, it has been announced that Herr Hans Wollinger will run in the upcoming election as the preferred candidate for the position of Chancellor." The announcement was followed by several minutes of comment and speculation by the news media on Herr Wollinger's suitability and chances in the upcoming election.

Erik never failed to be surprised at the level of intelligence that his superiors in the Puritan Organisation had access to. The Chancellor had only announced her decision to step down the evening before, yet Erik had received detailed planning notes about Hans Wollinger or as Erik had come to know him, the target, more than two days ago.

As the car pulled to a stop at the entrance to the hotel, Erik grabbed his rucksack and with no inconsiderable difficulty, extricated himself from behind the driver. Inhaling heavily, he released a long breath of air, bent to pay Klaus then after waiting for the listing taxi to rumble around the corner, Erik, slipped his carry-on rucksack onto his shoulders and headed off at a brisk walk in the opposite direction.

His meeting was in two hours and the location, a small fast-food outlet called Mustafa's Kebab shop. It lay about 1 kilometre away. Plenty of time Erik thought to scope out the surrounding area and ensure that he wasn't being surveilled.

From his view in the park, opposite Mustafa's kebab shop, Erik observed seven people in the café. Three middle-aged Turkish men sat playing dominoes and occasionally drawing long steady inhalations of tobacco from unfiltered cigarettes. Obviously, the rules about not smoking in eating establishments hadn't reached Kreuzberg. Or maybe, it just wasn't good community policing to send two white Policemen into the heart of the densest Turkish population outside of Istanbul, during their lunch break, just to tell them they weren't allowed to smoke!

Behind the counter, Erik observed an older man, Mustafa, the owner, he presumed. Balding and in his late fifties, Mustafa wasn't simply someone that worked behind the counter in a greasy café. No, mused Erik to himself, Mustafa was the beating heart of the café.

In the fifty minutes that Erik had been surveilling the café, Mustafa hadn't ceased moving. Behind the garish, chipped Formica counter, Mustafa glided between the expresso machine, the deep fat fryer and the tall, glistening stacks of kebab meat from which Mustafa expertly sliced long slithers of the spicy meat with his whirring rotating saw.

Somehow, this balding middle-aged owner, managed to maintain a conversation with the three domino playing men in the far corner, whilst making thick Turkish coffee to order and preparing Kebab to takeaway.

The fourth occupant was a transitory one, younger, by maybe twenty years, than the other men. The youth had entered and left four times during Erik's time observing the café. He now stood at the counter, hurriedly knocking back a coffee, helmet in hand, whilst, Mustafa, the man Erik believed to be the boy's father, expertly packed three large polystyrene boxes crammed with kebab into the kid's delivery bag.

Waiting until the moped carrying the food order had disappeared around the block, Erik crossed the road and strode into the Kebab shop. No point in having another person witness this interaction, if he could really help it. Giving a friendly nod to Mustafa, Erik ordered an Expresso to go.

Fleetingly. The three domino playing men, paused their game, and appraised the new entrant. The Berlin city tourist map, in the breast pocket of his rain jacket and the urban walking shoes, all marked this guy out as another tourist that had got himself lost in the wrong part of town. A glance outside at the rented Berlin City Bike confirmed their suspicions.

Gratefully taking the coffee, Erik paid and, in halting German, asked how he could get to Checkpoint Charlie. Grabbing his drink and exiting the café, Erik strode towards his City Bike. Coffee in hand, he proceeded to push the bike in the direction that Mustafa had pointed out to him. As Erik left the café, the two other occupants, threw some change onto their table, gave a light-hearted salute to Mustafa and followed Erik out of the café northward towards Checkpoint Charlie.

Once out of sight of the café, the two men increased their speed until they were walking directly behind Erik. The two men looked African, the older of the two was thicker set and slightly shorter, his pale ochre coloured skin and loosely curled hair marking him out as Moroccan, most probably, thought Erik. His companion, the younger man, was reed thin, the only imperfections in his ebony skin were pockmarks on his cheeks, probably from malnutrition or an illness as a child. The face was completed with cold dark emotionless eyes. Either Sudanese or Eritrean, Erik thought.

Erik deliberately turned into a slightly smaller street, the thin Sudanese man stepped in front of him. "Can you spare some change for a man with many mouths to feed?" The request was made with dark humourless eyes. Erik, surveyed the youth, then said, "here hold this coffee while I look for some change." A young couple walking hand in hand down the street saw Erik being accosted by the two men and crossed the street to avoid them. Neither of them made any attempt to intervene, or shout for help.

Obviously, this type of activity wasn't uncommon in Kreuzberg's poorer streets, thought Erik, as, with a resigned look on his face, he reached into his trouser pocket. Simultaneously, he felt the hand of the other older man brush against the pocket of his raincoat, where he had previously stored the street map. Pretending not to notice, Erik handed the thin man in front of him a handful of change. The youth sneered at the handful of copper coins in his hand and said. "I think I'll take your phone as well."

With another shrug, Erik pulled out his flip up phone from his inside pocket. The boy's bony hand streaked across the gap between Erik and himself and snatched the phone from Erik's grasp. Without saying a word to his partner who for the entire time, had been stood sentinel behind Erik, the boy turned, still clutching Erik's coffee in his left hand and strode off briskly.

Erik turned in the opposite direction and walking quickly, soon found himself back on the main road heading back towards the hotel, where he had left his bag. As he walked, he checked his pockets. Sure enough, his visitor's guide had gone and in its place was a cheap black and white street map of the area. A point marking an underground carpark had been highlighted with a marker pen on the map. Also in his pocket Erik found keys to a Volkswagen Passat.

After collecting his rucksack from the hotel's safe room, Erik visited a large electronics store, where he bought a professional video camera. Although no way near as bulky as the older videotape versions. The compact Panasonic camera still weighed in at over 5lbs and with the standard lens fitted, the sleek matt black camera looked bulky enough to pass as a professional cameraman's tool of choice.

Stood at the counter, wearing a baseball cap and thick rimmed clear-lensed glasses, Erik asked the sulky teenage sales attendant to confirm the price, and enquired if he could have a 10% discount. The point of the exercise wasn't about saving money, it was about appearing as normal, and therefore forgetful as possible. Erik had deliberately chosen to buy the camera in Berlin in order to try and confuse and delay any post incident investigation by the Munich Police.

Erik figured that nobody would walk into a store and shell out 3,000 Euros on a high-end camera without asking for a discount. The sulky attendant grudgingly nodded and as he entered the new sales figure into the cash terminal, expecting Erik to use his card.

"You know man, that ain't the best we got. That's old tech man. Solid state drives that's what you need man. You gotta keep up with the times man, you get me?" The young German teen obviously thought that Erik was American and that all American teens spoke like gangsters. Erik wasn't looking at the teen, instead he was finishing off entering a string of characters into his virtual Bitcoin wallet on his encrypted phone that he had just retrieved from his rucksack.

"That'll do the job just fine." Looking at the youth, Erik picked up the plastic bag with the camera inside and made to leave the counter. "Hey man, you gotta pay" the youth said. Erik turned and waved his phone at the youth. "I just did. Bitcoin man, never heard of it. You gotta keep up man." The clerk looked back at the touch screen on his till and saw that the digital display was now showing an outstanding balance of zero. In the lower right-hand corner of the screen, a small pop-up display read, Payment made via Bitcoin.

The journey south to Munich was uneventful, after heading through Potsdam, he followed the Route 9 all the way past Nuremburg, and onwards to Munich. Cruising at 150 km per hour, Erik reckoned that the Passat could cover the nearly 600 km distance in just under 5 hours. A few stops to stretch, fill up and grab some food, was all Erik needed.

Inside the Passat's spare wheel, which was stored under the car, the Organisation's contact had placed two sticks of military grade plastic explosive. The timing detonators were stored separately inside the cover for the plastic warning triangle. Apart from Erik's bag and the newly acquired video camera the only other items in the untraceable car were a DAT sound machine and collapsible boom mike for recording outdoor interviews.

The DAT machine was a clunky piece of equipment that wasn't commercially available. In essence, it recorded and synchronised the audio feed from a speech or interview with the images captured on the camera. It wasn't strictly necessary with the newest models of cameras, but it was recognised in the film industry, that it produced superior sound quality to the camera's built-in microphone.

Part of Erik's plan involved posing as a journalist to get close to tomorrow's event, where Hans Wollinger, the Chancellor elect, aka the Target, would be holding a midday press interview after opening of another refuge for asylum seekers in his hometown of Munich. Just as the Organisation had predicted, Hans Wollinger, like most politicians, would start his campaign for the leadership from his home base of support.

Erik had checked the Passat's glove compartment which had contained, flight tickets back to Zurich, via Dublin, a new passport, some money, and press credentials with photos of two of the three men he would meet in Munich. As he drew close to Munich, a faint sun was just beginning to peer into the world of men. Erik, was surprisingly alert after his long drive, the trip hadn't been enjoyable and certainly not as exhilarating as if he had done it in his BMW i8, but it had given him time to review and refine his plan.

He had wanted to deal with as few people as possible, but it was essential to the plan that the thin sinewy Sudanese had been at the first meet in Berlin. Erik had learned long ago that if you wanted to co-opt people to help you, then you needed them to believe that the rewards outweighed the risk. In fact, you had to convince them that the rewards were something that they couldn't achieve without you.

The Sudanese man was a Hawala broker. Hawala was the practice of sending remittances from Europe back to Africa and it had been around a long time. It was essentially a chain of brokers who held either cash or promissory notes. These notes were balanced against cash holdings at set intervals.

The system was actually as old as the very first Italian Bankers whose network of brokers were pivotal in helping Florence, Milan and the other Italian Renaissance City States amass so much wealth and power.

In this instance, the broker, in location A, (Berlin) would receive hard cash. Then via a network of brokers who all held promissory notes, the money could be collected in location B, (Sudan), by the family member, (the recipient). Erik had engineered one extra step in the process. The Sudanese man he was going to meet in Munich, was another Hawala broker, who had received the note to transfer $1000 to the families of the other two men who lived in Juba, the capital of the newly formed state of South Sudan.

The Hawala agent's job was to show the reward to the other two Sudanese that had been co-opted to help Erik. They would see that, to them at least, a huge sum of money was secure and on its way to their families in Juba. The sum of $1,000 represented just over one year's income for the average Sudanese family. The money would be sufficient for the family to live comfortably, whilst the men now residing in Munich, who had been trafficked across the Mediterranean Sea in appalling conditions, could concentrate on paying back the network of people smugglers for their passage. Like many refugees, these two men were effectively in bondage to the smugglers until they had paid back the grossly inflated cost of their transport out of Africa.

Grünwald and Hasenbergl, are both residential areas in Munich. That is however, where any semblance of similarity ceases. They are figuratively and geographically polar opposites. The leafy suburbs of Grünwald lay on the extreme southern border of Germany's third largest city. Previously inhabited by Germany's leading film stars, Grünwald is known locally as the German Beverly Hills.

Hans Wollinger and family lived in a 7-bedroom villa overlooking the river Isar, with access through the gate at the end of the extensive and immaculate lawn to the leafy trails and footpaths of the Grünwald woods. The house where Lotta, his wife and their two children; Ingrid and Karl lived, wasn't large by Grünwaldian standards, but with a current market value of just over 3 million Euros, it certainly compared more than favourably with the house of the average German citizen.

Almost directly due north of Grünwald lies the less salubrious suburb of Hasenbergl, or little Rabbit Hill, as it is known to insiders. As with Grünwald, the suburb sits at the very outer edge of the city. The population comprises of a mixture of first, second and third generation refugees. It was here, where the Asylum Centre, which Hans Wollinger was going to inaugurate, had been built, and not, in the pristine streets of his Grünwald.

It was 8 am as Erik slowed the Passat as he turned into Ratoldstrasse. He parked the car, got out and stretched like a cat. The opening ceremony, that the Target was performing was at 2 pm. The local council had built the centre on a piece of derelict ground, in the east of Hasenbergl. If the sun ever did actually shine in Munich, then the new residents of the centre, would have a great view of the sunrise.

The eastern aspect of the centre looked out over rolling fields and woods. From his vantage point, at the Aral petrol station opposite the soon to be opened asylum, Erik observed the morning's preparations for the grand opening ceremony.

Whilst filling up his car, Erik glanced at the team of people hurriedly making the final preparations to a small dais, which stood in front of the south wall of the building. The optics were great, thought Erik. The entire assembled Press Corps trapped in the enclosure would be forced to take in the gleaming new building, its clean, red brick facade, the immaculate patioed terrace and the view beyond across the fields and onwards into the woods.

Using one of the company's clean and untraceable pre-payable credit cards, Erik paid for his fuel at the pump and with his baseball cap pulled down tightly covering most of his face, he thought he had done everything he could to get a close look at the target area without being caught on camera.

The meeting with the three accomplices was at 11am. There wasn't much time between the meeting and the event, which was deliberate on Erik's behalf. The short interval allowed just enough time to be briefed, have a practice run through and get into position. Less chance for leakage of information, and also less time spent around the target area.

Leaving the forecourt of the fuel station, he drove slowly, but not excessively so, back along Ratoldstrasse, until he arrived at a non-descript detached house, with an adjacent garage. It was 11am, the three accomplices should already be in the house. Erik parked the car in the garage, which was open, and after closing the large roll-down outside door he entered the house via an internal connecting door.

The two men sat on the old settee, could have been brothers of the wiry Sudanese in Berlin, who had played the part of a street gangster. Their heads downcast, they stood when ordered to by the thicker set swarthy Moroccan.

The two rake thin men proffered their hands to Erik. "I'm Saleh and this is my brother Hassan. You are Mr Erik yes?" "That's right" Erik said, with a smile. After all he was playing the part of a TV news production agent and not a hired killer.

"Has Ali shown you the Hawala payment we are sending to

Juba for you?" "Yes Sir, yes," they both responded in unison. Erik continued talking to the two Sudanese men explaining how his TV company wanted to make a documentary film about the poor African asylum seekers that have given up and risked so much, leaving their families and lives behind in sub-Saharan Africa to make their way to Europe.

"You see, we want to tell your story and we were going to open the film with some footage of the opening ceremony being performed by the man that many believe will be Germany's next Chancellor." smiling his most sincere smile, Erik added. "Having him in the documentary will raise the profile of the piece."

Looking from one to the other Erik was confirming that they understood him. "The money we are sending through the Hawala brokers will be enough to look after your family for a year, or maybe even allow them to join you here in Munich?" At this last comment both men's eyes lit up, a flickering of hope passed through their frail bodies, then faded just as suddenly.

"So, let's get down to business shall we. All you need to do is to point the camera towards the stage and record the speech. Don't worry we have plenty of time to practice operating the camera. Because we are doing this outside, my sound engineers have told me we need to use another type of microphone. Here Hassan hold this." Hassan gingerly took hold of the long handled, fluffy headed boom mike. "That's it, encouraged Erik, you see it extends like this."

The young Hassan was by now stood in the room clutching the extended boom mike, next to him stood his brother Saleh with the video camera on his shoulder, mimicking the actions of a professional cameraman. "Good, good," encouraged Erik. "Hassan, that cable from the mike goes into this box." The boom mike and box were the only items of equipment that Erik hadn't let the Moroccan remove from the car.

The DAT sound recorder weighed only marginally more now than it had before. On the long journey south from Berlin, Erik had stopped the Passat in the middle of the night at a deserted motorway rest stop and removed most of the internal workings of the DAT machine. He had left the battery, after all he needed a power source for the electric detonators, which right now were buried deep inside the two moulded sticks of military grade plastic explosive, which Erik had shaped and sculpted into position inside the sound recorder. After confirming that Hassan knew how to, for appearances sake only, connect the sound recorder to the microphone, Erik gave them some more encouraging nods and looks as they play-acted out their new roles.

"Hassan, remember you need to get the boom mike as close to the speaker as possible, we need a really good sound quality on this one." The final thing Erik did before the two Sudanese men left for the opening ceremony two blocks away, was to give them their Press credentials. They were good copies of the real thing. On this occasion Erik wasn't that concerned with their security. I mean, who in their right mind would turn away two African reporters, themselves former asylum seekers from the opening of a new shelter. Wasn't it proof, if proof was needed, that the government's integration programmes worked?

Erik left the house, driven by the Moroccan, who still hadn't spoken directly to him, heading for the airport. They drove in silence, listening to the live broadcast on Radio Munich, which by running a short feature on the opening ceremony managed to achieve its actual objective, a more cynical observer may have noted, of supporting the local boy turned Chancellor, as he began his campaign to occupy the highest office of state in the most powerful country in Europe.

After the introductory pleasantries were over, the Target, Hans Wollinger, began, as Erik had expected him to, to talk about the forthcoming election, and how good it would be for the Bavarians to have one of their own controlling the reins of power in Berlin. On hearing the word Berlin, Erik's finger squeezed the haptic display on his smartphone, initiating a pre-programmed call.

Hassan and Saleh had arrived punctually at 1330, to be processed and escorted into the Press area. Their credentials, and their skin colour served to allow an expedient entrance into the Press area. Scattered amongst the local camera crews were several national carriers, and even an Associated Press team. The Chancellor in waiting's presence had turned a story that would carry a couple of column inches and a quick sound bite on local news station into a prime-time feature.

As directed by Erik, the two Sudanese managed to push their way to the barrier closest to the speaker. There were already a couple of teams at the rope barrier, but as Erik had already figured out, no-one in their right mind was going to start a shouting match with two Africans at the opening of an asylum centre, not even hardened Press photographers. So, with muted objections and disgruntled looks on their faces, the AP crew shuffled slightly to their left to allow the Sudanese youths to edge closer to the rail.

The optics were perfect thought Hans Wollinger, as he made his way slowly, through the congratulatory crowd, up the steps and onto the dais. He wore a crisp white shirt, open at the collar. His shirt sleeves were turned back slightly above his wrists and he complemented his man of the south look, not with a full set of Lederhosen, that would be ridiculous wouldn't it? and maybe a slightly too conservative. No, he, Hans Wollinger was the vibrant new face of the German leadership. Instead of the traditional Lederhosen, he complemented his pure white shirt, with a pair of soft brown leather trousers, something, understated but still with a nod to Bavaria and its heritage.

The two Sudanese boys were ready. Saleh struck his best professional cameraman pose with the new Panasonic camera balanced high on his shoulder, whilst his brother, who had connected the boom mike to the DAT machine, stood poised with the mike hovering high, but almost directly above the head of the speaker.

The boys had absolutely no idea who the speaker was, but they both agreed he looked like a film star. His perfect white teeth surpassed even the glow that his shirt projected. Hassan risked a stolen glance at his elder brother Saleh. He was holding the camera high and proud a smile cut from ear to ear. Hassan thought, this was probably the best day of their lives.

The speaker had finished welcoming everyone and to rapturous applause, had pulled the cord, to the small curtains, revealing a wall mounted bronze plaque. Hassan wasn't sure what he was talking about now. Something about Munich, Bavaria and Berlin. Whatever he was saying, Saleh was beginning to hope that he hurried up. Holding the boom mike extended above the speaker's head for so long had started to get very tiring indeed.

A round of applause, intersected the speaker's monologue. As it did so, Hasan noticed two rapid flashes of the red LED on the DAT sound box. Unsure, as to the meaning, he thought it might mean the battery was running low. Waving his free hand towards Saleh, he gesticulated towards the sound machine, to see if his brother could help with the problem.

The first of the two explosions occurred fractionally before the second, a small charge, which Erik had placed in the fluffy microphone head at the end of the extended boom. The flash and thundering sound of the explosion was the last image that the collected Press's cameras would record. Not that these images would ever be viewed by anybody. Less than $1/5^{th}$ of a second after the first explosion, which had quite literally decapitated Germany's future Chancellor, the second, heavier, main charge moulded into the DAT machine erupted.

Shards of metal and plastic from the DAT machine's casing were hurled violently outwards at over 8,000 metres per second in a radius of about 15 metres. These shards, cut deep into the flesh of the un-sensing people around them. It was the blast and the intense flash heat generated by the two sticks of plastic explosive, which was only slightly diminished after making their dual escape from the confines of the camcorder, that caused the most damage.

Escaping at over 1,000 degrees, the super-heated air, generated by the high explosive charges quite literally melted the skin of anyone unfortunate enough to be in the blast area. The accompanying blast wave served to tear chunks of seared flesh off the remnants of the charred corpses, spreading a conglomerate of different human body parts over an area of several hundred metres. The once pristine façade with the neatly printed brass plaque was pockmarked with thousands of tiny shrapnel scars, and a film of gooey, human fluid and flesh stuck to the jagged edges of the frames of the shattered windows.

A few shocked bystanders, who had been at the Petrol station, too far away to have been seriously injured, would later testify to seeing two black Arabs, with a camera, speaking excitedly in Arabic to each other only moments before the explosion. A spokesman from the BND, Germany's Federal Intelligence Agency, with the help of a forensic team from Munich's Criminal Police would later confirm that the explosion that killed Hans Wollinger had been perpetrated by Islamic terrorists. As yet no group had stepped forward to claim responsibility.

As the news of the attack broke on the local radio, the Moroccan stole a sideways glance at Erik. Indicating he turned off the slipway and headed for the drop off area of Munich's Airport. Erik wasn't sure, if the Moroccan had connected the dots. Probably, he thought, although he showed no sign of emotion whatsoever, no disgust, no anger, no joy. It wasn't until much later as Erik sat at Dublin airport waiting for his connecting flight to Zurich, that he considered that any man capable of trafficking humans and selling them into a miserable life of servitude and bondage, was probably inured to the deaths of two of his charges.

To the Moroccan, they weren't people. They were commodities. The last piece of communication between the Moroccan and Erik was completed as Erik was leaving the car at the airport drop off. The Moroccan leaned over and withdrew a black padded case, he briefly opened it before handing it to Erik. "I believe the paperwork is in order you should have no problems at the airport." Peering at the contents of the opened case, Erik wondered once more why he had been asked to transport two vials of cooled blood back to Switzerland.

It was several hours later, as Erik brought his seat back to the upright position, over the clear blue alpine skies as his plane began its descent to Zurich's airport that Erik finally managed to identify Hans Wollinger's single biggest sin. It was Gluttony. He hadn't just craved power, no Hans Wollinger had craved too much power and the secret file that the Organisation had supplied to Erik about the target, had outlined in some detail, exactly what lengths, this clean-cut politician was prepared to go to in order to satisfy his gluttonous desire for absolute power.

Hans Wollinger was the protégé of the Chancellor and life under him had promised to be a continuation of the Chancellor's policies. He had been famous for his outreach programmes, meeting and greeting immigrants as the German taxpayers were cajoled, partly through a Schuldgefuhl, or a feeling of guilt, for crimes that their ancestors had visited upon supposed undesirable members of society to spend ever more money on housing and clothing them.

The Organisation's preferred candidate, Berndt Eisenach felt differently, although a devout Protestant, he felt it was time Germany stopped having to apologize for the war and as in most other developed countries in the world, they should set quotas on immigration.

Seeing the blinking light on his office phone, Berndt excused himself from the caller "Sorry, Mr Vice President, I have to take this, it is the Chancellor." Berndt had been expecting the call. Reclining back in his office chair, legs crossed, with feet on his table, he took a moment to compose himself. "Frau Chancellor, how nice to hear from you." "Berndt, have you seen the news? Hans has been killed in an explosion." to Berndt's ears it almost sounded as if the dour and perennially solemn-faced woman was going to start crying.

Flicking on the TV to the national news. It never hurt to have a background track on these occasions, thought Berndt. He saw first-hand, the images of carnage. In an over-dramatic demonstration of ignominy, he slammed his fist on the table's glass surface. So forcefully in fact that he nearly spilled the contents from the crystal champagne flute. "Madame Chancellor, this is horrendous, we have to act. We must catch the culprits immediately."

In a more resigned and dispassionate tone the Chancellor replied, "We do Berndt, God only knows we do. But, insensitive as this appears right now, the election cannot be de-railed by this. I know this is a lot to ask Berndt, and I know that you and Hans didn't see eye-to-eye on everything, but I want you to take his place as our preferred candidate for the Chancellorship."

Unseen and unknown to the Chancellor a faint smile played at the corners of Berndt Eisenach's mouth. "It would be an honour Frau Chancellor. I know you and Hans were close, let me please extend to you my most sincere condolences at this, err difficult time." He replaced the receiver, raised the crystal champagne glass to his lips and sipped at the chilled Brut champagne.

Chapter Six

multiverse [noun]

Definition of multiverse

A theoretical reality that includes a possibly infinite number of parallel universes

- *How can life be understood without the possibility of a multiverse.*

UNCTC Lectures UNESCO Paris / UNCTC HQ Singapore

The Headquarters of UNESCO is situated on the Ile de France in Paris. In the shadow of this huge post-modern Tricorn shaped edifice, affectionately referred to as the Three-pointed Star, can be found a smaller building, known as the Accordion. The interior of the Accordion is an egg-shaped hall with an intricately worked pleated copper ceiling. It was here on a rainy Friday morning that Matthias could be observed, delivering the keynote presentation at one of the many plenary sessions of the General Assembly.

"Ten years ago, if I were to ask any expert in International Relations: What the world would look like in 2020? I probably would have received an answer very much in line with Francis Fukuyama's seminal essay entitled the End of History. Fukuyama presented a simple thesis; *'The failure of communism and the disappearance of the Soviet Union has resulted in the victory of liberal democracy and capitalism.'* There are, he claims, *'no more challengers. Security and freedom have been achieved, and consequently history has ended.'."*

Matthias stared intently out at the audience as he spoke, he had no need for notes, and as such, he managed to engage with his audience by keeping a steady focus on a point somewhere in the middle of the assembled group of spectators. Well, at least he hoped that was where he was looking. The truth was that the audience, weren't actually looking at Matthias, they were looking at a full-size 3D hologram of Matthias presenting his report on 'Global Structures 2020 onwards' to the UNESCO General Assembly.

The Hologram had been recorded at the CTC's media lab in Singapore and it was that file, that was right now, being projected onto the stage at the UNESCO HQ in Paris. It was the strangest of sensations watching yourself giving a presentation, Matthias thought to himself. From his desk at the CTC in Singapore he had 1st person viewer camera access through the hologram software to be able to observe the audience in real time.

Using this new Version 3.0 holographic software that Charu had developed, he was able to manipulate his own Hologram to be able to make small changes to its orientation, this gave the impression of the Hologram reacting in actual time to a live audience, despite the fact that the entire presentation had been recorded some two weeks earlier.

The camera gave Matthias, a keen observer of human behaviour, the ability to be able to understand the audience reaction to his talk and determine if he needed to skip sections or fast-forward to more salient points, based on the audience's response. Right now, as he gazed out at the audience, with his holographic image shimmering against the burnished wave-like copper roof, Matthias could see that his opening statement laced with scepticism about Fukuyama's view on history and about the potential multiverse that the 21st century offered had grabbed his audience's attention, with few exceptions the whole audience sat transfixed, not only at the ghostly hologram, emanating from the back of the stage, but more so, by the words being issued from its ethereal mouth.

"We are now living in a Post Truth world. nation states are having to work harder than ever in their media campaigns to convince their own and other nations' citizens that they are acting in their interest. This instability caused by this Post Truth construct has led us to the end of a way of living. In 1989 as Francis Fukuyama was writing the End of History, I believe what Fukuyama was actually witnessing and commenting on was the first tremors of a seismic change that have led us to this point." the hologram flickered slightly as Matthias steered it a few paces to the right.

"The point at which we are faced with numerous alternative futures, a potential multiverse, each equally likely or unlikely to be the chosen path. And for the first time in the history of the world, the chosen path, will truly have global ramifications. More important for you…" Looking across his desk at Charu, Matthias tapped lightly on an icon on his display and watched in wonderment as his hologram virtually extended its arm and swept his pointed finger across the rows of seated delegates. With a broad smile on her face, Charu signed a thumbs-up gesture to Mathias over the desk partition.

Matthias, continued talking "The most disturbing aspect of this multiverse is that you, or rather we, the United Nations in particular and most nation states in general, only have a limited ability to shape that path, it is actually the consensus of the billions of previously un-empowered and unconnected people around the world, now connected through social networks, who, based on whatever truth they choose to believe, that will decide which path our future takes."

"Communication and control of the truth has always been one of the most powerful tools for control and coalescence around an idea. Hitler, Stalin and Mao, were all master manipulators of this art. However, the influence they wielded was primarily internal, and had the greatest effect on their own populations."

"Due to the technological limitations of the time, these methods of propaganda yielded only limited effect on other countries. Today a blogger sat in his boxer shorts in Belarus or Beijing can have an effect many orders of magnitudes greater than Hitler or Mussolini could ever have dreamt of, harnessing their state media apparatus." The mention of a blogger in his boxer shorts drew a peel of stifled laughter from the assembled audience.

Matthias paused his hologram briefly for effect before drawing his speech to its logical conclusion. He knew he would draw criticism for this next part, particularly from the US delegates and their supporters. He glanced across his desk at the CTC HQ in Singapore to Charu and saw her wince with anticipation of the audience's reaction.

Sat thousands of miles away in his high-tech air-conditioned office in Singapore watching his hologram deliver his words, he recalled how he had once, long ago, been told that he lacked even the smallest veneer of tact, diplomacy and concern for other people's feelings and that he stormed through life, oblivious to his insensitivity towards others. The person who had made him aware of his shortcomings was his now ex-wife. Releasing his finger on the temporary pause button, he sighed and looked across at Charu and the other team members. "Someone's got to say it how it is, right?"

"The security of the current post-Cold War order is predicated on the stability, success and growth of a global liberal free-market economy and the willingness of its founder and sponsor, the United States, to be interventionist and be prepared to support this system."

"The financial crisis of 2007 and the past 10-years of increasing US isolationism have emboldened other actors such as Russia and China to become more assertive in their regions. What we are now witnessing is a return, back along the scale from isolationism to interventionism by the dominant power, except, the world that this power has returned to is structurally different to the one it left." as expected, Matthias noticed through the hologram's POV camera a lot of head shaking and scowling emanating from the seating area containing the US delegation. "Oh well, in for a penny, in for a pound and all that."

"Structural and political acts such as the US/Mexico border fence appear to be almost an act of denial by some, that we really are now living in an interconnected society. Walls, barriers or military strength no longer serve as the primary protectors of stability. These are, if you like, a very, pre-technological, way of presenting yourself on the world stage and influencing other nations." This last comment really had enraged at least one of the US delegation who promptly stood and marched out of the hall.

"Recent interference in national elections by foreign powers, manipulation of news and propagation of propaganda directly to the mobile phones and tablet screens of our nations' citizens has led to a situation where the truth and the minds of those reading their daily digest of news and social media feeds are being manipulated to serve several competing attempts to reshape and control the global order."

"We face two options; Fight to protect the current world order with all its imperfections or unleash a myriad of competing multiverses with all the chaos and instability that it will bring with it."

Matthias' Hologram flickered twice then abruptly disappeared. Through the lens of the still active 1st person camera view, Matthias watched with growing incredulity, as a quiet murmur of chatter began to ripple around the egg-shaped conference hall. Through the murmur Matthias became aware of a soft peel of clapping that quickly became a deafening crescendo of applause.

It had been the first time that the CTC had tried to communicate this way and the entire CTC team had been sat in the conference room eagerly watching the event. Li, Matthias' Chinese boss, who had only just managed to endure the 45-minute speech without being able to smoke, turned to Matthias with an extended arm, showing his mobile phone screen to the assembled group, he said "Well that's a first!! You just got a smiley face from the Secretary-General of the United Nations. Well done, Matthias, well done everybody, especially you Charu, that Hologram manipulation software, is incredible. Now if you will excuse me, I am in desperate need of some fresh air."

With that said he left the conference room, strode out into the main work area and headed straight into the glass smoking cube that dominated the centre of the room. As he sat down his phone buzzed once more. It was Guilherme, the Secretary General once more. The message was brief. 'Well done on today. Time is short, things developing quickly, I want your team to watch the forthcoming US announcement on the US Mexico Border wall completion. I would like a profile report from Matthias and the team on their view of the US President's mindset.'

'Also, I need a strategic report on the Lithuania affair. We are at deadlock over here at the Security Council and I need alternative ways that we can unlock the impasse. I am hoping that your team of cultural, technical and intelligence experts can offer me an alternative viewpoint?' Li clicked the screen to dark, dropped the phone on the table next to him and inhaled deeply on his cigarette.

puritan [noun]

Definition of puritan

A member of a 16th or 17th century Protestant group in England and New England opposing as unscriptural the ceremonial worship and the prelacy of the Church of England.

- *Paul was someone who certainly had a Puritan streak in him.*

El Paso sits squeezed into the southwestern-most tip of Texas, flanked to the northwest and northeast by mountains and bordered in the south by the Rio Grande. The city is no stranger to racial tension. Over the many years of the town's settlement the racial balance has seesawed between white American and Hispanic. On several notable occasions this racial tension has spilled over into violent clashes and organised campaigns of violence resulting in hundreds of deaths.

El Paso had formally become a part of the US in 1848 when the Treaty of Guadalupe Hidalgo finally fixed the Rio Grande as the US / Mexico border. Despite now sitting firmly within the USA, currently nearly 70% of the population of El Paso are Hispanic with Spanish being by far the most widely spoken language.

President Carlton P Simpson had specifically chosen this Texan city as the place where he would officially inaugurate the new US/ Mexico wall. Despite the Rio Grande serving as a perfectly obvious natural barrier at this point on the US / Mexico border, President Simpson, who had made a campaign promise to his fellow Texans to build a wall, had done just that.

"It's a thing of beauty isn't it?" exclaimed the President to General Curtis Lee Hayward, the Chief of the Defence Staff. The President was accompanied by his usual retinue, Helen Broxton, the National Security Advisor, John Linton his Press and Media Secretary and General Hayward. The only member of his inner circle not present, was Charles Henderson the Vice President who was attending a similar ceremony some 720 miles due west in San Diego. "It certainly is Sir." replied the General.

There had been considerable friction amongst the President's inner circle over the exact nature of the border wall. All his retinue were astute enough to realise that they couldn't directly oppose the President's campaign promise and long held personal desire to build a fortification between Mexico and the US. However, Helen Broxton, had been trying to get the President to scale down his plans. She knew from many briefings with the Treasury and FBI that the cost benefit analysis simply did not stack in the US' favour.

The conservative estimate lay at a little over 12.5 million dollars per mile, which when multiplied over the entire 2,000 mile border would come to a staggering 25 billion US dollars, and that wasn't counting the 17 million dollars per year in maintenance. The FBI had conducted its own private survey and come to the conclusion that the same net effect could be achieved by adding increased security to just 800 miles of the border.

However, the main reason for General Curtis Lee's enthusiasm and Helen Broxton's lack of enthusiasm was that the bulk of the funding for the wall would pass through the Department of Defense accounts. The General had fought long and hard to ensure that the border security project would fall under the purview of the DoD and not Homeland Security or the FBI as it might more normally be considered to do so.

The President had spoken to General Hayward as Air Force One was beginning its descent into El Paso on its final approach to the Biggs Army Airfield runway that sits as an adjunct to Fort Bliss in the north of El Paso. Helen had been unsure if the President and General Hayward had been referring to the distant scar, that had been gouged into the earth along the banks of the Rio Grande, that formed the newly constructed monstrosity of a wall, that made southern El Paso look more like the division between east and west Jerusalem than a southern Texan city, or the military-run, 18 hole Underwood Golf course, which was looked upon by the Franklin Mountains State Park in the North and West and flanked by the airfield to its south and east.

The President and the General were set to Tee Off at 4.30 pm straight after the inauguration ceremony. It had been on a golf course that the President and the General had sealed the deal that led to the DoD getting all of the funding for the wall. Helen, sat back in her chair as Air Force One slowly glided down to the warm asphalt below, closing her eyes, and with a wry smile on her face she mused to herself as to whether the President would ever even consider asking her to play golf with him.

I mean, did the President know that her handicap was just 4 over par? If so, did he see it as a personal threat, or as yet another area of life where women were insinuating themselves, removing yet another simple pleasure that men like himself and the General could enjoy in peace!

Penny had been sat transfixed for the last 3 hours replaying over and over again the US President's speech that he had just finished delivering in El Paso. Sat in a chair within the glass-walled CTC Conference room, she had expanded a snapshot of the President's face on the interactive conference table and placed it next to several more shots of the President's face in an area of the table that she was using to review individual frames of the speech.

Matthias exited the smoking booth and strolled back towards Penny who was sat engrossed in her computer screen in the conference room. He observed Penny closely as he neared the room. Even he was amazed at how much she had learned about reading micro-gestures and understanding body language. Of course, she still had a long way to go.

Unlike Maria, whose Secret Service training had allowed her to make quick, almost instinctive decisions about a small range of threat related micro gestures, Penny struggled to make quick judgements, however she had a deep breadth of understanding and had decided to focus her skills on ethnic Chinese. Her extensive knowledge of their language and time spent in country had made it an obvious choice for her.

Today's subject of scrutiny, the US President delivering his Border Wall inauguration speech, couldn't be more distant from the characters that Penny had become expert at studying. The Chinese senior political figures that Penny had honed her micro gesture reading talent on, were true adepts at delivering multi layered messaging, subtly hinting with verbal inflections and quite often misdirecting with deliberate facial gestures to deliver several messages simultaneously.

Reading one of these people was akin to viewing an oil painting by one of the old Masters, the layers of detail and meaning took many hours to peel away and truly comprehend. Today's subject was more comparable with reading a teenager's pencil sketching than an old master, Penny thought. The President's very arrogance engendered through a belief in his apparently unassailable position as the most powerful man in the world, caused him to not even try to mask his facial gestures and body language.

"So Penny what do we have?" Penny, jumped in surprise. She had been so engrossed in reading the President that she hadn't noticed Matthias walk up besidc her. "Bloody Hell Matthias, one of these days you'll give me a heart attack!" She began to review her observations with Matthias. "Here, you see," she said tapping the interactive tabletop surface and sliding across a close-up cropped image of the President's face for Matthias to see.

Affecting her best impression of a deep Texan drawl, Penny read out the President's words from his speech at the time the image was captured. "It is my duty as your elected President to defend these United States from all enemies internal and external that threaten our Constitution" Peering closer at the photo Matthias could clearly see the President's curled lip as he said the word enemies. "Disgust" said Penny. "The President is showing disgust."

"I agree" said Matthias, "it will be interesting to see what we get from the Vice President's speech. You see, the President simply wants to shut the Hispanics out of the country. He is thinking purely about jobs, and voters. For the Vice President, I believe, with his more Puritanical religious background, well, he is more serious about the Hispanics, for him it is a serious ethno-religious issue."

"He doesn't just want to segregate the Hispanics from the rest for political advantage, no, he firmly believes that the white protestant man is superior and destined to be master of these people." Shocked, Penny looked up at Matthias. "Really?" "Well, I could be wrong of course, I have been studying some of his past speeches and it certainly is beginning to look that way to me."

The pair continued to review the President's speech, moving

through the President's hidden gestures of disgust, pride and arrogance. "So that's about all I got. What do you think?" "I think you did really well. You missed only one key point. Sometimes when the speaker switches subject then you have to reframe your perspective to be able to pick up on the cues. Go back in the recording to the final part, where the President uses the opportunity to talk about the United States' reaction to the Kaliningrad annexation."

Penny swiped back through the recording until she got to the spot, where the President, flanked by his National Security Advisor and his military Chief of Staff, gave a short defiant statement on how the US was combatting a growing Russian resurgence in general and the Lithuanian affair specifically. "There" said Matthias jabbing his finger on the screen. "Look, do you see it? Weakness and Insecurity."

Penny was staring intently at the President's face, "Where? He seems defiant, bellicose even." "No, no" stammered Matthias in his excitement. "Look away from the face, look down at his left hand, when he says the phrase 'taking the fight to the Russians'. Look, right there, his left hand is covering his genitals. This is one of the most common subconscious actions that a man will make when he feels under threat or weak in the face of aggression."

"The President believes he is reassuring the American voters that he is the man that can face down Russia, when in reality, he is not sure himself if the depleted and under invested US Armed Forces of today can actually manage to mount a credible counter threat to Russia in Europe."

Nodding slowly as the picture became clear to her, Penny began to speak. Pointing to the Chief of the General Staff General Hayward, who was caught in the same frame as the image of the President. "You're right, now I see it. Look at the General, when the President says the word Russians, watch his eyes."

As if on cue Penny pressed the play button and they both watched as the General's usually defiant and intimidating demeanour, subtly shifted for a split second. The General's chin dropped slightly and he cast his eyes down and to the left. "You are right Penny, that is the face of a man who knows the reality of what is being proposed and he can't look you in the eye and let you know that he can deliver."

"You know they have sent a carrier group into the Baltic don't you?" "Yeh, I heard from Maria the other day, it is all over the British Press, it is causing chaos in the English Channel as it transits in full display mode up past France and England." "Right, well do you know how much it costs to run a carrier battle group for one day?" "No," replied Penny. "$6.5 million dollars, per day and the US currently have two on active duty in the south China sea, one in the Arabian Gulf and now this one here."

"How long do you think that is sustainable before the President has to go to Congress to raise the US debt ceiling, begging for more money to maintain this show of strength? That could be very counterproductive indeed. It will only serve to confirm to the Chinese and Russians that the American national debt is moving into unmanageable territory."

A little more than 720 miles away in San Diego the Vice President of the United States had just finished holding a Service of Thanksgiving. Vice President Charles L Henderson had opted for a Service of Thanksgiving at the First Lutheran Church of San Diego, preferring to eulogize to a congregation of like-minded people rather than to stand and bait the majority Hispanic population of El Paso as the President had done.

Archbishop Willem De Vries of the Gereformeerde Kerk, or Dutch Reformed Church looked over at the Vice President and listened intently as he spoke. Archbishop De Vries had known the Vice President in various capacities for over 30 years and Charles Henderson had seized the opportunity to invite the Dutch Lutheran Pastor to preside over the service.

Standing erect in a dark grey suit in front of the lectern, the VP paused briefly in his eulogy and cast his gaze slowly around the room. Finally, after what seemed to be an interminable amount of time he settled his gaze back on his long-time friend the Archbishop before concluding his sermon. "This wall should serve to remind us of what happens to different cultures, with different ethics towards work and civil society are forced to live so closely to each other. My sincere hope is that with the Lord's blessing, and with the right people leading Mexico, we will be able to tear down this wall and unite as brother's working towards a common goal."

Not known for their over enthusiastic displays of exuberance, the Puritan congregation all rose as the Vice President accompanied by the archbishop processed down the central aisle, out of the church. Of course, the visit to San Diego had never been about the border wall. Rather Charles L Henderson, Vice President of the United States of America and de facto leader of the secretive cabal known as the Puritan Society had actually used the church service and wall opening ceremony as an excuse to gather the upper echelons of the senior council for the global cabal in one place.

His eulogy in the church, whilst fulfilling its purpose of being seen to support the President on delivering on his key election pledge, had, for those who understood the deeper meaning behind his sermon, actually served as his Keynote speech to the assembled senior council, which represented the majority of the congregation of the church. The service and accompanying sermon had served to welcome the society members to their annual meeting whilst setting the tone and direction of the talks that would follow.

The Puritan Society had, in one form or another been in existence since around the beginning of the 30 years' war in Europe. This savage conflict, set in the first half of the 17th century, which had pitted the great European powers against each other, began ostensibly as a battle over the right to practice your faith as either a Catholic or a Protestant, but eventually as most conflicts tend to, it developed into a much more concerted battle for political dominance across most of Europe.

One of the first and most radical groups established to coalesce support for the minority Protestant groups, was the Puritan Society, as the conflict developed and grew in scale, over the first couple of years the Protestant groups formed a greater Protestant Union as a counterpoise to the unified Catholic league.

Many of the original Puritan Society became disenchanted and disenfranchised with the compromises required to maintain a larger Protestant union and it was this discontent coupled with the idea to spread Protestant ideas to new untainted areas of the world that was the driving force behind the sailing of the Mayflower to Cape Cod in the newly established territories of North America.

A distinction shared by only two of the modern-day Puritan Society was that Vice President Charles L Henderson and Archbishop Willem De Vries of the Gereformeerde Kerk, could both trace their direct ancestry back to original passengers aboard the Mayflower.

In the suburbs north of San Diego many large residences can be found perched atop the rocky escarpment overlooking the Pacific Ocean. Within the grounds of one of these properties a large single story timber barn-style building can be found. The building is reminiscent of many of the buildings first erected in Massachusetts by the first waves of European settlers. Originally designed to shelter family groups and their animals from the foul north Atlantic rain and wind, this building was ostensibly built to house the 40 ft yacht and speed boat of the residence's owner.

On this particular day the boats had been drawn outside and the inside of the barn had been simply decorated with a long heavy oak table, upon which was placed some simple food, carafes of wine and 3 large candelabras in the form of an elongated dagger-like crucifix. Sat along each side of the long oak table, dressed in simple black suits and white shirts were 10 of the most influential and richest people to be found in Europe, Africa, Australia and North America.

As the US VP and his long-time acquaintance, the archbishop walked between the main residence, where they had changed clothes, across the expansive and perfectly manicured lawn, the VP, placing his hand on the shoulder of his old friend as he did so, said "You know Willem, your boy Erik has done outstanding work for the Society over the years." Squeezing the older man's shoulder a little more firmly, the VP continued, "His particular talents will be crucial for the next phase of our operation."

The elder Pastor, didn't reply, he simply nodded his head in acknowledgement and smiled inwardly at the thought that his own son, who had spent so many of his formative years in the wilderness of South Africa under the harsh tutelage of his Uncle Rudy, had grown into the man that he had and was now able to serve his God and church with his special talents.

After walking around the table and shaking the hand of each of the ten assembled men in turn, Charles L Henderson took his seat at the head of the table with the archbishop sat immediately to his left. "Gentlemen I know many of you have travelled a long way for this meeting and I thank you for your time and attendance. We are at a key stage in our plan. We alone stand as the vanguard in this rapidly changing world. We alone are the only ones capable and dedicated enough to be able to rebalance the world order. First, we have to control the enemy within, before we can challenge the enemy from afar." The 11 other men congregated around the table nodded fervently as the VP spoke.

The two newest members of the cabal's highest council and the two who had travelled the furthest were Kurt Vorster and Doug Macintyre. The Cabal had originally been a European creation, but as the biggest threat to the Puritan's ideals and overall aims now came from Asia, it had been decided to invite like-minded brethren from the southern hemisphere.

Kurt, a large ruddy-faced South African, had travelled from Bloemfontein in the heart of the South African mining country. Vorster Enterprises owned three diamond mines and a swathe of land around half the size of Wales, which Kurt jokingly referred to as his pet wine project.

It would be disingenuous to label a company with an annual turnover of $1.5 billion as failing, but as head of Vorster Enterprises, Kurt had certainly seen his company's fortunes decline, and he knew exactly where to point the finger of blame. Ever since the end of Apartheid, he had only been able to sit back and watch as one incompetent government after the other, introduced new laws to loosen his control over his business empire.

Doug on the other hand was a rail thin, tough man in his early 60s from the Northern Territory of Australia. His family had held land in the far North of Australia since the beginning of the 1800s. Although not quite staking claim to be one of the original group of settlers landing in Botany Bay, his family had been one of the first that had made the perilous journey from Sydney through the central deserts and up into the deep tropical zone of the Northern Territories.

Doug Macintyre, who as well as being the Chief Minister of the

Northern Territory sat at the head of a copper mining conglomerate whose mines ranged over an area twice the size of Wales. Doug was the newest member to be promoted to the senior ranks of the society and was personally driven by an increasing paranoia, as he saw himself being surrounded by Chinese interests and investments in his own country.

He had tried in vain to invoke legislation in the Northern territory to limit the amount of stock a foreign country could hold in an Australian company but had been beaten back by the soft city lawyers and law makers in Canberra.

Ultimately mining was the biggest driver of GDP in Australia and China was their biggest customer. There was no way that any Australian Prime Minister sat in Canberra was going to do anything that jeopardized the flow of dollars from Australia's biggest cash cow.

"Turning first to our fight against the enemy from within." The VP was now in full flow, sat amongst his closest confidents, recalling fact after fact from his eidetic memory. If his earlier speech in the church had been a eulogy, then this speech now was delivered in the style of a CEO addressing his Board. "The operations in Germany and Austria were executed, no pun intended, perfectly." He turned to acknowledge the archbishop as he said these words.

Two of the men sat at the table, Norbert Mansheim, the German pharmaceutical baron from Munich and, Joseph Stilltmeyer, the Austrian, who was the head of the Tirol Privat Bank, one of the most discreet private and investment houses to be found in Austria, both nodded in agreement. Both men had privately donated millions to ensure that after the unexpected removal from politics of the Austrian Chancellor Kurt Waldinger and the despicable murder by North African Asylum seekers of Hans Wollinger, the Chancellor elect in Germany, the Society's own candidates had comfortably won their respective national elections.

Just as the VP turned to speak, Norbert stood, "err sorry brothers this is my first meeting so please excuse me if I have not followed protocol. I would like to thank the cabal for the two vials of blood that were recovered from Germany. I can report that they arrived in a fully viable form, and I can confirm that both samples contain the virus. I have a team of my people working on the agreed upon modifications from the lab on Brother Kurt's estate in Bloemfontein as we speak." Still a little unsure of himself Norbert sat his large frame back down into his chair.

"If I could invite our English brother to give us a consolidated update on the last few initiatives against the near enemy?" Charles Henderson always simply referred to the fellow council members by their nationality and the term brother. The man he had invited to stand up was a tall, impeccably dressed man in his late 50s, known within the organisation in which he was the head, simply as C. Sir David Simmingford-Bell was the Head of MI6, the British Secret Intelligence Service. Although Sir David came from 'old money' he was one of, if not the least, wealthy people sat around the table.

Sir David's power and therefore contribution, to the Puritan Society came from his unparalleled access to information. Rising and buttoning the top button of his suit jacket, Sir David addressed the room "I can say with considerable certainty that the actions taken to install our preferred heads of the German and Austrian governments have gone completely undetected." Peering over his silver Pince-nez and gazing intently across the table, Sir David nodded at two of the three Scandinavians represented in the cabal.

Anders Jensen the Danish Foreign Minister had recently become the Prime Minister elect, ever since the peaceful coup that saw the current Danish Prime Minister, who was terminally ill with cancer, hand over the reins of power and day to day running of the country to Anders Jensen. His Scandinavian brother sat to his right, Thor Christiansen, was the Norwegian Finance Minister who effectively controlled the largest Sovereign Wealth Fund in the world.

"Due to the lack of any coordinated decision making coming from what is left of the EU, I believe Oslo will be holding a summit next month. In light of the recent Russian invasion of Lithuania and the threat a resurgent and confident Russia poses to other northern European states the Scandinavian states, are seeking a closer and reformed political, economic and security alliance with the Baltic States, Germany, Austria, and the UK of course."

"Representatives from both Belgium and the Netherlands will

be invited to attend, initially as observers. Should they demonstrate to us that that they share similar goals on such issues as immigration, security and the economy then they will be accepted into the alliance. Should they show hesitation, then similar plans as were employed in Austria and Germany are already in an advanced state to ensure that the correct people will be in place to represent these countries the next time we speak." Sir David smiled wolfishly at this last comment.

"Finally, before I hand back to our American Brother, I would like to share some new information that my organisation has recently discovered, that will once again reinforce the importance of our activities against the distant enemy." Removing his Pince-nez Sir David Simmingford-Bell stared around the room, allowing his gaze to linger fractionally, on each of the 11 brothers in turn.

"I hope the significance of what I am about to say is truly understood? Last week the Chinese People's liberation Army Navy's only Aircraft Carrier, the Liaoning, sailed with her escort ships through the Straits of Malacca and entered a Chinese built port near Karachi in Pakistan before sailing across the Indian Ocean to berth in the newly built Chinese port in Djibouti."

"The Aircraft Carrier then remained in the sea off the coast of Djibouti conducting maritime and amphibious exercises with the large Garrison of Chinese troops permanently based in Djibouti before sailing back to its home port of Dalian."

The Head of Britain's Secret Intelligence Service raked the room with his owl-like glare, to ensure the message was being received. "Two things are of significance. The last time that any Chinese military vessel sailed outside the South China Sea and into the Indian ocean was under the Command of Admiral Zheng He, in the early 15th century!" Sir David raised his voice slightly and spoke a little louder to emphasize the date.

"The second point is, that the garrison of 2,000 Chinese troops in Djibouti represents only approximately 2% of the over 200,000 Chinese labourers, teachers, engineers, and advisors" Sir David raised his hands and bent his fingers in air quotes as he said the word advisors. "These people live and work across Eastern Africa. They live in compounds or in Chinese owned agricultural land and pay little to no regard to the local governments or customs officials."

"Much like in Southeast Russia, Mongolia, Malaysia, Tibet and northern India the Chinese are invading by stealth, growing like a cancer inside a foreign organism until they eventually take control." Pausing slightly to confirm his point had been understood, Sir David unbuttoned the top button of his suit jacket and took his seat once more.

"Thank you, Brother for the perfect segway to our next speaker." Charles Henderson positively purred these words as he thanked Sir David for his update. "If our Canadian Brother would like to give us an overview of developments on our Africa Project?" The Vice President emphasized the word 'our' as he looked over at Ethan Macdonald. The youngest member of the council stood and addressed the group.

Ethan had made his money by investing early on in the new crypto currency called Bitcoin. He had then got out of the Bitcoin market before the bubble burst, realizing millions in profit and put his considerable engineering talent and his PhD in quantum physics to work, applying the unique encryption that lay behind Bitcoin to work on a far more ambitious project. Well at least it had started like that, then after making even more money by selling his 'unbreakable' series of blockchain cryptography to most of the major banks in the world, he set about developing a form of cryptography that like many of the most cutting-edge theories in physics only resided in a theoretical form in the heads of half a dozen academics in the world.

By the time Ethan was 40 he was rich and bored, so he set to work on his next physics problem. He aimed to develop the ultimate cryptographic tool. Using his knowledge of quantum mechanics, he had developed an encryption and processing device that worked on the superpositionality principle of Qubits.

In essence unlike a regular binary computer which could only ever exhibit one state at a time, either 1 or 0, the Qubit processor could be either 1, 0 or both simultaneously. Already an incredibly wealthy man, Ethan had decided to use his quantum encryption for the sole benefit of the Puritan Society.

Addressing the members gathered around the table in his mid-

Atlantic accent with inflections of a soft Scottish burr, he delivered his report on the African Project. “So, as you know our facilities based on brother Kurt’s estate in Bloemfontein are now working at full capacity. We have two facilities there. The first is the meeting and distribution point for our medical cadres that are engaged in the East African vaccine programme and the other cadre is where we train our Soldiers of Christ commando groups that have been so effective in defending the Christian minority groups in Syria and Northern Iraq.”

“The political leadership candidates that we have trained in Salem have been in place now in Bloemfontein for just over two months. They have now all been fully briefed and have met up with their respective country liaison officers. In the next couple of weeks, they will begin their coordinated move into their target countries and establish their vaccine clinics.”

The Puritan Society had silently gained influence and power in the global community through the manipulation of three levers; Political influence, control over tremendous economic resources, and access to the most incredible supply of information / data. However, its most powerful asset by far was the freedom it had in manipulating these levers towards a common goal.

The Society had a clearly identified goal and every decision required to reach this goal was made by the 12 men assembled in this room alone. These 12 ‘apostles’ were not answerable to an electorate, to shareholders or world opinion. They were answerable to God alone, and as in the days of the Holy Crusades, God, to the Puritan Society at least, appeared to allow plenty of latitude in how they could achieve their aims as a society.

Some members of the group brought political power and influence, others, such as Sir David, brought access to unparalleled levels of information. Several leveraged their considerable industrial or economic strength. Ethan Macdonald, brought genius. Put quite simply, Ethan Macdonald’s intellectual capacity was off the charts.

The quantum cryptography that he had developed for the sole use of the society had begun as a hobby to keep his mind stimulated after he had finished developing his blockchain cryptography for the banking sector. His greatest strength was also his biggest weakness.

Unless constantly stimulated Ethan got bored quickly and when bored he turned increasingly to illegal chemical stimulants to assuage the desires of his hyperactive brain and indulge his misogynistic tendencies.

It was during one of these self-destructive periods of chemical stimulation that Charles Henderson had first met Ethan. As the representative for Massachusetts, soon after declaring his bid to run for the Vice Presidency of the United States, it had been brought to Charles Henderson's attention by one of his campaign staffers that the wife of his chief Republican political rival had been found naked and unconscious in a hotel room.

A hotel maid had found her laying in the hotel room with several empty vodka bottles and clear evidence on the powder-streaked table's surface of cocaine use. The Congressman's wife had not been alone. Laid in the bed next to her, also unconscious, was Ethan Macdonald.

After receiving a quiet phone call from the hotel manager, Charles Henderson had managed to allow one of his campaign staffers to get 5 minutes access to the hotel room before the hotel management dealt with the situation.

The campaign staffer did as he had been instructed to do. He took several pictures of the couple laid in bed together and searched the smartphones of the couple to look for any incriminating evidence. It was at exactly 10am on that Sunday morning 3 weeks before the primary elections were to be held, that Charles Henderson knew with absolute certainty that he would be the Republican nomination for the Vice Presidency of the United States of America.

The short video file sent from the Congressman's wife's phone showing the Congressman's wife performing a sex act that she certainly hadn't ever performed with her husband had been shot by Ethan as the act was being performed in a mirror. It also vividly showed that the person upon whom she was performing the act, was not her husband.

It was after the conversation between Charles Henderson and the Republican candidate, where the former had persuaded the latter to step down from the leadership bid, that Charles Henderson turned his attention to Ethan MacDonald. Charles Henderson's biggest single ability in life was mastery of the art of manipulation. He knew he could never use the video evidence against Ethan.

Ethan was financially very wealthy, not married and super smart, Ethan would not be hurt by the revelation of the sex tape in Charles Henderson's possession. In fact, it might even provide Ethan with a couple of weeks of bragging rights as he did the rounds of the Washington and Boston social scenes.

No, thought Charles Henderson. Knowing that he could always use someone as smart as Ethan, Charles decided that he would be Ethan's mentor and guide, helping Ethan to find God and break once and for all these destructive drug fueled misogynistic episodes in his life. This is how Ethan MacDonald, one of the smartest men in the world, found himself sitting around a table with 11 other men, all of whom shared one unified focus and purpose.

Chapter Seven

Go [game]

Definition of go

Go is an abstract strategy board game for two players, in which the aim is to surround more territory than the opponent. The game was invented in China more than 2,500 years ago and is believed to be the oldest board game continuously played to the present day.

It had been two weeks to the day thought Li, since his friend Guilherme had turned to Li and his team as a last resort and tasked them with writing a report on the Lithuanian crisis. The Secretary General having exhausted all other channels hoped and prayed that Li and his team of unusual experts might just be able to unlock the bitter and protracted stalemate that had existed in the UN Security Council ever since Russian tanks had rolled across the border of Lithuania, destroying everything and anything in front of them on the pretext of protecting ethnic Russians. It had been the first time, recalled Li, that he had ever seen real despair on the Secretary General's face.

Li was stirred from his thoughts. "You know you could at least try to make it look challenging when you beat me" scoffed Mathias. The two men sat ensconced in their glass-walled smoking cube engrossed in a game of Go. Apart from providing a sanctuary for the smokers in the CTC, the cube was a place where, Li, Matthias and Philippe did their serious thinking.

With a smile curling playful on the edge of his lips, Li glanced up at his opponent. "You really are getting much better, Matthias, remarkable actually for someone who has only been playing the game for a year. Your problem is, that this isn't poker! you read me and my gestures and then make your move based on my actions. You are simply reacting to me. You might be brilliant at reading people and that is why you have developed so quickly, but ultimately you are being reactive, which always puts me one step ahead."

Matthias was about to perk up a little at Li's tepid praise and encouragement, when he noticed the faint playful crease around the older Chinese man's mouth, that gradually spread into a broad grin. You didn't have to be the world's foremost expert on reading micro-gestures to realise that Li was teasing Matthias. Becoming a little agitated and pushing his chair back to stand as he lit another cigarette, Matthias stood staring out of the window into the open office area beyond.

"You know Li, I have been thinking about this report we have to write for the Secretary General." Reclining in his own chair and exhaling a steady stream of smoke from his cigarette, Li was staring at the grid-lined wooden board with its tiny black and white pebbles arrayed upon it. "Go on Matthias, what exactly have you been thinking." "Well, maybe we are going around this report writing bit the wrong way?" "OK.... Continue" prompted Li as he lazily traced his finger around a pattern of the tiny black stones that were concentrated in the corner of the Go board.

"You see, I know we have some smart people here and almost unparalleled access to information. It's just I don't see how we are going to find anything new to report to the Secretary General that countless other agencies and Think Tanks haven't already reported." Not wanting to interrupt Matthias, Li sat quietly, drawing deeply on his cigarette and feigning only mild interest in what Matthias was saying.

After a brief pause Matthias continued. "The more I look at what happened in Lithuania, the more hours of video I watch of the Russian President talking to different audiences, the more I am convinced that for the rest of the world we are somehow playing a game, the rules and end state of which we don't fully understand, and, rather like my efforts at this Go game of yours, at the moment we are simply surviving and clinging on by luck and by reacting every time some new development happens."

This last comment had pricked Li's attention. Rising from

his chair, the older stooped Chinese man walked to stand next to Matthias, without looking him in the eye, he said "Matthias my old friend. I don't quite agree with you." Li stressed the word 'quite' as he gripped the back of Matthias' chair.

"We know the rules to the game. The rules are as old as civilization itself. What we don't know is the strategy. The game we have just played is the oldest board game in the world. It is the ultimate game of strategy that has been played for over 2,500 years. Brilliant in its simplicity, having just two piles of counters and taking it in turns to place them on a simple wooden board, it doesn't sound too difficult does it?"

Matthias knew the question was rhetorical, having played Li nearly every day for the last year, he hadn't even come close to beating him. Some days it felt like Li toyed with him, allowing him to believe he was getting the better of him, before swiftly closing down all of his avenues of attack and isolating his counters on the board.

"Exactly, it doesn't seem too difficult to you maybe, but it bloody well is!" Placing a conciliatory hand on Matthias' back, Li stifled a laugh allowing his friend and colleague, Matthias to vent his frustrations. "I am convinced we can only add value to the Lithuania situation if we only reframe our thinking and whilst still using the same facts that everyone else has in mind, examine these facts through a different paradigm."

It was just then dawning on Li exactly where Matthias was going with the conversation. "You know," said Li, almost conversationally, "The game of Go incorporates nine basic strategies. Each strategy deals with global influence, and the interaction between distant stones, you must keep the whole board in mind during local fights. Only then is it possible to allow a tactical loss when it confers a strategic advantage."

"Tell me about it," mumbled Matthias sheepishly. "I just pick one or two strategies each time we play and try and force the play that way." "I know, Matthias, that is why it's so easy to beat you." Li placed a reassuring hand on Matthias' arm. "You know, it took me the best part of 50 years to understand how to play Go effectively."

Li could see Matthias was interested so continued. "Learning to play Go is like learning to play the piano. You begin with one finger of one hand tapping out a simple rhythm, only after years of practice can you conduct the intricate and complicated serious of thoughts and actions required to play a piano concerto."

Li was now pointing at the Go Board in front of the two men. "In the game of Go you have to learn to employ an overall general strategy, which allows you to incorporate all of the nine individual strategies when they are best suited. A bit like writing an algorithm. What I am saying, Matthias, is you can't start the game without already having in mind the overall effect you want to achieve in the long term, or rather in this case by the end of the game."

Li who was still gripping Matthias' arm, turned to look at him. "You know however abominable a one-party state or quasi-dictatorship appears to us, countries like Russia and my country, China, have one great advantage over us, here in the West. Without interference or interruption, these countries can embark on a multiple decade-long strategy and devote massive resources to achieving their goals."

"As they play out this strategy, they simply fine tune its execution by employing one of the nine specific strategies that appear in Go." Cutting in and continuing Li's thoughts Matthias spoke "So what you are saying is; We need to understand Russia's end game, their decade long strategy to understand why they have been employing the tactics and strategies that they have." "Exactly." exclaimed Li. Matthias could see the glowing energy building in Li's eyes.

Suddenly becoming animated, as if seized by a revelation, he bent to put on his suit jacket and stubbed out his cigarette. "No time to lose Matthias, rally the team. I have an important announcement to make." The door swung shut and Matthias stared in bafflement at his elderly Chinese boss as he hurried towards the briefing room, pausing only briefly at Charu's desk to beckon her into the briefing room.

Just over one year ago, Li had introduced the strategic board game of Go to the team and had proscribed playing the game as an essential part of his team's regular training. Whole games had been recorded, so that, rather like the great chess games, a move by move playback could be watched by the team at review sessions.

Li had repeatedly stressed that he didn't mind if the team didn't keep on playing the game, as he had, until he had nearly mastered it. He merely wanted them to understand if they lost, how it was that they had lost.

The whole team were now assembled around the Interactive Briefing table, Andrei and Maria sat close together on the side by the window, with Penny and Walt seated opposite them. The shimmering surface of the pulsating interactive table lay between them.

"Say, anyone know what this is about?" asked Maria. "Absolutely no idea" replied Penny, "I guess we're about to find out", said Andrei, pointing with his eyes towards the open office through the glass wall of the Conference room.

Li, Matthias and Philippe who had spent the last 30 minutes standing over Charu as she manipulated different pieces of software on her computer, had all turned and were now making their way towards the conference room.

Li looked far more animated than normal. His usual calm, unreadable exterior was transformed, he seemed to be bursting with energy, and stood before them with a mischievous grin on his face.

"Thanks to our resident anthropologist's persistent skill in coming second every time we play Go together" Li, glanced at Matthias, who smiled sarcastically back at him. "and more importantly due to his unrivalled ability to view the world from a very unique perspective, I believe we now have found a way that we can potentially add real value in the report we are going to send to the UN on the Lithuanian affair."

The team sat speechless around the table, none of them had ever seen Li so animated, and none of them had a clue where he was going with this. Seemingly ignoring the look of bemusement on the faces that stared back at him from around the table, Li continued his outpouring.

"You see, I think when the Secretary General asked the CTC to analyse the Lithuanian crisis, what he should have been asking us to do, was to analyse why the UNSC is in a state of intractability over the crisis." Li noted the continued look of incomprehension on his team's faces.

"What I mean is, we need to understand the key players' strategic intent and work out how that relates to the events in Lithuania. Actually, it's quite intriguing really, what he wants is the impossible. The Secretary General of the United Nations wants us to predict the future." By now the blank bemused faces had begun to form creases of incredulity as they struggled to comprehend what Li was asking of them.

"Now I'm not sure if this request comes borne out of his own frustration with the current situation, or as I would prefer to think out of his belief in our ability as a team. Either way, thanks to Matthias here," Li placed a thin hand on Matthias' shoulder and gently squeezed. "I think we might just be able to do the impossible, maybe not perfectly, but good enough for what's required."

Still beaming, and now only just noticing that he was still clutching Matthias' shoulder, Li slowly removed his bony hand and looked around the room at his team. Recognition and understanding was slowly relaxing the frowns on the faces of the assembled group and Li looked on at the collective eye-widening and jaw dropping on the faces as they slowly absorbed what Li had said.

Li took a step backwards and clapped his hands. "So, time is pressing, and we have a report to get to the Sec Gen in two weeks' time. Charu, if you would please?" Glancing over at Charu, with an impish grin on his lined face, Li nodded to the Indian maths prodigy, who was just finishing setting up her table-based workspace.

Standing up and stepping back from the table, Charu appeared to squeeze her fingers together and a perfect 3D facsimile of a wooden Go board, complete with its little white and black pebbles, was thrust violently up from seemingly deep inside the table, high into the air. As it fell back towards the table's surface it stopped suddenly, chaotically throwing all of the small black and white pebbles into the air. As they in turn landed, they fell into seemingly random clusters across the wooden Go board that was now slowly revolving around an imaginary point on the middle of the table.

"Strewth Charu, would you give us a heads-up next time you do that? You nearly gave me a bloody heart attack." Although, Walt, the team's newest member was smiling as he said these words, a look of genuine incredulity was etched into his face. “I thought I was ready for it this time, after the first time I saw it and nearly fell of my chair. I just didn’t see it coming, I mean you weren’t even touching the table. How did you get it to do that?”

Charu looked at Walt, then the rest of the team as she held up her right hand and showed off the smart black ring, she was wearing on her index finger. The ring had tiny LEDs which pulsed white as she spoke. “It’s basically like a mouse or track pad, you twist it, tap it, swipe it etc, ‘e voila’ via Bluetooth it can give commands to the table.”

“Cool,” drawled Maria. “I want one” shouted Penny. “Calm down guys” Charu, was beginning to get a little flustered and embarrassed by now. “You’ve all got one, they are in the draw compartment by your seats.”

“OK guys, now that we have all recovered from Charu’s little circus trick, then let’s focus please?” Philippe’s voice was commanding, yet always somehow managed to keep a warm and friendly tone.

Addressing the group Philippe outlined the task. “I want you to consider recent world geopolitical events from, say, the last 10 years and consider them as if they were a game of Go. Analyse these events and the Go strategies you see employed in isolation first, then we’ll get together and see how the individual games may be linked and hopefully we may be able to divine future intentions from these events.”

“Philippe, Maybe I’m being a bit thick, but I’m still not quite sure what you want us to do.” Walt, the newest member of the team was the only team member that hadn’t regularly been playing Go. “No problem Walt, with the help of Charu’s magical Go board, I’m going to speed through the nine strategies that will frame your thinking, then let you all know which events each of you are going to focus on.”

“In essence though it is simple. We are looking for patterns and trends in the data, then we will see if by using the nine Go strategies, whether we can identify the algorithm, process or strategy whatever you want to call it to predict what the Russians might be trying to do in the future."

Turning towards Charu and inclining his head slightly, he began his guided description of the nine strategies. "So, in total we have nine strategies: *Connection, Cut, Staying Alive, Mutual Life, Death, Invasion, Reduction, Sacrifice and Sente.*" As Philippe read through the nine Go strategies, an icon representing each sprung from the table and hovered in a fixed position rotating around its central axis.

"I would like you to look closely at the Go board, you will see a time lapse sequence of moves that show the strategies in action." As he spoke the first series of moves began to play out on the holographic Go board in front of the assembled team. "Essentially guys, you are seeing first-hand the overall effect of what happens when you employ each of the strategies. Stay with me, I promise this will make sense."

With a confident smile Philippe talked the team through the strategies. "*Connection,* this is really simple it is about keeping your own stones, or territorial possessions connected. It's actually about conserving energy." As Philippe spoke the black counters slowly began to form into a contiguous amorphous group reaching into each sector of the Go board. "If the territories are connected then they are easier to govern, require less logistical resources, and of course are easier to defend."

Philippe looked up from the board. "Can anyone give me an example of this happening recently?" Philippe looked at the assembled group. Walt raised a hand, "Yes Walt" tentatively Walt proffered his answer. "Err, the annexation of Crimea?" "Exactly, Walt, by annexing Crimea and essentially occupying part of Ukraine, the Russians essentially gained permanent access to their key warm water navy port, thus mitigating the need to seek permission from the Ukrainians to extend treaties and to transit through the Ukraine."

Abruptly, yet politely, Li cut in "Walt, do you think this was a rational act or an irrational one?" Becoming more flustered, and after stealing a barely concealed glance at Andrei, Walt began to stammer, "It was a perfectly rational action" cut in Andrei in a cold precise tone. "Hey! you're just saying that because your Russian," retorted Maria.

Matthias was the next to speak. "Actually, I agree with Andrei.

Sorry, just to clarify, it was rational but illegal. Consider this, since the end of the Cold War, despite a specific promise that it would not happen, NATO has been expanding eastwards at a rapid rate, now, for the first time, encompassing some Slavic peoples and touching against countries with large Russian diasporas."

"Next, throw into the mix, the fact that Ukraine, one of Russia's former key bulwarks against NATO and a country that is historically indivisible from the history of Russia itself, decides that it is going to join this creeping, threatening mass called NATO."

Matthias could see the conflict and confusion building on his team's face as they looked from one to another across the table. "If this, on its own wasn't enough, now imagine that pretty much your only reliable warm water port, which allows your navy year-round access to move freely around the world sits in the Crimea, a half island, formerly a Russian possession and separated from you by your ex-ally. What would you be inclined to do?"

Matthias looked at Maria first, then turned his gaze to each team member in turn. "Thank you, Professor," Li said with a mischievous glint in his eye. "Guys, the little exchange we have just experienced exemplifies perfectly a point that I wanted to make. We, that is the CTC, are unique, we are a close-knit international team. If we can add any real value to the issue of Lithuania, then it must be by employing the type of analysis that is being explained to you now. However, regardless of how powerful a tool this approach may be. It simply won't work if you allow national biases to interfere with your analysis."

"You must detach yourselves from any form of bias and consider your research like a case study. The names of the state actors, or who did what to who, is not important. The only thing of importance is understanding how the actions were done and which of the nine strategies were followed. If we can distil the events down to these nine categories, then hopefully Charu and her team can begin to 'do the impossible' and model patterns over time in the data." Still smiling, but slightly flushed, Li sat down.

Looking across at Li's seat, Philippe sought approval to continue with his brief. As Philippe spoke, he used the names of the nine strategies as key words to activate a stunning 3D visual display of each. The mesmerising display was completely immersive and fully interactive. Philippe paused regularly to allow each team member in turn to manipulate the Go board to get a different perspective on each strategy as they were being outlined. As he drew towards the end of his presentation, Philippe was keen to key the team back into their tasks.

"So, to summarise the strategies; *Cut*; is the opposite of *Connection*, either the effect of *Connection* to the other party or a deliberate act to keep an area separate, rather like Berlin after the Second World War. For those of you who remember your history around the Berlin Airlift, Berlin was actually deep in Soviet territory and the Russians certainly made life difficult for the allies to maintain a lifeline there."

"Staying Alive, I guess the easiest way to summarise this one is that it is about planting seeds or bases of power. Again, in the Second World War when the Nazi's were at their height, in order to stay alive, the Allies supported the Russians on the Eastern Front whilst they just managed to maintain a foothold in Britain before they were strong enough to begin a second western front." Looking around the room to see if everyone was following him, Philippe continued with his summary.

"*Mutual Life* and *Death,* may seem to be opposite sides of the same coin, however there is a subtle difference. *Mutual Life* pertains to activities conducted that may seem contrary to the overall goals of the country but are necessary to ensure survival in the short term. Any ideas or examples?" Philippe threw the question to the floor.

Most of the team were still staring intently at the Go Board on an area where both black and white pebbles were touching each other but no contest appeared to be taking place. Penny raised her hand tentatively, "Well, I guess most of Europe is still kept warm thanks to sales of Russian gas, whilst at the same time NATO seems to be rebuilding and repositioning its forces to counter an increasingly confident Russia."

"Good point" said Li, "it is still mutually beneficial for this trade to continue even though several western nations are very close to war with Russia. What I want you to consider when you get your individual tasks is what it would take for this situation to change?"

"Death" said Philippe, trying to keep his momentum, "*Death,* as a strategy Is not so much about the state a player may find themselves in, rather it is about the removal or death of other players to make them ineffective as allies or redundant as enemies. Any suggestions for examples of this strategy?" Philippe put the question to the table.

This time it was Andrei's turn to comment. "The strategy of the Soviet Union effectively caused the death or paralysis of many of the Warsaw Pact States. Russia effectively exerted so much political and military control over these states that they were effectively not viable as independent actors, therefore could not be manipulated against Russia by the West and could be used by Russia against the West."

"Perfect example Andrei" Matthias cut in. "I am guessing if the end result is the same, then it doesn't matter how we get there? What I mean is many countries such as Pakistan, Uzbekistan, Kyrgyzstan, and many East African nations are so heavily indebted to China due to loans for massive infrastructure projects that they have no hope of ever paying off, that they are effectively *Dead* as independent political actors and serve only to benefit China and its policies in the international arena."

deepfake [noun]

Definition of deepfake

Deepfake generally refers to videos in which the face and/or voice of a person, usually a public figure, has been manipulated using artificial intelligence software in a way that makes the altered video look authentic.

- *Deepfakes can be convincing enough to pose a real threat to democracy.*

Philippe continued through the remaining four Go strategies until he reached the final one; "OK, thanks for sticking with it, team, I'm going to hand over to Charu for this last one, as I know that, Charu is the only one who really understands the example we are going to work with." With his ever-present broad grin, Philippe turned to Charu and hand extended, bid Charu to stand and finish off the presentation.

Charu stood, gazed around the room, then with a raised arm, drew her thumb to the side of her finger which bore the interactive smart ring and with an exaggerated flourish span the ring forcefully, so that it whirled on its own axis, around her finger and the tiny white LEDs glinted as they pulsed in the subdued lighting of the briefing room.

Matthias, who as usual, was observing Charu closely, noted her more confident performance in front of the group, the way she held her head a little higher, not arrogantly so, but high enough to engage the team in eye contact, her body was inclined slightly more towards the group in a less defensive pose, again not legs wide, hands on hips, alpha male dominance, rather, just enough to signal to the group that she was in control.

Smiling to himself, Matthias made a mental log of her behaviour, and realised he was smiling because he was happy for Charu, after her awful ordeal after being attacked and nearly raped as a student at MIT in Boston, it finally seemed that she was starting to find some of her old confidence back.

As Matthias turned his head away from Charu back to the table, he was surprised to see his own image, hovering and flickering above the table's surface. It took him a moment to take in the scene. It really was him, but where was he? Then it came to him, and he understood why it had taken him so long to connect the dots. It was the imagery, of him presenting at the UNESCO HQ in Paris, where only a couple of months ago he had delivered the keynote speech on the future political shape of the world, his so-called Multiverse.

Of course, he had never actually been there, what he saw in front of him was a hologram of his hologram that had done the presentation in Paris. OK, he thought, where was this going? Charu began "So the final Go strategy is *Sente;* this is best defined as a play or action that forces the opponent to respond. Remember, rather like in the game of chess, if you are always responding to your opponent's move, then you never gain the upper hand, and you only ever can be reactive. If you can effectively employ the *Sente* strategy, then you control the flow of the game."

Charu, paused briefly to see if the rest of the group had grasped the concept, before tapping her smart ring once more and bringing Matthias' Hologram to life. As the hologram began to move and speak. It was definitely Matthias talking and it was definitely at the UNESCO HQ, but no one around the table could believe what he was saying. Matthias was staring intently at the audience and sweeping his arm around the assembled crowd.

"Everybody here in this audience should be thanking the Russian President. It is President Mikhail Mikhailovich Voronin of the Russian Federation that has saved us from this weak debilitating liberal order. It is only President Voronin that can guide the world safely away from our decaying over-indebted free market system and lead us to a safer more prosperous future. I fully support the necessary actions he bravely took in Lithuania, to begin this correction that we all need so dearly." The crowd in the UNESCO hall, were standing clapping loudly and cheering after Matthias had finished speaking.

Charu had stopped speaking and had allowed the rest of the group to concentrate on Matthias' hologram. They had all watched his presentation from their office in Singapore, yet each team member sat transfixed at what they were now seeing. "Bloody Hell" exclaimed Penny. "No bloody way" whispered a stunned Maria to Andrei.

Charu continued her brief. "You see, in the world of international relations when we think about the *Sente* strategy, we typically think of a concrete act, such as one country imposing sanctions on another, or launching an attack against a specific target. Once either of these actions occurs, the government is obliged to respond. Typically, in the short term at least, whoever begins the chain of events *Sente,* maintains the upper hand."

Pausing the hologram momentarily, Charu addressed the group. "I want us all to think about a fourth dimension in international relations. If you like a new way to apply *Sente,* or to influence world opinion. Welcome to the world of Deep fakes." "Deep what?" spluttered Walt.

"Deep fakes replied, Charu calmly. You see in our interconnected globalised world, individual actors and nation states are now manipulating media to influence opinion, cause outrage, disrupt political discourse or even cause unrest and revolution within countries." Charu now knew she had their attention, the team were following every word she uttered.

"So, to your specific question Walt, Deep fakes are the product of recent advances in a form of artificial intelligence known as deep learning, in which we can manipulate sets of algorithms called neural networks to learn to infer rules and replicate patterns by sifting through large data sets."

Seeing even more confused looks around the table, Charu broke it down further. "More specifically, Deep fakes emerge from a specific type of deep learning in which pairs of algorithms are pitted against each other in generative adversarial networks, or GANS.

In a GAN, one algorithm, the generator, creates content modelled on source data (for instance, making artificial images of cats from a database of real cat pictures), while a second algorithm, the discriminator, tries to spot the artificial content. "

"Since each algorithm is constantly training against the other, such pairings can lead to rapid improvement, allowing these GANS to produce highly realistic yet fake audio and video content."

Spinning her ring once more on her finger, Charu switched off Matthias' hologram. "What you have just witnessed, I think you will all agree, appeared realistic? After I had written the algorithms and set up the GANS, that short clip took our system about 4 days to achieve." Smiling, like a mother who had seen her child utter its first words, Charu finished speaking and sat down.

Allowing the team to process what they had just seen and heard, Li stood slowly, leant forward, pressed his hands against the table's surface and surveyed each member of his team one by one. "500 years before the birth of Christ, a Greek philosopher and founder of modern logical and philosophical thought called Heraclitus, made one of the most profound utterances ever made by a human. He said, '*change is the only constant in life*' It is with this statement in mind that I am going to give you your individual assignments."

"Essentially, we are going to try and model the most likely

version of future events based on our understanding of past events and most importantly based on our understanding the strategies that the major powers are using to shape future events." Looking once more around the table, Li could see doubt and scepticism reflected back at him from his team. Only Charu, seemed to have a half curious smile curling at the edges of her mouth.

"We only have 2-3 weeks to get this work done, timescales are tight I know, but one of the advantages of doing this work in a short time space is that we leave less time for change to occur. Phillippe, Matthias, I want you to look back at events in Iraq, Afghanistan and Syria. Don't just focus on the obvious US involvement, we need to understand who is pulling the levers of power now that the US have withdrawn."

Walt, can you and Maria follow the money?" "Sure, anything specific?" Walt asked. "Actually yes; the change in cost of world trade, since tariffs kicked in, military expenditure around the globe, rare earths and precious metal prices and the strength of individual sovereign wealth funds or national reserves." "That's a lot of data Li, it may take some time to pull together." "I know, but remember we are interested in change over time, it is trends we are looking for, this is the key to understanding which strategies are being played out."

Li looked over at Maria and said, "Maria, I have one further task for you. I want you to act as Andrei's control, we are sending Andrei into Ukraine. It seems the Russians have been emboldened by our lack of response over their annexation of Lithuania and they now want to make even more territorial gains in eastern Ukraine."

Maria's eyes flashed at Li, but Andrei placed his hand gently on her arm and looked over at her. "It is OK, Li and I have already spoken about it. I will be fine, we just need to get some first-hand info on what is happening there. The Op should only take about ten days." Li continued, this time turning to face Penny.

"Penny how is your Mandarin coming on? You and I are going to be looking at developments in China. More specifically, the new Silk Road project and the new island infrastructure projects that the Chinese are building." Li made the universal two-fingered speech mark gesture as he said the word, infrastructure.

Turning finally to Charu, Li said "Charu I need you to look into small wars, high profile assassinations and serious international organised crime. Focus on Europe and Africa. As I said to Walt and Maria, I am looking for trends and correlations. I need that brain of yours to search for patterns linking actions to actors." Lowering his voice to a whisper and squeezing Charu's arm a little too tightly for her comfort, Li fixed her with a stare.

"But before you begin, I have a far more pressing task. I want to know how the data files you manipulated from Matthias' talk found their way onto the internet." Charu's eyes flashed and her jaw physically tightened as she tried to process the news. Stuttering slightly, she cut in "What the hell do you mean?"

Li turned his mobile phone to face Charu and watched her expression carefully as she took in the view of Matthias' hologram as it vehemently seemed to espouse the virtues of the Russian President for anyone who cared to click the link. "I don't need to tell you Charu how embarrassing it is to receive something like this from the Secretary General of the UN. I want to know when our system was breached".

Charu's face began to flush a burnished crimson. Now, deliberately avoiding eye contact with her boss, she spoke. "I'll get it taken down straight away. I swear it wasn't me. You have to believe me I'll have to do a complete security sweep." Li, could see already the genuine frustration and annoyance building on Charu's face, he took a swift sideways glance at Matthias who had been instructed to watch the confrontation and let Li know how he read Charu's reaction.

Matthias turned away from the pair, before doing so he nodded briefly to Li. Releasing his grip on her arm, Li took a step backwards. "I know Charu, don't worry I am not casting doubt on your abilities. Unfortunately, this only leads to one very unfortunate conclusion. What was it that the famous Sherlock Holmes was so fond of saying? Ah yes! 'Once you eliminate the impossible, whatever remains'..." Charu quietly cut in, barely conscious that she was uttering the rest of the phrase "...Whatever remains, no matter how improbable, must be the truth."

Li saw the understanding dawning on her face. "Charu, I want you to check access logs from all people who have had access to the building. Obviously, I want you to begin with visitors, maintenance staff, technicians, cleaning support, catering. Look everywhere." It was now that Charu shifted her gaze uncomfortably to look Li direct in the eye. "Do you want me to check on the rest of the team?" "Regretfully, if we don't find anything before that, then yes, you have my permission to do that. Let's hope it won't come to that."

Charu silently acknowledged Li's order and briefly stared up at the ceiling. "Are you Ok?" "Yes" Charu replied. "I was just calculating how long it will take me on my own to do all the checks. There are over 90 support staff and God only knows how many visitors we have had since Matthias' lecture. You do know, if you want this doing discretely, then it will take me around 6 hours per person at a minimum?"

"I hadn't actually considered that. And I know you are busy with other tasks. Look this is serious, but not critical, do your searches, be discreet and let's say I give you a month to get back to me. Would that work?" Charu, visibly relaxed slightly, "OK, it will be tight, but I figure I can do that." Li gave Charu a sincere appreciative smile as he withdrew a crumpled cigarette packet from his pocket. "Right, now that's settled I have to go do some thinking."

Chapter Eight

> **ambiguous figure** [noun]
> **Definition of ambiguous figure**
> A picture of a subject which the viewer may see as either of two different subjects or as the same subject from either of two different viewpoints depending on how the total configuration is interpreted.
> - *At her peak she was an ambiguous figure, hard to define.*

Donbas

Andrei had been on the ground in Ukraine for exactly 4 days. After a series of frantic calls to the British Foreign and Commonwealth Office and then one personally to General Sir Rupert Heeringly, the Chief of the British Defence Staff, Penny had managed to get permission for Andrei to join a small group of Russian speaking, British Special Reconnaissance Regiment (SRR) troops, that were operating in the area.

The group had been given tacit permission to operate on and around the Crimea and the industrialised eastern part of the country, both of which, since the invasion of the 'little Green Men' the involvement of whom the Russian Government claimed no official knowledge, were now de facto Russian territories.

Despite having tacit permission to be on the ground, the Ukrainian government had explicitly stated that they would strongly deny any knowledge of these NATO troops acting on Ukrainian soil, if they were ever discovered by Russian Forces. It had taken some great personal effort and not a little obfuscation, by Sir Rupert, to gain permission for a Russian national to join the British team.

Sir Rupert had wisely glossed over, or rather omitted to mention Andrei's history as lead team member of Russia's most special of Special Forces, instead he had merely stated that Andrei was part of a UN Cultural Research Mission.

Andrei was now in his third day of live operations with the British team, and hard as it was for a Russian Special Forces soldier to do, he had to admit, these Brits were good, very good. Operating almost exclusively in plain clothes and expert in Small Arms tactics, Close Target Recce, Surveillance and Counter Terrorism Ops, the unit had gained its prestige and fierce reputation under another name and in another time, on the tough streets of Northern Ireland.

Having since been renamed and expanded, this highly specialised and secretive unit now worked far more closely with Britain's other Special Forces, the SAS, SBS and SFSG. The Special Reconnaissance Regiment (SRR) had been an active part of every UK overseas operation since it was founded as the then 14 Intelligence Company back in 1973.

Paul, a wiry, Liverpudlian, the SRR team leader had been equally impressed with Andrei's skill set. The Russian absorbed the British tactics easily, contributed well to team planning sessions and seemed to have an almost supernatural ability to maintain focus. The very nature of the work that the team undertook, was both mentally and physically demanding. Andrei had endeared himself immediately to the group after his impromptu induction shortly after arriving in Western Ukraine.

The Team had partaken in a few sociable beers, this in British parlance actually meant, an excessive night of hard drinking. Then, as is common, around the world, with such specialised units, they had conducted group physical training early the next morning. The training had consisted of a ten-mile run with a daysack containing 10kg. The men had been impressed at Andrei's ability to keep pace, despite looking a little worse for wear.

However, their opinion rapidly altered from simply being impressed to astonishment, when after about 5 miles and just as Paul the team leader was beginning to pick up the pace and put the hurt on the team, Andrei calmly asked to confirm if the route back was going to be a repeat of the route out. Between harsh breaths Paul grunted and nodded. At that, Andrei seemed to effortlessly accelerate, and indeed to the remaining team members, he appeared to continue to accelerate until he was out of sight.

Andrei was on the phone to Maria, leaving the shower with a towel wrapped tightly around his waist, when the rest of the team, tired and sweating after their exertions, arrived back at the apartment. He had a smile on his face, he was happy with his performance, or maybe relieved would be a better word, he thought. Relieved indeed, that the enhanced Haemoglobin upgrade his Version 2.0 through-life upgrade as Dr Aziminov had jokingly referred to it, had been successful.

If anything, thought Andrei, this V.2. upgrade was better than the original formula. He wasn't sure, but he had the feeling that he was recovering from exercise even better than before. He made a mental note to contact Dr Aziminov and ask him about the new formula.

It was good to hear Maria's voice again he thought, as they caught up on life back at the CTC HQ in Singapore. Maria was sat in her office space in the large open plan work area and as she was preparing to finish her call with Andrei, she noticed Matthias running over to her gesticulating wildly. "Say Andrei, hold on a minute will you. I think Matthias wants me for something."

Removing the phone from her ear, Maria span in her chair to face the rapidly approaching Matthias. "Is that Andrei on the line?" spluttered Matthias between breaths. "Yeh, but he has to go now they are back out on the ground later on today." "Tell him to hold on please. I need to speak to him. We may be re-tasking him." More intrigued than alarmed, Maria handed the phone to Matthias.

Still breathing heavily, Matthias spoke with Andrei. "Andrei have you seen the news? A peace accord has been signed in Afghanistan. It was signed between the Taliban and the Afghan government but it was brokered by a joint coalition of Russia, Iran, Pakistan and China." There was silence on the other end of the line. "Andrei are you there?" "Yes, err, I mean what the hell, where did that come from?"

"We don't know, it has stunned everyone here. The UN had no idea, the Americans were ambushed and as you can guess are seriously pissed about what has happened. Bottom line is, we need you back here asap. You and Charu are going on a little trip. Do you think you can wrap up your work there in 3 days?"

Philippe and Matthias had begun their task of analysing the key State influencers in Iraq, Afghanistan and Syria. They had chosen to concentrate their efforts on Syria initially, as this was the most dynamic situation and as such most prone to change, with the punitive Civil war still doggedly dragging on in some areas of the country outside of the major cities such as Aleppo and Damascus, despite the recent ceasefire agreement. Just as they had begun to turn their attention to analysing Afghanistan, they had heard the shock news bulletin.

The TV pundits were blaming everything from an increasingly ambitious and assertive Chinese foreign policy to the Iranians trying to gain more influence in the simmering Sunni-Shia schism being played out across the region. For most commentators the net effect was the same, it was yet another poke in the eye for an overly hubristic US foreign policy. Highlighting yet again, after the recent Syrian Peace Accord the ever-decreasing US global influence and perceived weakening in its position as the world's pre-eminent superpower.

Li had supported Phillipe's request to have access to the UN weather and agricultural survey satellites, and from this rich data source and thanks to Penny's contacts at the UK's GCHQ Image Analysis department, the UK equivalent to the NSA, the team were quickly able to build a picture of exactly how the coalition of Russia, Pakistan, China and Iran intended to back up their promise to act as guarantors of peace within Afghanistan.

The new Afghan Peace Accord had been achieved through compromise. An act, which as had been noted by more than one observer around the world was something which nearly twenty years of western military intervention had failed to do.

Effectively a north south line had been drawn through Afghanistan from Quetta in Northern Pakistan, running just east of Kandahar directly north, passing to the west of Mazar Sharif ending in the far north of the country at the intersection with the Tajikistan, Turkmenistan border.

Both parties had conceded ground that had been hard fought over, and the Afghan government had remained titular leaders for the country as a whole, however the areas ceded to the Taliban were now autonomous areas and effectively the Taliban could act as they wished within this area. The biggest diplomatic and geo-political win however, was in securing the agreement of Pakistan to seal their infamously porous North Western border with Afghanistan.

In matter of fact, the four peace guarantor powers appeared to have provided considerable forces aimed at securing the external borders of Afghanistan and capable of surging into the country to separate the two parties if either side attempted to encroach on the territory of the other.

The part of the deal that was as yet unclear and remained a mystery to many western observers, was exactly why and how Pakistan had been persuaded to convince its own remote and mostly self-governed Northwest Frontier provinces to close its lucrative border with Afghanistan.

The Iranians had already reinforced existing Garrisons in Zahedan, which sits only 50km from the extreme southwest border of Afghanistan with some of their best troops. The 1st Battalion of the 23rd Special Forces Division, backed up by another 4 Battalions from the 55th Parachute Division along with most of their heavy lift aircraft.

Their stated purpose according to a press release from the Revolutionary Guard Corps' Office for Public Information was 'to be able to act as a quick reaction force capable of parachuting aggressive forces over the southern Afghan border or along the north – south demarcation line, should they be required.'

The main Pakistani contribution wasn't as expected in the Quetta border region, instead the Pakistani's had committed a large contingent of some of their most hardened mountain fighters. In total 9 full Battalions of the Pakistani Northern Light Infantry from Kashmir.

These troops had already begun working up and exercising with the first Chinese units which had been given permission to enter Afghanistan quite legally through the Wakhan Corridor, a thin spit of land in the northeast of Afghanistan, bordering Tajikistan in the north, Kashmir to the south and importantly for the Chinese military logistics machine, with its own natural border with mainland China in the east.

As with the rest of the region, the Wakhan corridor area was highly mountainous and the Chinese had sent their largest ever overseas deployment consisting of mountain troops from the 57th Mountain Combined Arms Brigade, 3 of the six airborne brigades of the 15th Airborne Corps and of surprise to most observers their most elite troops the Special Operations Brigade.

These troops numbering over 10,000 in total represented, as one TV commentator put it, 'the forces deployed to Afghanistan by China were just the 'sharp point of a very long spear'.

Back in Singapore, Matthias, Phillipe and Li were trying to make sense of the rapidly developing situation. In the background a constant cycle of live TV news was being broadcast on a large monitor displaying multiple tiled panes that increased or decreased in size depending on the amount of concurrent channels being viewed.

"So, team, what do we have?" Li said quietly to his two colleagues as they sat staring at a large-scale digital map of central Asia that was being displayed on the Table's surface. Charu tapped on key locations in the north of Afghanistan and in the southwest and blown-up satellite imagery popped up of the Iranian, Chinese and Pakistani troop movements. Tapping her index finger onto a digital colour palette she began drawing red circles around key sites along the Afghan border.

"Ok, guys, this is what we can make out so far." Charu continued to hurriedly daub red dots of varying sizes onto the table's surface. "Each dot relates to either Chinese, Pakistani or Iranian troop deployments. Part of the ceasefire agreement was that no foreign troops, with the exception of the Chinese forces in the Wakhan Corridor, were to be based on Afghan soil. We would expect to see a serious contingent of troops with rapid reaction and heavy lift capability around".

She prodded the map at a small bulge of land that seemed to extend into Afghan territory. "here, in Shalozan, which is a federally administered region of Pakistan and lies about 150km due west of

Peshawar. Considering the terrain, this is probably the closest point to the Afghan capital, Kabul, and I guess it will be used as the main troop concentration for a Quick Reaction Force capable of supporting the government in Kabul."

Matthias stared at Charu intently as she gave her brief. She certainly was a lot more confident giving these sorts of talks than she was a year ago he thought. However, despite this display of confidence, Matthias noted, or at least thought he observed something else in Charu. He couldn't quite put his finger on it, he thought he had discerned glimpses of anger, no it wasn't anger it was that other equally strong emotion; fear.

"Finally," Charu said, relieved to be getting her speaking part over with. "So, in summary, the three powers seem determined and very serious about enforcing this ceasefire. However, when we examined the satellite imagery for a second time, Maria spotted something we had all missed. Up here."

Charu stretched forward her long hair cascading forward and obscuring the view temporarily and tapped a couple of points on the map that lay in a tiny, and often forgotten about piece of territory that lay squeezed between Nepal in the west and Bhutan to the East. "This is the Doklam Plateau and forms a key part of the of India / China line of demarcation. It's quite some distance from the areas we were focussing on, I guess that's why we missed it the first time around."

Turning to Maria, Charu asked her to expand on what she had observed. Spinning her black ring on her finger and tapping at the LED surface, Maria brought up a series of high-definition photos of the areas. Maria began to speak, and the congenial atmosphere disappeared abruptly, it was replaced with a brusque, no-nonsense military Point Brief. Matthias glanced over at Li and caught the edges of a wry smile on the older Chinese man's face.

"As I was saying," Maria repeated, glowering at Matthias who she had caught not paying attention. "Nature doesn't make many straight lines," As she spoke, she began highlighting specific areas of the photo with red borders, "These we believe are bunkers built into the rock and these" she pointed due north with her pointer. "These straight lines represent a new railway and road connection from

Yadong, here in the south of Tibet, all the way to the border."

"The Chinese government's official explanation," Maria formed the two-handed inverted comma sign in the air and drew a sarcastic smirk across her face, "The official explanation is that the work forms part of the new Silk Road infrastructure, although it doesn't appear to lie on any of the previous maps or plans that we have been privy to."

"Best guess, as to its use?" Philippe asked. "Well," Maria paused slightly and unusually an element of doubt crept into her normally straight forward briefing style. "Through estimating the amount of material that was removed from the excavations, we figure the caves are roughly the same size as 3 football pitches each and there are three of them. So you can only guess at the amount of military hardware they could hide away in there!"

"Of more concern, to me is this here." Slowing twisting the LED ring on her finger she zoomed into a long strip of land which at first look appeared to be a wider than usual fire break in a forested area. "With a little help from some contacts of mine at the NSA, I've managed to look up a complete series of imagery of the same area for the last 5 years. Charu has stitched it together in reverse chronological order, into a nice little reverse Gif for us." Clicking her fingers Maria commanded the Gif to play.

Before everybody's eyes the Gif began to play revealing detailed images of the forested area in reverse chronological order. The forested area with its long neat fire break slowly began to cleave in two eventually forming two separate forests. Li winced, and Philippe looked on dumbfounded, eventually he managed to utter "you mean they have created this one forest to camouflage an airstrip?" Maria nodded.

"The Russkies routinely practice flying their aircraft from makeshift runways, often using their major roads as landing strips during their major annual exercises. Many of these roads have removable lights and collapsible barriers purposely designed for that reason." Matthias cut in "It appears that the Chinese have taken a leaf out of the Russian playbook and created their own strategic lift landing strip right under the noses of the Indians!"

This last comment by Matthias caused Li to sit a little more erect in his chair as if jolted by a subtle surge of electricity. He quickly scribbled a note in his pocketbook before returning his attention to the table's surface.

Penny who had been watching the Gif play out from her desk, walked over to the assembled group. "You know the Indian government have been worried about this for a long time. They have made repeated requests to both the British and American governments for drone and satellite monitoring of the area. According to a file I read before I left MI6, over the last year the Indian defence forces have repositioned a considerable amount of their most capable troops to the area. A full heavy division supported by a considerable proportion of their ground attack air power, missile defence systems and artillery. They are nervous as hell about a repeat of 1967 war."

Maria nodded in agreement and Matthias casually observed Li as he assimilated the new information. No longer able to hold it in any longer Charu blurted out "I have family in Amritsar, way up in north Punjab and very close to Kashmir further north and Lahore across the border in Pakistan, they messaged me this morning, they are all really scared because everyone has been talking about these massive troop movements and large-scale exercises." That explained it, thought Matthias, that explained the fear he had read in Charu this morning.

Penny cut in "I bet they are worried. I was reading up on some of the Chinese media sites this morning and they have announced large scale exercises to practice working with the Iranians and Pakistanis. I guess it is only natural they have never worked together as allies and will have many communication, logistic and weapon systems that they will need to synchronise if they want to work effectively together. They are calling the manoeuvres, Exercise '*Qūyù hépíng*' sorry err I mean Exercise Regional Peace!!" Once more Matthias glanced over to the elder Chinese and saw the growing comprehension beginning to spread across his demeanour as his razor-sharp analytical mind filtered and reordered the information they had just been given.

destabilize [noun]

Definition of destabilize

To make unstable

Alternate: To cause something such as a government to be incapable of functioning or surviving.

- *Their sole aim is to destabilize the Indian government.*

"I'm not sure if it's pertinent?" Maria offered, quickly looking down at her tablet quickly scrolling through pages of text and tables. "But I did check the Secret Service's daily terrorist threat matrix and out of curiosity I flicked through the stats on India this morning."

"Apparently, there has been a marked increase in attacks in the East of India. Some group called the..." Maria struggled briefly to pronounce the group, "the err, Naxalites. They managed to detonate a couple of devices outside government offices, in towns called Patna and Ranchi and two devices were intercepted a day later much further away in" she slowly read out the names again tripping over her pronunciation. "Kolkata and Hyderabad. My God you guys pick some difficult names to pronounce," Maria said grinning at Charu.

"Actually," Matthias, cut in "Both towns are great examples of the move away from the past of colonialism and unfortunately, more scarily towards a potentially more radical nationalism. Kolkata is what the British called Calcutta, as in the Black hole of Calcutta. It was renamed only in 2001, And only last year did the ruling Hindu nationalist party, the BJP, threaten, sorry I meant promise to rename Hyderabad, Bhagyanagar." Mimicking Maria's sarcastic air quote hand gesture, Matthias smirked as he said the final part.

Philippe was next to speak. "Guys, you all know that I have no military experience. Everything you guys have said seems to make perfect sense. But I am looking at all of these nice red blobs Charu has drawn on the map. Something is bothering me, I mean, we are only looking at this one way because we were told that the forces arrayed around Afghanistan were being positioned there to support the recent peace accord."

Unaccustomed to having her analysis challenged, Maria cut in a little too abruptly. "Obviously, I mean anyone can see that it makes sense. It might be a little bit of overkill, but those Taliban are tough bastards."

Unruffled, Philippe continued "No Maria, what I mean is we are only looking at this in a certain way because we have been directed to think like that. I'm an engineer by training and in my industry, we are always taught to look at the upstream and downstream effects of what we do. I guess to put it simpler, I don't see things travelling in one linear direction. The Chinese and Iranian media releases have told us that they are supporting a peace accord and that for regional peace they will be conducting joint training exercises. What if that is simply the narrative they want us to believe? Could all of these troops be used in an offensive manner instead of defensive?"

Charu, who personally had more at stake than anyone else in the room immediately saw where Philippe was going and picked up the thread. "Guys, I hope Philippe is not right. What do we know about the troops?" Charu started to list the characteristics: "Highly specialised in mountain warfare, highly mobile, well equipped and with excellent air and missile support." She had barely finished when Penny spoke.

"You don't mean, what I think you mean do you? They are forming a coalition to help the Pakistanis take Kashmir?" "I don't know it's just when you look at the increased Naxalite activity, the build-up of troops in Yadong in southern Tibet and this new development, all I am saying is, these forces could be used to seize Kashmiri territory, Indian forces will be stretched really thinly with multiple threats around the country."

Now it was Li's turn to speak. He rarely interrupted his team at such discussions, preferring instead, to observe his team in action, absorbing their ideas and allowing them scope to develop different theories. "Philippe, very inciteful as ever. I really do hope you are wrong. At the moment, legally China, Iran and Pakistan have acted within international law. I am speaking to the Secretary General at the beginning of next week and will be sure to appraise him of this. Meanwhile, I have asked that Charu and Andrei get on the first available flight to northern India. They are going to enter Indian Kashmiri territory and conduct a fact-finding mission and get some atmospherics."

"I want to know what is happening on the ground and I want you to study the terrain and demographics and provide me with a report on the effects of any potential attack will have on subsequent displacement of peoples." Pausing to look around him at his team and visibly appearing to tense his slight frame, "Whatever is happening, we can be certain of one thing, the world is teetering on a precipice, a pivotal moment of unknown change is upon us and on an unimaginable scale."

"We, that is the UNCTC must be prepared to fulfil our main role. We must be capable of delivering the right technological solutions to these newly carved out quasi-states so that the people, many of which had no say in the cleaving up of their territories, have the resources they need to not only survive but to develop." Suddenly conscious that he had been leaning heavily on the table and gripping its edges a little too tightly with his fingers, Li straightened and with some effort tried to relax his demeanour.

Matthias was the last to speak before the group dispersed. "So, just to be absolutely clear, if I can summarise. The Iranians, Pakistanis and Chinese have achieved in less than a year and by seemingly peaceful means, something the Americans and their allies failed to do in 20 years of warfare. The price for this stability is accepting a Shariah law-based government in the north of Afghanistan and the continued existence of the Taliban as a force."

Matthias paused briefly to let comments sink in. "The American forces have been completely squeezed out of the area, very soon after they were ejected from Syria, and it seems if Walt's report is correct that the Chinese threw in debt abeyance or in some cases complete forgiveness for Afghanistan and Pakistan as a deal sweetener. Did I miss out anything?"

The team nodded in solemn agreement, none of them wanting to verbalise what everyone was thinking. The map in front of them spoke volumes. Effectively, from the Syrian / Lebanese border a swathe of territory extending east through Syria, Iraq, Iran, Afghanistan,

Pakistan and through into China was now effectively under the political influence of America and the West's undeclared enemies.

As they departed from the briefing room each person present at the brief tried to assimilate what they had just witnessed, struck by the realisation that they just may be witnessing the first murmurings of a massive geopolitical powershift. The only question remaining was, what America and the West's response would be?

equation [noun]

Definition of equation

The act or process of equating.

Alternate: a complex of variable factors.

- *New plans have taken chance out of the equation.*

The team left the briefing room and slowly drifted back to their desks. Li, Matthias and Philippe instead headed straight for thc glass smoking cube. As they walked together in silence, Li felt ashamed at his loss of face in the briefing. This act of raising his voice and showing emotion, reminded him once more that at his heart he was Chinese, it also caused him to wonder what his father was doing right at that very moment.

The last time he had spoken with his father had been right there in the very smoking cube they were heading towards now. Touching his own cheek reflexively, Li brought back the bitter memory of his father's slap across his face and his cold words as he verbally pronounced his permanent disassociation from his adopted son.

Having entered the Smoking cube, Philippe now sat opposite Li and Matthias who sat side by side on an old leather sofa, between the three men stood a small table with a Go board, still showing the result of the last game between Li and Matthias.

As usual Philippe was the last to actually start smoking, he always spent considerable time cleaning and preparing his pipe before he spoke. Matthias mused to himself that the big French Canadian did indeed take as much pleasure from this ritual preparation as he did from actually smoking his pipe.

Still staring intently at Philippe, Matthias quietly spoke to Li. "I'm concerned about Charu." Li didn't speak he just barely nodded his head in acknowledgement of Matthias' words and allowed the anthropologist to continue speaking. "This is personal for her, she has family. In the region and I am worried that her emotions will skew her judgement. We need her at the top of her game you know."

After what seemed like an interminably long time, Li spoke. "Charu is stronger than you think Matthias. You need to stop thinking of her as a victim. What happened to her in Boston, will stay with her for the rest of her life, but she will and is learning to reframe herself and you can see how her confidence is growing."

Matthias considered Li's words and feeling slightly more reassured, sat back and continued to inhale deeply on his cigarette. As he was lazily exhaling a deep lung full of smoke, he gazed absently at the Go board sat on the table between the three men.

"Say, Li how are those Go strategies coming on in your head? Have you worked anything out yet?" At the sound of the words Go Strategy, Philippe, still reclined in his seat, opened one eye, with his pipe still clamped firmly in his mouth he lifted his head and joined Matthias in looking at Li. The older Chinese man still hadn't moved, yet both of his colleagues could see that behind his calm exterior a hive of activity was going on.

"Matthias, before I begin any game of Go, I build my own strategic equation in my head." Both Matthias and Philippe sat forward and began listening intently to Li who was still sat slumped back on the sofa, eyes closed. "First, I consider the variables, who am I playing, how do they play, how much time do I have etc, only then do I consider and decide on my end state. This will be the overall strategic state I want to be in by the end of the game. Finally, I simply work out which of the other strategies I need to employ to reach my desired end state." Philippe looked to Matthias with a quizzical look on his face.

Slowly opening his eyes, Li spoke once more "From the thundering silence engulfing us it seems that I will have to explain myself a little more clearly." Standing abruptly, still with his ubiquitous cigarette clenched between his lips, and with surprising agility for a man of his age, he pulled a white board marker pen from his cardigan pocket and began to scribble a simple equation on the glass walls of the smoking cube.

"For the purposes of this exercise I am playing the role of the opposition and considering the facts and current situation. Let's chalk it all up here; Crimea, Lithuania, Kashmir. That would be 3 x Invasions, let that be $3I$. The events in Afghanistan, Silk Road infrastructure building in Africa, Pakistan and throughout Central Asia. Now, let me think, that would give us; let's say 4 x Connection, and the reciprocal minus 4 x Cut. We'll call that $+4Co - 4Cu$. And all of this: $3I + 4Co - 4Cu =$ gives us what?" With a flourish, Li finished scribbling down the last of the equation and turned with a triumphant look on his face to gaze intently at his two closest colleagues.

"There!", Matthias and Philippe just looked at each, then back to Li, both men wore bemused looks on their faces. "Sorry Li" began Philippe in a calm level tone "you may need to expand a little on your equation" Li looked a little deflated that the two other men hadn't followed his reasoning. "Ok, guys, so if I replace the question mark with this 'S' then we have $3I + 4Co - 4Cu = S$ here **S** is Sente."

Both men nodded at Li, although Li could see that they hadn't truly understood the equation yet. "Remember Sente is the state when the other side is forced to respond to what you are doing. You know rather like playing chess the ideal position to be in, is where you are making a play or dictating the moves and the opponent is forced to try and defend or counter your moves rather than dictating the game themselves."

Suddenly, a lightbulb came on in Matthias' head, "Ok, so if I am reading this correctly, you are saying that the bad actors are using Invasion to Cut or divide territory formerly controlled or influenced by the opposition and Connect a new series of territories to create a large bloc?" Matthias was stressing each of the key Go words as he recounted back to Li his understanding of Li's thinking.

Now it was Philippe's turn to jump in. "and the result of this aggression is for the bad guys to get the upper hand right? I mean they, at some point when enough territory comes under their influence, will be able to dictate the rules of the game?"

Peering back at his two protégés, over his round glasses, which, as ever were perched, owl-like on the end of his nose, Li spoke once more. "Unfortunately, Philippe, I think you may just be right on both accounts." Matthias raised a hand, "hold on guys, we've seen this before, haven't we? I mean, what you're saying here is basically Cold War v 2.0." Li then spoke once more. This time in a quieter more foreboding voice.

"Matthias remember your lecture on future multiverses and the end of a unipolar world?" Both Matthias and Philippe nodded in solemn agreement. "Well maybe what we are witnessing here is the beginning of a tipping point away from this unipolar world. However, unlike the beginning of the Cold War which saw the formation of NATO and the absolute fear of another Great War starting. We are now in the position where NATO is weakened and leaderless and several of the world's younger 'alphabet' generations have a very fuzzy memory or any idea at all of the horrors of total war." This time it was Philippe's turn to speak.

"OK, as my hero; Detective Columbo never tired of saying, we need to know the Who, How and Why. We know the Who because these actors have been directly behind all of the recent events. Russia, China, Iran, I'm still not convinced this is an organised coordinated series of events. It might just be that these three states who have been under extreme sanctions of one type or another from the US and by extension most of the West for some time have seen that the time is now right to start to shake things up a little."

"As for the Why, well as I said, I am not sure they are coordinated events. I mean the Russians are still sore about losing the Cold War and see themselves as regional or even global leaders. Iran has always strived to be a regional force but has been kept at bay by the Israelis, Iraqis and Americans. As for China, well what can I say. The country is developing so fast and on such a scale that it almost seems obvious that some accommodation will have to be made to allow them a leading position in the world."

"Now for the How, well that still baffles me, if I am being completely honest. But if we follow Li's thinking in his equation, using Invasion and the Connection and Cut strategies to create a great contiguous bloc of states and territories, connected through natural borders, sea lanes and road and rail. From what we can see so far, this contiguous bloc is rich in energy, mineral and agricultural resources along with a growing population. To me at least it seems like a pretty sound plan."

Stubbing his cigarette out, Li moved to leave the room. "I need to speak to Walt and Penny and see if they have those economic forecasts on the Silk Route Project. I need to review them before I speak with the Secretary General next week. Matthias, Philippe you are both correct I believe in your assumptions, although I dearly hoped you weren't. What I want you guys to do now, whilst the others are off keeping an eye on Kashmir, is to look at what we believe these States are doing and try to determine the next moves. We must try and get ourselves on the front foot. We simply can't allow them to achieve Sente." Li walked briskly out of the smoking cube and strode over to a small alcove desk where Walt and Penny were working on the economic data.

Chapter Nine

Somewhere on the Silk Route

> **depose** [verb]
> **Definition of depose**
> To remove from a throne or other high position.
> - *She must be deposed for the sake of democracy.*

At the same time that China began work on its One Belt One Road project, using roads, ports and railways that would eventually create the greatest single integrated trading bloc the world had ever seen, in parallel, unbeknown to most observers, it had begun to develop a more powerful complex of communications, banking and data networks.

Over the past ten years, this secondary, less overt network, had been assiduously used to deeply embed political and diplomatic influence as well as physical and cyber security and media influence throughout the entirety of the One Belt One Road Project area. Such an area of political and geographic influence would soon surpass even the size and scale of the British Empire at its zenith. All of which, well nearly all, had been achieved without any overt military action.

Bishkek, the capital of Kyrgyzstan, sits in the far north of the country. It is framed to the south by an imposing chain of snow-covered mountains called the Ala Too range. To the north just over the border in Kazakhstan lays a vast seemingly endless desertified steppe-land, probably the very same land that Genghis Khan swept over with his Mongol horde on his way to sack Baghdad nearly 900 years ago.

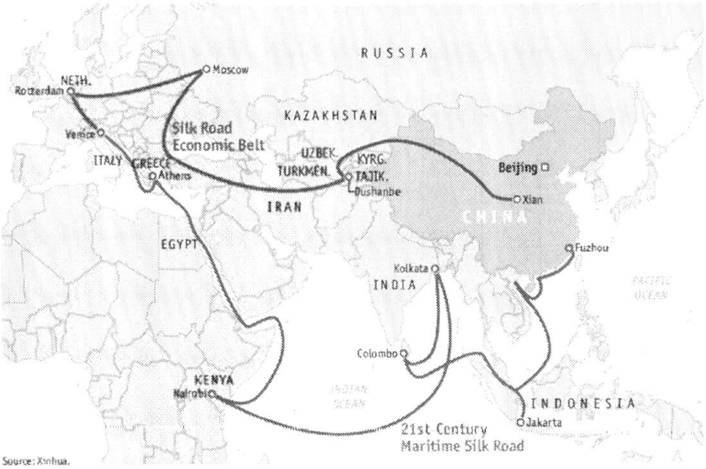

Source: Xinhua.

Of a more prominent geographical note, the capital of Kyrgyzstan, or at the least the surrounding area was to be a key nexus on the One Belt One Road Initiative, and it also just happens to sit equidistant to Tehran, and Beijing, or at least as equidistant as any place on earth that wasn't actually located in Russia, Iran or China.

Minister Zhang Wu mused this point as he stared absent-mindedly out of the bulletproof window of the Hongqi N501 Presidential limousine over towards the hive of frenzied activity surrounding President Voronin's Russian-built Aurus Senat limousine. As with the Chinese Premiere's vehicle, the Russian President's car had been flown in especially for this event.

Zhang paused for thought and reflected that his President's personal limousine had been flown to every single Silk Road meeting that had been held. This included most of East Africa, and almost all of Central Asia. A wry smile lit up his face. The car had visited more foreign countries than Zhang himself he mused.

The reason they were all still sat in their vehicles on this rather bleak and desolate runway was simple, the Presidents of two of the world's superpowers were waiting for the President of Iran. It was well known that Iran's Supreme Leader, the ageing Ayatollah, would never leave Iran, instead the country's highest elected official, the President, was due to attend the meeting.

That is, he should have arrived over an hour ago but the President's ageing Airbus A340 had recently been a target of sanctions by the Americans and this had forced the President to make the ten-hour flight from Tehran in one of the Air Force's even older and more decrepit Boeing 707 planes.

This particular plane had been in service with the Iranian Air Force since 1974 and it had taken two aborted take offs, some extremely frenzied mechanical work and a lot of luck and trust in God's benevolence to finally transport the President safely to the meeting.

The ancient 707 lumbered, groaned and strained as it lined itself up for its final descent into Bishkek. Homayoun Ghorbani, who was coming towards the end of his first term as President, clutched the arms of his seat and prayed a silent prayer to his God that he would survive this flight to be able to fight for a second term as the country's President.

He knew one thing for certain, if things continued to go to plan on this project then the crippling US sanctions would no longer affect his country and he promised himself that the first thing he would order would be the purchase much needed new aircraft for his country's Air Force.

Zhang, who had been watching with interest the precarious descent of the Iranian President's plane, was woken from his private reflections by a sharp dig in his ribs. Taking just a fraction of a second to compose himself and quell the rising annoyance at being treated like a lowly functionary, Zhang turned to face the Chinese President Zhao Leji. Zhao had only occupied the most senior position, that of Paramount Leader, in China's overly bureaucratic political system for a little over 6 months.

Despite his predecessor having been elevated to the position of Core Leader, a title only ever bestowed on 4 of China's leaders. It had been felt by several members of the Standing Committee that the former leader was concentrating too much power in himself. The more wary Standing Committee members, too smart to openly confront the former leader, instead set about carefully building a quorum of like-minded members.

Zhao, who was amongst this group of old men who silently opposed and feared the now ex-President, had been approached by the other members who had all offered him their full support in removing the former President.

Zhao, in turn, had turned to the man who now sat beside him, Zhang, for explicit help in toppling his political rival. Despite the ex-President having almost complete control over the Armed Forces and country's security apparatus, he did have one achilles heel. He had always shown only a vague passing interest in the country's highly developed State Cyber Security Division. Why should he? After all he was the most popular President China had ever had and he commanded the largest Army in the world.

Zhang's task had been a relatively simple one. Step one was to fly to Shanghai and engage a small trusted team of civilian hackers who worked on contract to the State's secretive hacking organisation PLA Unit 61398. After using them to set up dummy bank accounts they then proceeded to electronically transfer an obscenely large sum of money into an account in the name of the former President's wife.

Step two, in Zhang's opinion was the really creative part. Using his team of hackers and their military contacts within PLA Unit 61398 based in Shanghai, they scripted and wrote a series of news articles about a scandal involving the embezzlement of tens of millions of Renminbi by the President's wife.

The really ingenious part had been to use the President's own 'Xueliang', or Sharp Eyes programme of surveillance against the man himself. by subtly ensuring that another department of the same Unit 61398, responsible for monitoring foreign electronic media content that could prove harmful to the state were allowed to discover the circulating stories.

The President's fall from grace was brutal and swift. Having personally overseen numerous corruption cases against his political rivals, the President knew full well how this would play out. Despite cajoling, threatening and even in two cases temporarily imprisoning senior ministers, the former President could not establish who was behind the plot. Although speculation over the embezzlement was pretty much stopped within China itself, due to tight controls of the internet by the very organisation that first discovered the stories.

The Communist Party knew only too well that if they as a party wanted to remain relevant and maintain an unassailable position at the top of China's political hierarchy, then they could ill afford an incident of embezzlement on this scale involving the highest position in the land. Put quite simply, the Chinese Communist Party were a victim of their own success. Years of reform and development of a uniquely Chinese economic model had resulted not only in a raising of living standards and wealth for much of the population but equally in a raising of the people's expectations.

At the next Politburo Standing Committee meeting the seven men who controlled anything and everything that happened in the world's most populous State voted 5 to 1 to remove the seventh member, the country's President. The country's second highest position, that of Premier was the only member of the Standing Committee that voted for the President.

"You know Zhang," Zhao whispered to him, "Do you know what China's greatest invention is?" The question was rhetorical. Of course, Zhang knew, he simply looked back at the man who he had been instrumental in placing into power and waited "Paper, simple paper. We invented the stuff hundreds of years before the West discovered our invention. Paper has many properties, but only one that will make China great."

Zhang had no idea where the older man was going with this, but it actually had him curious. "Because paper is brittle, friable, it crumbles and decays over time. The result is that most Westerners believe that China has only ever been a backward peasant nation riven with internal strife."

"Students in the UK and America who fawn over stories of Egyptian Pyramids and Pharaohs, Greek civilization or the Roman Empire, learn absolutely nothing about our great nation's amazing achievements and history. Quite simply, no real evidence exists of much of our science, politics or great military events. It is just dust, buried deep in the earth. You can dig all day and you won't find any written evidence of China's achievements on our beloved delicate paper."

Cinching his thumb and forefinger together Zhao rubbed them

back and forth. "That Zhang, exactly that! Those fine, delicate, crushed wooden fibres which simply turn to dust over time, is our strength. The West underestimate us, they think us primitive and underdeveloped. And I for one want to encourage this thinking, until we are truly ready and at a time completely of our choosing, which is fast approaching my friend."

Zhang stared at his superior and knew that he had made the right choice to elevate him to power. This man, Zhao, with the Zhang's guidance of course, would lead the Middle Kingdom to its natural position of pre-eminence in the world and he, Zhang would be there every step of the way.

Zhao noted Zhang's interest and continued his monologue. "Our age of dominion, Empire, hegemony, call it want you want, will be different. We will exert hegemony over the largest contiguous landmass ever controlled in recorded human history, the Americas," he spat the word derisively from his mouth, "the Americas can rot for all I care, they will be nothing but a disorganised feuding mass of peoples struggling to survive without access to the world's resources."

"As for Europe, they will have one simple choice to make; join us or wither and die!" Zhao banged his fist down hard on the centre console of wood between the two men as he said this last part. The action startled Zhang and he silently cursed himself for flinching.

Most of the other delegates attending the One Belt One Road Coordination summit were already in the Congress centre being treated to a display of traditional Kyrgyz dancing whilst sampling the local Kyrgyz cuisine. Not everything on offer was to all of the delegates' taste.

The Burmese delegate, having already imbibed a little too much of the local alcohol, a fermented mare's milk called Koumiss, closely avoided an international incident as he fought to stop himself vomiting over the Turkish delegate's table, after a show of bravado, when, in an attempt to impress his Turkish colleagues, he took a large swig of the warm frothy horses' milk.

As with everything organised by the Chinese, every action was conducted with a specific purpose. The entrance of the Russian, Chinese and Iranian senior delegates was orchestrated to put on a show of unity of purpose to the other delegates. A large brass gong sounded in the main congress hall and the entrance of the three senior delegates was announced.

Processing in a rather awkward group of three, the Russian President, Chinese Premiere and Iranian President entered the hall and climbed the small steps leading to the raised platform from which they would lead the afternoon's meeting. As to be expected, in an overly-zealous attempt to demonstrate their virility both the Chinese and Russian leaders almost seemed to compete in their efforts to bound up the small flight of stairs in the most athletic manner possible. The unfortunate pale-faced Iranian President was forced to clutch the handrail firmly as he struggled to fight off the effects of the air sickness caused by his traumatic flight from Iran.

The purpose of the Congress was partly for the obvious publicity that an event of this scale attended by such important world leaders would generate, secondly, it was to reinforce bonds between the member nations and encourage deeper cooperation, whilst acting as a forum to focus everyone's attention on the achievements and future tasks. However, most importantly Zhang realised, it was, above all about maintaining momentum.

Zhang new from his time as a young man at the People's Liberation Army Officer Training Academy, that above all for an attack to be successful, the conservation of momentum was the most critical factor. This, law of war, was proudly attributed to Sun Tzu, Zhang recalled, and now nearly fifty years after this concept was drilled into him, here he was using the same idea himself to guide the One Belt One Road Project to a successful conclusion.

Standing and walking to the microphone to begin the introductions and open the Congress Zhang remembered the other Sun Tzu dictum taught to him so many years ago during his Officer training. "Energy may be likened to the bending of a crossbow; decision, to the releasing of a trigger." Indeed, he thought the energy that this project possessed, wielded by the right person, would surpass any country's ability to withstand its impact. The release of the metaphorical trigger on the One Belt One Road project would unleash a paradigm-altering force.

Intently aware of the Russian President's eyes boring into him as he moved towards the dais, Zhang tried hard to focus and concentrate on what he was about to say. Looking around the room he took in the various nations represented in front of him. Casting his gaze over one half of the room he noticed the sizable African delegation.

These people, Zhang mused to himself, more than others, had benefited most so far from the One Belt One Road project. The introduction and the building of the extensive port and rail networks had connected almost the entirety of East Africa, not just with each other but more importantly with the wider trading world, in an extremely efficient manner.

Ports from Mozambique in the South all the way up to Sudan in the North, were disgorging a hitherto unimaginable volume of manufactured goods to the eager and willing new markets of Africa. East Africa was hungry, not for food this time, they were gorging themselves on consumable electronics, domestic appliances and the latest fashions, indeed they were happy to devour anything and everything, just as fast as the Chinese factories could produce it.

Of course, the container ships returning to China weren't going back empty. No indeed, they were taking rare earth minerals, grain, textiles and cattle to not simply put food in the mouths of the growing Chinese population, but just as importantly to satiate the hunger of China's enormous industrial complex.

Zhang had thought long and hard about how to make this speech. The secret he had decided, was to put on a display of humility and benevolence in equal measure. Glancing, one more time at his notes in front of him, he raised his head and began to speak. "Gentlemen, welcome to the 3rd Congress of the One Belt One Road Project." A ripple of polite applause flowed around the Congress centre. "Our new Silk Road aims to connect almost half of the world's population and one fifth of global GDP this will set up trade and investment links that will eventually stretch across the entire world."

It had taken considerably more effort than Zhang had believed to say 'our new Silk Road' and not 'China's new Silk Road'. Now time to get even more inclusive, he thought. Opening his hands wide in the universal gesture of inclusivity; "We, the Asian and African peoples, should be capable of constructing international playgrounds…"

Zhang paused briefly to allow the audience to respond. He was rewarded with a burble of excited chatter. "and most importantly..." Pointing skywards with his index finger raised high above his head. "Most importantly, we, the Asian and African peoples should be capable of creating the rules of the games played on these playgrounds." This time the Burmese delegate, who had narrowly avoided the unfortunate accident with the warm horse's milk, and his newly found Turkish colleagues, rose to their feet and began clapping.

Zhang guessed that only a handful of people in the room knew that the exact same words he had just spoken, were taken directly from the previous Chinese Premiere's final speech at a plenary session of the People's Standing Committee of the Chinese Communist Party National Congress. The only difference between Zhang's words and the former Premiere's was the insertion the term Asian and African peoples instead of the word Chinese.

By now, most of the audience were on their feet, applauding every nuanced phrase Zhang spoke. Now, thought Zhang, the icing on the proverbial cake; "And unlike every hegemon before us. You will not be asked to change the way you run your country, to adopt a different system of government, give up your cultural values or allow external interference. No! the rules of this new playground we are jointly building are simple, commerce, not religion or politics will be our defining value."

"Every member of this Project will benefit from the open trade and communication between its members regardless of political or ideological differences." The rapturous applause began to synchronise into a pulsing rhythm that reverberated around the large hall, slowly fading to a gentle, yet constant murmur. Zhang stood, smiling as he surveyed the audience in front of him.

A curt cough from Zhao, behind him, sent a jolt of guilt through Zhang's body as he realised that his boss, the Premiere of China and the Russian President were sat not ten feet away watching as their underling received personal acclaim for their efforts.

Zhang felt his face begin to suffuse with blood as both fear and embarrassment rose in equal measure from deep within him. A tiny bead of sweat began to grow on his temple, threatening at any minute to develop enough mass and momentum to begin its own self-propelled journey, creating in its wake a tiny rivulet of sweat down the blood-infused side of Zhang's face.

Knowing that he could not afford the loss of face or ignominy of taking out his handkerchief to remove the self-minded bead of sweat that threatened at any moment to show itself to the world, in a hoarse voice he quickly began to outline the rest of the activities for the day. This of course would involve many different plenary sessions broken up into different groups by nationality and a few keynote speeches later in the afternoon.

Turning from the dais and still unable to look his boss squarely in the eye, Zhao began to consider his tasks for the day. The main task for his team would be to secure Burmese, Pakistani, Iranian and Yemeni political agreements on the shore-basing of Chinese warships in the newly built ports.

If, or rather, when, Zhang reminded himself, these countries signed the agreements, the effect would be to give China an uninterrupted and mutually supportable chain of military naval bases stretching in the East, from Vladivostok on the Russian / Chinese border all the way through the contested South China sea and around the southern tip of India, across the broad expanse of the Indian Ocean to the shores of East Africa.

Zhang was highly confident that the respective country delegates would get the deals signed by their leaders, despite some lingering internal political disapproval. Due to America's strong-arm tactics and ability to manipulate world bank transfer system, the effects of economic sanctions against these countries was really beginning to affect the stability of each of the respective regimes.

After observing the collapse of the Berlin Wall from afar and more recently and intimately the reaction by the Chinese government to the Tiananmen Square protests, Zhang knew very well, that any political system could only repress internal dissent for so long, before the governed began to threaten the governors.

Naturally, one of the chief considerations when China had established the Asian Infrastructure Investment Bank (AIIB) was how the bank could support China's broader strategic political objectives. All four of the countries had already begun receiving considerable financial aid in loans and grants supplied through the AIIB.

Zhang knew this to be a fact, because it was he personally, that had endorsed the release of funds. The AIIB's international exchange system had been deliberately set up as a discrete and isolated system to the one used by the rest of the world for just this eventuality.

Still slightly cowed, Zhang trailed on behind, as the Russian, Chinese and Iranian Leaders descended from the raised platform and were led by their respective security details to a private conference room.

The room had been designed and decorated in the style of a traditional Kyrgyz Yurt. The soft furnishings and low tables were arrayed in a circular fashion, with a round low wooden table in the middle of the yurt which held an array of drinks and food.

The thing, that immediately struck the Russian President, was the complete absence of chairs in the room. 'Was this another little dig by the Chinese? Another subtle way of signalling who was in charge?'. The Iranian President gracefully knelt down in his traditional Islamic repose and looked relaxed as he began to serve tea for the other two leaders.

The Chinese leader followed suit, preferring to adopt a more typical cross-legged seated position. Once seated, both men casually looked across as the bull-headed Russian president as he struggled in his tight-fitting suit to sit in a more or less comfortable cross-legged position.

Mishka Voronin, President of the Russian Federation, did indeed feel uncomfortable, struggling to breath as his belt dug deeply into his waist. However, he continued to smile, not willing to give either of these unworthy dogs the satisfaction of seeing his discomfort. Inwardly, although he was seething, despite this he reminded himself of the advantages, both to him personally, and to the Rodina; the Russian motherland.

Russian Defence manufacturers: companies in which he personally had sizeable equity invested, were working at full capacity. Indeed, they were rushing to build new factories and expand current ones just to keep up with the demand for orders for their new air defence missile systems, armoured vehicles and anti-ship missile defence systems.

Just as Zhang's team was busy gathering signatures to shore base their naval assets in the various countries, Voronin's own team of functionaries were busy getting signatures from Sudan. Mozambique, Myanmar, Pakistan and Iran for orders of the latest S-400 Air Defence Systems.

It was widely known, but not openly admitted by the Americans, that the S-400 was far superior to the US Patriot system and effectively denied access to Western air to air fighters or ground attack aircraft. Not just because the West currently had no effective countermeasures against the S-400 system, but principally because of the S-400's ability to learn and adapt.

If a plane came within range of the system's powerful radar, then the tracking data would be uploaded and analysed within minutes by Russian radar specialists. If, indeed the US was stupid enough to fly too close with one of its much vaunted and obscenely expensive F-35 stealth jets, then before too long the Russians would be able to map and understand the faint trace signature left by the plane and re-programme the S-400's software to effectively counter the F-35. This would at one stroke, virtually nullify all of the investment made in the most expensive aeroplane ever designed.

All three men sat, sipping their tea and waiting patiently for the Russian President to begin the discussion. "My friends, I am pleased to announce that we have successfully installed our air defence systems in Eastern Ukraine, southern Lithuania, Kaliningrad, and Belorussia. That I believe will give NATO something to occupy themselves with as they try to work out a strategy for containing our supposed westward expansion." Voronin used the ubiquitous two fingered hand gesture and stressed the word 'supposed'.

The Russian President understood all too well that his country's actions in Ukraine and Lithuania was merely a sideshow, a distraction designed to support a much larger strategic goal. If he were to be honest with himself, despite despising the Chinese as a race, he actually admired the Chinese leaders' ability to develop and sustain a multi-decade strategy.

Unlike Russia's seemingly life-long struggle to be a great power, which despite them inventing an entirely new political system to try and achieve world dominance they had eventually failed due to an inability to control and adapt the system. They had watched, with some jealously and more than a little concern over the years, as the Chinese effectively took the Soviet's original Communist ideas and, thus far at least, seemed to be able to successfully manipulate the state and its people to effectively develop the Russian Marxist-Leninist political thought into a potentially world beating system.

Although, Voronin reflected, as with Stalin's purges, the use of the Gulags, and the horrific loss of life in the Great Patriotic War, the Chinese system had also achieved its current state through incredible individual human sacrifice.

The Chinese President politely bowed his head in acknowledgement of the Russian's achievement, before beginning to speak. "For our part we are slightly in advance of our predicted timescales for the next phase of our plan. Teams within PLA Unit 61398, have successfully produced a series of Deep Fake media assets. I am quietly confident that they will serve our purpose in achieving our strategic goals in Kashmir."

"I have had our analysts pass the files over to both your Russian Cyber warfare specialist group and the Iranian Revolutionary Guard Corps (IRGC) Quds Force cyber warfare group," Zhao, turned and looked slightly condescendingly at the Iranian President as he made this point. Calmly and without returning the eye contact, the Iranian President stirred his green tea once more before replying.

"Thank you, Mr President. My team have reviewed the files and are currently assigning suitable points of origin for each of the story files. We find it more effective, as, from my understanding, do the Chinese, to allow this type of media influence to seem to emanate from sources, more closely accepted and associated with the target country audience."

Voronin fought to keep the smile from spreading across his own face after watching the expression of incredulity on the Chinese President's face on hearing the Iranian President's succinct summary of Chinese Cyber warfare operating protocols and capability.

Maintaining his momentum, the Iranian President offered up his own contribution to the discussion. “Following your request, we have been investigating and monitoring the recent spate of Islamic attacks on Chinese agricultural plantations in Africa. I would like to confirm that these attacks were not inspired by our own Quds Force, neither was it any of our affiliate groups such as Hezbollah.”

“Indeed, we are perplexed, our networks within ISIS, Al Qaeda and Boko Haram, also report no involvement in these attacks. We are not yet certain, but we cannot rule out outside interference.” Looking slightly puzzled, the Chinese Premiere asked “Are you saying that these are not Islamic terrorists attacking our workers in Africa?”

Calmly, the Iranian President replied “As far as we can ascertain you are correct. It appears that somebody else is doing the attacking and attributing the attacks to Islamic groups.” The Russian President interrupted. “I have read the reports myself, it could be the work of African nationalists, but it is still too early to tell.”

Over the last year a series of limited and small-scale attacks had occurred targeting Chinese farming infrastructure in East Africa. The early attacks had been small in scale and been limited to Eritrea, Conveyer belts had been sabotaged and generators had been disabled. These minor inconveniences had been put down to disgruntled African workers, being displaced by the ever-increasing stream of Chinese labour.

However, the attacks had persisted and not only grown in sophistication but also crept across the border to Ethiopia and Sudan. The latest attack in Sudan had targeted a bus full of Chinese workers as it headed from a residential compound to the farm. It was still a minor irritation, but it nevertheless was an itch that the Chinese leader would dearly love to scratch.

“Gentlemen.” The Chinese leader had once again fully regained his composure and was calmly bringing the session to its natural conclusion. “I think, notwithstanding these petty attacks against our workers in Africa, we are in a good position. I look forward to our next face to face meeting when we will be able to celebrate a further consolidation of our plan.”

Gracefully, the older Iranian President lifted himself to his feet, The Chinese President followed him and, with considerably more effort the Russian President also stood to bid farewell to the others.

Zhang found himself once more, sat on the airport runway, next to his President in the Hongqi N501 Presidential limousine. Somehow the car seemed a little more claustrophobic than earlier.

Zhao, had been polite with Zhang, not explicitly mentioning Zhang's performance on the stage, however, Zhang knew full well that the event would have been permanently etched into the brain of his superior, waiting for just the right moment to be recalled.

"Zhang, we have, or rather we expect to have, a group of 34 countries involved or connected by the time we complete the One Belt One Road Project. I want you to personally oversee the following." Although the President took personal delight and acclaim for the success of the overall project, it was actually Zhang himself that dealt with the real detail.

Patiently, biting his lip, Zhang waited for the President to enunciate the key activities that Zhang was already in the process of delivering. "Zhang are you making a note of this?" snapped the President, noticing that instead of sitting up and paying attention, Zhang had seemed to slump slightly in his seat and relax. "Certainly Sir," Zhang responded suddenly sitting upright and producing a small notebook from his pocket.

The President continued to outline Zhang's tasks; "I need someone I trust to ensure the following strategic activities occur to connect up all of the infrastructure we are building; I want a timeline for when we expect to gain actual control of the ports we are building, back from the national governments."

Although a couple of billion dollars to build a port was a lot of money, and the thought of effectively losing that money was difficult to stomach, it had always been the Chinese' intention that, 'when' and not 'if' the East African, Yemeni, and Pakistani nations defaulted on their loan repayments, as they inevitably would, then they would be politely reminded of the contractual clause that they forfeit direct control of the port in lieu of payment.

"Secondly, I want you to ensure that we generate effective cyber control over all of the networks that we are building in each of the host countries. I want the ability to be able to switch off a country's access to any data network. You know Zhang, the next war, will be an information war, control of communication and data flows will be decisive."

Hoping desperately that he was portraying a suitable expression of awe and subservience on his face, Zhang nodded along enthusiastically. In fact, the third lesson that Zhang had carried with him ever since his time at the Officer Training Academy was, that one particular law of war was repeatedly ignored by countless nations all throughout history. Simply put, the knowledge and experience of successfully fighting the last war was no guarantee that you would be equally successful in fighting the next war.

Settling into his seat on the Chinese President's personal airliner, Zhang fought to recall something he had once heard that annoying Danish Anthropologist that worked at the UN say. 'What was it again? Oh yes, that was it.' Now Zhang clearly remembered watching the speech at UNESCO. It stuck in his memory for two reasons, firstly the use of the Danish anthropologist's hologram to deliver the speech was truly impressive.

A cold sneer rippled briefly across Zhang's lips. *'An uncertain 21st Century, a century of possible Multiverses!,'* Zhang was certain he knew how the 21st Century would be defined. Not as an unstable continually morphing series of multiverses, rather as the new era of global dominance by China.

Chapter Ten

hegemon [noun]

Definition of hegemon

Something, such as a political state, having dominant influence or authority over others.

- *These were the periods in which England and then America filled the role of hegemon.*

The South China Sea

Synchronicity, is, in the opinion of some, simply put down to random events that just happen to coincide. For the more educated, or in some cases the more machiavellian, synchronicity is the product of deliberate coordination, manipulation and planning.

The timing of the 3rd Congress of the One Belt One Road Project had been coordinated and orchestrated, some might even say synchronised with the expansion of a chain of artificial islands that China had been building in its, and yes in the mind of the Chinese it very much was 'its', own territorial waters.

The chain of small artificial Islands had been built over ten years by the Chinese government. When pressed on the work they were doing, they had claimed it was part of the One Belt One Road Project and that the Islands would serve as convenient mooring, repair, and refuelling sites to be able to deal with the expected surge in shipping leaving China's Eastern seaboard.

Returning from the One Belt One Road Congress, the Chinese leader's personal aircraft had deliberately extended an already long flight of over 4,000km, by essentially, flying south along the hypotenuse of a giant right-angled triangle which began in Bishkek and with Beijing directly to its east had the tiny speck of land in the south China sea as its destination at the end of the hypotenuse.

Gazing down at the sea from the comfort of his lavishly adorned private cabin, the Chinese President watched, with unbridled pride as an old, non-descript cargo freighter, sailed towards Fiery Cross Reef.

Sitting almost equidistant from, Borneo, Vietnam and the Philippines, Fiery Cross Reef formed part of an archipelago called the Spratly Islands. In China's eyes, the islands were the undisputed sovereign territory of the People's Republic of China. Unfortunately for China, Malaysia, Brunei, Taiwan and the Philippines also claimed sole territorial rights over the same archipelago.

Three seats behind the President and seven miles above the old container ship, Zhang quietly sat and observed the older leader. The non-descript Chinese freighter that was carefully drawing close to Fiery Cross Reef was carrying the most advanced anti-air and anti-ship missiles that his Russian partners could manufacture. The events that were about to occur, could most easily be likened to the Cuban-missile crisis. The President of the People's Republic of China was about to land on an artificial island some 4,000km south of Beijing.

If this in itself wasn't a strong enough statement of political intent, the wider and far greater significance of effectively being able to deny maritime access from an unsinkable aircraft carrier through the Straits of Malacca, essentially meant that Japan, South Korea, Taiwan and any other nation dependent on being supplied with oil or gas from the West would be at the whim of the Chinese government.

The official reason would, of course, not be an offensive one, designed to coerce or aggravate China's neighbours, instead it would be touted as a purely defensive move designed to protect China's access to its own supply of oil and allow its millions of tons of annual exports to pass freely through this congested and essential waterway.

In a private meeting with his inner circle, just prior to his leaving for Bishkek, The Chinese President had proudly proclaimed that the years of China having to 'hide their strength and bide their time' were past. With an uncharacteristic flourish, he had stood and explained that China was entering a new era; the era of 'China Forward, China First'.

It had in fact been Zhang's strategy, the President would be taking credit for. The idea was beautiful in its simplicity, it was China's version of the US's own Monroe Doctrine. Back in 1823 the USA had effectively declared its own right of sovereignty over the western hemisphere, gaining either direct, or political control over territories such as the Philippines, Cuba, Puerto Rico, and Guam, followed not too much later by Hawaii.

Internally this was viewed as removing interference from Spain by taking back many of its territories in the region. Externally, it was seen as America's coming of age and its decision to become a global player, starting, quite naturally by securing its own 'backyard'.

Some five time-zones distant, in the Kremlin, Grigori Grigorovic Popov leant precariously forward from the deep leather seat embossed with the seal of the President of the Russian Federation, fumbling slightly, he slowly removed a razor-sharp folding knife from his pocket. His eyes never left President Mikhail Mikhailovich Voronin as in one swift and well-practiced movement he sliced the gold wax seal cleanly off the ice-cold bottle of vodka.

Pouring two generous measures he wiped the tears once more from his eyes as he held his glass aloft. "Nostrovia, Misha!" Unable to contain his laughter any longer. "Tell me again about the Chinese ant's face when the Iranian President let him know how much he knew about Chinese cyber warfare?" "Grisha, old comrade, it was priceless. I swear if I wasn't already sat on the bloody floor, I would have fallen off my chair with laughter."

Victor Voronin had summoned his oldest friend and the architect of Russia's 21st century Information War to meet him at his private Kremlin apartment as soon as his plane landed. Both men had just sat and watched via live satellite feed, the arrival of the Chinese leader's private plane as it slowly circled then touched down on the newly constructed runway.

"You've got to admire their ambition, Misha. You know, if I had searched for those latitude and longitude coordinates just 3 years ago, all our satellites would have seen would have been a coral reef with a few rocks devoid of life protruding above the surface of the ocean. Now..." Grigori Grigorovic Popov, struggled momentarily whilst, still tightly clutching his vodka glass, he unsteadily raised his slight frame from the leather chair and clumsily made his way across the room towards the wall mounted monitor.

Jabbing a finger at the screen he proclaimed. "Now, this speck of rock and coral is transformed." He clumsily flung his arms wide in a flourish, as a conjurer would when revealing a trick, in the process managing to launch the remaining contents of his vodka glass over the crimson red carpet. "You know Misha, this spot of concrete and sand, this Fiery Cross Reef, is now probably the single most important strategic defensive post in the world!"

Standing considerably less clumsily and seemingly unaffected by the vodka, the Russian President stepped forward to help Grisha back to his seat. Gently grabbing the cyber chief by his arm, and slowly leading him back to their chairs, the Russian President said, "Yes, my old friend, thanks to Chinese ambition and Russian technology, we have given NATO one more problem to deal with. Tell me Grisha, has the satellite uplink started yet?"

Reaching forward with a now much steadier hand Grisha picked up a small tablet device that had been sat on the table. 'Amazing' thought Victor Voronin to himself. How did his old friend do it? One moment he was bouncing off the walls and spilling his vodka, the next he is as sober as a judge. Grigori deftly tapped and swiped at the screen on his device then gestured with a glance of his now fully focused eyes towards the wall mounted monitor.

Replacing the images of the Chinese President's aeroplane on the tiny island's airstrip, was now a continual feed of vectors, triangulated positions and speeds. The screen was alive with scrolling pages of text and equations. "Misha, what you are seeing is the telemetry data for the Chinese President's private aircraft. It was uplifted to our satellite directly from our air defence systems on the island."

A broad grin creased the President's face. "You mean we can do it?" "Yes Misha, in fact it was simpler than we originally thought. We have the ability to learn everything that our systems on the island are doing in near enough real time. More importantly we can remotely switch the systems on or off by satellite."

The Russian built S-400 air defence systems on the island, apart from acting as a lethal threat to any foreign air or naval assets in the area, served a far greater strategic purpose. The systems would effectively prevent any use of the US F-35 Jets within a range of 400km. With a chain of these systems located around the southern tip of Asia. It gave both China and Russia an incredible strategic advantage.

Voronin was never going to be inclined to fully trust his Chinese partners and as an insurance policy, he had tasked his Chief of Cyber Operations, to create a link capable of monitoring the systems in real time and to be able directly take control of the systems if it was required.

"So what now Misha?" Picking up the still half full bottle of vodka, the President stood and smiled. "Now, Misha my old comrade, now we go see if Katarina and Tatiana have been behaving themselves in the other room." The President winked at his old friend and strode across the crimson red carpet to a door, as he placed his hand on the door and leant forward to push it open he could hear the clink of glasses and the giggling coming from the girls behind the door.

Like the ripples on the surface of a lake, the news and images of the Chinese setting up their radar and missile systems on the tiny reef in the Spratly islands spread wide and far in all directions.

Cabinet Office Briefing Room A (COBRA) Meeting, Downing Street, London

Following a rapid series of rather terse phone calls, the principle members of the UK Government's emergency response team had been assembled once more in the Cabinet Office Briefing Room Alpha, better known as COBRA. As usual the Prime Minister chaired the meeting, sat with him were the Foreign Minister, Defence Minister, the Head of the UK Armed Forces, General Sir Rupert Heeringly, and sitting quietly off to one side was the Head of MI6, Sir David Simmingford-Bell.

Before standing to address the meeting, the Prime Minister glanced around the room at his colleagues. Toby Morrison, the Defence Minister was his usual fidgety self, The General looked tired thought the PM, no doubt worn down with the dual pressures of deploying a sizeable chunk of his most capable units to the Lithuanian border, whilst trying to mobilise his Reserve Forces to backfill their positions. One thing was for certain, the news he had to share today wouldn't make the General feel any happier, or less tired.

The Prime Minister was, in what is known in politics, a modern progressive, yet behind his public progressive face he was every inch the staunch nationalist when it came to any issue that threatened the United Kingdom as a whole. Immediately on becoming elected, he had decided that the country needed re-energising and demanded a fresh team around him. This translated into removing every department head or Civil Servant who wouldn't or couldn't be bent to the PM's own way of thinking.

After his very first briefing with the Head of the United Kingdom's Secret Intelligence Service, the Prime Minister, had taken an instant dislike to its Director, Sir David Simmingford-Bell. In the PM's view, C, as he was colloquially known, came across as overbearing and paternalistic. Some in the PM's new progressive cabinet had likened him to a zealot, rather too holier than though. The Foreign Secretary had gone one step further, calling him puritanical and self-righteous.

Whatever people's views on the Head of MI6 were, one thing was certainly true, wanting to remove and replace the 'Keeper in Chief' of the nation's deepest darkest secrets, and actually having the ability to do it, were two very different things indeed.

The PM stood and greeted his colleagues and then turned to C, who was still languishing in the shadows of the room instead of sitting at the table like the rest of the group. "C, can you bring us all up to date on the details of yesterday's events?" C stood slowly and in the Prime Minister's view, rather too reluctantly, to address the group. 'My God the arrogance of the man', thought the PM.

Peering raptor-like over his pince-nez, C began his briefing. "At 1900hrs last night my office received the images that you can see in front of you." "Each of the COBRA members was franticly swiping through their own personal tablet looking over the imagery. The imagery was sent to us from GCHQ in Cheltenham, who in turn received it from the Australians, using one of their..." In, what for the Head of MI6 was an uncharacteristic display of emotion, Sir David, raised both his arms and bent the first two fingers on either hand in the universal gesture of quotation marks. "One of their Agricultural monitoring satellites. This information was shared under the 5 Eyes Agreement."

Sir David was interrupted by a stuttering Defence Minister. "Sorry C, you said '5 eyes agreement?" Inwardly seething, Sir David replied. If there was one thing, he hated more than arrogance, it was laziness or sloth as he had been brought up to think of it. And this man, this puppet of the PM had both attributes in bucket loads.

Trying yet failing to remove all traces of condescension from his voice, "Yes Toby, as you were briefed on entering office, the 5 eyes agreement is a Signals Intelligence sharing agreement between Australia, Canada, New Zealand, the UK and the US."

"What that means in this instance is that each of these allies has exactly the same information as do we and more importantly we will have continued access to the satellites, at no expense to the British taxpayer, for as long as we require it." Picking up on the tell-tale reddening of the jowls around Sir David's jaw, the PM swiftly stepped in to recover the situation.

"Thank you C, I think we all get the picture, as it were. I'll now ask the Chief of the Defence Staff, Sir Rupert to describe our overt reaction possibilities." The rather frazzled looking General stood, straightened down his dress uniform and addressed the group. As usual the General delivered his thoughts as he would any other military brief, beginning with a review of the Ground.

"Gentlemen, you have all reviewed the imagery, the Ground, unfortunately couldn't be more challenging, as of 1900 hours last night we find ourselves faced with two direct threats to NATO's alliance and to the integrity of its members' borders, not to mention the free right of passage. What's more," The General used a laser pointer to highlight to circled areas on a large map of the world projected onto a screen behind him. "What's more, the two threats are located in diametrically opposed locations on the planet."

The group stared at the world map as the General highlighted his Task force's locations in Lithuania and the supporting naval assets, then very slowly and very deliberately, traced the red dot diagonally down across most of the world until it settled on the Spratly Islands. He was using the map as a prop, exaggerating the way he clumsily had to rotate the globe to point out the vast distance between the two circled areas. It added no real value to the briefing rather than to serve to emphasize exactly how much of a logistical problem the dual threat posed to the military planners.

Having made his point, and trying to lighten the situation slightly, he flippantly commented "It's textbook really, the sort of thing we all get hammered into us at Staff College. Spread your enemy's resources thin etc…" This comment received several nods and a couple of chuckles from those around the table who had served in the military and endured their own versions of the Intermediate Command and Staff courses at the UK's Defence Academy. One man who despite never having served in the military, Sir David, seemed to sit a little more upright in his chair when he heard these words.

Continuing with his military style brief the General turned to the situation. "The Situation Gentlemen is rather bleak I am afraid, the closest likeness in my memory was rather like in the 1980s when we had tens of thousands of men and women stationed in Germany facing down the Soviets and Warsaw Pact, and then at the drop of a hat we were ordered to recommission everything and anything that sailed to launch a Task Force on a wing and prayer to retake the Falklands."

Seeing the nods of grim assent around the table the beleaguered General continued. "Today's situation sees us, err how shall I put it, just as inclined, yet, less able to react. We have far fewer troops and most of those are currently engaged in maintaining pressure on Lithuania." The Foreign Secretary bullish as ever interrupted. "Yes, but Rupert let's not forget you have two brand spanking new Aircraft Carriers to play with now!" The riposte which had been designed to soften the General's pessimism had the opposite effect.

"That would be fine Foreign Secretary if we were going into bat against the bloody Argentinians again. But the proposition of sending arguably our country's most potent and I might just add, most expensive display of strength to within range of an unsinkable island which has been designed with the sole purpose of sinking such assets is bloody lunacy!"

With tempers beginning to rise around the table once again, the PM felt obliged to defuse the proceedings once more. "Good points made by all, I think you will agree. It is my feeling that we cannot be seen to do nothing, but I also take Sir Rupert's point about placing such an expensive and potent piece of equipment in harm's way."

"Now as you know I will have to face the ire of my own back benchers as well as the Opposition leader in the House tomorrow, not to mention the Press. So, I have decided that, based on the information available from our discussion today, I will be informing the House tomorrow that a Task Force led by the Aircraft Carrier HMS Queen Elizabeth II will sail for the region within a fortnight."

The PM first heard and then saw the snapping pencil gripped in the General's hands as he made his declaration. "Don't worry Sir Rupert, your mission is to show intent, until we have built up some form of coalition and plan of action. That means sending a task force to the area but at all costs keeping it well out of range of the Island's defences." The meeting trailed on for a further 45 minutes as the inevitable discussions over resources, funding and how they should manipulate the story for the media, were discussed.

As they filed out of the Briefing room, the PM asked the Foreign Secretary for a brief word. "John, before you go, can you let me know where we stand on Lesotho?" The Foreign Secretary tried but failed to hide an expression of bemusement. "Not sure what you mean PM. As you well know the country is inherently unstable, the former President had been in and out of power at least three times by last count. At least this new chap seems sensible and dare I say, at current reading, marginally less corrupt than his predecessor."

"Right," said the PM, raising a quizzical eyebrow. "Don't you think it is a tad suspicious, even by African standards that the entirety of the former President's entourage cabinet and wider family all succumbed to this virus at the same time?"

Speaking a little slower as if trying to recall a distant memory, the Foreign Secretary responded "Come to think of it, at the time I did find it peculiar and I recall tasking C's bunch to look into it for me. He sent his man from Durban to investigate and by all reports there's nothing to it, just one of those poorer little African countries whose kleptocratic government suffered at the hands of their own nepotism." "Go on" said the PM.

"It appears that during their most recent resurgence of that horrible virus we've all been fighting, the President and his acolytes thought that the social distancing rules didn't apply to them. Our man in Durban reported that by all accounts whilst most of Lesotho was in enforced lockdown, the President and his cronies were seen meeting up most evenings at lavish parties and banquets." The PM nodded and added. "Not too dissimilar to how my predecessor acted then?" The Foreign Secretary who had despised the previous PM harrumphed and bellowed. "Yes, bloody conceited lunatic."

The Foreign Secretary paused for a moment then glanced skywards trying to drag something from the depths of his memory. "yes, that's it, I remember quite clearly now, I recall it struck me as rather odd when I heard it the first time. When that puritanical pompous ass C gave me his report, he said I've looked into it and it's a clear case of death by gluttony".

"I wasn't quite sure what he meant at the time. I guess he simply meant that it was the President's overindulgence that killed him." "Thank you John, yes, I agree C is an odd fish, but he is very diligent, whatever we think about him, he is rarely wrong."

Washington

As the end of President Carlton, P, Simpson's first term in office drew closer his interest and inclination in the playing the role of the most powerful leader in the world dropped exponentially. In recent weeks, he had moved away from shortening meetings by feigning migraines to openly practicing his golf swing in the Oval Office during his morning briefings.

His first couple of years in office had been a great success, simply because he had solely focussed on any short term strategy he could find to improve the outlook for his US voting base.

It could be said that he took exactly the same approach to the Presidency as he did in his former business life. He leveraged the country's balance sheet by borrowing eye-watering amounts of money to invest in tax incentives for US-only businesses and large infrastructure projects.

He slammed tariffs on nearly every trading bloc imaginable in the aim of making US products more appealing to his domestic market, and as the most powerful man in the world, he did what all oil tycoons would do given his position. He stripped away any pretence of abiding by any environmental or trade agreements that stood in the way of his narrowly focused plan.

The net effect was that he was, if the results of the previous election were to be believed, hugely successful in making exactly half of the US electorate happy and in improving their take home pay. However, as his first term drew to a close, he was becoming increasingly unpopular with the other half of the electorate as well as most of the rest of the world, who had all suffered from his America first policies.

The usual retinue, with the addition of the Treasury Secretary, were gathered in the Oval Office for the morning brief and this time it was Helen Broxton, the National Security Advisor who led the morning's proceedings.

"Go for it. Helen." The President demanded, as he completed his second practice swing of the morning staring out of the Oval Office window and across the White House South lawn at the imaginary ball which, in the President's mind, virtually hurtled straight as a die arcing gracefully over the South Lawn and slowly beginning its descent into the President's Park to land with an imaginary splash in the large round waterfall.

"Sir, I see an opportunity here, for us to get on the front foot." The recent series of events including the Afghan and Syrian peace deals coming so soon after the Russian annexation of the Lithuanian land corridor had led to a sharp drop in the President's approval ratings.

From inside the Washington beltway, it seemed that America wasn't getting the respect it deserved from the rest of the world, from outside the country it appeared that America had stopped acting as a leader and either didn't care about what happened outside its borders anymore, or maybe potentially more frighteningly than that, America might be impotent to do anything about it.

“Sir” Helen continued. “As you know it is the opinion of my department and the Department of Defence.” Helen glanced across at General Curtis Lee hoping for some tacit nod of support or agreement. The General surprised the National Security Advisor by standing and striding across the Oval Office to stand next to her.

Standing well above 6-feet tall with a square jaw and a barrel for a chest the General cut an intimidating figure. “Mr President, what the little lady is trying to say.” inwardly seething at being called a little lady, Helen bit her tongue knowing how much she needed the General’s support on this one. “If we don’t act now, we may lose the Pacific”, boomed the General. The President paused mid-swing and turned to face his team.

A little-known fact is that, if the US can be accused of having any long-term strategic foreign policy, then it certainly must be to gain and retain control of the Pacific. The adventures of the US in the Pacific were the sort of schoolboy history that had evolved into mythology.

Some of the nation’s most influential Presidents had been involved in securing territories across the Pacific and Carlton P Simpson, the 46th President of the United States certainly was not going to go down in history as the man that lost the Pacific.

America’s period of hegemony had begun, or maybe a better term is ‘been engineered’ through the calculated seizing of control of the Pacific. This series of wars and hostile actions catapulted the US from a relatively unimportant yet dynamic country to a serious regional player with ambitions to be a world player.

General Curtis Lee Hayward drew himself up to his fullest height and began his diatribe on the history and importance of the Pacific to the US, “My granddaddy served in Teddy Roosevelt’s. own Cavalry Regiment in the Philippines and I am proud to say that my Cavalry Regiment served our country in Guam, Iwo Jima, Korea and Vietnam. Of one thing I am dammed certain, I will not go down in history as the General who forsook all of that blood and treasure.”

Beginning soon after the purchase of Alaska from Russia for the poultry sum of $7.2 million, around $120 million in today’s money, America’s dominance of its ‘own sizeable back yard’ dates back to the 1898 the Spanish American War which saw President Simpson's personal idol, Teddy Roosevelt in action in the Philippines.

This was soon followed by the effective takeover of Hawaii under William McKinley in 1900. Under Franklin D Roosevelt, another of President Simpson's favourites, some of America's most bitter fighting during the Second World War was conducted in the Pacific rim. The result being a Pacific Ocean dotted with tiny island outposts now belonging to the US government and a heavily US influenced Japan and South Korea.

The detail and zeal with which General Curtis expounded on the American conquest of the Pacific decreased in exponential intervals with the recency and some might say popularity of the methods used to acquire and maintain US dominance of the Pacific region.

After lecturing in some depth on the Korean campaign of the early 50s, a campaign that was technically still ongoing, the General skirted swiftly through the energy-sapping Vietnam war ending in 1975, and only mentioned in passing America's strategy to keep their own hemisphere of the Pacific in check.

Under the Truman doctrine, all governments along the entire Pacific coast of central and South America had at one point in time seen aggressive US support for the US' 'preferred' choice of leadership.

Standing a little straighter as he finished his brief. "So, you see gentlemen, whatever we might think of the President's predecessor, our pivot to the Pacific and basing of US troops in northern Australia is essential to keeping a fix on China."

Seeing her opportunity noting that the President had finally put down his virtual golf club and smiling inwardly as she noticed how the President even seemed to inspect the head of the non-existent club before seemingly handing it to a non-existent waiting caddy, Helen Broxton thanked the General with what she believed to be her most winning smile and turned to address the President.

It was an unusual moment indeed and had to be capitalised upon thought Helen. For the first time in months they seemed however temporarily to have the President's full attention. It was obvious to everyone in the room that the President had been captivated by the

General's telling of how the US won the Pacific. He had even briefly perched himself on the edge of the Resolute Desk as he listened to the antics of his idols being regaled by the General.

"Sir, I have put together a range of options and discussed them with the Joint Chiefs. It is my personal opinion and that of General Hayward…" Helen hadn't made it to the top in Washington by not understanding how to leverage people to her own advantage. If she couldn't ever get to play golf with the President, then she needed the man that did, to be on board with her plan.

Seeing she still had the President's rapt attention she continued. "Our best policy in light of the recent Chinese show of strength in the Spratly Islands is to show overwhelming force. For that reason we are proposing that we immediately despatch another carrier group from San Diego to sail west and harbour-up off the east coast of Vietnam, the Vietnamese have given us their agreement, they are as pleased to get support for their claim on the Spratly islands as we are. The second carrier group will sail out of Okinawa and head for Darwin Australia. Initially, both fleets will preposition themselves close to these ports but will begin work up manoeuvres as a show of hostile capability."

Pausing briefly to glance over at Paul Sheridan, the Treasury Secretary, she received a nod from him to continue. "With our troop bases in Okinawa, this strategy effectively creates a series of US 'islands', albeit floating islands, stretching from northern Australia to Japan. It essentially gives us and our allies solid bases from which we can deter any future Chinese posturing in the South China Sea. Faced with such overwhelming firepower, these actions we believe will be sufficient to get the Chinese to come to the table and talk."

Unbidden, the Vice President, Charles Laurel Henderson took the floor. Sly glances passed surreptitiously around the room. In recent weeks, the President had confided to his closest aides that he thought the VP was becoming more distant from 'the team's message' and was no longer acting as the sort of team player that the President liked to surround himself with. He had even secretly tasked his own Chief of Staff, Chuck Lewis, a man who knew more than most about the inner dealings of Washington to put a feeler out to see if the

Vice President was considering running himself for the Presidential nominee slot at the upcoming election.

Everything about the Vice President's demeanour was conservative thought Helen as she watched him stand to address the group. He was the archetypal grey man. A featureless face, his body wrapped in a neat, yet instantly forgettable Jacket, shirt and tie ensemble and exuding not even the merest hint of charm or character. Maybe that is how he climbed so high in his previous profession at the CIA before running for office, she mused to herself.

Unbidden, the Vice President began to address the room. "While I applaud wholeheartedly our strong approach to facing down the threat posed by Communist China, we must also remember our fiscal responsibilities to the American people. How much extra will it cost to send two complete Carrier task groups to the region and sustain them indefinitely?" The challenge had been expected and in response a carefully orchestrated series of actions followed. Helen, on a cue from Paul Sheridan, spoke.

"Good question Mr Vice President and you are right to point out the not insurmountable cost of this strategy." She now briefed the group on the two pieces of information that she had deliberately left out of her opening brief, having kept them in reserve for just such a moment.

"Our Vietnamese partners have committed to allowing us to resupply and refuel our ships from Nha Trang and have even offered port refitting berths if we need them. This will significantly reduce our logistical burden for the fleet leaving from San Diego. The Australians likewise have offered considerable logistic support for our fleet along with a small but potent contingent of their Commandoes and a squadron of their F35's that they have just bought from us." Glancing briefly over at the VP she saw that he wasn't overly moved by her offerings.

OK, she thought let's see what you think to this then. "In an unprecedented act of solidarity, the Japanese Prime Minister has strongly indicated that when our fleet sails from Okinawa, it will be accompanied by a sizeable Task force including two of its Izumo class Helicopter Carrier Destroyers."

The news caught the Vice President by surprise and Helen briefly saw a flicker of concern flash across his face before it returned itself to its customary dour, expressionless countenance.

The Japanese Helicopter destroyers, when coupled with the newly purchased F-35B Vertical Take Off capable stealth fighters effectively gave Japan a capability that had been denied to them since the end of the Second World War. Never spoken out loud in Washington or Tokyo. The two ships classified as Helicopter Carriers were, all be it rather limited in scope, deadly Aircraft Carriers.

The final act of this pre-planned charade was played by the Treasury Secretary, "Charles, I admit that at a rough order of magnitude cost of $6.5 million per day, per fleet, and let us not forget our fleet stationed in the Baltic off Lithuania."

It was the worst kept secret in Washington that the Vice President detested the Treasury Secretary, to the Vice President, Paul Sheridan represented everything he loathed most in the world. This spineless bureaucrat, who had grown up as an accountant for some nameless New York consulting company had never served his country for a day in his life and wouldn't know the Old Testament from the New Testament if they hit him in the face. Indeed, cursed the Vice President inwardly to himself as he endured the sneering accountant's nasal eulogy on the ease by which the US could finance its latest adventures.

"You see Charles the cost of borrowing is at an unprecedented low, we can effectively get the Fed to print the money we need, we, then 'borrow' this money from the Fed and pay it back at our leisure, or maybe not at all" he smirked at his own smugness at this last comment. 'Usuary, Greed, Pride', The Vice President mentally reeled off this odious man's vices whilst managing to maintain a visage of only mild interest at the treasury Secretary's words.

"Thank you Paul, I hadn't quite grasped the economic alchemy we were using today, I guess you guys at Treasury have it covered."

The sarcasm wasn't lost on the others in the room and in a rare display of leadership, the President stood thanked everybody for their contributions and finally gave his official seal of approval for the plan which had already been put into motion.

As they filed out of the White House Oval Office, leaving the President sat once more on the edge of the Resolute Desk, although no one openly voiced it, it wasn't lost on anyone in the room that the US was relying on the support of, historically at least, two of its most bitter enemies to act out their latest strategy of intimidation in the Pacific.

As was usual with the morning briefings Helen had selected 6 agenda items, whilst fully realising that she was highly unlikely to be able to retain the President's attention for all six items. As she went to leave the Oval Office she glanced back over her shoulder and noticed the President still sat on the edge of the Resolute desk looking wistfully into nowhere.

Dipping back into the office she decided that she would seize the opportunity to finish off the last couple of points on her briefing sheet. I mean after all hadn't the President's briefing team had a long running bet that nobody would be able to get through all of their briefing points in one session.

"Sir, Mr President Sir?" It took the President a couple of seconds to descend from his reverie. "Sorry, err yes Helen, is there anything else you want?" Taking a step further into the Oval Office she quickly read off the final couple of points on her briefing sheet and as she turned to leave, paused briefly at the door. "Sir" "yes" came the significantly more exasperated voice, this time from behind the desk.

"Sir I know you are having dinner with the South African Ambassador tonight, I just thought I would remind you about the fact that Lesotho recently lost its ruling Presidential family and cabinet to the virus and they now have a new President. Lesotho is a touchy subject with the South Africans at the best of times, probably best if you give the subject a wide berth at tonight's dinner."

The President looked up briefly from his papers. Noting the look of semi-bemusement on the President's face, Helen thought quickly of a way to prevent having the President ask the question that he really needed the answer to but was never going to ask. "Sir it's about twice the size of the greater DC Metropolitan area and sits plum in the middle of South Africa." With a broad smile on her face, she turned swiftly and hurried out of the room.

Striding down the corridor away from the Oval Office and to the bemusement of the pool of secretaries she jerked her clenched fist back towards her in the exaggerated movement now commonly known as the 'yes, nailed it' gesture. Smiling to herself as she regained her composure, she withdrew her cell phone and messaged the WhatsApp group. "Guys, you owe me…

Chapter Eleven

trojan horse [noun]

Definition of trojan horse

A person or thing intended to undermine or secretly overthrow an opponent.

Alternate: A program designed to breach the security of a computer system whilst ostensibly performing some innocuous function.

- *With one mouse click the trojan horse was activated and entered the system.*

Bloemfontein South Africa

It was actually quite unnerving, thought Charles Laurel Henderson, locked away in his study in the Vice President's official residence at the US Naval Observatory in Washington DC. Despite his study possessing a commanding view of the entire park, the US Vice President was currently sat at his desk, blind to his immediate world.

Through the use of a Virtual Reality headset, which was fixed, a little too tightly for the Vice President's liking, firmly onto his face, the Vice President found himself virtually transported to a large colonial style mansion in the lush rolling wine country outside of Bloemfontein South Africa.

Through the vast panoramic window of the meeting room, Charles Henderson could see the imposing Kimberley mountains to the Northwest. And although he couldn't see it, he knew that just 150km away to the East, barely over the border with South Africa sat Maseru, the capital of Lesotho.

Not a city that Charles Henderson was personally familiar with or for that matter ever likely to visit, however it had now become one in which he now had a rather large political stake.

Kurt Vorster leant over to the Australian, Doug Macintyre "Brother Doug, it's pretty spooky isn't it?" Both men had been gazing over at the seat reserved for Charles Henderson at the Puritan Society's meeting. A ghostly pale shimmering hologram sat in the seat. The hologram was deep in discussion with Ethan Macdonald.

"Scares the crap out of me, if I'm honest" replied Doug, unable to pull his gaze away from the flickering apparition before him. "I mean, do you think he can see and hear everything?" "You'd better ask brother Ethan; it's his brainchild. Apparently, the hologram is generated at source in Brother Charles's office and the data is sent using Ethan's encrypted quantum computer."

"You see that little black cube, built into the desk in front of Brother Charles' image? Well that little box is his connection from us back to him. It sends sound to him and tracks his eye movements. If he moves his eyes, then the box relays a feed from one of nearly 40 cameras we have in the room."

As if sensing he was being discussed, the ghostly pale holographic visage of the US Vice President gazed up and towards the two men sat at the over the table from him. A short nod sufficed to tell Kurt that he should get the meeting underway.

Gentlemen! As the first point of order on the agenda today, I would like to introduce you to a new member of the Society, the new Prime Minister of Lesotho, Mr Relebohile Molise. The assembled Brothers all rose in unison from their chairs and began to clap as the diminutive figure of Relebohile Molise, nervously smiled in acceptance of his welcome. Raising his hand to silence the group, Kurt Vorster began the meeting.

"Brothers, our main reason for being here today is to discuss the Africa operation and to give you an update on the actions of those ungodly locusts, the Chinese." Murmurs of agreement and disdain for the Chinese rippled around the room.

"I am proud to report that our operation to remove the 'Chinese puppet', Prime Minister Mohapi from government in Lesotho went as smooth as clockwork."

Continuing with their global campaign to effectively influence or control the global political order and after installing their own preferred political leaders in most of the Christian European nations with sizeable Protestant populations, in their most audacious and ambitious move yet, the Puritan Society had begun to exert their influence in Africa.

Their aim was simple, in the absence of a weakened and disinterested USA and with a shattered European Union unable to hold itself together never mind exert foreign influence, the Puritan Society saw it as their God given mission to curb the growing incursion of the atheist Chinese state in South-Eastern and Eastern Africa. A region which had endured one post-colonial corrupt leader after another and still with large populations of devout Protestants was ripe for the picking.

The Puritan society knew full well that the fertile lands of East and South Africa could once more become the most productive agricultural areas on the planet, if only they were properly managed and governed.

Lesotho had been a trial. A landlocked nation surrounded entirely by South Africa. The fearsome people had bravely resisted British colonisation in South Africa and maintained their independence ever since. However, since the mid 1980s the state had been riven with corruption and had already suffered from three debilitating military coups, with the ruling elite stuffing their own pockets by selling off the rights to the country's wool and meat resources to Chinese state-backed investors. The job for the resource-rich Puritan Society was reasonably simple. Identify their man in Lesotho, put him in power and use him to kick out the Chinese.

That man, who now possessed a substantially greater personal wealth than he did a month ago was now sat at the table with the very people that put him in power. Relebohile Molise, was indeed a devout Christian, the son of a minister and personally possessed of a keen sense of right and wrong.

Although popular he would never have even been considered as a candidate without the backing of the Puritan society who through the manipulation of local media had skilfully created a climate of fear and loathing for the increasing numbers of Chinese workers entering

Lesotho and at a higher level, against the Chinese government.

Particularly they had focused their energies on exposing a believable scenario that the Chinese had deliberately manufactured a SARS-style virus and weaponised it in an attempt to weaken foreign governments and allow the Chinese state ever greater access into the affairs of these weakened African states.

Of course, as the old adage goes 'a picture paints a thousand words' even better than a picture is a rolling Gif embedded and distributed throughout the major African social media platforms that allegedly shows Chinese scientists in full protective gear transferring metal canisters of highly hazardous biomaterial from their laboratory onto unmarked trucks.

This had been enough to scare the ex-Prime Minister into trying to finally obtain some decent protective face masks for his country. As all around the world, these items had become scarce and were rapidly becoming unaffordable to small economies such as Lesotho, so it was to the great relief of the now ex-Prime Minister when a small group of charitable Christian workers in the country offered to give the President a limited supply of high-grade face masks along with several shipping containers of the simpler, less effective single use masks.

True to form and in perfect alignment with the Puritan plan, the ex-President wasted no time in distributing the high-tech masks to his family, political allies and cronies, whilst handing out the cheaper masks to the front-line workers in the country's hospitals.

The disturbing truth of the matter was, that a strain of the SARS virus had been weaponised, just not in the crude way depicted by the social media Gif. In fact, using the blood sample retrieved by Erik, it had taken Brother Norbert Mansheim's team nearly six months of dedicated work at his Munich-based pharmaceutical company to engineer a strain of the SARS virus with an R number of zero, effectively reducing the virus' replicating ability to nothing.

Bidden by the glimmering ghost-like hologram of the puritan leader, the corpulent Bavarian stood to address the collective. "As I was just commenting to Brother Charles yesterday, cutting the virus replication rate to zero was the simple part. Creating a gel lattice that could be 3D printed and inserted into the filter of our face masks was a much bigger challenge. You see training a virus is a little more difficult than training one's own pet dog!" As was his custom Norbert bellowed and guffawed loudly at his own joke.

Uncertain laughter rippled through the room. It was at that point that Doug Macintyre happened to glance across at the Vice President's hologram and noted, with some degree of unease, how the leader of the Puritan society's gaze was fixed, and his countenance portrayed an air of rapture as he listened to the bloated Bavarian explain in minute detail how he had developed a lethal killing tool.

Uncannily, and as if he could sense he was being watched Charles Henderson's ghoulish hologram turned to peer across the table at Doug. Although the hologram was smiling, it portrayed no warmth. Doug shuddered inwardly and returned his gaze once more to the speaker.

"Ja, as I was saying. training a virus to lie dormant and do nothing until you activate it with warm moist air is no easy matter. In fact, we did more than that. After lunch we are all going on a special tour of brother Kurt's wine cellar, where we have set up a scaled-up version of our 3d printing operation. Yes, that's right, directly under your feet we are printing the mask filters that are to be loaded onto the container ship for phase 2."

"Thank you brother" said the Vice President, his hologram flickering briefly as he stood and initiated a round of applause. Doug turned to Kurt and muttered, "you know in the 15 years I have known that man, that was the first time I have ever seen him demonstrate emotion. I'm just not quite sure what the emotion is, pride, happiness or arousal." Noticing that the Vice President had once more turned to look at the pair, they quickly pulled their heads apart and stood to join the clapping.

The meeting was temporarily adjourned as the assembled group of Puritan leaders were guided down the stone staircase into the labyrinthine cellar passages that lay between the estate's grand house to be led on a tour of a near silent workshop of death.

On command, behind a heavy oak door, a steel bio safety door with biometric entry recognition swished open to reveal row upon row of industrial scale 3-D printers humming quietly as they created layer by intricate layer the virus-laden filters for the face masks.

It was whilst the rest of the group were being led on the tour by Brother Kurt that Ethan Macdonald stepped into a private room to contact Erik for their scheduled brief about Erik's next mission.

As the quantum feed engaged and came live on Erik's laptop he sat up from his dining table, where he had just been enjoying the first few mouthfuls of succulent tender wild boar cheeks marinated in port wine and served with rosti potatoes. Reluctantly he glanced longingly once more at his plate before standing and striding to the breakfast bar to receive the call.

Erik, as is so common amongst people in his trade, usually preferred to control how and when he engaged with people. This person, this controller, whoever he was, had begun to annoy Erik with his insistence on controlling the time and content of their meetings. Under normal circumstances Erik would have pushed back and refused to work until he gained control, however given that all meetings were held using the quantum encrypted computers he had no choice but to attend when told to.

As he hit the Enter key to receive the call, he consoled himself that this meeting would, at the very least, be shorter than the last one. He had received an in-depth brief about the background and logistics of the operation and was expecting or rather hoping to receive a simple mission brief, focussing on times, places and actions. "Hi, Erik how are you?" said the mid-Atlantic voice belonging to the, as yet unknown, speaker.

This was another fact that annoyed Erik about the situation. The speaker sounded more jovial than usual, had he been drinking? "I'm fine thanks do you have the details for me?" Realising he had been a little too abrupt in his greeting, Erik settled back on his bar stool and whilst looking longingly back to the dining table where his braised pork cheeks were rapidly growing cold he took a long sip on his velvety rich Rioja and settled back to be talked to for the next hour.

"So Erik, I just wanted to clarify that you have the bigger picture before I give you the specifics, OK with you?" No it bloody well wasn't, Erik thought, do you realise I sat concealed in a hide on freezing ground for 2 days to shoot that boar, which I then physically manhandled over 10 kilometres of rough ground to get it home. Now, of all times, when the fruits of my labour are sat within touching, or should that be, tasting distance, slowly growing cold on their plate, you ask me if it is OK for you to repeat everything you said last time? "Sure, go ahead" Erik replied in what he hoped was his most positive sounding voice.

"This will be quick I promise, the others are reconvening in half an hour. So, you got the outline, the freighter sails straight up the East coast of Africa from Durban in about 10-days' time. Our target ports serve Mozambique, Tanzania, Kenya and Uganda. The shipments for Zimbabwe and South Africa will be dealt with by land transport from here. Got it?" Not expecting to have to contribute to the monologue, Erik was still savouring a rather large mouthful of his Rioja when the question came.

Slightly flustered and hoarse-voiced he responded "Yeh, sure East Coast, got it," Keen to wrestle some control over the meeting he asked a question. "How long will the trip take, I have calculated that with a journey of a little over nearly 2,200 nautical miles we'll need about 8 days, then when you add on waiting time for unloading at the docks and briefing of the delivery teams, I guess we are talking about nearly two weeks?"

Quietly confident and happy with his attempt to gain control over the meeting Erik sat back and drew once more on the deep rich Rioja. "Actually, we plan to do it in 10 days flat. The boat we have selected has just had an engine refit and can cruise at 35 knots comfortably, maybe 37 or 38 knots with good weather."

This time Erik nearly spat his wine out. Before he could recover and respond, his controller continued. "You see Erik, if we want the element of surprise on our side, and we do, then we want to strike as simultaneously as possible, otherwise people might begin to connect the timing of our presence with the events. Don't worry, we have people at each dock waiting for you. You will waste no time queuing up to be unloaded."

"We have retrofitted the freighter with a large landing pad, by basically welding a huge series of steel plates over the top of a grid of 6 x 3 TEUs, that's containers to me and you. From most angles the ship will look like any regular medium sized cargo ship. The landing platform is only visible from the air." Not noticing that his controller had paused his monologue and still listening intently, Erik pondered the intricate plan with its exacting timescales.

"Erik are you still there?" wrenched back to the here and now Erik replied "err sure, I mean yes of course. 10 days you said." "Yeh, look I know the timings are tight but your job is simply to brief the teams and deliver the goods by helicopter to the local country Charity Aid HQ, then fly back to the ship and be ready for the next drop off. Our teams there will ensure delivery to the right government people for our little surprise to have its effect."

"OK, so you don't want me 'shore side' at all?" queried Erik. "Not unless we run into any issues that need your particular skill set to be dealt with." "OK roger that, I stay on the ship unless the shit hits the fan and then you want me to go and clean up any loose ends?" "I'm glad we are on the same page Erik. You are a valuable asset to our Society. Someone with a rare skill set like yours, we need to use only in extremis."

Turning once more to glance over at the dinner table, to see if his braised pork cheeks were salvageable, Erik responded. "OK got it. When do you need me in Durban?" "Let's say someone will meet you there in a fortnight. Listen I have to go now Erik, the others are reconvening, and I need to be in on this."

Erik thought the speaker sounded disappointed at not being able to prolong the conversation. In his most tactful voice, whilst replenishing his glass with a rather generous serving of Rioja and glancing at his still, maybe salvageable meal, Erik replied. "OK Durban in two weeks."

As the Puritan leaders took their seats once more at the conference table, the holographic apparition that was the Vice President stood to begin the second half of the session. "Brothers, you have all witnessed Brother Norbert's incredible work. I am sure you will all agree, with the successful trial in Lesotho behind us and with the detailed organisation that has gone into this operation we are well on the way to achieving a considerable amount of political influence and not a small amount of long-term profit across the region."

The Vice President cast his soulless gaze across the assembled group, lingering slightly longer than was comfortable on Brothers Doug and Kurt. "The events in Lesotho and the social media influence campaign we have been waging have only served to reinforce the demand for our masks. Our aid stations all across East Africa have been inundated with official government requests to supply them with the masks."

The Vice President's otherworldly gaze fixed momentarily on each of the assembled group. "We have been nurturing our preferred political replacements through extremely generous funding for their parties and by generating support for their anti-Chinese policies. You see our Brothers, who we spent considerable time training at our education and Development centre in Salem, are now fully operational."

"Using their cover as Regional aid workers for our well-funded Christian charity, they have been putting their training to good use and have launched a series of what look like Islamic terrorist attacks against Chinese workers and property in our target countries." This time the Vice President gave an acknowledging nod towards Sir David Simmingford-Bell.

"Our sources reliably inform us that these attacks have caused outrage from Maputo to Mombasa. We have been quite skilful in creating a narrative that links our candidates in the target countries with the groups that have been carrying out the attacks. Obviously, we don't want our candidates too implicitly linked, just enough for the average concerned citizen to believe that our candidates have some control or link, however tangential with the terrorists. Or should I say Freedom Fighters."

With a rare grin, which was received more as a grimace by the collected group the Vice President glanced up briefly from his notes. "You see the 'Freedom fighters'…" This time the Vice President used the two-handed bent finger gesture to imitate speech marks. "These Freedom Fighters are being seen as an anti-colonial uprising 2.0. Fighting to rid their countries of the oppressive yolk of the most recent wave of colonialism to affect their lands, this time not from

Europe but from the East. These words by the way are simply what I have just read from one of the social media feeds which, by the way, I have to thank Brother Ethan and his team for generating."

The Vice President looked across at Ethan who nodded his head in acknowledgement. "In short, the ground has been laid and once our virus does its God divined work, we are highly confident of our candidates rising up to claim their respective leadership positions."

"Now if you excuse me, I believe Brother Kurt has two more agenda items to discuss and I have to leave." With that the Vice President switched off his VR headset and his hologram instantly disappeared. Back in the Vice President's residence overlooking the Naval Observatory, the Vice President inhaled deeply, glad to have the infernal VR device no longer clamped to his face.

Rising from his chair to leave his office he felt a warm feeling rising through his lower belly as he visualised once more the small army of 3-D printers in the cellar of the South African vineyard, quietly and obediently weaving the deadly matrices. He made a mental note to privately thank Ethan for setting up the hologram facility, only he and Ethan knew exactly how sensitive the microphones spread around the room actually were.

"Brothers, I will keep this short, the food is waiting and we still have to do the proper cellar tour." Kurt's words were well received around the table and their cheers were accompanied by loud banging on the large wooden table. He then stood to address the group. "Brothers, what you are about to watch is a short clip taken from an edited video we posted online 6 hours ago. The final item of business is once more a piece of work developed by Brother Ethan, so I will hand you over to him to explain."

Ethan, clicked a button on his laptop screen. "Yes, by last count it had received over 5 million hits. Now if you wouldn't all mind opening the tablet in front of you and pressing play, you will see what it is all about."

The assembled group did as they were told and a series of sharp intakes of breath peeled around the room. The video showed the US President on his favourite golf course being filmed by what appeared to be a distant mobile phone. The conversation the President was having with his Chief of Defence could, by design, only be intermittently heard.

The essence of the conversation most definitely appeared to show the President of the United States of America denigrating the Mexican President in the foulest language imaginable. With the Army General beside him seemingly howling with laughter at the President's language. At one point the President referred to his Mexican counterpart as a greasy dago, shit eater who defiled little boys.

"I see you have all finished watching." Ethan continued. "It's not Hollywood, I know. But it is generating a lot of debate. Obviously, the Republican networks are claiming it as fake news. Which it is of course". Grinned Ethan. "The more liberal networks have got their hooks into it and are calling for impeachment. Either way, true or not, it has achieved our aim which was to raise the ire of the American voter ahead of next year's mid-terms and hopefully drive a deeper wedge between the US and one of its closest trading partners.

Chapter Twelve

interfere [verb]

Definition of interfere

To enter into, or take part in the concerns of others.

- *The UN cannot interfere in the internal affairs of any country.*

If you really had to take an 18-hour flight into a contested hostile territory surrounded by the most militarized and unstable areas in the world, then you would want to do it in your own private Gulfstream G550 jet, flown by two very experienced military pilots and crewed by the exceptional Christi Gudmundsson, who served as something between a personal Ambassador, Team Medic and experienced on-the-ground Operator.

Drowsy from her 6-hour sleep, Charu reached her left hand down the side of her chair and gently pushed the button to bring the chair back to its upright position. Glancing up at the wall-mounted clock. Charu estimated they had around 3 hours left until they landed at the small regional airstrip in Ludhiana, Northern India.

Twisting in her seat to stretch and look out of the window, she noticed Andrei and Christi stood over the interactive tabletop reviewing maps of Jammu Kashmir and discussing the finer details of their plan.

Li had once described his team at the UNCTC as being divided into two halves: the Doers and the Thinkers. Charu sat firmly in the latter group. It was only her personal family contacts in the region that had convinced Li to allow her to go on this Op at all.

If she was truthful to herself with every passing mile she was becoming more and more unsettled at the thought of driving up into the contested area of Indian controlled northern Kashmir.

Technically nothing had really changed since the 1947 partition and despite at least four armed conflicts over control of the area, relative peace was maintained within the Jammu Kashmir region, if not always at the border itself. The new twist had been the Afghan peace deal struck between, China, Pakistan and Iran.

These three enemies of India encircled Indian-controlled Kashmir geographically, and since the peace deal, they now had tens of thousands of highly trained troops, with the declared intention of acting as guarantors of Afghanistan's ceasefire, exercising in a coordinated way all along the Jammu Kashmir border areas.

Loosening her seatbelt Charu stood to join the others, over the drone of the engine, she caught snatches of Christi and Andrei's conversation, snatched phrases such as, 'Actions On', 'Medevac' and 'Emergency RV', did nothing to relax her mood. As she neared the two figures who were intently peering over the 3D relief mapping that was being holographically projected above the table's surface, the pair stole a furtive glance at each other, and their conversation abruptly stopped.

"Hi guys" Charu tried to hide the nervous shrill to her voice. "Say, do you both have time to go over the plan one more time with me?" "Sure thing Charu", replied Christi. "In fact, it's perfect timing. Andrei and I have just wrapped up all the boring stuff. Let's go over the plan." At this point Andrei cut in. "I was meaning to ask you Charu, Li told us to get into Indian-controlled Kashmir to get a feel for what is happening since the Afghan ceasefire. How close to the border does he want us to get and are we to try and cross the border?"

Charu felt her pulse quickening at the thought of crossing into Pakistani-controlled Kashmir. "Actually, guys I think we don't need to go anywhere near the northern border. According to the most recent intelligence report from Penny, there is no sign of any immediate threat to the status quo there. It seems, to the intelligence community at least, that the troop build-up is exactly what the Chinese, Iranians and Pakistanis say it is. Simply Quick Reaction forces training and preparing for the event that someone breaks the Afghan ceasefire."

"But what about Phillip's point, that the same troops could be used offensively?" Andrei cut in. "That's exactly why we are here, and exactly why I have ventured out of my office. Something I am beginning to regret." Christi overlaid the image of the travelling Gulf stream onto the 3D map. A small blinking red light leaving a trail of red dashes behind it could be seen on the map.

Leaning over the map to point out the dot, Christi began speaking. "OK, this is us now. By the way I will be able to track you both and any vehicles in real time whilst you are out there, so don't worry." Although Christi's words were meant to be reassuring, it only served to raise Charu's anxiety another notch, she was now beginning to feel nauseous. Christi continued "We touch down here." With a dab of her finger on the table's surface a small green pulsing ring began emanating from Ludhiana Airport in northern India.

Checking her watch and doing a quick mental calculation she said "We should arrive in approximately 3 hours from now. From there your cousin Vihaan will pick you both up in his twin cab Hilux. Look there he is now." Christi pointed to another small red dot lazily winding its way westwards from the regional capital of Chandigarh. "How….?" Andrei didn't finish his sentence. Charu cut in. "He gave us his GSM info before we left, we are tracking him via his cell phone."

After grinning at Andrei's face, Christi continued. "So, your first stop is the city of Jammu." With a waft of her hand, the map illuminated the route north from Ludhiana to Jammu. "They are pretty good roads and the journey should take about 5 hours. The city isn't really deep into Jammu Kashmir itself, but it is a great nexus and really close to the Pakistani border. It should be ideal for Charu's plans to capture some atmospherics." "Yeh, about that Charu" Andrei interrupted, "What is it we are doing exactly when we land?" "Right, OK, sorry I should have gone over that shouldn't I."

"Actually, I can do most of it myself, you're just the hired muscle in case we have any problems." She punched Andrei playfully on his arm and was shocked at how hard his arm was. Pulling her hand away and rubbing her knuckles, she continued. "Anyway, as I was saying. Thanks to Vihaan's father, my Uncle Rajeev, we will be able to track the movements of much of the population of Indian Kashmir."

"The Indian Intelligence Bureau have granted us, for a limited time only, access to their cell phone data. So a picture of their real-time movements is being built up back at the CTC on a platform I built before we left. We have a meeting planned with my uncle, who as you know works for the Indian Intelligence Bureau. He has promised to give us a truthful account of how the government in Delhi is reacting to the situation."

"Finally, we want to get a feel for life in the city itself, because it is so close to the border with Pakistan, I want to find out what the gossip is from the cross-border traders, they often know more than the Security Services."

"OK," replied Andrei, nodding in understanding. "How do we do the last part?" "Right, well whilst I chat with my uncle…" "Hold on, surely I should be there with your Uncle?" "Err yes" Charu blushed. "In an ideal world sure I agree, however my uncle isn't quite as enlightened as we are at the CTC and he certainly was not happy with the idea of baring India's fears to a Russian Spetznatz Officer." Andrei looked putout and simply grunted.

"So you and cousin Vihaan have an enjoyable couple of days planned walking around the various textile markets. Our family have a lot of connections in the Kashmir wool industry and so you and Vihaan will be sounding them out to understand what the word is on the street or over the border." Andrei's initial reaction was to be visibly irritated at the lack of trust, shown by the Indian Intelligence community, however, ever the pragmatist, he winked at Charu and grinned as he made his way back to his seat to prepare for the landing.

Awkwardly, Charu returned his wink and then immediately returned her attention to her tablet. Peering over towards the table from his seat, Andrei asked "What is it with you and that tablet? You have had your head in it for weeks now."

"It's err, kind of interesting in a geeky sort of way. Look" she twisted the tablet screen to Andrei to see the Game of Online Battleships she was playing.

"Err Battleships, a kid's game trying to guess where should put a bunch of crosses on a screen. How can you call that interesting? There're way cooler games than that nowadays." "Yeh, I know" she replied with a wry smile. "But this is Quantum Battleships. I have no idea who the guy is who I am playing but he is hosting the game on his self-built quantum computer." "What's so special about that?"

"Well, because it is a Quantum computer it means that each time a guess is made the actual position of the battleship could exist in more than one place at any one time. Meaning you have to try and maintain and remember multiple different configurations for each vessel as you play." "OK, I guess that is kind of cool, but isn't it a bit weird playing a game with someone you know nothing about?"

"Kind of, I guess" she replied brushing her long hair away from her face. "Anyway, who said I don't know anything about him? He has opened a messaging app and we have been exchanging messages. He's kind of flirty, in a nerdy sort of way." This time her hand slid up involuntarily and pulled her hair back across her cheek to hide her blushes. "Do you even know where he is?" "Not really, although I am guessing by his use of idiom that he is from the US or Canada."

Guenther Kramer, the ex-German Air Force pilot had just handed over the controls of the Gulfstream to his former Italian Air Force co-pilot Fabio Cancerelli. "There you go Fabio, I will let you have the honour of landing her." That said, Guenther switched channels on his intercom and spoke with Christi, "Christi, do Air Traffic control actually know who we are?"

Christi responded immediately, "We sort of have a plan Guenther, there is only one runway anyway, land as directed by air traffic control, then as you taxi off the main runway, I am told we will be met and escorted by a Military Police vehicle which will take us to a hanger in a quiet part of the apron."

"Roger that Christi." Seemingly unfazed by the lack of precise detail in Christi's plan, switching channels once more, Guenther turned to his co-pilot and gestured that he should begin his descent.

A barely perceptible tremor rattled briefly through the fuselage as the Gulfstream G550 lightly touched down at the small airstrip in Ludhiana. As promised, hardly had the plane slowed to turn off the main runway than a bulky Nissan Patrol Police vehicle careered onto the runway next to them with its blue lights flashing. Odder still, was the sight of Vihaan, Charu's cousin, leant out of the window grinning broadly and waving at the plane to follow them.

Charu glimpsed her cousin as she peered out of the window and quickly began loosening her seatbelt as the Gulfstream eased to a stop inside the hanger. Christi had barely begun to open the Gulfstream's main door when Charu squeezed past her and rushed down to the steps to Vihaan. Andrei and Christi exchanged a knowing look as they both calmly exited the aircraft.

It was good to see Charu happy, mused Christi to herself. Charu and Christi had quickly formed a close friendship and early on Charu had confided with Christi about the attempted rape in Boston. Although it had been over 4 years since the assault, Christi knew that Charu still bore a lot of deep mental scarring and it would take some considerable time and therapy for her to be able to live anything close to a normal life, with what had happened.

Glancing over to the aft of the aircraft Christi caught a glimpse of Andrei levering open the huge crate which had just been lowered from the plane's hold. Christi had always thought Andrei to be handsome, his slender hips, tall physique and broad shoulders crowned with a strong jaw and high Slavic cheekbones, what was not to like?

"Say Andrei, need a hand with that?" "I'm good" he grunted as he ripped open the lid and tore down the side walls of the packing crate. The crate was the reason for the plane needing to land in a secure area. Around the bulk of the main item in the crate were nestled a collection of small arms and a new rifle on loan from the British Forces.

The sharpshooter rifle, designated the L129A1, although not a pure sniper rifle, was semi-automatic and carried a 7.62mm round, which in the right hands was easily capable of stopping a target dead in its tracks at 800m. The trade off with the extra range and stopping power of a sniper rifle was the relative light weight of the sharpshooter rifle at dead on 4.5kg and the semi-automatic option.

For somebody with Andrei's skill and training the 6 x 48 ACOG sight was more than up to the task of stopping anybody stupid or ignorant enough to pose a threat to him. "Let's hope you won't need to use any of those nice toys you've brought along." murmured Charu, half to herself.

Whilst completing his quick inspection of the weapons, Andrei heard Charu releasing the tie-down straps on the bulky object that nearly filled the crate. "What the ....?" Vihaan, who had been peering over Charu's shoulder exclaimed, as Charu carefully pulled the tarpaulin off the squat object that sat dormant on the floor of the crate. "Vihaan, let me introduce you to P-C Track 2-18, better known as Snappy!"

The squat autonomous tracked vehicle, did indeed look like a snapper turtle, thought Vihaan, as he stared in awe. "It's Andrei's favourite toy. Maria complains that he spends more time and attention on it, than with her" "Hey that's not fair! You said I had to train it." Charu grinned and glanced across at Andrei, who had just placed a pair of wrap-around clear-screen glasses on and had begun to check Snappy's system diagnostics.

"Train it?" muttered Vihaan. "Yeh sure, it's based on machine learning. Basically, the more Andrei interacts and conducts training connected to Snappy through the glasses interface, the better Snappy becomes at understanding what Andrei wants and how best to achieve it." Despite a look of incredulity on his face, Vihaan nodded his understanding. "But Andrei still controls Snappy right?" "Sure. I mean, maybe one day we could get him to do some autonomous actions, that's Snappy, not Andrei I mean!"

Charu's grin deepened as she caught the feigned look of hurt on Andrei's face. Continuing, she said "But he's not there yet, I think." "Sorry cousin. You think?" "Well it's not an exact science like we normally understand. It isn't just about a set input giving a set output. Sometimes we get to see some really cool emergent behaviour. You know, when Snappy basically comes up with an idea or action that works, but that we didn't actually directly ask him for."

Charu continued, explaining to Vihaan all about Snappy's electric propulsion system, its range and speed and load carrying capability. "You see those glasses Andrei is wearing? That's how Andrei interacts with Snappy. We can set a series of parameters before we move, let's say that Snappy must stay within 500 metres of Andrei at all times, and the buggy just does its own thing."

"What do you mean?" asked Vihaan with a quizzical look. "OK, remember the machine learning algorithm I told you about? Snappy is a fully autonomous vehicle, he has all of the onboard mapping, geo data and weather info he needs to make his own decisions about which route to take. He simply follows the one command we set him, which in this case is stay within 500 metres of Andrei." "Cool," exclaimed Vihaan, looking up at his cousin admiringly.

"But what happens if Andrei loses sight of, err, Snappy?" "That bit is simple," replied Charu, with a broad grin on her face, she stepped over to Andrei and gestured for him to remove the glasses. "Try these on for size." Gingerly Vihaan placed the glasses over his eyes. "Charu! You are kidding me. This is bloody awesome!" "I know! everything that Snappy sees, Andrei also sees through the left lens of those glasses. Cooler still, using eye gestures he can bring up a menu of options for actions that Snappy will carry out."

"What do you mean actions? I can't get into the menu." Charu smiled at her cousin as he blinked and contorted his face trying to access the interface. "No cousin, you won't be able to. The glasses use retina verification to ensure the user ID before allowing access" "Ahh, said Vihaan, you could have told me before I started pulling all those stupid faces. Anyway, what's he used for?"

Carefully taking the glasses back from Vihaan, Andrei spoke. "He was designed at our Tech Transfer Centre in Namibia by one of our awesome engineers called Petrus. Originally, we thought about using him as a way of delivering aid to remote areas in dangerous conditions, we also tried him out as a remote mine detector." Andrei pointed to the large covered storage area under Snappy's outer shell.

"You see we can programme him to drop small plastic explosive charges next to any mines he finds and then, once we get him clear of the area we can trigger the electric detonators with these glasses." Andrei tapped the side of the glasses. Vihaan looked completely awestruck. Charu cut in, "On this trip we have fitted him out with an EMP." "An EM what? Do you mean what I think you mean? An Electro-Magnetic Pulse device?"

"Err, yeh," said Charu, "Some of the people where I work, and I really hope they are wrong on this, but these people believe that Kashmir could be in far more danger than usual." Not wanting to alarm Vihaan further, Charu chose her words carefully, trying to remain non-specific about the threat to Kashmir. Vihaan was himself exceptionally bright and had completed the first two years of his electronic engineering degree in Delhi, before he had been forced to return to his family's business.

"But surely an EMP would destroy Snappy as well?" As he said this, he placed his hand affectionately on the Snappy's shimmering surface coating. It was amazing how that effect worked, mused Charu to herself. During the design stage Matthias, the organisation's chief anthropologist had suggested designing the Buggy, then purely designated as P-C Track 2-18, in a zoomorphic way, so that it looked as much like an animal, in this case a turtle, as possible.

The effect was instant. Everyone that saw the buggy, instantly felt a protective bond towards it and most felt inclined to touch and caress it in some way. It was after these startling results were revealed that the team redesignated P-C Track 2-18, simply to Snappy.

Dragging herself away from her thoughts, Charu faced Vihaan once more. "Sorry, err, yeh, normally you would be correct. However, when we built Snappy, we basically built a Faraday cage around his electronic parts, shielding him from any harmful effects of the EMP." Vihaan looked admiringly once more at his cousin as Andrei began to walk to the other end of the hanger.

After a brief delay, Snappy silently rotated on its tracks and glided a little closer towards Andrei. Charu giggled briefly, then quickly covered her mouth, as she saw Vihaan's disbelieving double take.

Just then, Christi sauntered over in her tight-fitting flight suit. Charu gave Vihaan a stern look then smiled, "You can close your mouth now Vihaan. Let me introduce you to my colleague Christi Gudmundsson." "Are you guys set?" Christi asked. Charu turned to glance over at Andrei, who was watching as Snappy navigated itself up the ramps and onto the back of Vihaan's pickup truck. Andrei gave Charu a thumbs up, then unconsciously patted Snappy on its back before walking over to re-join the group.

It was Christi that finally called the group to order. Although she spoke to the group her eyes were fixed on Andrei. "Right guys, we will be here to pick you up in 3 days' time. Remember we can see where you are at all times, and we have worked up a couple of alternate extraction plans if everything goes south."

Christi saw that this physically unnerved Vihaan. She touched his cheek softly as she said "Don't worry Vihaan. It's standard practice, we do it every time we go anywhere." Blushing slightly and unable to take his eyes from Christi, Vihaan nodded his understanding.

The twin cab Hilux, with its precious cargo of Snappy, safely hidden under a tarpaulin in the loading bed, rolled out of the airport entrance to begin its nearly 5-hour journey to the regional winter Kashmiri capital of Jammu. Andrei sat in the back with Charu sat up front with Vihaan. Gazing out of the window.

The journey north through the flat lightly forested grasslands was quite pleasant, thought Andrei. Glancing out of the side window at the majestic and still quite distant Himalayan peaks that dominated the entire Northeast of their route, Andrei couldn't quite shake the feeling of foreboding, as if it was these peaks alone that were physically holding back China's push for westward expansion.

Twilight was slowly fading as Vihaan entered Jammu. As they neared the broad open water expanses of the Tawi river which bisected the town, Vihaan veered right, still driving on Highway 44 and began to steadily climb the northern edge of a long ridge that embraced Jammu from the East.

Vihaan slowed once more and turned off onto a dirt road. The abrupt change from the smooth tarmac of the Highway to the rutted dirt track jolted Charu awake. Immediately she wound down the window, leant her head out of the window and breathed in the strong fragrant aromas of the rich forest that surrounded them.

Opening her eyes and glancing forward she saw the first of the small strings of lights that guilded the forest path and bathed the onlooker in a warm comforting glow. An impressive white-walled colonial style mansion stood regally in a small clearing, erect and proud, yet strangely at one with the surrounding forest.

As the vehicle left the confines of the track and drove into the clearing Andrei, who had strained to look past the warm lanterns deeper into the forest, noticed the silhouettes of various armed figures hidden just inside the wood line. "It looks like your uncle is expecting us" he whispered to Charu.

Barely had the Toyota come to a halt, than the great house's front door swung open and Charu's Aunt Surinder burst out of the house, her intricately embroided sari swirling in the wind behind her as she ran to the car to embrace Charu.

Slowly releasing his grip on the pistol in his waistbelt and sensing no threat, Andrei relaxed and was immediately struck by just how elegant and graceful the older Indian lady was. Her hair although flecked with strands of grey was long and lustrous and the woman carried herself with such poise and grace. Now I know where Charu gets her looks from, he thought to himself.

Charu hurled herself out of the car and rushed to embrace her aunt. Behind her standing regally in the doorway stood Uncle Rajeev. Standing erect, almost to attention, Andrei thought, his pale orange turban made him seem even taller than he was.

Although it was not his physical bearing that drew Andrei's attention it was the older man's intelligent eyes, that seemed to glitter in the moonlight. Eventually, after much hugging and kissing the group were allowed to enter the house.

Auntie Surinder immediately went to the kitchen to prepare tea and refreshments for the weary travellers as Uncle Rajeev led the group into his study. "It is so good to see you Charu my dear" began her uncle. "Err, sorry and of course you too Vihaan, tell me how are your family?"

Without waiting for an answer he continued "I was sorry to hear about you having to quit your studies like that, my sources tell me that you were a first class student. Something I am afraid that in these dark times our country and armed forces need more of. You know I can have a word with your parents if you like. Maybe we can get you a military scholarship?"

Vihaan looked appreciatively at his Uncle. "Thank you Uncle, that means a lot to me, maybe in a couple of years? I think Mama and Baba really need me in the family business for the moment." Uncle Rajeev's eyes softened and fleetingly appeared to sadden as he acknowledged his nephew's situation.

"And you must be Andrei?" The older man said, turning to

appraise Andrei. "I have heard much about you, and of course I have made my own enquiries. Tell me that super soldier program of yours is it as effective as we think?" After glancing swiftly over at Charu, Andrei's gaze faltered for the briefest of moments as he internally recoiled at what the old spy chief had just said. Had Charu been saying more than she should have?

"As you know sir, these things are always measured by the operational results, which as I am sure you will understand is not something I am allowed to discuss. Anyway, as I am sure you also know, I am no longer part of that world." "Uncle Rajeev raised a consoling arm and said "I am sorry, I didn't mean to pry, old habits, I guess. Actually, I was more concerned that my niece would be well looked after in Kashmir."

At that moment Charu's aunt came into the room bearing a huge tray laden with cakes and tea. Glancing over at her husband she placed the tray on the coffee table and excused herself.

"We will have time to catch up and eat properly later" began Uncle Rajeev, "however, unfortunately I believe events may be moving faster than we thought." Uncle Rajeev settled himself into his well-worn armchair.

"I say, I believe, because I am yet to persuade my colleagues of my suspicions and that is where I need the help of my gifted niece Charu." Charu looked up quickly nearly spilling her tea. "My help?" "Sure, maybe we can talk tomorrow in a bit more depth about it when these two men are off enjoying their stroll around the market stalls of Jammu?" Andrei understood the intelligence world's obsession with compartmentalising everything, however if he was honest to himself, it still irked him not to be included at the highest level.

"Without going into specifics or sources I can give you all a brief overview of where we stand. Of course, this is just an old man's view of our situation, sadly it is not a view shared by our political masters. So first the bigger picture..." Uncle Rajeev went on to explain the strategic threats facing India.

"India cannot be separated from her geography. We have always feared invasion along our land borders. To the north-west, thanks to a poorly executed partition of our country lies a series of majority

Muslim states that harbour no great love for India, chief amongst them Pakistan. Then directly to our north we have what the international community like to call the disputed territories of Kashmir." Like an experienced Professor, Uncle Rajeev, expounded eloquently and fluently on the history and circumstances surrounding India's current predicament.

"The fear of invasion for most of the 19th century was invasion through Afghanistan, Tajikistan and Pakistan by the Russian Empire. We have our British colonisers to thank that this never happened" He glanced briefly around the room ensuring that the irony of his comment was not lost on his audience.

"The new threat to India comes however, from the East. China has already constructed high altitude Himalayan routes through the Wakhan corridor into Afghanistan as part of their Belt and Road initiative. Furthermore, one of our reconnaissance satellites picked up disturbing construction and earthworks on the Doklam plateau."

"For those of us whose geography needs refreshing. This plateau is a thin section of land squeezed between Nepal to the west, Bhutan to the east. The territory is one of our few actual border areas with China proper." Charu cut in. "Maybe we can chat more in detail tomorrow about this, but our own imagery also shows considerable excavation and roads and airstrips in the area."

"I agree" Uncle Rajeev, relieved not to have to give away any more of this sensitive information he nodded to Charu. "Our team's estimate is that they have excavated deep into the mountainside and have removed enough waste material to have excavated an area the size of three to four footballs fields inside the mountain. What we don't know is why."

Rajeev nodded "Yes, err that is pretty much what we think as well, we also have a couple of ideas as to what they may have inside the caves. Needless to say, the whole affair raised a lot of alarm bells in Delhi and over the last year we have moved a considerable portion of our heavy armour and offensive air capabilities over to east of the country to protect against any incursion there. Then of course we can't forget the common border with the Chinese in Kashmir." Andrei, an avid student of military history himself, was immediately spellbound by Uncle Rajeev's narrative of recent events.

"You know it's been 60 years nearly to the day since the Chinese came pouring over that border. With everything that has been going on in Afghanistan recently our top brass are pushing hard to have the entire north-eastern part of Kashmir reinforced militarily. But the fools in Delhi that hold the purse strings, many of them who were not even born when the war started, aren't prepared to stump up the extra funds to reposition another garrison up there." Charu glanced across at Andrei and exchanged a glance as her uncle's temper began to rise.

"And as if that isn't enough," Charu had rarely seen her uncle so agitated, he stood from his silk covered stool and strode over to the fireplace. "The same fools in Delhi who refuse to strengthen our defences in Kashmir all sit on different committees and never see the full picture. They also play down the Communist inspired Naxalite threat that has recently resulted in a series of coordinated attacks on regional police stations all down the north-eastern edge of our country and when you couple that with the reports from our Navy about Chinese and Russian submarine sightings in the Bay of Bengal and Arabian Sea then, well..." releasing his arms from behind his back and relaxing his shoulders a little, Uncle Rajeev refocused his gaze on his small group of visitors.

"Hmm, it seems I got a little carried away doesn't it. Sorry, it's not often that I have an audience to air my grievances, my poor wife, your Aunt Surinder, has heard this same rant a hundred times, poor woman." The faint glint had returned to her uncle's face as he deftly moved back across the room sat once more on his silk stool and prepared to serve tea to the group.

It had been a long time indeed since Andrei had slept so well, he mused to himself as he watched the sun lazily filtering its way through the net curtains and begin to fill his room with light. He wasn't sure if it was the almost complete silence that had engulfed the house after dark or the cool mountainous forest air that had filtered through the small gap in the window as he had gone to bed. Whatever it was he now laid on his back in his bed breathing slowly and concentrating on the warm doughy smells that were wafting up the stairs from the kitchen below.

‘That’s it’ he thought, unable to resist the tempting smells, he jumped up, slid into his cargo pants, pulled on a t-shirt, and ran down the stairs. He nearly knocked Charu over who was unsteadily processing from the kitchen out onto the verandas to a table with a tray piled high with garlic and mince filled naan breads fresh from the tandoor oven and tangy crispy potato-filled Samosas fresh from the frying pan.

The pair were joined by a sleepy-looking Vihaan who bade them all good morning with a half-hearted wave of his hand before slumping into a spare seat at the table. The group were joined by Charu’s aunt as they set to, diving into the tasty feast. “Your uncle told me you have a busy day ahead of you and that you weren’t to leave the house on an empty stomach” Aunt Surinder said with a glint in her eye.

“Where is Uncle Rajeev Auntie?” Charu asked, “Oh he’s been up for hours now, he is in his study calling all his contacts in the markets. He is organising Andrei and Vihaan’s agenda for the day.” “Great” spluttered Charu whilst trying to finish off a mouthful of spicy Keema Naan.

“You know I might head into town and join them once I’m finished setting up the mobile phone software and satellite feeds that Uncle Rajeev is sharing with us. I haven’t been to the market since I was a little girl and used to come up here for holidays. It’ll be fun to explore again.”

By two in the afternoon, Andrei was beginning to detest the person who had invented tea. The pair had gone from cloth vendor to cloth vendor according to their uncle’s plan and sat patiently talking to them trying to build up a picture of what the traders had seen and witnessed whilst over the border in Pakistan and further north in Pakistani controlled Kashmir.

Despite official borders and government demarcated zones, as is typical in many such areas, the people such as the cloth merchants, who actually lived there and traded to survive, mostly saw the border simply as a beaurocratic nuisance that merely meant greasing a few more palms each time they wanted to buy and sell their cloths and silks.

Each time they entered a new vendor's house, they would follow the same procedure, Vihaan would lead and make the introductions, then Andrei, who was mostly treated with great distrust would sit quietly at the back of the room making notes as Vihaan asked the pre-discussed series of questions.

They had actually made far more progress than Andrei had believed they would and as the clock moved slowly towards three and Andrei drained the dregs of yet another cup of tea, they had built up a pretty good, and to Andrei's military mind, a rather disturbing picture of the state and preparedness of the Iranian, Pakistani and Chinese forces that had been conducting 'coordination' exercises over the border.

Looking through his notes Andrei was most disturbed by some of the more recent sightings from north of Islamabad. Although descriptions varied, several of their sources reported seeing mobile artillery that purportedly fired shells which detonated in the air releasing hundreds of tiny drones.

They had also seen row upon row of heavy-lift helicopters lined up waiting to be fuelled. Most startling for Andrei was the repeated assertion that whatever formation the traders said they had seen, and regardless of location or nationality, they all reported seeing heavily armoured command vehicles with multiple antennas and satellite dishes all bearing the unmistakeable lone red star of the Chinese People's Liberation Army.

This was the one consistent fact reported by everyone they interviewed. Stepping outside into the street, they spotted Charu waiting by the Hilux, chatting to an older woman. "Hi guys, I thought I would come out and get a feel for the market myself. I'm trying to seal a deal on some Pashmina scarves for the girls at work, but my haggling skills leave a lot to be desired." She handed over a crumpled bunch or rupees to the older lady and thanked her for the silk scarves as she turned to face the guys properly. "So, where to next?"

Vihaan spoke first, "Actually we are just about done, we just have one more contact to visit who was recently in the border territories with Afghanistan, Uncle Rajeev says he is a bit of a rogue but just might have some useful info for us. He lives a little way north of the town on the road up to Domel. Do you fancy riding along? I guess we should be back before nightfall."

"Sure thing" Charu said jumping into the front of the Hilux next to Cousin Vihaan, "I'll give Uncle Rajeev and Aunt Surinder a call and let them know what time to have dinner ready for us." The call didn't connect. That's odd, we should have a signal here she thought to herself peering intently at her phone as the Toyota slowly left behind the cacophonous traffic of Jammu and started to pick up speed on its short trip northward towards Domel. Charu removed her phone once more and pressed Call to speak to her uncle. "Say Andrei, do you have a signal, my phone still isn't working?"

Andrei was the first to react. Maria called it his Spider-sense, his innate ability to sense danger however remote. Glancing at his phone then up at the traffic lights ahead that seemed to be out of order, he screamed "Stop!" Vihaan nearly jumped out of his skin when he heard Andrei's shout from the back of the truck. Swerving wildly with the heavy weight of Snappy in the cargo bed he wrestled the vehicle to a stop on the dusty hard shoulder.

Once the vehicle had settled and stopped rocking both Vihaan and Charu turned in their seats to stare at Andrei who was already loosening his seatbelt. Binoculars in hand he lowered the rear window and began scanning the sky. "Hey man, what's going on?" Vihaan wanted to know. All he got from Andrei was a terse "Shhhh, cut the engine."

Barely audible over the slow ticking of the hot engine, the three occupants of the car could hear a rumbling droning sound. Her voice barely a whisper, Charu asked "Are they aircraft?" Pointing upwards to the West she could just make out a chorus of thin vapour trails streaking across the clear Kashmiri sky.

Andrei tracked the shadowy objects with his binoculars until they passed over the car and onwards on their journey South-eastwards. He leant down and rummaged through his pack, as he did so he started calmly issuing commands. "Buckle up guys and follow my instructions." Withdrawing a handheld GPS from his pack, he handed it to Charu, "Charu, turn it on and navigate Vihaan to Waypoint One please".

Doing as she was told Charu fired up the GPS and began giving Vihaan instructions. They carried on north until they were nearly in Domel then took a dirt track which connected after a few miles with a larger metalled road that would eventually wind its way south-east back to the Kashmiri / Indian border and hopefully back towards their waiting plane and crew.

As they left the main road several large detonations could be heard resounding in the distance. From the front seat Vihaan mumbled "OK Guys, I'm officially a little bit freaked out now. What just happened back there?"

"D.O.S attack" Andrei said as he pressed speed dial on his encrypted Sat phone. Seeing the uncomprehending look in Vihaan's eyes Charu explained. A Denial of Service attack (D.O.S) is typically an attack aimed at the software of an operating system to prevent it from doing its job or shutting it down. It seems that somebody, and we don't have to play guess who? for too long to work out who, has shut down the communications network and power supply, that's why the traffic lights weren't working."

She could see the comprehension dawn on Vihaan's face, "You mean someone is actually attacking Jammu? Why?" "I think it might be bigger than just Jammu and as for why, because it's what I would do" Andrei calmly stated. "It's a bit like turning the lights off. First you blind and disorientate the opponent then you attack him physically. Those missiles you saw they were either to destroy the main crossing points from India to Kashmir or maybe to mine the roads and rivers. Either way the effect is to seal off Kashmir from reinforcement by India."

Andrei broke off and began enumerating a staccato series of numbers and letters into the Sat phone. After a brief pause, they heard Christi's voice on the other end." Hi guys, what's happening?" "We need an Evac from ERV 1. Our estimated time of arrival is 50 minutes. We will prep the landing zone." "Roger that, we are going to need a little longer. The Air Traffic Control people have reported outages in their system and are reluctant to allow take offs."

With a confidence in her voice that in no way matched her mood, Christi Gudmundsson signed off and turned to the two pilots who were asleep at the rear of the aircraft. "OK boys, who wants to show me what a skilful pilot they are?"

Driving alone, the Hilux made easy work of the metalled road, Cousin Vihaan was actually a good driver and it was only the increasing thunderous explosions of artillery and rocket shells that seemed to be creeping slowly southwards that made him lose his focus.

In retrospect, it was, if she was being honest with herself, actually Charu's fault, she had been trying to watch out for danger when she noticed a dark cloud behind them in the vicinity of the last town they had passed. Pointing this out to Cousin Vihaan caused him to look up for a split second too long.

The pickup veered sharply towards the edge of the metalled road and the front left-hand tyre was ripped apart by a piece of old reinforcing bar that lay on the side of the road. The tyre blew immediately, and Vihaan only just managed to wrestle the vehicle to a halt.

"Shit, shit shit shit shit shit shit!" cried Vihaan. Although shaken by the near miss, Charu managed to remain calm. "Hey cuz, don't beat yourself up about it. It was my fault I should never had distracted you like that."

Meanwhile, ever vigilant to the approaching danger, Andrei was peering through his binoculars. The Hilux had covered a lot of ground and they only had about 10km to get to the border crossing. Climbing swiftly out of the vehicle, he dropped the tailgate and began to lower Snappy out of the Hilux on its ramps.

"Charu, Vihaan, do you think you can change that tyre on your own?" "Sure" they shouted in unison. OK get to work, as fast as you can. Me and Snappy are heading over to that mound over there to get a better look at what's happening."

What Andrei had not told the pair, who were now obediently changing the Hilux's damaged wheel was that through his binoculars he had seen pick-up trucks with what looked like flatbed mounted anti-aircraft guns mounted on them hidden in a small depression about 4km north of their location. There was no direct road between the heavily gunned pick-ups and their Hilux, but it wouldn't take the vehicle long to cover the ground if they were spotted.

Grasping the sniper rifle in the low carry, at arms-length in one arm he set off at a swift jog using the ground to hide his movements as he ran around the small mound that lay some 500m to their right. Snappy had followed Andrei some of the way but using his smart glasses Andrei paused the short stocky vehicle. He manually reversed it into a small irrigation trench behind some trees and left it to monitor the activity of the pair fixing the wheel.

Andrei moved the final 200m metres to the crest of the mound on his belly. Methodically, yet efficiently sliding forwards towards his vantage point. He stopped just short of the ridge and peered through the long grass. Edging forward slightly he scanned the horizon, first taking in Charu and Vihaan who had managed to get the damaged wheel off the vehicle but seemed to be struggling to get the spare wheel in the right position to fasten it back on.

Scanning further north the small depression where the enemy vehicles had been, was now empty, instead he saw small dust swirls zig zagging across the dry earth heading in the direction of Charu and Vihaan.

There was probably about 2 hours of light left, Andrei calculated as he began to adjust the sniper optic fitted to his rifle. The low sun was to his back which highlighted in profile one of the vehicles cautiously navigating over the rough ground towards the Hilux. There was a gentle breeze blowing to the west, around 5km per hour Andrei reckoned. He continued his calculations and observations as he prepared the rifle to fire if necessary.

There was still a chance that the vehicle hadn't seen their pick-up and was actually heading south towards the same small border crossing as they were, in order to seal it off. A well-positioned 4x4 vehicle, heavily armed and well crewed, would be more than up to the job of holding a small dirt road crossing, particularly when the track and old wooden bridge wouldn't be able to take the load of armoured vehicles, and once anti-personnel mines had been remotely scattered to form a small but highly dangerous obstacle for any reinforcements wanting to use the track to get into Kashmir.

Just as he thought the vehicle was going to drive past Charu and Vihaan a couple of hundred metres to the north, the lead vehicle swerved violently to the left and changed its course heading directly at the pick-up.

Through the sniper scope, Andrei saw Charu who had spotted the vehicles, gesticulating manically at Vihaan who was desperately trying to remove the vehicle jack which had somehow become jammed under the truck.

Through his sniper scope Andrei counted down the metres as the pick-up closed with their own vehicle. At 500 metres his left eye glanced upwards and then to the left. The motion triggered a pre-programmed command in his smart glasses. Within seconds on the ground below him Andrei watched as Snappy whizzed silently through the tall grass on a trajectory directly towards the Hilux. Through his scope Andrei now saw two objects converging at speed on the Hilux.

It's impossible to begin to explain to someone who hasn't experienced it first-hand, just exactly how terrifying it is to be on the receiving end of heavy calibre machine gun fire. There is no fizz or whizz as rounds fly past you. Instead, what the recipient focusses on is the impact. The 12.7mm rounds plough into whatever they hit with such terrifying force tearing huge gashes into everything they touch.

The first burst of fire from the heavy machine gun was wide of its mark, but the well-trained gunner balancing precariously on the back of the accelerating pick-up truck managed to walk his aim slowly onto the targets in a series of short bursts. The third burst ripped a lump out of the back of the vehicle and blew the driver's door which, had been open, clean off its hinges.

Charu screamed more in shock than pain as Vihaan in full flight struck her in her stomach propelling her backwards into the tall grass on the verge of the road. Shaking with fear, they clung to each other, heads buried in the dirt as the sound of the pick-up drew closer.

Andrei had identified three targets in the vehicle. The gunner, the driver and the passenger who was trying as Andrei watched to manoeuvre his AK47 out of the open window to bring down fire on the Hilux. In Andrei's mind, each target had been prioritized according to the threat it posed.

From this range the first threat was the heavy machine gun,

closely followed by the driver, then finally the passenger. There were now barely 500 metres between the pick-up and the Hilux.

Before sighting on the gunner Andrei once more used his left eye to select a function on the smart glasses and activate it. The function, which would enable Snappy to charge and fire its EMP had a 5-second countdown to activation. The first projectile in Andrei's five round magazine missed the gunner but struck the weapon itself rendering it useless. Smoothly re-cocking the weapon and testing and adjusting his position, he released another shot. He followed the shot through his sight watching it pierce the magazine carrying bandolier the gunner wore around his chest, enter his chest cavity, then tear through his spine and rip a gaping hole in the back of the dirty white Shalwar Kameez the gunner was wearing. Calmly noting to himself that he would have to add his report the fact that some of the enemy units were dressed like tribal militia.

The countdown in his glasses reached zero and through his scope Andrei noticed Snappy rock violently on its tracks then watched as the fried electrical circuits on the pick-up truck ceased working and the vehicle began to lose speed. The gunner was dead, and now with the vehicle disabled, Andrei changed his priority from the driver to the passenger who was preparing to fire at Charu and Vihaan who had foolishly decided they would make a run for their own vehicle.

Vihaan was inside the cab trying in vain to start the vehicle unaware that the same EMP that had destroyed the militia pick-up had also disabled their vehicle. Andrei's first round missed as the gunmen unexpectedly pulled his head back through the window of the vehicle. With only two rounds remaining Andrei waited for his chance. The militia vehicle had now ceased moving and both the driver and gunman flung the doors open and began running towards the Hilux.

His next shot struck the running figure of the gunman in the centre of his chest. The figure was physically thrown backwards by the force of the impact and lay like a distorted puppet lifeless on the ground. Rapidly shifting his aim and with only one round left, Andrei snatched off a shot at the final figure who had nearly reached the Hilux.

Vihaan had jumped out of the far driver's side door and bravely stood ready to meet the assailant with a tyre lever in his hand. Andrei's final shot ricocheted off the rear fender of the Hilux as the driver dived down and took cover behind the far side rear wheel.

Dropping the sniper rifle and withdrawing the pistol from the back of his trouser belt, Andrei stood and launched himself at full speed over the crest of the mound and down through the long grass towards the Hilux. The driver had just managed to get himself to his feet as Vihaan swung down violently with the tyre iron. The swing was hard and well-aimed but it failed to impact on its target. As the man rose from the floor he quickly raised a concealed pistol and fired off a rapid shot. The round struck Vihaan in his thigh and spun him to the ground.

Andrei was now 200 metres away and closing fast, the problem was that the target and Charu were both obscured by the bulk of the vehicle. Slowing his pace as he approached, Andrei stopped briefly to listen for his enemy, he could hear grunting and scuffling coming from the far side of the vehicle.

Glancing under the vehicle he could see Charu prone on her back and what he thought were the sandals of the figure straddling Charu. Cautiously he crept around the rear of the vehicle as he reached the rear his shirt sleeve caught on a piece of the torn rear fender where his final round at struck. Hearing the noise, the gunman who had by now straddled Charu and begun to choke her, turned his head briefly at the sound.

What followed surprised everyone, Charu more than the rest. She would later claim to have no knowledge of what happened however, unfortunately for Charu, the whole spectacle was being recorded on the HD camera embedded in the Smart glasses.

The action of turning his head had temporarily removed some of the gunman's weight from Charu's chest. The slight change in equilibrium had been enough for Charu to slide out one of her pinned down arms. It was, just as Penny had taught her on the exercise mat back in Singapore.

In one fluid motion her free arm shot out and upwards. Charu's tightly-balled fist striking up and through the exposed throat of the surprised gunman. The blow had smashed into the man's trachea and forcing the cartilaginous tissue back towards his spine. Dropping his weapon in shock and clutching his hands to his shattered throat the man leant forward. His hateful glare fixed Charu for a moment in a terrified rigor.

Briefly Charu had been reminded of the assault she had undergone in Boston all those years ago. However, although about to be overwhelmed with fear their appeared to be some new sub-routine working away in the back of her unconsciousness. Without knowing she bit down hard on the man's thigh and reached upwards once more with her free hand. Grabbing the man's dirty beard, she pivoted and deftly levered the man sideways.

The man rolled off Charu and as she tried to stand she heard another gunshot. The reaction to seeing a person's brain matter sprayed up against the side of a vehicle barely two feet from your face was to be expected. She vomited ejecting the bile and fear from her body in equal measure. She looked up in time to see Andrei binding Vihaan's leg with a tourniquet and bandage.

"Well look at you, quite the little Ninja now aren't you?" Andrei said winking as he glanced over to Charu. "Are you OK to move?" "Err, I guess, I mean I don't know." Slowly Andrei bent to help Charu to her feet, trembling and tear-stained she stood. They gazed briefly into each other's eyes. Charu saw compassion and understanding, Andrei saw dignity and restored pride. "Hey, are you guys coming or what?" Vihaan had just awkwardly settled himself onto Snappy's cargo rack and was beckoning to Charu to join him.

Andrei helped Charu over and she climbed on next to Vihaan. "It's not exactly what we designed him for, but it'll do. I guess." Charu grunted as she tried to get comfortable. She had a sharp pain in her rib from the attack and suspected it may be broken. "OK we have about 7km to go to get to the border crossing and we don't know who else is out there. I have the terrain map projected on my smart glasses."

"Vihaan I will be trying to get there as quickly as possible, but I also want to use as much cover as possible. Can you keep talking to Christi and the flight team and give them updates as we go?" "Sure thing Andrei."

Whilst Andrei and Vihaan were talking Charu was opening a small hatch on one of Snappy's hexagonal panels. "What are you doing cousin?" "Giving us some eyes in the sky." With that she flung a small matt black plastic looking object high into the air and using her thumb quickly span her haptic ring on her middle finger a couple of taps later and the small black object had opened out its propellers and begun whirring, almost silently as it held position over the moving buggy.

"Good call Charu" Andrei said as he set off at a brisk run. Obediently, Snappy, with its two passengers lurched forward and followed on behind. The delay with the attack had cost them too much time Andrei thought as he gradually increased his running speed. 'We have to get over the border and prepare the landing strip before Christi and the team arrive'.

Once Charu and Vihaan had got used to the rising and falling motion of Snappy, they began to plan how they would create an airstrip in the middle of nowhere. The plan was relatively simple they needed to find a straight stretch of the highway with at least 900 metres of length. The problem Charu knew would be finding a stretch of road wide enough to accommodate the aircraft's wings. When or rather if, they found a suitable strip then they had to clear it of any debris and highlight the runway with smoke flares due to the fading light.

Vihaan nearly lost his balance and made a muffled cry of pain as his injured leg jarred against the buggy's irregular shaped shell as Snappy surged forward and swerved violently to avoid a large rock. He turned to Charu and said "Hey is it me or is he running even faster now?" Glancing up briefly from her mobile which she was using as a monitor for the drone, Charu looked back at Vihaan.

"I think he's only just getting started. He knows as well as we do that we need to get across the border before they decide to either mine the bridge or destroy it. I don't know about you, but I would also like very much indeed not to meet up with any more of those tribesmen that attacked us back there."

"Say, how far is it to the border from here?" Vihaan glanced down at the GPS screen and made a quick calculation. "Err as the crow flies about 3 kilometres" Charu looked back over to Andrei who was some 50 metres to their right. Shouting hard above the noise of the buggy, Charu cried "Andrei, we need to go faster if we can. 3 kilometres to the border. I'm sending you the drone feed to your glasses."

Andrei simply raised a thumb in acknowledgment and in a seemingly effortless action slightly lengthened and quickened his running stride. The effect was felt rather than seen by the pair sat astride Snappy as the little buggy accelerated again to keep pace with Andrei. Andrei knew he could make the border in less than 15 minutes he only hoped that would be enough as he reviewed the drone video in the corner of his glasses' lens.

The other three pick-up trucks were now clustered around the one that Andrei had destroyed and the men were busy loading their dead comrades into the other trucks. More alarming to Andrei was the sight of piles of large green regular shaped plastic objects in the back of the pick-up truck bed.

Damn, he cursed to himself. Mines! Now they had to beat the pick-up trucks to the border. His only advantage was that he and the buggy could cut a large corner off the route where the road swept in a large arc to the east.

They may just be able to make it as long as the trucks didn't see them and try to intercept them directly and just headed straight to the border. Once more he picked up the pace. He was now running flat out weaving around the low scrub land. A light sheen of sweat covered his back and he was now taking full deep lungful's of air and beginning to feel the slight acidic feeling in his throat as the lactic acid built up.

He moved closer to the buggy and in ragged gasps shouted his instructions to Charu. Fly the drone over to the bridge at the crossing I need to take a closer look at the site. I have an idea how we may be able to delay them a little. Charu did as she was asked and was surprised to see how close the little wooden bridge was.

Clinging on even tighter now to Snappy and wincing every time her ribs were jolted by a pothole, she grabbed Vihaan's arm and said, "I think we might just make it. Just do exactly as Andrei tells you to and be as quick as you can OK?" Vihaan smiled back. She could see his face was much paler now and knew he must have lost a lot of blood from the gunshot wound to his leg.

500 metres, 400 metres, Andrei counted down the distance to the bridge. As they reached the bridge Andrei brought the small team to a halt right in the middle of the bridge. "Charu help Vihaan and move over the bridge and follow the road around to the right until you enter the tree-lined area." Charu nodded and inhaled sharply as the twisting motion of climbing of the buggy caused her broken rib bones to grate against each other.

The pair hobbled pathetically off over the bridge leaving Andrei and Snappy together. Andrei reached inside the cargo compartment and withdrew a satchel containing flares. Before closing the hatch, he engaged the buggy's anti-tamper self-destruct switch and after fondly stroking the outer casing of the buggy's exterior trotted off after the others.

Charu had left the drone in loiter mode high above Snappy's position on the bridge. Luckily for the team the road turned sharply to the right just after they left the bridge and this turn coupled with the tree covering would obscure them from sight.

However, Andrei was fully aware that it wouldn't be able to mask a medium sized private jet approaching to land barely 500 metres from the border. Now it's down to luck and timing. As he caught up with the injured pair, he grabbed the Sat phone and called Christi.

"Christi we are over the border. But only just. I will prep a runway on the road. The surface isn't super smooth but it should take the weight. Watch out as you approach there may be a bright flash on the bridge as you line up for the approach." "Roger that Andrei, we are 12 minutes away. The boys are just drawing straws to see who is going to land the plane. My maps don't show a lot of room for error."

"Roger Christi. It looks like you have at most 1km of straight road, I just hope and pray it is wide enough. By the way be prepared for a couple of casualties when we board. I think Charu has cracked some ribs and we have an extra passenger." Unflustered, Christi patiently waited for the details.

"Young Vihaan, he took a gunshot to the thigh." "What the… You guys really have been having some fun. OK I need to get strapped in for the descent. We will be with you very soon Andrei. Out." Folding the antenna on the phone Andrei slipped it into his jacket pocket and turned to look at the others. He was about to distribute the flares and issue orders on what each person had to do, but he noticed that they were both glued to Charu's smart phone screen.

The silent black and white video they were watching was accompanied by its own live soundtrack as the remaining three pick-up trucks loaded with mines and at least ten tribesmen looking to revenge the deaths of their fallen comrades approached the bridge.

Andrei stared intently he knew that they would not be able to resist inspecting the low squat buggy that was blocking their way across the bridge. He only hoped that Snappy's last defiant act of self-destruction would be enough to save them all and prevent the tribesmen from crossing the bridge or shooting at the plane.

Charu jabbed with her finger at the screen as a group of the tribesmen parked their pick-up a few metres short of the buggy and got out to inspect it. It was difficult to make out a lot of detail as the light was slowly fading, however it was possible to discern the bulky shape of one of the fighters as he tried to lever open one of Snappy's hatches with a cruel looking blade. As the hatch lever was pried free and the hatch swung open it broke an electric circuit which in turn triggered the electric detonators to ignite the Buggy's in-built explosive charge.

The charge was relatively small, one flattened square of plastic explosive with 6 phosphorous grenades embedded in it, but it was enough to completely rip apart Snappy's central casing and for the phosphorous grenades which burnt with an unbelievable white-hot ferocity to cover the surrounding area with molten metal and debris. The three men closest to the Buggy had been blown back by the force of the blast and blown clean over the side of the bridge.

In images which themselves burned themselves into the mind of the three observers. The three watched as the stunned, charred bodies bounced and spilled down the craggy ravine edge, eventually laying distorted and twisted in the small stream below.

The intense heat of the burning phosphorous and the force of the plastic explosive had rent a huge hole in the wooden bridge and as the flames began to engulf the rest of the bridge the remaining fighters urgently tried to reverse their remaining vehicles off the bridge. Finally, a thunderous crack was heard as Snappy and the lead pick-up truck both broke through the floor of the bridge and plunged downwards, as they fell and were bounced from hard rock wall to hard rock wall the mines that were in the back of the truck began to explode.

These detonations were enough to finally shake the main bridge supports loose from their fixings and in one final act the entire central span of the bridge groaned and collapsed in on itself falling like tinder wood into the chasm below.

With no time to waste Andrei quickly began issuing orders. Giving Vihaan two red flares he told him to sit himself in the centre of the road and hold the lit flares high above his head when signalled. He was to be the final stop marker. Sharing the remaining flares out between himself and Charu he said. "OK you take the left I'll take the right, every hundred metres we need to place a flare. Place them as wide as safely possible."

The pair began running down the wood-lined road dropping the flares as they went. Charu cursed every time she bent to drop a flare as the small fragments of broken rib grated against each other. Andrei got to the end before Charu and pulled out his phone. "Christi, do you read me?" "Loud and clear Andrei. We have you in sight and we are making our approach now."

Looking skywards Andrei saw the plane's landing lights begin to line up with the pattern of flares on the ground. He turned to Charu and shouted. "OK we gotta get back to Vihaan before the plane gets here. Are you up for it?" A broad grin broke out on her dirt smudged and tear-stained face. Turning and beginning to hobble back down the flare lined road she shouted, "Just try and keep up old man."

Despite both pilots wanting to make the landing it had been decided that Fabio Cancerelli, the former Italian Air Force pilot would make the attempt as he had logged more hours landing on the short narrow decks of aircraft carriers than nearly any pilot outside of the US Navy. Easing back on the throttle and beginning to lift the aircraft's nose slightly, he calmly asked his co-pilot for wind and altitude readings.

The plane began to accelerate then drop sharply as the skilled Italian brought the plane down to ground level in the limited space that the winding road afforded him as the plane drew near to the ground the flare-lined straight section finally revealed itself.

"OK guys all we have to do now is stay on the road and not hit any trees." Christi who was strapped into the cockpit's jump seat stole a nervous glance across at Guenther Kramer. He winked at her and turned back to face his controls.

Much later, back at the CTC HQ in Singapore, when asked what the scariest part of the whole mission was Charu was heard to reply "Sitting in a huddle with my cousin and Andrei at the end of a dark tree-lined road watching a jet plane descend at speed towards us. I was sure we were going to die. There was like no way they should have been able to stop in time. All I saw was these three lights. One on the nose cone, the other two in the extended wings. It was like something out of ET. These bright lights came hurtling towards us seemingly brushing the surrounding trees out of their way in a blast of wind."

"The deceleration noise of the engine was immense and grew louder as the huge object hurtled towards us. I tell you it can't have stopped more than 10 metres from us. We were just sat their frozen to the spot, exhausted, expecting this huge metal beast to plough through us at any moment."

Charu, despite the trauma she had been through, hadn't been exaggerating, before the drone's power had finally drained it had recorded the event and it had been downloaded and played over and over again by the team back inside the plane and again for everyone's entertainment, once they were safely back in the CTC.

The team had been back at the CTC in Singapore for three days. Vihaan's leg was healing well and although he would be walking with a limp for some time, he was glad to be spending some extra time with his cousin in Singapore. After an exhaustive couple of days of debriefing led by Li and Matthias the team had managed to piece together a blow-by-blow account of the events in Kashmir.

Penny had reached back to her old colleagues at MI6, and they had allowed her to spend a day at GCHQ in Cheltenham where she was allowed access to analyse the signal intercepts captured over the period of the battle for Kashmir. Maria had also come up trumps and managed to persuade the NSA to share some of their Satellite imagery of the events on the ground for the 72-hour duration of the battle.

It was Philippe who now stood in front of the assembled team ready to give them a digest of just exactly what had happened in the hills of Kashmir. An ever-present smile creased his eyes as he looked fondly at his team sat around the large Virtual Reality table in the conference room. "Well, apart from a few near misses and some minor injuries we are all back safely, that is the main thing."

Li, looked a little more pensive than usual as Philippe prepared to deliver his brief on how events had unfolded in Kashmir. Matthias gazed across at his old friend and boss and pitied the old Chinese man. Even though Li himself was considered persona non grata in China, he still seemed to be personally carrying some sort of hidden guilt or embarrassment for the events that had occurred in Kashmir.

"The following is a short digest of the report we have sent to the UN Secretary General. I will begin with the now infamous video clip that 'kicked off' the events after it was posted online". Unusually for the big French Canadian, Philippe spoke with a bitter sarcastic tone when he said the words kicked off.

"For those who haven't seen it, it is very distasteful but it is important for context." Snapping his fingers, a short video clip streamed on the table surface before each of the assembled team members. Charu had already seen the clip when she had helped prepare the presentation for Philippe, even then she couldn't prevent herself from feeling sick and was forced to turn her head briefly away as the clip played.

The short clip that had been streamed across almost all the major social media platforms showed in graphic detail a group of Indian soldiers in Border Guard uniforms stood around smoking before a group of kneeling and prone captured Chinese and Pakistani soldiers. The scene was purportedly filmed in Kashmir high up on the north-east border where the territories belonging to India, China and

Pakistan are closest. Philippe stood silently as the film played out.

The clip started with one of the more senior Indian guards stubbing his cigarette out on the neck of one of the captured Chinese soldiers, whose hands, like all of the captives were bound with barbed wire behind their backs. Next the camera panned over to show another younger Indian soldier laughing whilst urinating on the prone bodies of two Pakistani soldiers who had been hogtied together and lay on their sides in the dirt.

The remaining group of soldiers began laughing, then inexplicably and almost as if choreographed they drew their bayonets and began savagely hacking at the throats and necks of the bound captives. At this point Charu turned and wretched, vomiting the contents of her stomach into the bin behind her. Even the unperturbable Li turned his head away in disgust. The video ended with the Indian soldiers seeming to take enjoyment from kicking the severed Chinese and Pakistani soldiers' heads around the grassy field like footballs.

6 hours after this video was released the Chinese and Pakistani governments simultaneously declared their intention to enter Indian controlled Kashmir under the UN Responsibility to Protect (R2P) stating their commitment to prevent any further genocidal acts by the Indian governments on other captured troops." Philippe gazed around the room ensuring he had their attention.

"The people at the NSA and GCHQ both independently confirm that the video is a Deepfake, a very good Deepfake, certainly good enough to convince anyone sick enough to download it or share it that it was real. In fact, it took the analysts at Fort Meade and Cheltenham several days of work to be able to say with certainty that it was a Deepfake."

"We are confident that the Deepfake was planted deliberately to act as the trigger to enable the invasion. The assault was so well coordinated that it must have been planned and prepared months before. What followed, I will let our military expert Andrei, explain in more detail."

Standing, Andrei began to explain in as much detail as he could to the mainly non-military group how the events unfolded. "What we have just witnessed was unique in the history of warfare, we have just seen the first example of true network enabled kinetic warfare against a near peer enemy coupled with a complex hybrid operation. I will keep things simple and hopefully the graphics on the Table's 3d map will help explain how things unfolded."

Using his interactive smart ring, Andrei span the ring on his finger and a large three coloured terrain map of Kashmir bounced up from the table's surface. In the green and blue areas in the north-west and east respectively prepositioned military formations could be seen spaced around the border.

"Before we get too focussed on the events in Kashmir itself, we need to zoom out a little to see how the Chinese and Pakistanis initiated the hybrid element of the assault. The map now expanded to cover the whole of India."

"Here in the East," Andrei pointed to small flashes or explosions that were detonating seemingly randomly in small villages and towns all down the north-eastern edge of India. "These explosions are a series of coordinated terrorist attacks on local police and military bases by the Naxalite separatists. They have been running operations against the Indian government for years but never on this scale and never coordinated like this." Then, rather like viewing an old second world war planning map, the team watched as large Indian military formations moved across the map to combat the terror attacks in the East.

"Whilst the attention was focussed on the uprisings in the East, the Chinese, we believe, launched a crippling series of cyber-attacks against the Indian power and communications infrastructure. Essentially turning out the lights, cutting power to critical sites and jamming all cellular communications. We witnessed that first-hand in Kashmir when the cell phones went down and the traffic lights stopped working. Stage one, which was to divert military resources to the other end of the country was completed 3 days before the video was released."

"Now, timed precisely to coincide with the Chinese and Pakistanis declaring their R2P intent with the UN, another series of coordinated events occurred with the aim of neutralising India's quite formidable Air Force. In the north-west ICBMs, some Iranian we believe, were launched at the northern Indian air force bases." As he spoke the team gazed at the floating map as streaks of yellow light arced from southern Iran and Pakistan and touched down with devastating effect destroying the Indian air strike capability base by base in Amritsar and Pathankot.

"Now please look East if you would." Andrei pointed to the mountain-side bunkers dug out of the solid Himalayan mountains by the Chinese in the Doklam plateau that the team had discovered several weeks ago. Here we can see Chinese CJ10 cruise missiles being launched from hardened shelters in the mountainside." The team watched as again a series of yellow lines streaked across the north-east of India detonating with brutal effect at the Air Force bases at Jodhpur, Gwalior, Uttarlai, Pathankot, Adampur and Sirsa.

"Finally, cast your eyes to the ocean off the coast of Mumbai. Look carefully." They all stared fixedly at the water "Exactly 3 hours after the assault started, a Chinese CM-708 submarine rose silently out of the depths off the coast of Gujarat and targeted Jamnagar air force base with 6 CM-708 cruise missiles." This amount of coordination takes months of planning and training. Which brings us nicely to the network-enabled part of the attack."

With a wry smile on his face Andrei glanced over at Philippe. "It seems we should have listened more closely to what Philippe had to say when we were observing the Chinese, Iranian and Pakistani troop movements after the Afghan Peace Accord signing. They used their exercise 'Qūyù hépíng' (regional Peace) to preposition and coordinate this attack."

"The reports from the merchants that Vihaan and I interviewed in Kashmir spoke about Chinese command and control vehicles with many antennas dispersed amongst all of the fighting formations around Kashmir. They also reported what seemed to be multiple-launch rocket systems capable of deploying drones."

"Do you guys recall the Russian invasion of Ukraine last year. When they effectively carved off a huge piece of Eastern Ukraine creating a land corridor connecting Russian territory directly with their newly reacquired naval bases in the Crimea? Well, it took our guys," Andrei immediately reddened and briefly paused speaking realising his verbal faux pas. "Err, sorry, what I should have said was. It took the Russian military 11 months to preposition the troops, material and supporting logistics for that campaign."

"We remember all too well." cut in Matthias, "we also remember how everyone just sat around watching them do it without trying to stop them." "Exactly, well effectively we have just been guilty of doing the same thing again."

"Deliberately masquerading behind politically and legally ambiguous notions such as protecting their own citizens, the Chinese, Iranians and Pakistanis have pulled off what can only be described as a devastatingly effective and rapid conquest of Kashmir. I'll quickly run through what happened. Please focus your attention now solely on Kashmir and the surrounding border areas."

Andrei rescaled the table map and began to spin his interactive ring. "Stage one, after the lights were switched off, and the Indian Airforce were neutralised was to seal the border to prevent Indian reinforcement. This was done quite ingeniously using pre-programed rocket fired guided mine systems. They effectively laid anti-tank and anti-personnel at all the major border crossings where the Indians could possibly drive their heavy equipment over to reinforce their troops."

"For the smaller foot and light vehicle crossings they used, as we know very well from our own personal experience, small groups of tribal militias to deliver and lay the mines by hand. We got some close-up footage of the mines before we destroyed them using Snappy's drone camera."

"Penny and Maria have done some analysis and we believe the mines have time actionable fuses. Basically, it means the minefields can be deactivated after 24 or 48 hours. Which from a military standpoint is perfect if you are planning on pushing on further in the future." This last point wasn't lost on Li and Andrei noted him scribbling furiously in his little pocketbook.

"Look closely at the map now if you would. The next phase was really clever." As Andrei spoke a series of 30 large grey missiles streaked out of the hardened mountain bunkers in the Doklam plateau and navigating close to the terrain they wove their way through the valleys until the finally detonated releasing clouds of smaller explosively packed drones over the skies above each of the major military bases in the region.

Moving far more slowly but timed precisely to coincide with the horrific fire-engulfing detonations of the explosive drones on the mainly wooden barrack structures were heavy-lift military transport planes cruising from the Pakistani military bases north of Lahore laden with Iranian and Pakistani Special forces soldiers.

The team watched with fascination and horror as hundreds of parachutes began floating down from the sky just downwind of each of the burning Indian bases. "There was never any chance that the Indian forces could have done anything to stop such a well-coordinated surprise attack."

"This phase took place overnight, so yes, we have learned something else. It is not only the Americans and British that can fight at night. It seems that the Chinese also have excellent night vision capabilities. The whole affair was over in a matter of hours."

Bringing his brief to a close, Andrei pointed once more to the very far north of the map. "See here, in the Aksai Chin Kashmiri region, well, by conveniently using the super-fast rail and highway roads they have been building for their Belt and Road initiative, the Chinese have managed to stockpile thousands of tons of heavy armour, artillery and spares."

"Both Penny and Maria's review of the Sat-Int from GCHQ and the NSA confirm in some detail just how much kit the Chinese managed to move, right under our noses. As we speak all of that heavy armour and artillery is being moved by road slowly down into Kashmir to reinforce the Pakistani, Iranian and Chinese positions in Kashmir and also developing a large concentration of armour and armoured infantry right down on the southernmost Kashmiri border, just to the north of the minefields, that to my mind at least, can only be considered a potential invasion force.

Chapter Thirteen

invasion [noun]
Definition of invasion
Incursion of an army for conquest or plunder.

- *The invading armies smashed all in front of them.*

With China being a permanent member of the UN Security Council and with the accompanying all-important veto power, the Indian ambassador to the UN knew his actions would be futile, but he called for a meeting of the Security Council anyway to officially lodge India's anger and state their position.

Sat back in his chair as head of the Security Council, Guilherme Oliveira quietly mused to himself how clever the Chinese / Pakistani strategy had really been. With one ear he listened to the Indian Ambassador's tirade closely followed by the American Ambassador's fist thumping monologue about defending a true democratic nation against dictators and communists, internally Guilherme considered what was actually going to happen.

By setting a 48-hour timeframe using the time-delay minefields they had laid. The Chinese had effectively given India an ultimatum and a limited time window to respond. With India's Air Force in tatters and the might of the combined Chinese, Pakistani and Iranian militaries poised on the southern Kashmiri border there really wasn't much India could do.

They certainly wouldn't be in any position to retake Kashmir by force for several years and the PM wouldn't stand the political fall-out, if he delayed his response for more than 48 hours and allowed the combined armies to continue their march south eventually threatening the Indian capital of Delhi.

More importantly thought Guilherme to himself it hadn't gone unnoticed that the Chinese had been the first country to successfully deploy hypersonic missiles in a real conflict. He knew the Americans wouldn't dare risk the sinking of one of their aircraft carriers by doing what they usually did in such situations, which was to park an entire Carrier Fleet off the offending nation's coast.

As he stared at the increasingly reddening face of the US Ambassador, he saw in the man's eyes that the Ambassador knew this as well. With a resigned shrug, he leant forward to bring the session back to order. Although it would take many more hours of discussions, he already knew the outcome. India would bluster and complain for 48 hours then eventually provisionally cede the territory to Pakistan but commit to maintaining an interest to the territory and its Indian population in perpetua.

The only way Chuck Lewis had convinced the President Carlton P Simpson to hold a Western Coalition Summit at all, was by holding it at Camp David in Maryland. It did mean of course that the daily programme was unusually short for such a summit as the President insisted that he must be allowed to tee off at exactly 4pm at Camp David's own private golf course.

The principle reason for calling the summit was to finally come up with a workable plan for dealing with the, as yet, unresolved Russian incursion and land grab in Lithuania as well as the new developments in Kashmir.

From the US' side all the President seemed to be interested in discussing was trying to share the financial and military burden for resolving these issues. The President had come to power on a platform of using US taxes to benefit US citizens only. Each of the attending countries had been allowed to suggest one of their own agenda items.

By day three of the conference an uncomfortable atmosphere was descending over the participants. The President was quite taken aback when the Japanese PM stormed out of the room after the President in his usual brash unthinking way blurted out that it was about time the South Koreans and Japanese form their own East Asian military alliance.

That event was only eclipsed by the British PM standing up to square off with the EU Commissioner, a French Bureaucrat, who had disdainfully sneered and scoffed, when it was suggested that the UK take the lead on a European Defence Force.

Unusually it was the normally reclusive Vice President, Charles Laurel Henderson who wrested control of the summit from the disinterested President and got things back on track. In a rare show of emotion on day 3 of the summit he quietly stood and walked over to a huge world map hanging on the conference centre's wall.

"Gentlemen, if I may have your attention please. I would just like to underline the gravity of our current situation. The only word suitable to describe the future for all of the nations represented here today is irrelevance!"

To emphasise his point he struck the map so forcibly with the wooden pointer that it shattered. "Good now I have your attention I will explain my point." Pointing at the EU Commissioner and the UK Prime Minister.

"Gentlemen, after two World Wars, Western Europe has depleted all its easily accessible natural resources. You are at the mercy of Russia each winter being dependent on flows of natural gas and oil from the East. Your heavy manufacturing industry is practically nil and you rely on China for nearly all of your manufactured products."

He then turned his unsettling gaze on the Japanese and Korean leaders. "After your failed experiments with nuclear power, both of your countries are more reliant than ever on imported oil from the Gulf. This Gentlemen…"

Once more he returned to the map and nearly skewered the tiny city state of Singapore with the remnants of the pointer. "is the Malacca Strait. All of your oil has to passage through this tiny strait and at the same time navigate perilously close to the recently built Chinese artificial islands all of which, I have been reliably informed have hypersonic missiles installed on them." He glanced over at Helen the National Security Advisor for confirmation at this point. Imperceptibly she nodded back.

His next target was the Australians. "You Sir, he said pointing to the Australian PM, you may think that several thousand miles of ocean make you impervious to threat from what's going on in the rest of Asia, but you know full well that your entire economy is dependent on coal, copper and iron-ore sales to China."

Finally, he addressed the Saudi Crown Prince. "Your Highness, instead of making things better, your unsuccessful military involvement in the Yemen uprising has triggered more, not less, instability in your region.

"You have rioting and insurrection by the Shia majorities in your major oil producing regions in the East of your country and our estimates are that the current rulers in Bahrain have at most a year before they are ousted by a coalition of Shia opposition leaders." This time he turned to General Hayward for confirmation. "Indeed, I believe we have already begun contingency planning to rebase our 5th Fleet from Bahrain, further south to Oman."

Lifting his gaze from the now very uncomfortable looking Saudi Prince he peered menacingly at the assembled group. "My point being Gentlemen, due to a severe lack of joined-up strategic thinking by the West over the last 20 years we have managed to sleepwalk into this precarious position where we have been cut off from each other and the enemy controls all of the ground in between. In short, whilst we have been weakened by our geography. The Chinese/Russian Alliance has strengthened its position." The Vice President was in full flow by now and nobody in the room dared interrupt.

"The Belt and Road initiative has built goods and communication networks from Shanghai to Kaliningrad in the north and all the way through the Mongolian steppe to the shores of the Arabian Sea off the coast of Pakistan. They even have a growing foothold and military bases in Eastern Africa."

"Within this huge land mass those godless heathens, the Chinese and Russians control the natural resources and production of technology and manufactured goods for a growing market population of more than half the world's population." He glanced down at his own hand and the pointer which he was still gripping maniacally with whitened knuckles.

Breathing out hard and willing himself to relax, he lightened his tone and concluded his speech. "So you see. If we want to try and find a way to resolve the Lithuanian issue and to help our good friend the Indian President here with the Kashmiri debacle, then we need to have a strategy that is equal to that of our enemy. I suggest we spend the remaining time at this summit deciding how we are going to act in a strategically offensive way to counter this growing threat. If I may suggest we might want to stop the rot by beginning the battle for influence in Africa before it is too late."

modus operandi [noun]

Definition of modus operandi

A method of procedure.

Especially: A distinct pattern or method of operation that indicates or suggests the work of a single criminal in more than one crime.

- *It was his usual modus operandi.*

The leg sweep had caught Penny off guard. Barely able to maintain her balance she collapsed to her knees, as she raised her head her opponent drove a knee into the side of her head. The room began to spin. The attacker slipped round behind Penny and jamming a knee into her back, grabbed a handful of Penny's auburn hair and pulled back hard. With her soft pale neck exposed, Penny's opponent skilfully reached their slender arm around Penny's throat and began to squeeze.

Her world was becoming black, the darkness that enveloped her only occasionally punctured by brilliant flashes of light as her oxygen-starved brain, slowly shut down. In a final act of defiance, Penny closed her eyes and willed her body to relax.

As her body sank forward, it drew the unwitting attacker's centre of gravity, ever so slightly forward. Feeling the change in pressure and using the last of her strength Penny grabbed a firm hold on the arm that was wrapped tight around her throat and heaved her body forward twisting as she did with all her might.

The effect was stunning. Still attached to Penny by the arm around her throat, the opponent's body was thrust forwards and upwards and was catapulted over Penny's head. Her mistake was not to let go of

Penny's throat. She landed hard on the thinly matted floor, with no means of breaking her fall and Penny landed directly on top of her, her body driving down hard onto Charu's injured rib as she piled onto her opponent.

Charu gave a sharp exhalation of air and released her grip immediately, striking the floor with her hands in submission. Both girls rolled onto their backs on the gym mats and breathed deeply. Still laid on her back, Charu pulled apart her Gi and rolled up her T-shirt to inspect her ribs. Penny turned and lifted her head, glancing over at the bruised torso of her training partner. "I'm so sorry Charu I really wasn't thinking properly. You dazed me with that head strike and I was running out of air with few options left."

Charu turned her head on the mat and stared back at Penny. "No worries, I guess I was frustrated and angry and was looking to vent my anger on someone." "What, because of what happened in Kashmir?" "No, no. That reminds me I need to buy you dinner. Your training saved my life in Kashmir."

"So, what is it?" "You remember that game of Battleships I was playing online? Well, the guy started messaging me and he was getting kind of flirty." "Yeh, I remember, it was that Quantum thing. Anyway, what's wrong with a bit of flirtation now and again?" "Well, it was going OK, then he asked me about my favourite food and what type of films I liked. I told him I loved Bollywood and adored freshly cooked Keema Naan." "Mmm, delicious," said Penny, "I have just thought of where you can take us for that dinner you just promised me."

Charu chuckled softly, "Well no sooner had I told him, then he started ranting at me, I mean really abusive stuff. Look." Charu reached to the side of the mat and grabbed her tablet. Opening the chat app she showed it to Penny. Penny's face twisted in disgust. "That's horrible Charu. What's that he wrote at the bottom?" "he called me a little brown godless whore." Charu was close to tears now, and Penny put a reassuring arm around her.

"He wrote that the reason that India had still never managed to develop was because it was no longer run by white Christian men." "Fucker! You know what they say Charu. 'Don't get mad. Get even!'

Isn't there something you can do with your super hacking skills?" "Well, err," Charu blushed slightly. "Actually, you see my last comment to him?" "It's just a row of angry looking icons. What's that? A small Hindu cow, a sad smiley face and if I'm not mistaken an image of Shiva, that's one of your Hindu gods, isn't it?"

"Exactly, except they are not just little icons. Actually, each image represents a piece of coded malware. Together they create an open-source data mining tool. They are designed to worm their way onto his servers and every time a computer that is not too heavily encrypted is connected to his server it will send packets of data directly to one of my own servers."

"You naughty girl Charu" said Penny grinning from ear to ear. "I know but it's his fault right? The only problem is, I will only get access to certain data dumps and it might be a bit random, but it will hopefully be enough for me to find his identity and location and 'out' this misogynistic racist prick on social media." "Wow, talk about a woman scorned!! Let me know what you find out, I already hate him and would love to see him embarrassed online."

Life at the CTC had quickly got back to normal, with the team resuming their research tasks given to them by Li. Meanwhile Li was comfortably ensconced in his usual chair in the glass smoking cube, with, as usual, Matthias and Philippe for company. They had been spending a lot more time than usual in the cube and it had not gone unnoticed by the other team members. It was always the case when there was serious thinking to be done.

With Charu's help. Li had adapted a virtual Go board to incorporate a map of the world. He had used white counters to represent Chinese and Russian areas of influence and black counters to represent the rest. Some countries were still not covered in counters. These Li declared were the neutral countries or as Li put it. The last hope of winning the Game. He now cast a simulation of the game from his tablet onto the myriad of flat screen monitors dotted around the CTC.

For Li, this adapted Go board with its silhouetted world map represented the state of the strategic conflict. Normally such a map would be useless as geopolitical events usually moved at a glacial pace. However, Li, who had a nose for such things, felt that the world was in the midst of an endgame.

A dramatic restructuring was happening right in front of everyone and this time the usual glacially slow spread of global influence had been replaced by a raging torrent cascading and spreading with a furious intensity. Li reckoned the world would look very different from now in maybe just a year from now.

Turning to his two proteges he asked. "This is what Sente looks like gentlemen. Now we are playing against an opponent who is forcing us to be reactive. Tell me. How would you try and win this game?"

It was Philippe, the Engineer who was the first to comment. He didn't waste any time on the huge swathe of contiguous white counters spanning from the Barents Sea in Russia's far north to the Sea of Okhotsk to the east of Russia's huge land mass and directly north of Japan.

Indeed, the territory extended as far south as Hainan in the South China sea and stretched across the vast fertile plains of the central Asian steppe reaching as far as the Persian Gulf just off the coast of Iran, crossing the Caspian and Black seas and jutting straight upwards to the Baltic off the coast of the now considerably smaller Lithuania.

Ever the Engineer, Philippe focussed on the detail. Taking a stylus from his pocket and choosing green for Russia he drew 10 neat circles on the map and one long line in the Arctic Ocean. These symbols represented the Northeast passage which thanks to a fleet of new nuclear powered ice breakers, Russia could keep open for 8-months of the year.

The circles represented Russian resurgent global military presence with military bases in Venezuela, Syria, Crimea and Kaliningrad. Not to mention the six new bases under construction in the Central African Republic, Egypt, Eritrea, Sudan, Mozambique and Madagascar.

Tapping the stylus on the palette, he selected yellow for China. An unconscious decision, Matthias mused to himself, but it still demonstrated once more how ingrained some prejudices are, even in the most kind-hearted and compassionate of people.

He now proceeded to deftly highlight the Chinese naval base and effective control of the Nicaraguan canal in Central America and the five heavily armed artificial islands in the South China Sea and the military base and free port access in Djibouti. "To me these are the critical elements which we need to neutralise." Looking across at Li, who smiled and nodded, he handed the stylus to Matthias.

In a bold gesture Mathias, the anthropologists, simply drew huge rings around South America, the Arctic, Australia, and Africa. "I disagree. I think we should concentrate on winning the undecided states in these countries down here over to our side. It won't be easy considering our past colonial involvement in both Africa and South America. I mean who would you want to partner with? Look at China and Russia. One country which is running around the globe handing out huge financial development packages and building infrastructure projects with no apparent political strings attached and the other country which helped many African and South American countries finally throw off the yolk of colonialism during the Cold War?" Li smiled at both men and pulling his lighter from his baggy cardigan pocket he lit another cigarette.

"Unfortunately, I fear in a way, you are both correct. I haven't fathomed out a strategy yet, but it certainly will include ensuring the markets and natural resources of South America and Africa become accessible to Europe and North America. It is the areas that Philippe circled, that have deliberately been placed in our way to try and make this task impossible."

With his eyes firmly closed, reclining back in his chair and slowly exhaling the hot smooth tobacco smoke through his nostrils Li calmly pronounced; "We have arrived at one of those seminal moments in history. We are embarking on a new Super cycle. 30 years ago, at the end of the Cold War, the West simply stood still after the Berlin Wall came down. One famous academic even wrote an article called 'The End of History'. The heart of the old Soviet Union, Russia, was bruised and battered and too busy tearing itself apart from the inside." Li raised one eyelid a fraction to measure his friend's reaction.

"That just left China alone, who insidiously followed a strategy of hiding their strength and biding their time. Until now of course." He abruptly opened his eyes and stared at his two colleagues. "You know what the really crazy thing is that they even announced their intentions at the beginning of every 5-year planning cycle and the West simply ignored them. Do either of you know what the most recent national unifying slogan is?"

In unison both Matthias and Philippe whispered, 'China Forward, China First'. It was Philippe that stood and banged his fist in anger on the side of the glass cube wall "It was there in front of our faces the whole time and we were too arrogant to even give them a second thought!"

"Ahh, there you are, looking energized I see. How was the sparring session with Charu?" "it was, err interesting today. Charu is getting really good and it gets harder and harder to beat her." "But you did right? You beat her?" Penny's face began to flush with embarrassment.

"I still have a few tricks up my sleeve." "I bet you do" Walt said winking at her. 'Is he flirting with me?' Penny wondered, 'for God's sake woman pull yourself together he's nearly 20 years older than you. But he is kind of hot though.'

"Come over here if you would." Walt said indicating a pair of soft chairs in front of a monitor. "We're going to watch a movie together." Walt and Penny had been tasked by Li to look at global finances, particularly defence spending, and use of globally important materials used in the manufacture of electronics or space programs.

"Now, strictly speaking I shouldn't really be showing you this. An old buddy of mine back in Beijing kind of lent me a copy. It's not Hollywood, granted. It was made as part of a presentation pack for the Politburo by..." "the Chinese National Space Administration" Penny cut in.

"Wow, how the hell did you know that?" "I read the symbols on the back of the CD cover" "Ahh, yes. Well, it's a good job you read Chinese because the whole movie is in Mandarin." "Great it'll be good practice, Let's get started, shall we."

Penny settled back in her chair and silently thought to herself. 'Who the hell does Walt know in China with the connections to be able to smuggle a copy of this material out of China? Sipping her coffee, she returned her attention to the documentary.

30 seconds into the movie, Penny coughed and nearly sprayed a mouthful of coffee all over Walt. Despite the film being made in virtual reality, the graphics really were pretty lifelike. Indeed, it was the fact that it had been made in VR that caused Penny to not believe what her eyes were telling her.

In front of her on the screen a conical-shaped spacecraft could be seen departing from an orbiting space station and propelling itself with huge solar sails through space until it attached itself limpetlike to one of the myriad M-type near-earth asteroids.

The text explained that asteroids with a diameter greater than 500 metres were ideal candidates for mining as the extraction work could be safely done without fear of destroying the structural integrity of the asteroid and creating huge piles of drifting space debris. The graphic showed the spacecraft drilling deep into the asteroids surface then sucking the loose material into its cone.

Arrayed around the cone extended and oriented directly towards the sun were huge heat mirrors. It was these mirrors that managed to superheat the extracted mineral ores and using this heat separate out each element by its melting point. Silos of copper, gold, platinum and cobalt were filled without the added burden of having to transport millions of metric tons of raw ore back to earth.

The remaining superheated waste ore was injected back into the asteroid and naturally refused itself to the rest of the asteroid as it cooled. To say the operation was efficient was an understatement. Penny turned to Walt. “Is this real?” “Yep,” he replied cheerily. “You know all that time they told us they were building their own Space station along with the Russians?” “Yeh” “Well they were. Kind of, it’s just they were never going to use it for research. All the time they were building the world’s, or maybe I should say Space’s most efficient rare earth mining programme.”

Penny wrinkled her forehead. “Is that why the Chinese and Russians didn’t seem to have the same semiconductor and rare earth shortages as the West during the peak of the most recent Covid wave?” “Yep, those clever buggers are sitting on the largest stockpiles of these vital materials in the world. You name it, Lithium-Ion batteries, smart phones, electric cars, computers. Didn’t you ever wonder how they manage to produce more of these things and at far lower cost than the rest of the world put together?"

Penny's razor-sharp brain was now spinning at full capacity. "So, they would have had no restrictions building more guided drones, hypersonic missiles and satellites?" "Li told me you were a smart girl." Walt nodded in confirmation. "Do the rest of the team know about this?" "Not yet, but they will once we get this report over to Li."

Penny's brain was whirring, thinking through the strategic consequences. She also had a nagging concern in the back of her mind about the source of the CD. She couldn't put her finger on it. It was really more of a gut feeling that something didn't add up. Excusing herself from Walt, she strolled over and sat down beside Charu and Maria, who were both busy putting the finishing touches to their team presentation.

Chapter Fourteen

infiltrate [verb]

Definition of infiltrate

To enter or become established in gradually or unobtrusively, usually for subversive purposes.

- *The intelligence staff had been infiltrated by spies.*

Zhang looked over at his President. President Zhao looked drawn and tired. 'Only the Spirits know where he gets the energy from' Zhang thought. It would be a misrepresentation of the truth to say that thc pair had been locked in a hotel room together for the past four days. In actual fact, by means of making a statement and much to the annoyance of the Americans and many other UN delegates, the Chinese President's retinue had taken over an entire hotel.

The Millennium Hilton at One UN Plaza sat a mere 200 metres from the iconic ageing UN edifice on New York's Upper East side. The President and his immediate team occupied one floor with his retainers, secretarial staff and senior ministers occupying a further two floors. His security team were spread at strategic points throughout the hotel's 56 floors and it went without saying that the Ministry for Internal Security team had ensured that all rooms were electronically swept on a daily basis.

The remaining floors hadn't been left vacant. It was simply that as the People's Republic of China had effectively rented the entire hotel for the week, that they got to decide which guests could use the hotel. These guests consisted of a carefully selected cast of delegates for the upcoming UN General Assembly meeting. All of the hotel's guests had one thing and one thing only in common. This shared characteristic would become glaringly obvious throughout the course of the forthcoming Assembly.

Slipping his hand surreptitiously into his pocket, Zhang withdrew a slim paper sachet containing a fine white powder. The last several weeks had been non-stop, regular 16-hour days had taken their toll on Zhang's less than youthful body and it was beginning to wear him down. Before they had left China. Zhang had asked his personal doctor to prescribe something for him that would keep him going.

Inconspicuously he ripped the top from the paper sachet and allowed the amphetamine to slide into his tea. The small amount of prescribed Dexedrine would do its job, Zhang knew. He also knew that once this business was over with, he was going to treat himself and that new secretary of his, to a week at the Party's exclusive Sanya beach resort on the southern tip of Hainan island.

"That really isn't good for you, you know?" Startled, Zhang reflexively tried to shove the empty sachet into his trouser pocket, spilling some of the white powder onto his trousers as he did so. 'By my ancestors, does that man have eyes in the back of his head?'

Hurriedly composing himself he turned to face Zhao. "Chairman…" whenever Zhang thought he had annoyed his boss, unknowingly in English he automatically deferred to his leader and used the more appropriate title of Chairman rather than President.

"Err Chairman, I thought you were sleeping?" "Not yet, I will rest on our flight back after the Assembly, once we have achieved our ultimate goal. Zhang, come here, stand with me for a moment."

Leaving his amphetamine-laced tea to stew, Zhang dutifully stood and walked over to the window. The President was staring out of his 52nd floor window straight down East 42nd St, at the heart of Manhattan. "What do you see Zhang?"

Zhang twitched nervously, he hated these interrogations. Realising that the President simply wanted someone to listen to his diatribe, he relaxed slightly and replied. "A modern dirty city." "Hmm, let me educate you then Zhang my old friend. This city is the beating heart of America. It is this city that represents all the power and history America has to offer."

Jabbing a skinny nicotine-stained finger at the window and working from the north to the south he pointed out some of New York's finest landmarks. "The Rockefeller Centre, built in 1903,

Grand Central Terminal, 1871. Just to the left there, the Chrysler building, 1928 and that there," he inclined his head and peered a little further southwards.

"That is the famous Empire State building, constructed in 1930." The old man was in full flow now and Zhang knew not to interrupt. "These impressive buildings are nothing but vanity projects from the age of American industrialists, the Vanderbilts, Rockefellers, Chryslers, and their ilk."

"To the thousands of tourists that flock here each year they represent what passes for US history whilst simultaneously representing American power and prestige." Zhang looked across the clear blue sky at the glittering facades of thc tall stone-clad buildings. Zhao scoffed. "Can a country really call itself great if it considers something built in 1871 old?" Zhang knew his boss was being rhetorical and wisely chose to remain silent.

"And can this country really claim to be the world's economic powcrhouse when they haven't built anything of scale in the last 60 years?" Keen to show his interest in the discussion and even keener for it to be over so that he could get back to his tea, Zhang interrupted. "Chairman, according to our latest infrastructure report. With 88 skyscrapers China built the most in the world last year. And if my memory doesn't fail me the USA came second with just 13 new skyscrapers. Is this not proof of what you are saying?"

"Indeed it is Zhang, indeed it is. Unfortunately, the Americans haven't realised it. Yet. Maybe, they will think differently by the end of next week's conference? Tell me Zhang? Is everything prepared for the conference?"

"Yes Chairman. I actually wanted to discuss a couple of details with you. We have guarantees from the relevant countries that they will support our declaration at the Assembly. The only outstanding issue is the CTC." "Sorry, Zhang, the CTC you say?" "Yes minister, remember the UN has this division called the Centre for Technology and Culture?" Zhang knew the Chairman was well aware of the CTC, he simply wanted to embarrass Zhang by drawing attention to what he was going to say.

"Ahh yes, I recall, your son heads up this division, doesn't he?"

The Chairman stared fixedly at Zhang when he said this. "Err, yes, my adopted son, who as the Chairman knows I have completely cut off." The Chairman gave Zhang one of his very best reptilian smiles. Keen to get the conversation over with and to be able to return to his room with his now cool cup of amphetamine-laced tea, Zhang continued.

"Well Chairman, we have been tracking this division. It seems they have been asked by the Secretary General to investigate our activities and it seems they may be getting close to uncovering what we are doing. We have a man on the inside, an Australian who, how shall I say this, who's desire to gamble and play the tables at our Macau casinos far outstripped his talent or ability to pay his outstanding debts. Needless to say, he was approached by our security services and offered a way out of his embarrassing financial position."

"He has been feeding me CTC files. My team from Unit 61398 have prepared a nice media clip ready for release. It shows copies of reports from numerous CTC agents who appeared in both Lithuania and Kashmir as the fighting started. Even better we have a recording of the team sat around some strange holographic table discussing the European Union being carved up into tiny little independent states." Zhao's ear pricked up at the last comment.

Noticing that he had the Chairman's attention, Zhang continued. "I am sure once these files are leaked, journalists everywhere will put two and two together and be climbing over each other to infer that it is the CTC, an unelected and shadowy division at the heart of the UN who seems to be orchestrating and coordinating all of the chaotic destabilising world events."

This time the Chairman's reptilian smile broadened baring some of the Chairman's crooked yellowing teeth. Zhang had always wondered why the leader of probably the most powerful country in the world had never decided to have his teeth's aesthetic appearance improved. "I think that should be enough to keep the CTC busy and out of our affairs for a little while. Good work Zhang. Now off you go and drink that tea of yours."

"Hi girls," Penny said, leaning over the back of Charu's chair. "How's it going? I say that looks interesting." Penny was pointing at Charu's screen where a web of fine interconnected lines emanated from just north of Boston USA to multiple points around East Africa the Levant and the Middle East.

"It looks like one of those nail and string pictures my Mum used to make. You know where you hammer nails into a geometric pattern on a board then weave the golden or silver thread around the nails in neat geometric lines." Maria and Charu looked first at each then at Penny. It was Maria, for whom tact had always been an afterthought, who spoke first "You really need to get out more Penny."

"Actually Penny" said Maria as she stood to offer Penny her seat. "I think you might be interested in what we have here." "Ohh, OK," Penny took the proffered chair and sat in front of Charu's bank of monitors. Charu began sketching out what they had learned, using her long-nailed fingertip to describe wide arcs on the screen.

"So, we started investigating the terror attacks from Egypt down to Mozambique and even into Lesotho. Then extending northwards from Egypt through Israel, Lebanon and into Syria and southern Turkey." Penny's eyes followed the thin tendrils that spread like a spider's web across the screen.

"We started with a clean piece of paper and asked what connects these areas?" Maria cut in "One thing we do know for sure is that there is substantial Chinese investment in all of these countries and nearly all of the attacks have been against foreign Chinese workers and their compounds. It seems that someone, and we are not really sure who yet, is against the Chinese encroachment of influence."

Maria lazily traced her considerably less glamourous fingernails up from the tip of the east coast of Africa across the Suez Canal all the way into the belly of Turkey. "They have drawn a line in the sand, quite literally in some places. But what I see here is a ..." Penny cut in "The FEBA." "Exactly," said Maria, glad that someone else spoke her language.

Charu simply stared back at the other two with a bemused look on her face. "FEBA?" "Ohh Sorry." Cut in Penny. "The Forward Edge of the Battle Area. I know it's a pretty big area, the entirety of Eastern Africa and as far north as Turkey. But I guess it makes sense."

"Damn right it does. If you had asked me to draw a line on the map of all the areas that are ripe for takeover as part of China's One Belt One Road initiative, and also fall outside the obvious area of Russian influence, then well that's as good a line as any."

"So do you girls have any ideas who is initiating these terror attacks yet?" It was Maria that chimed up first. "It certainly isn't the US. There are simply too many different countries with different ideologies for us to deal with and anyway, haven't you heard we are taking a break from policing the world."

She smiled sheepishly as she said the last few words. Now Penny spoke, her analytical brain spinning up to full speed "OK so if it is not you guys, and it certainly isn't the UK we simply don't have the resources for that. It's obviously not the Chinese or Russkies, then who?"

"Yeh we kind of came to the same dead end," said Charu. "We searched our databases for all terror groups, Islamic at first, then we widened the search for any terror groups that operated across the area and came up blank. There simply isn't any group with an interest as broad as all of Africa and the Levant."

Now Maria cut in "So, clever old Charu here," "Hey less of the old if you don't mind." "As I was saying our resident expert had the bright idea of searching for any organisations that were common to all areas."

"We got the usual cluster of hits from the big NGOs like Médecins sans Frontiers etc and a several large Agro companies. You know big firms looking to test out their latest GMO crops, well away from the streets and fields where their shareholders live."

All three girls exchanged a contemptuous look at this comment. Now Charu concluded, "So apart from the NGOs and the Agro guys the only other group that kept on coming up is a couple of smaller scale Christian Missionary outfits. One based out of the Boston area and the other out of Eindhoven in the Netherlands."

"Yeh, but surely they don't have the scale or reach do they?" Now Maria was in full briefing mode. "That's what we thought, and as there were only two Missionary groups against 12 NGOs we figured we would rule them out first."

Like a well-rehearsed team, Charu took over. "That's where we got our break. You see all of these organisations have to register as charities and there are records of their board members filed in each domicile. It turns out they are both actually connected!"

Penny interrupted, "Let me guess our super hacker here found some breadcrumbs?" Now it was Charu's turn to blush. "Actually, it was a team effort and we had to call in some favours from a few of Maria's contacts in the US. So, the Dutch missionary Group is called the Nederlandse Hervormde Kerk, Missie voor de Wereld. That's the Dutch Reformed Church Mission for the World to you and me, and interestingly they also have a large organisational presence in South Africa."

"The other group based near a town called Salem in the US is simply called the Mission and is headed up by a collection of foundations under the title the Puritan Board." "Ok I'm with you so far." Penny said. "Well after a bit of digging through some quite dodgy looking shell companies based in the Turks and Caicos and after spending too much of our lives reading through several disks' worth of data on these foundations that support our Missionaries, it turns out that the Dutch Reformed Mission group is actually more like a local European and African arm of its sister, or should I say Brother organisation in the US."

"Right," said Penny, whip smart as usual she asked the right question "So they are not Islamic. Do we have any names or any way of tracking what they are up to. I still can't believe that an Organisation like this is capable of these terror attacks. And I can't for the life of me think of a motive?"

Maria answered Penny's questions. "We are not certain on motive or if they actually are related to these incidents at all. However, we did manage to dig up some interesting names that kept coming up as non-executive directors for the foundations."

Maria stole a glance at Charu before continuing. "Some very interesting names indeed." "Come on don't keep me in suspense spill the beans." "Well, it's actually hard to believe, we have the usual retinue of Australian and South African miners and Industrialists, properly using the connection to charity to appease their conscience and give their company shareholders something to smile about."

Looking around once more to check no-one was listening in, she continued in a hushed voice. "But even more interesting than that; no other than our very own Vice President of the USA and that creepy guy, your old boss at MI6, you said didn't even know your name when it was time for you to leave the Service." "Who C?" explained Penny. "That old bastard. So how do we follow these people?"

It was Charu that answered, "We don't really, I mean I have installed a metasearch on my machine to notify me of any major press announcements or stories concerning the people of interest. But Maria had the best idea. To follow the money. Maria has persuaded some of friends at the DEA to lean on the bank in the Turks and Caicos, telling them that the accounts were part of a wider investigation into drug shipments entering into Florida and we now have a trace on any monies being wired into or out of these accounts." "Great," said Penny instantly seeing the logic. "So we will be able to follow the action in real time."

"Anyway that wasn't why I came over actually. I have just watched a very disturbing film with Walt" "You naughty girl Penny" chided Maria. Blushing profusely, Penny retorted "No, actually it was about the Chinese Deep space mining programme."

"Oh yeh" responded Charu, stiffening slightly at the mention of Walt's name and the link to China. "Look, the bottom line is that despite the massive upfront investment costs of setting up their own Space station. Between them China and Russia have successfully been mining rare earths and God knows what else for the last year."

"Shit" Exclaimed Maria, glancing over at the now permanently evolving world Map Go board displayed on all of the common flat screen monitors in the CTC. Penny glanced at her, "what is it Maria?" "Look at the map on the screen." In unison both girls turned to follow Maria's gaze.

"So basically, from what Penny has just told us most of the important elements needed in modern high-tech production, Gold, Lithium, Platinum, copper etc can only be found in certain countries on the planet. Sure, Russia and China have some of these elements in small quantities but the majority can be found in... Well let me think."

It was Penny that interrupted first. "Well, about half the world's Cobalt is found in the Democratic Republic of Congo, a notoriously difficult and volatile place to do business." Now it was Charu's turn, "Yeh and Gold well there's a lot in the USA, South Africa and Australia. All of which are areas not currently under the influence of Russia or China."

"And finally, if I may conclude," Said Maria, with mock irritation. "Our newest most valuable rare element, Lithium. Pretty much every electric car that will be produced in the future will have this element at the core of its battery. And despite China having about a quarter of world supply, over half of the world's supply is in South America. Another of the non-aligned continents on our little Go board over there."

Finally, Charu quietly, almost to herself murmured. "It kind of defines the shape of our map doesn't it. I mean our board is covered with white pebbles covering all of the territories that come under China and Russia's regional sphere of influence. Anything else that they need to survive and prosper in this technology driven age, such as these rare earths, Well, it's quite brilliant. Instead of wasting a lot of time and money here on earth slowly persuading countries scattered around the world that they should be selling the commodities exclusively to China and Russia, knowing full well the push back they would get from the US Government and Europe. They have simply put that money into securing their own reliable and almost inexhaustible supply from space."

The three girls sat silently nodding in agreement as what they saw on the monitor began to crystalize in their minds. It was meant to be a glib throwaway comment when Penny suggested "Maybe we need a 3d map to include space and the battle for its resources?"

Neither of the other two girls laughed. Realising the change in tone, Penny spoke once more. "Actually, that wasn't the reason either why I came over here. It was Walt I wanted to speak about. My spider sense tells me that something is wrong. I mean how did he get his hands on that film. It is super highly classified?"

Maria and Charu glanced at each other; Maria nodded then they both looked at Penny who was still sat in the chair in front of them.

Charu briefly outlined the problem. "Remember before the world went mad, we watched that deepfake of Matthias' lecture at the UN? Well, that was possible because somebody leaked the root file from our servers. I'm not talking about the internet clip of the event. I mean they needed tons of extra data to be able to manipulate the file and they got it, or rather were given it by someone accessing our servers."

"Well it wasn't the only file that was sent and Li asked me to track down the culprit. I checked out all of the usual suspects, temporary staff, private security, cleaners etc, but came up empty. Then I started on our own team." Seeing that Charu was about to embark into a super technical explanation, Maria cut in. "Right, bottom line, Charu tagged all outgoing files and logged the sender and receiver. It was Walt Penny, fucking Walt."

Charu had to place a hand on Maria's arm to get her to lower her voice. "Walt has been sending bundles of files to an untraceable receiver. We now know that it is the Chinese Government." "Why that sneaky little so and so." "But wait, it still doesn't tell us why the Chinese Government would leak such an important file to him." argued Maria.

"You are right, Control never gives away important info to their agents. Unless err hold on a minute. In my old job at MI6 I was trained to understand that Information is important for two reasons. Not just for its content and meaning but for its time sensitivity."

It was Charu that put two and two together first. "If an event has already happened or is imminent then the information has no value." "Exactly! Does Li know?" asked Penny. "Yeh, he told me to lock Walt out." "Maybe hold fire for a bit. Remove access to anything super sensitive, if he asks just blame it on server outages or maintenance or some such thing. If Walt doesn't know he's compromised, we may be able to use him to pass on the information that we want them to see. I'll chat to Li and get him to clear it."

Before Penny turned to head towards the smoking cube, she paused briefly. "Say Charu, any news on our little shit of an online friend?" "Strange you should ask. I've been getting quite a bit of random junk from his servers. I can't place his location exactly, due to the encryption package. But I built a probabilistic model and the most likely location is somewhere on the East coast of the US."

"It is difficult to unpack a lot of the files, again due to the encryption, however I am recognising a pattern. Maria saw it first. We have managed to correlate a noticeable build-up of traffic and transactions including long video conference calls prior to each of the African terror attacks."

Now Maria spoke. "Before we start running away with ourselves. The fact that Charu's racist stalker happens to be connected to servers that seem to show huge volumes of traffic prior to each terror attack on its own may not mean anything. It could be purely correlational and not causal. Simple Chance."

"Or Observer bias?" Penny prompted. "You mean like we were looking at all of these events and trying to find patterns that fit?" " Yeh". "But what would be the chance that this same sort of traffic would also match the European assassinations? I did some digging and every one of the European leaders that came to power after the sudden demise of their predecessor is a self-declared deeply faithful Protestant."

Charu swung her monitor around and showed the others an updated trace map. This time showing in green all of the data traffic linked by probable source location to the known terror events in Africa and assassinations in Europe.

"Bugger me!" exclaimed Penny. "That's beginning to look much more like a pattern" On the screen the green lines from Charu's data grab all emanated from the same attack locations as the arcing red lines of the known attack sites and the Missionary Groups' location near Boston.

The different coloured arcing lines only diverged as they neared the Northeast coast of the US. And this was only because they couldn't place the source of the abusive gamer's location with certainty.

"So what do we do next? I mean who do we tell?" "Good questions Penny." responded Maria. "I guess before we start going off half-cocked with some Western global conspiracy theory. You know dark forces, a deep-state cabal, working behind the veil of democracy and religion. I guess we need some verification. I think what we have could be enough for me to go to the Secret Service with. They may be able to do a physical inspection and seizure of the actual server farm." Penny cut in "If we find that both Charu's creep and the Puritan brothers share the same servers, then it gets us a step closer.

Chapter Fifteen

separation [verb]

Definition of separation

A point, line, or means of division.

Especially: termination of a contractual relationship.

- *He believes in the separation of the races.*

Li's report to Guilherme had been short and to the point. It contained four sections. How they had gone about doing the research the Secretary General had asked for, (the method), What they had discovered and a certainty rating beside each item (the results), The future developments based on what was known (the effect) and finally recommended courses of action (policy recommendations).

Although well written and easy to read, it didn't make the news any easier to digest. Guilherme, sat uncomfortably in his office, his cold coffee long since forgotten about, digesting Li's analysis. The analysis was sound. Guilherme was sure and however uncomfortable the reading was, the Secretary General knew deep down that the narrative in the Report perfectly described what had been happening on the ground.

Sat high in the UN Building overlooking the East River, Guilherme hit speed dial on his smartphone and lifting the device to his ear spoke rapidly. "Li," "Hi Boss, did you get the report?" "I did thanks. I must say it makes for disturbing reading."

As Guilherme was speaking, loud shouts and car horns could be heard down below at the entrance to the UN Plaza. The Secretary General knew it was probably only the usual sounds that were to be heard when large convoys of delegates arrived for the annual General Assembly.

The New York locals, who at the best of times were mercilessly unforgiving of slow traffic or diversions were making their feelings known. Recently, Guilherme reflected, there had been more than just angry motorists when the world's delegations arrived at the UN. There had been growing anti-China demonstrations. It had begun with the usual 'Free Tibet' crowd but had really taken off when a hard core of professional activists began protesting against the much reported treatment towards the Uighur minority in Xinjiang Province.

Guilherme continued speaking over the cacophony below. "Thank you Li, I have no idea how I am going to approach speaking to the parties involved. I mean Christ if even half of what you have written in your report comes true then we could end up living as almost two separate global communities with only limited access and contact with each other's territories."

Li cut in. "Please Secretary General, remember, this is our best guess model. Try and see it more as if things continue to go the way they are then this is the most likely outcome. What we need to remember is that the longer these self-reinforcing actions by the Chinese / Russians and their allies on the one side and by the US and the West on the other are allowed to continue then the more likely things will turn out as you say."

"I know Li, God knows I know." Tentatively, Li proffered. "If I may, I would recommend that you delicately suggest to the US and its partners that they focus their efforts on stopping Africa falling to the Chinese alliance and to do some bridge building with the South Americans? If you want, I could get some people from my team to do a sort of high-level tour of the senior leaders in these countries. You know a sort of wake up, or awareness campaign?"

Guilherme had stood and walked to the opposite window to try and see why the UN Plaza was noisier than usual. "Normally I would jump at the chance Li. You know how much confidence I have in you and your team. But actually, the reason I am calling you is not about the report. Well, it's kind of is related."

In that instant, phone stuck tightly to his ear over the growing chanting of the crowds below, Guilherme froze. His eyes were witnessing the events but his brain was stubbornly refusing to process the images the eyes were recording. Somewhere in the back of his subconscious he registered a deafening crashing noise. Still his conscious mind failed to assemble the information.

"Mr Secretary General! Can you hear me." 15,000 km away in Singapore, Li was shouting down the receiver. He too had heard the explosions. "Li, the UN is under attack!!" Slowly his brain began to assemble the information his senses had presented it with. Fearful for his old friend Li shouted down the phone.

"Tell me what you see Guilherme." "Two, no wait three heavy vehicles. I think they are armoured cars, like the ones used for transferring cash around a city. They have rammed the UN fence line and smashed into the visitor centre. I can hear shooting. Oh my God."

Timed perfectly to coincide with the arrival of the delegate's convoy of armoured cars, the attack had been brutally simple. Orchestrated to coincide with the physical attack, the attackers posted the stolen images taken from the CTC which apparently according to the accompanying commentary were proof that a secret cabal deep inside the UN was dead set on destabilising the world. The spokesperson, who claimed he was speaking on behalf of the Anonymous Collective, said that his brave martyrs had given their lives to save the world from itself.

On the ground, it was carnage. Three Armoured cars had forced their way off the road and through the picket line of steel bollards. The first vehicle with a specially modified front bumper had been used as a battering ram to smash through the first series of bollards. It had got stuck and was bulldozed out of the way by the bigger truck behind.

Once the iron railings outside the UN visitor centre had been breached the trucks began disgorging their payload. 6 balaclavered people streamed out of each van, each person carrying an assault rifle.

It was clear by the build and movement of the masked attackers that there were both men and women within the militia force. For no good reason at all, this unusual point stuck doggedly in Guilherme's mind. He had never really perceived or even heard of women committing mass acts of shooting.

His overworked and confused brain, whilst trying to take in the scene beneath him started to flippantly play with the thought that seeing the women in the scene below was maybe just a logical extension of the Me-Too movement.

The masked militia flooded into the Visitor Centre and began shooting. Meanwhile the final vehicle had tied its recovery cable around the base of the famous non-violence sculpture, the huge brass sculpture of a revolver with its barrel tied in a knot. Revving the engine violently, the truck's wheels began to screech on the sidewalk. Slowly, imperceptibly at first, the brass statue began to quiver, then its oscillations became more violent until, it gave up its resistance to the enormous force the truck was applying.

The vehicle's tyres found their traction and the sculpture was ripped from its mounting plinth. The truck with the huge brass pistol still attached, hurriedly drove away, heading down East 45th directly towards Grand Central Station.

The two teams of six armed militia in the Visitor's centre had finished their deadly shooting spree. Magazines expended, smoke and the smell of cordite filled the usually calm air inside the visitor Centre. 27 visitors laid dead or dying between the shattered glass display cabinets and broken shelves. Blood splatters created vulgar patterns on the walls and floors.

As one, in a well-choreographed movement, the team stepped outside of the shattered building's façade back into the glorious September sunshine and onto the pavement. Placing themselves in two lines facing each other, as one, their rifles clattered onto the hard stone floor, as they withdrew their side arms and in the grossest act of defiance and vulgarity the balaclavered militia turned their own pistols on themselves and pulled the trigger for the final time.

The individual reports of the 9mm round being released and drilling up through their jaw and into the brain shattered the silence amongst the crowd of transfixed onlookers filming the event on their smartphones. The playback of the images, which took mere minutes to go viral was barely 45 seconds long.

It began with the loud thrashing sound of the huge armoured trucks as they collided with the UN's metal fences and finished with a softer sound almost like a Champagne cork being popped, followed by a group of 12 black-clad militia involuntarily losing their ability to support their body weight and slumping to the floor.

A similar fate awaited the crew who had dragged the screeching damaged handgun statue down East 45th. The sparks flew as the brass of the gun's twisted barrel ground against the hard asphalt, the statue remaining behind the truck only occasionally banging off a parked car to correct its course. As the vehicle arrived in front of Grand Central Station the heavy truck slew to a halt in front of a cordon of Police cars. This time, it appeared the Police were prepared.

Groups of Officers took cover behind their vehicles, weapons out, pointing as one at the stalled vehicle. Once again, this time without even leaving the vehicle, the driver and passenger simply raised their side arms to their heads and calmly sent a 9 mm bullet crashing through their skull and deep into their brain stems before the Police could even get close.

The fog of surprise was starting to lift from Guilherme's brain, gone were the random and whimsical musings he had had, on seeing women shooting innocent tourists. "Li, my God I don't believe it. For the first time in our history the UN has been attacked. I don't mean one of our teams in the field. No this is different. We have been attacked for what we represent as an organisation." Li was struggling to hear over the sound of the alarms. He knew Guilherme was simply processing what he had just witnessed, vocalising his abhorrence and disbelief.

"It is what I was trying to tell you Li, before this happened. You've seen the videos that have been leaked about the CTC, well switch on your TV and look at what the group who claim responsibility for this massacre are saying."

Li fumbled for a remote control, one shoulder holding the phone to his ear. Before his eyes on one of the 24-hour news shows, Li saw the live scenes of devastation. Below on the headline bar scrolled the message. Anonymous Collective claim responsibility for attack on Secret UN Cabal. Now it was Li's turn to be dumbfounded.

"NO, No, No No. The fools! They don't understand. They're being manipulated …" "Li listen, as I was going to tell you. I want your team to keep working for me in the background, but there is no way on this earth that you will be able to do your roadshow. You have been totally discredited as an organisation."

"But it's lies." "I know that, and you know that, but we aren't operating in a reasoned age anymore. We are living in a Post Truth World." Resigned to the news Li slumped back in his chair and listened.

"People choose to believe anything they want. We are no longer the good guys in the eyes of many. This fake news has spread around the world, not through respected edited journalists or from Government agencies. No, this news has spread like a cancer from host to host passed on through our shared digital DNA. Are you following me Li?"

Li simply grunted, he was in shock, completely drained. Everything he stood for, his whole career in the CTC was gone. Simply disappeared. Why? because somebody or some group decided they would spread fake news about the CTC.

"Li, you understand don't you? People today recognise their family and friends, their social groups as the only reliable source of advice. It's like we have devolved 250 years to the days before the enlightenment. Rational thought, science, reasoned debate all count for very little nowadays."

"Remember the fiasco during the height of Anti-Vax campaigns? Rational people, choosing not to get vaccinated, their decisions were not based on peer research or facts or even government advice. No, simply a meme shared by someone with their own agenda in their social group somewhere, or through misplaced solidarity with an ethnic group."

Li interrupted, "Sir, I know, I really understand. My team are calling it; the age of Information Warfare. Agents ranging from individuals selling their souls for clicks and likes, to nation-state actors are able to speak directly to you at your home whenever they want through your smartphone."

" It is like a digital cancer metastasizing in the body of the global system that will soon consume us and overtake our ability to function. Very soon we will start losing control of our actions. Our ability to coordinate effort, engage people to do good, to strive together with common purpose."

Now it was Guilherme's turn to slump back in his chair as his Security personnel burst into his office to take him to safety. He signalled with one hand for them to give him 2 mins. "You are right my friend. Now work out a way to prove to the world that the video about your team was a lie and I will try and do what I can at this end during the General Assembly."

In the queue to enter the UN grounds, only the Chinese and Russian security details remained in their cars as the gunfire erupted. The huge convoy of heavily protected vehicles waiting to gain entry into the UN stretched back two blocks to the north and another two blocks to the West.

Armed agents sprang from each of the support vehicles, guns out, ready to protect their respective Principle's. Huge lumbering armoured limousines jostled, strained and ground their gears as they hastily tried to perform 3 point turns in the tightly packed New York traffic.

Only one particularly large convoy which had all left from the Chinese occupied hotel, sat without movement. Indeed, the distance was so short and the convoy so long, that some vehicles had barely left the hotel's car park as the front of the convoy were trying to enter the UN Compound. The lead section comprised the Chinese and Russian delegations.

One eyebrow raised, President Voronin turned to his companion sat next to him in the President's newly designed Aurus Senat limousine. "Grigori Grigorovich you seem anxious my old friend. Do you not trust Russian engineering to protect us? Maybe another vodka will help."

Grigori Popov turned to face his long-time friend and President. "You know I am not a fan of all this needless violence. I prefer much subtler methods." "That you are my old friend, that you are. Indeed, we wouldn't be here today witnessing this knife being thrust into the heart of so called modern democratic Institution, if it wasn't for your work directing our Information Operations."

Sipping slowly on the chilled vodka from a lead crystal glass engraved with the Double-headed Eagle crest of the President of the Russian Federation both men gazed languidly through the bullet proof glass as the vehicles containing the First Responders hurtled past their stationary car to try and secure the scene.

Four vehicles in front of the Russian President's vehicle sat the Chinese Premier and his trusty aide Zhang. "Excellent, Excellent repeated the Chairman." Barely able to contain himself, he was clapping as only a small child would do, bouncing up and down in the large leather seat. Zhang didn't know where to look he had rarely seen Zhao Leji express any emotion at all.

To Zhang the Chairman seemed at times like an automaton. Indeed, the hardest part, Zhang thought, about getting him elected to the highest office in China was the fact that the man simply possessed no observable character. He was quite devoid of emotion.

Seeing his mentor bouncing up and down in his chair like a school child worried Zhang. Had the stress of the last few weeks been too much for the old man? 'Is this what a nervous breakdown looked like?' Zhang thought to himself. "Mr Chairman, are you alright Sir?"

Suddenly stirred from his reverie China's supreme leader sat back once more in his chair. "Sorry Zhang, I quite forgot myself for a moment. This little display that our Russian friends orchestrated here today is the perfect pre-cursor for what is to come."

Knowing when to speak and when to remain silent, Zhang simply nodded his acknowledgement. "We stand on the verge of a new dawn. China is the future. The future is Chinese." Sitting patiently behind the Chinese and Russian delegate's vehicles were a further 22 national delegations all emanating from the Chinese hosted hotel.

Due to the Security incident the main UN building had been locked down tight and the increased security checks would mean that the locals would have to endure even more painful traffic jams and delays as the delegates faced long delays in entering the main building.

This was a small price to pay. It was even more important than usual that the general Assembly sit in session thought Guilherme as he was busy being manhandled by his protection detail into his secure room.

The atmosphere in the General Assembly Hall was feverish.

From an outsider's perspective it appeared more like a Moroccan Bazaar than a meeting of the Heads of the world's governments. Figures stood animatedly addressing their closest neighbours.

The buildings own security team had only just broken up a confrontation that had turned physical between Kenyan and Somali junior delegates in one part of the large chamber than they had to hurry across to the other side to quell a fight between none other than the Georgian President himself and his Azerbaijani counterpart. The conference usually scheduled for seven days would either be over extremely quickly or would run on for more than the maximum nine days typically allowed for these events.

Notable by his absence was the US President. Dcspite having the least distance to travel he had deferred the task to his Secretary of State. It wasn't just that in his mind the boring and ineffectual conference would severely curtail his golf practice. He was seriously concerned about how the recent world events were affecting his popularity ratings.

So, as politicians the world over are want to do, he had side-stepped the meeting avoiding having to answer any uncomfortable questions about America's lack of leadership and had cocooned himself away at his Camp David retreat with his retinue of close advisors to try and come up with a plan for America to regain its advantage and most importantly for how he could improve his polling figures.

The British Prime Minister was sat in a huddle with his Foreign Secretary and the US Secretary of State as well as the EU Foreign Minister. Under discussion was an even stricter set of economic sanctions against Russia. Monsieur Blamont, a rather portly, but cheery figure had been the EU Foreign Minister for the past 3 years and as such had been deeply involved in the torturous and infamous Brexit negotiations.

Placing a condescending hand on the British Foreign Secretary's arm, in impeccable, yet heavily accented English he began to lecture the Foreign Secretary on the virtue of patience and dialogue.

"You see, Mr Secretary, your brash Anglo-Saxon approach simply won't work. This is exactly what we should not be doing.

Tightening the economic sanctions on Russia is the last measure we, the EU, would like to adopt. I would propose more face-to-face dialogue. You must remember they are our neighbours."

Almost purple with fury and about to descend into one of his legendary apoplectic fits of rage, the Foreign Secretary threw off the portly Belgian's hand and taking a step closer, stared directly down at him. With spittle erupting from his mouth he hissed. "It is a bloody good job that we are out of this Franco/German subsidy club. Now let me tell you what her Britannic Majesty will do about this situation. If it were up to me, we would be increasing sanctions on China, Iran and Russia, the whole bloody lot of them."

It was the PM who had turned his head briefly away from the US Secretary of State at the raised voices. "Now then Jeremy, I think it is I, who will be speaking on behalf of her Britannic Majesty today, not you." chastened, the Foreign Secretary took a step back from the European delegate hastily adding. "Very sorry old boy, many apologies and all that."

The PM briefly turned back once more to catch the US Secretary's eye before continuing. "It is obvious that whatever has been happening, this new boldness of Russia and the expansion of Chinese influence needs to be checked. The Secretary and I were just discussing the best way forward and we believe that we should open with the offer of face-to-face dialogue as our European partners have suggested, under the stewardship of the UN of course."

"If that fails then we are in agreement that we should stop these limited financial sanctions that seem to be having little effect and go straight to the nuclear option." The Belgian diplomat blanched at the word nuclear. "No, no Monsieur Blamont, I fear you misunderstand. Let me explain. What I, err, we mean, by the nuclear option is to close down the Society for World Interbank Financial Telecommunication (SWIFT) banking system completely to the target nations."

The SWIFT banking system was an international communication network that allowed over 11,000 international banks to quickly and securely conduct international transfers. The Achilles heel as far as China and Russia were concerned is that the payment transfer system was denominated in dollars and as the transactions were cleared by

American banks it gave the Americans jurisdiction to wage what amounted to financial warfare using this system.

"I truly hope it does not come to that. And I would have to discuss our agreement on this with our member nations." replied the still heavily perspiring and visibly unsettled Belgian Ambassador.

Flanked by two minders. It was the Secretary General himself and not the President of the General Assembly that strode onto the stage to open the General Assembly. Even with Guilherme's commanding presence on the stage it took a further 5 minutes for the fracas in the chamber to quieten down and for the delegates to take their seats.

"Ladies and Gentlemen of this Assembly." Guilherme's eyes flicked around the crowd, judging the mood. "I would like to open this year's session by taking a moment to consider the attack upon our institution and the terrible deaths of what I can now report are 27 civilian visitors with a further 7 in a critical condition in hospitals throughout New York. We, ..."

This time, recalling the report he had just read, his gaze held more steel and it was fixed on the Russian and Chinese delegates. "We, collectively as the United Nations want to make it absolutely clear that such an attack has no place in a decent and civilized world. On behalf of the United Nations of the world I would like everyone to stand and take a minute's silence to remember those that died today." The Hall fell silent as every delegate sombrely stood. With heads bowed the room fell silent.

Typical Assembly meetings follow a similar format. An agenda based around disarmament, economic issues, social and business issues is produced and the plenary session always begins with general opening remarks by member states. It is the President of the General Assembly's task to decide on the order of speakers and to control the debate. Guilherme now turned to the 65-year-old Barbadian and nodded, thus officially beginning the general debate. The old wiry Barbadian slowly stood to his feet and opened the debate.

"Delegates I call forward the representative President of Brazil to speak first." It was typical of the UN with its focus on equality to allow nations of differing power status to speak without regard to their global importance. Since 1995 Brazil had begun these sessions closely followed by the USA, after that the order of speakers was completely random, with the only caveat being that if a country's leader was present then they would speak in advance of other countries only represented by their ambassadors.

The Brazilian President's tone differed markedly from his predecessors. Typically, the Brazilian's added a great deal of value at the Assembly. A large country and the dominant political power in South America, they were what had been referred to as a Goldilocks country. Not too big to interfere in other countries' affairs and not too small, not to be listened to, when they did speak on such issues. They were generally impartial and reasoned, in their discussions of political issues.

This year, their President, a hard-line nationalist and unusually not a close ally of the current US President, began his speech in his own inimitable bullish style. To the disgust of many in the hall, he began by describing the recently slaughtered visitors as lambs and life's losers that should have been carrying weapons to defend themselves.

He moved swiftly on to denounce the interference of the UN in developing countries and even went as far as to hint that the recently released video footage of the CTC clearly showed that it was the UN itself that was at the heart of global power and manipulation. He was largely ignored by the delegates in the room. At the mention of the CTC, Zhang leaned forward and glanced to his left, nodding his head barely perceptibly at Grigori Popov.

The US Secretary of State took the stage next and almost to reassure himself, he lightly touched the British PM's shoulder as he passed by his chair on the way to the stage. How times had changed he considered as he negotiated the stairs onto the stage. Ten years ago, the USA positively owned the UN. The world's delegates hung on their every word and the US was seen as leading the world. Now, he knew many of the people assembled in the room actually blamed America's lack of inaction and withdrawal from global leadership as the reason for a rising China and resurgent Russia.

This he knew was why he was presenting today and not the President. It was always the case when something unpopular needed to be done or said, then it fell to others, not the President of the USA to say them.

"World Leaders, Ambassadors, Colleagues, fellow delegates." He retained his broad all-American folksy smile throughout his talk. Shining perfect white teeth bared. His speech which strictly speaking was meant to be limited to 10 minutes began with what had come to be known as the State of the Nations speech by those outside America. It was where the once all-powerful leader of a Unipolar world stood and told the rest of the world exactly how things were and what America expected.

This year's effort was markedly more muted. In the space of 18 months the US government had been seen to be unresponsive, unconcerned or incapable of meaningful action on no less than three armed conflicts; the as yet, unresolved annexation of Lithuania, the Kashmir incident as they liked to refer to it and the resolution by the Triparty agreement of the longstanding Afghan war. The Secretary of State knew he couldn't simply stand up and be defensive. No, his brief from the POTUS himself had been to go on the offense.

So with his wide grin still firmly fixed on his face, he began. "I am now communicating a message on behalf of the democratic countries of the world and it is firmly directed towards those who wish to destabilise the current world order. You will fail!" He slammed his fist on the dais as he pronounced the word fail. "The economic might of Europe and America, our buying power our loans our aid is what keeps this world spinning."

He raised one finger in the air and rotated it clockwise. "If these mis-thought-out provocative actions of the Russian Federation and the Chinese Communist Party leadership continue then we will have no option but to cut you off completely from global trade and wealth transfers. I am speaking of excluding you from the international SWIFT system until you have changed your behaviour."

His once gyrating index finger was stabbed violently through the air in the direction of the Russian and Chinese delegates. It wasn't simply unconventional to call out other world leaders in such a forum, it was positively against any norms of international diplomatic behaviour. The room was briefly stunned into silence. As if synchronised, of the 194 states represented in the hall, all but 24 groups of delegates erupted into heated debate and discussion.

Phones were pressed to many delegates' ears as they phoned back to their leaders asking for guidance on how the country wanted to react and more importantly if they were going to support the Americans in following through on their threat.

A more observant spectator would note the dispassionate, some would even say bored stares of the selected 24 groups of delegates who remained silent. Some would later comment that they seemed to possess a serene almost detached countenance.

Hearing what the US representative had just said, the wily Barbadian President of the General Assembly was now scribbling furiously on his notes to rearrange the speaking order. He knew that the most important issue to be addressed and that everyone wanted to hear a response to, was the growing divide between the US and the Russians and Chinese and that until they had spoken in response to the US' thinly veiled threat, the conference would not be able to move on to discuss the multitude of other important issues.

The Barbadian President of the proceedings almost winced as he called forward President Voronin to the stage. In another time and another place, it would have been viewed as comical, The short bull-like Russian President having to reach up almost at arm's length to lower the microphone to a more suitable height.

"I thank our American speaker for his candid words and also his invitation to open up focussed discussions on the real issues affecting Mother Russia. For too long we have skirted around these issues and watched as the US has squeezed us, territorially through NATO and economically, through their sanctions."

Guilherme who had been watching from the side-lines noted the Russian President's terse tone and getting the Barbadian's attention signalled to him that he should be ready to interrupt the speaker and move the conference forward if things started to get out of hand.

"I am pleased to announce that today we are changing this balance. Your petty economic sanctions," Victor Voronin was staring directly at the US Secretary of State as he spoke. "Your sanctions will affect us no longer. I have a series of announcements and I would like to invite the Chinese Premier and the Iranian President onto the stage to join me in these announcements."

Now outwardly flustered, the Barbadian President of the General Assembly stood and took a step towards the speaker. "This is most unusual Mr President." barked the Barbadian President. "I must ask you to finish your speech and return to your seat. It is I who will control today's events thank you very much." The Russian rounded on the lean old Barbadian and fixed him with an intimidating stare. The Barbadian skulked quickly back to his seat at the side of the stage.

"I am pleased to announce the establishment of the Russian Rouble and the Chinese Renminbi as the formal reserve currency of the Eastern Alliance Investment Bank." Murmurs swirled around the room. The British Foreign Secretary glowered at the Belgian EU Ambassador, and pointedly remarked. "I'm sure he means East Asian Bank. We should have used our economic tools whilst they still had some use. Because of your crowd's dithering and insistence on negotiations we are now sat here toothless and embarrassed."

As the news was sinking in, the Iranian President, resplendent in his long flowing robes was struggling to negotiate the small staircase to the stage. Very soon he stood by the side of the Russian President. Looking across at the President he grabbed the microphone and twisted it towards his own mouth. He gently stroked his beard before speaking.

"As a founding member of the Eastern Alliance bank." There it was again, the Foreign Secretary pricked up his ears. Surely both Presidents wouldn't get the name wrong? "The Islamic Republic of Iran, along with all other founding members, is formally announcing the removal of all its banks and their assets from the SWIFT system and demands repatriation of all funds stolen by the Americans. If these monies are not returned, they will be considered as spoiled currency and new currency will be digitally printed to replace the value of these funds and deposited in the new EA Bank."

It hadn't taken the Secretary of State more than a minute to piece together what he was hearing. He hurriedly sent a message to one of his aides to fetch all the information he could about this

Eastern Alliance Bank. If this bank really existed then, the US had just witnessed their only remaining political leverage tool taken away from them in a matter of a few short words.

His head buried in his hands he dreaded to hear what the Chinese Premier would say. Rubbing his face and wiping his eyes the US Secretary of State looked up once again to the stage and found the Chinese Premier stood side by side with the Russian and Iranian leaders. The Chinese leader stood composed in-between the two men. It was clear to all that were observing this spectacle who the senior partner was.

"Secretary General, Mr President, world leaders and Ambassadors. I realise that today's proceedings have been a little, shall we say, 'out of the normal', however they represent actions that have taken years to bring to fruition and represent for the parties that have agreed and hopefully for those on the cusp of agreement 'our new normal'. I would like you to bear with me whilst I introduce some people to you."

The older Chinese leader's tone was measured and he had chosen to speak in Mandarin instead of English. Every member of the audience and the millions watching the live screencast of events from their homes was spellbound. Some listened in enlightened resignation, others utter disbelief, but they all listened to what China had to say.

"Could the representatives of Belarus and the Central Asian states of Tajikistan, Azerbaijan, Uzbekistan, Turkmenistan, Kyrgyzstan, Afghanistan, Pakistan, Mongolia please stand up?" He raised his hands in an uplifting gesture as he called on the leaders to stand.

The room was buzzing with excited chatter. Such behaviour had never before been witnessed at the UN General Assembly. "Thank you, gentlemen. Now, if I could ask The Turkish President, The Bahraini Prime Minister and the delegates from Iraq, Egypt and Syria to stand with us. And finally, not forgetting our East Asian and African brothers. Could the leaders of the delegations for the Philippines, Myanmar and Indonesia please make themselves known and the dear leaders of Ethiopia, Somalia, Uganda and Malawi also stand please?"

Heads swivelled around the huge chamber, as large clusters

of delegates stood. This was truly unprecedented. The question on everyone's lips was; What did it mean? They didn't have to wait long for an answer. Coughing briefly into the microphone to attract everybody's attention the Chinese President continued. "I ask the remaining members of this Assembly to formally recognise the founding members of the Eastern Alliance!"

Zhang had done good work indeed, thought Zhao as he looked across the crowded Assembly at the islands of people stood tall and facing the stage. It had been his idea to bring all of the founding nations together under one roof in the Millennium Hilton at One UN Plaza. Having everyone under one roof had made it much simpler to deal with the last-minute membership negotiations and to seal the outstanding deals.

Despite having not spoken for ten seconds, Zhao was pleased that the Hall remained silent. 'This is how it will be going forward' he thought to himself as he pressed his lips closer to the microphone to begin to speak once more. "China, has" Zhao, suddenly checked himself. Looking around him he continued,

"Err China and her close partners have built our own self-sufficient Union. It is not a new idea, I know. Western Europe has had a once steadily growing and now quickly fracturing Union for well over 60 years." The British Foreign Minister, hackles raised, bristled with anger that the Assembly's discussion had been positively hijacked, by of all people, the Chinese. Although, he pondered, the Chinese leader did have a point about Europe.

Allowing his words to settle and be absorbed by the audience, Zhao continued. "We have built our commercial and industrial infrastructure on a scale never before seen on this planet. Our communications network spreads our influence halfway across the globe. We have our own currency union, independent banking system and access to all of the raw materials and resources we will ever need. In short, my point is that the Eastern Alliance which by the way contains well over half the world's population is, as of today effectively in charge of running its own internal affairs. From today, the West has become an irrelevance to us." It was this final phrase that later became the headline across many of the world's news bulletins later on that day.

The Chinese Chairman continued to speak as the delegates tried to digest and comprehend the magnitude of his words. "We no longer respect the right of this biased, interfering institution called the United Nations." He smiled sardonically as he almost spat the words out of his mouth, his yellowing nicotine-stained teeth bared to the crowd.

"We will no longer tolerate interference in our affairs from this institution, the EU or from the USA. In the future we will decide when and how we interact with you." All the delegates that had been standing had made their way onto the stage by this point.

Standing in a unified bloc they made for an imposing sight beneath the harsh stage lighting. The Chinese leader punched out his hand, forefinger extended as he screeched the word 'You', fine strands of spittle connecting his upper and lower sets of yellowing teeth.

The Chairman of the Standing Committee of the Chinese Communist Party didn't exactly drop the microphone as he finished his speech and turned to greet each of the delegates on stage personally with a handshake, however the effect was similar as he roughly placed the mic, back into its holder causing a loud screech of feedback to reverberate around the hall.

It was the portly Belgian EU Ambassador that was the first to speak in the American and British contingent's party. "Life is an island in an ocean of solitude and seclusion." He had stood and was surveying the scene as he gazed around the chamber.

"What are you jabbering on about man? muttered the Foreign Secretary. The British PM was first to answer, "He's quoting the author Kahil Gibran if I'm not mistaken. Don't you see, look around you." The PM cast his arm in a wide sweep around the conference hall.

It was the US Secretary of State using a photo of the events from an American news channel that brought new symbolism to the debate. "Look guys. Look closely at this photo. It's a death by a thousand cuts." This time the Belgian interrupted, "Rather apt don't you think. It is after all an ancient Chinese form of torture n'est pas?" The image which showed the crowded stage in the foreground, full of Eastern Alliance delegates tightly packed behind the dais all smiling and greeting each other warmly.

As the shot zoomed away it revealed a dark void, once full of people, now with a few small clusters of delegates, spread sporadically and seemingly randomly around the hall. Their faces in contrast to the men on the stage showed various emotions, some were shocked, others showed genuine disbelief, in a few of the remaining others, calculation and the dawning of opportunity could be glimpsed.

Back in the UNCTC, the photo from the news report had been projected onto a wall-mounted screen in the conference room. The Group were all in their usual positions around the holographic table. There was one notable absence. Walt had been quietly but quickly picked up from his apartment by UNCTC Security Staff and taken to Singapore's Changi airport where he had been placed unceremoniously on a cargo plane bound for Australia, where the embarrassed Australian Immigration authorities were waiting to take back his passport on his arrival.

The Go board with its world map overlay and black and white counters representing what had now been defined and declared as the Eastern Alliance bloc and the rest of the world had been transported from the wall mounted screens and rendered into an interactive hologram.

There, the team stood leaning over the table's surface checking and confirming as new countries were added to the EA bloc of contiguous white pebbles. Matthias called the room to order once they were finished updating the board.

As they stood back to survey their work, Matthias asked the question. "What do you see? What's the difference?" Philippe, ever the optimist, was the first to speak. Jabbing at the hologram with his empty pipe. "Well, the EA's white pebbles only cover just over half of the world's landmass and look there. The whole of the America's from northern Canada down to Patagonia are not white." "Good try Philippe," Matthias, who, by nature was much more cynical. You are right the Americas is not white, but it's not all black either.

Look here in South and Central America, look at how many

countries are grey or undecided. "He slid his hand down the Eastern coast of the America's from Guatemala down to Argentina. Now Andrei, who usually remained quiet during these briefings spoke. "Coordination of Effort." "Sorry Andrei can you expand," Matthias encouraged. "Da, Coordination of effort. The EA has a purpose-built infrastructure, they have a set of rules, ready-made and growing markets for their products and access to vast swathes of fertile land and natural resources."

Stopping to casually sip his tea, he continued. "In the military, coordination of effort is critical. Boring but critical." This caused a brief chuckle to ripple around the room. "I mean, effective communications, good logistic connections, a unified political purpose and sufficient resources is pretty much the recipe for success from a military point of view."

"That's an interesting perspective Andrei, I hadn't considered that. I was actually talking about something more simple than that. Think of the map as a picture, what do you see?"

This time it was Penny that picked up on Matthias' thought train first. "Islands" she shouted, a little too loudly. "Err sorry, Islands," she repeated a lot quieter. "Islands, remember from Go, there are the two compatible strategies of Connection and Cut. One can achieve the other. By connecting all these countries together either physically or through military bases, railways and better port systems the EA have effectively carved up the rest of the world. Now I understand what Andrei meant."

"See, they have interrupted the already ad hoc communications between the remainder and divided their resources." Admiringly Li, who had been stood back observing his team began clapping slowly as he moved towards the table. "For the last 30 years a giant game of strategic Go has been played, except we on this side, were unaware that we were even playing." The ramifications dawned on the group and Maria, ever the pragmatist, was first to ask.

"So, if I am following you correctly, Li, and if I really have understood anything from all of those Go games you made us play. We..." as she continued she cast her hand around the holographic map at the isolated land masses covered in black pebbles. "We, the non-

EA countries are now in a position where we have been caused to be reactive." "Bingo," said Matthias. "The Chinese and Russians have achieved *Sente*! The question is what do we do first, how do we react?"

The question was rhetorical and Matthias now in full lecturing professor mode, continued to explain. "We need to convince the nations in grey to come over to our side. This will not defeat the EA but it will even the odds slightly and stop them from getting even stronger at our expense."

Maria slumped back in her chair and sighed "Yeh but look at how many countries scattered around the world there are to be convinced and I don't know if anyone remembers but the CTC isn't exactly flavour of the month you know. Apparently, we are the evil masterminds plotting the collapse of the world order."

Charu, who had been silently tapping away on her keyboard listening to the conversation unfold, laughed. "You're right Maria, but we are working on that. Sorry, that came out wrong, I mean we are obviously not working on global domination, I mean we are trying to fix our reputation after the release of the video. We have a plan to neutralise its effect by inviting the Press here to us and releasing the full version of the planning video to show everything in context."

Matthias, looking slightly irritated at being interrupted, coughed quietly before speaking. "I know how we can help. At least until our reputation has been restored and we are allowed to go out there again. Look at the photo behind me if you will." The team stared up at the screen at the now famous shot of the United Nations Assembly with its small islands of delegates surrounded by darkness.

"I have had the photo enhanced and it is going to be our reference point. Now if I can invite my glamorous assistant up here to join me please?" He indicated with his hand to Penny, who took a brief double take before standing and slowly moving towards the screen.

"So what we can do is prioritise the countries that we need to influence first. We will give them a simple ranking from 1 to 5 for how close they sit to a current non-EA state and how close they are to wanting to join the EA." "Err, wait a minute Professor." Maria interjected, her voice laced with sarcasm. "The first part we can do real easy, just by looking at a map, but guessing how close they are to deciding to join them or not, well unless someone here is telepathic I can't for the life of me figure out how we can guess that part."

"You're right to disagree Maria," Matthias responded, with only slightly less sarcasm in his voice. "However, with the help of Penny here, I am going to give you the Anthropological Best Guess. We have footage of the entire event. We are going to read their micro-gestures and try and imagine what they were thinking at this time." he tapped the screen with his index finger as he spoke.

Matthias who was a world-renowned expert on reading micro gestures had been tutoring Penny for several years now. Penny's love of Asia and knowledge of China had made her more than an expert than even Matthias at reading faces and body language from Asian cultures.

"This may take some time, you are free to stay or I can call you all back later if you want." Some team members drifted back to their workstations other remained, fascinated by Penny and Matthias' skills.

"Let's start right here shall we, with the Vietnamese President." He was reasonably tall for his nation with clear penetrating grey eyes and a receding head of dark black hair. Matthias enlarged the image. "What do you see Penny." Penny stared for a moment at the image. "Scorn, rage, disgust maybe," She indicated the President's downturned mouth, as if he had just bitten into something that he didn't like the taste of.

"I think I would go along with that too Penny." "but what does it mean? Does it mean he is disgusted with the Chinese and therefore on our side or with something else?" Matthias carefully enlarged the shot to take in the full extent of the scornful President's body. "Look more closely here."

He ran his little finger down the side of the President's image. "Look at his body's orientation. At the time the photo was taken he is looking over at the Americans, however his feet and lower body are still pointing directly at the stage. His contempt and scorn is for the Chinese not the West. I'd bet my wife's left arm on it." The facial mapping exercise went on well into the middle of the night as the pair roved in a cultural arc around the world, analysing and interpreting the gestures of the leaders.

Chapter Sixteen

alliance [noun]

Definition of alliance

A bond or connection between families, states, parties or individuals.

Especially: a confederation of nations by treaty.

- *The two parties were still too much apart to form an alliance.*

Elegant, thought the President grudgingly to himself, he found himself staring at the newest member of his inner Golf clique. As the driver was smoothly drawn backwards and upwards, torquing the player's torso into a tightly wound spring, the President found himself drawn to the flat smooth belly of the player as their Polo shirt rose slightly above the trouser line during the backswing.

Of course, he would never say it to her face, after all Helen Broxton was part of his staff, no less than his National Security Advisor. He turned to the man sat in the cart next to him. "General! Huhum, General!" General Curtis Lee Hayward, the senior US Soldier and the President's Chief of Defence Staff was also having difficulties concentrating on his game today. Reluctantly he peeled his eyes away from Helen's svelte figure and tried, with no little effort, to refocus his attention on what the President had just been saying.

Despite the President's objections, Helen had insisted on playing off the same tee as the two other men and was now handing her driver back to the Caddy and climbing into the rear of the two Golf Carts, which had been especially adapted for the President and his entourage. Each cart was driven by a Secret Service agent and had been modified to travel at least 10 m.p.h faster than a regular cart.

The just over $350,000 per year costs of adapting and maintaining this fleet of extraordinary golf carts wasn't something widely shared with the US taxpaying community. Instead, it was obscured as a single line item on the annual Secret Service Presidential Protection budget request.

Obviously, it was the General that shared the ride with the President. 'baby steps' reminded Helen to herself. It had taken two years for the President to even invite her to play a round of golf with him, despite her having a lower handicap. Or maybe it was because she had a lower handicap that it had taken so long. It was an open secret that the President didn't like to play people he couldn't beat.

"Now, Helen, that's a mighty fine swing you have, however that wasn't the reason I invited you along today. If I may, we need to talk a little business." Although both carts were nearly silent as they drove side by side between the 17th and 18th holes. Helen still found it difficult to hear the President over the wind. "Chuck says we need to build our own coalition. What do you think Helen?"

Chuck Lewis the President's senior advisor and closest confident was a Washington survivor. However, Helen knew that things weren't good between him and the President at the moment, indeed things hadn't been good for some time. The President's popularity ratings were in free fall as his Presidency appeared to be incapable of reacting to the daily international news headlines.

The shouts from the pundits in the Press and on the talk shows was for a new strategy to combat the rising Chinese threat. The truth was that since the end of the Cold War, America didn't seem to possess a strategy, never mind a grand strategy.

Instead, it had simply relied on bumbling between 4-year electoral promises which sometimes gave a nod to those outside the US, but more often than not and certainly more often in the recent past, it had withdrawn money and support for the global system that it was so pivotal in engineering and focused its interest on appeasing lobbyists and in propping up its declining and increasingly outdated manufacturing sectors.

As the National Security Advisor Helen was more aware than anyone of the looming crisis. She had been reading reports from the Pentagon and the CIA on an almost daily basis for over 6 months now, outlining the threats posed by the insidious creep of Chinese and Russian influence in Africa and South America.

The problem, as always, was in holding the President's attention span for long enough to get him to understand. Well, here she was now, on the golf course with the President and it was an opportunity she was not going to pass up. Even if it meant leaning out of a golf buggy swerving around a golf course at 30 m.p.h.

Shouting over the wind. Helen replied to the President. "Sir, Mr President Sir. We need to secure our southern flank urgently." The President looked back at her with a complete lack of comprehension. "If we want to get a jump on the Chinese and Russians then the first thing we need to do is to stop them gaining any more territory and influence. And,"

Helen paused briefly and shot the General a quick confirmatory look. "as the General and I have discussed we need to start on our own doorstep, beginning with Mexico and working our way down." As they had pre-arranged General Curtis began nodding vigorously in agreement next to the President. "But, but," stammered the President, "we just got finished building a goddam wall to keep them Mexicans out, damn it. Now you're telling me we want to go and cosy up to them?"

This was always going to be the tricky part, Helen knew. "I wouldn't quite put it like that Sir. As we speak, Chuck is busy preparing some Press releases and booking some TV slots to explain our new strategy of engaging with South America on our own terms, instead of, how did you put it Sir, Yes, instead of being used as the teat of the sow that every bastard piglet in the world uses to suckle." Helen had hated the phrase, when she had first heard the President use it, but if it got her what she wanted then she was prepared to use it.

"OK, we'll try it Helen's way." said the President in response. He turned to face the General as he spoke. It was a time worn tactic of accepting the authority for someone else's idea whilst ensuring that any responsibility should it backfire lay squarely with the originator of the idea.

"I will suggest a tour of Mexico's finest golf courses with the El Presidente. Obviously, I will need you to come with us Helen and to bring your clubs. The Mexican President's wife is a keen golfer and the only chance I will have to get him alone will be if you two ladies play along behind us. I'll try and make sure we keep a couple of holes distance between us. Having you two ladies playing alongside us would only serve as a distraction."

Back at the Camp David lodge house, the two men currently most out of the President's favour, the Vice President and Chuck Lewis had been busy making the last few phone calls and putting the finishing touches to the first draft of the new US Security policy initiative. Which essentially boiled down to creating a NATO+ grouping that was going to be rebranded as the Western Alliance (WA).

So far, the grouping included the US and Europe, the UK, Australia, New Zealand, Japan, India and Malaysia. As far as policies went it wasn't that original but at least it was a safe strategy, calling on people they could already count upon to join the alliance. That was of course until Turkey had decided to stir up more trouble.

Over the past decade, the once staunchly secular Turkey had been gripped by an overwhelming tide of Islamic nationalism, the whole movement was being driven by its current President who having already been in power for seven out of ten of the past years, showed no signs at all of ever leaving office.

It was the same story the world over. Old Empire, spends years in obscurity and finally after many years of hardship, naval gazing and being forgotten about, the economy has finally taken a turn for the better and the country now expects to be treated as a major regional power again. The only problem in Turkey's case is that the world has moved on since 1922 and nobody seemed to be listening.

The Vice President turned to Chuck and with his usual demeanour devoid of any overt emotion, he pointedly suggested that Chuck would be best placed to tell the President about the recent communique from Turkey, and that it should most probably be done as soon as they return from Golf.

Inwardly, Chuck Lewis withdrew, He knew damn well how the President would react when he heard the news, but on the other hand the Vice President really creeped him out and he simply wanted to agree with him just to stop the damned man from staring at him.

Chuck was saved from the Vice President's withering glare as they both looked up at the sound of vehicles approaching the cabin. Breathing out in relief as he walked away from the VP to put on his suit jacket, Chuck looked over his shoulder and asked. "Which part do you think I should lead with. The bit about Turkey pulling out of NATO? Or the part where they threatened to give the Russians all of the telemetry captured from the F35 fighters flying in and out of the US air base at Incirlik by the Russian-made S400 Surface to Air Missile batteries they had just bought?"

As it happened the second point was a moot one. Prior to export the Russians had installed the same data-upload capability into the air defence systems as they had with the Chinese and they already had the faint, yet characteristic radar shape of the F35. They had in fact spent the past six months trying to reconfigure their system to optimise it to be able to detect, track and ultimately destroy, the single most expensive piece of flying hardware ever built.

The President had taken the news about as badly as anyone had expected and was in such a foul mood that, despite trying everything he could to deflect the President's ire by setting up Chuck to deliver the news, the Vice President had decided to take his own plane back to Washington, rather than share the claustrophobic environment of Air Force One with the President. Although, unbeknownst to anybody in the President's inner circle, he did have another more pressing reason for getting back to Washington ahead of the President.

The Church of the Pilgrims is a staunchly Presbyterian Church. Situated, less than a mile and a half from the White House, it was the Vice President's preferred meeting spot. A short drive up Pennsylvania NW, then six blocks north, the Church, which had dominated the local area for over 100 years could be found set in a wide grassed area.

It was an elegant building, its clean smooth limestone blocks were intricately carved and shaped as they combined to form the huge bell tower which dominated the eastern flank of the church. Long thin windows adorned each face of the square tower which, by design decreased ever so slightly in stepped increments as it rose towards the clear blue sky around it.

Despite being located so close to the centre of Washington's power, the VP had chosen the church quite simply because it was most definitely not one of the few churches in the heart of Washington that political power players attended in the need to be seen doing so.

The Service had been well attended and from his reserved seat at the front of the church, despite trying to casually glance over his shoulder at various points in the service the Vice President had failed to spot the person he had come to meet. As the service finished, the Vice President was deferred to and a path was cleared as he and his Secret Service entourage strode down the church's central aisle.

He was beginning to become agitated as he neared the church door, without seeing the man he had arranged to meet. The lead Secret Service agent stepped out onto the street and into the bright crisp air, scanning for threats as he did so. The Vice President forced himself to relax his tightly-clenched jaw and smile as he briefly shook hands with the minister.

He moved on towards the light filled entrance hall and stepped off the stone-laid church floor, out through the ornate wooden doors and onto the first of two flights of stone carved steps that led down to the pavement level.

Just as his feet touched the final step a wraith-like figure stepped into line beside the Vice President and began walking next to him. The usually composed Charles Laurel Henderson, Vice President of the United States of America nearly jumped out of his skin.

It took several seconds for his mind to confirm what his eyes were registering. Quickly recovering his composure as only a man like the Vice President could, he shot Erik a hard stare and unspeaking, continued to walk towards his waiting vehicle.

The front most Secret Service agent still hadn't noticed the intruder quietly walking next to his principle, the second agent out to one flank saw the threat and realised how late he was. He pulled his gun and rushed towards the Vice President. The Vice President raised a hand to signal that he was OK and the now thoroughly angry and frustrated agent returned to his position on the VP's flank.

It had been Uncle Rudy that had taught Erik one of the most impressive skills that the boy had ever learned, the ability to become invisible. The lesson had been learned during one of their long hunting trips on the plains of South Africa.

The pair had been trekking along a dried-up river bed on their way back to their camp when, as the sun was beginning to cast long shadows over the bushland, they came across a female black rhino with her calf who were stood in the midst of some scrub and thorn, tearing the few remaining succulent leaves from the lower branches.

They were lucky to be standing downwind of the Rhino, but she had already heard the two humans as they walked within 10 feet of her, talking loudly to one another. Raising her head and moving it from side to side she tried with her myopic eyes to focus on where the sound was coming from.

Uncle Rudy froze and turned his head slightly away from the nervous female rhino. Erik watched on in amazement as his uncle slowly bent his torso and began almost imperceptibly swaying in rhythm with the surrounding vegetation. Erik quickly tried to copy his uncle's slow pendulous motion.

The effect was nothing short of amazing. Despite lumbering forward to try and detect the threat, the mother rhino seemed completely incapable of sensing their presence. After nearly two minutes she lost interest in the pair of swaying objects in front of her and returned to her task of wresting succulent leaves from the thorn tree with her calf.

Much later, when the two had returned to his uncle's homestead, Uncle Rudy explained how they had avoided the Rhino. He explained that during his time in the Selous Scouts they had once received a very special training exercise conducted by, of all people an illusionist.

Nowadays we might call him a Mentalist, but the simple fact is that so much psychology is tied up with our ability to accurately see and interpret the images from our eyes, that if an object does not conform to its context or seems out of rhythm or place with its environment then, for a short time at least our brains are temporarily confused and simply ignore that piece of information. They have seen the image, it simply fails to be processed by the brain.

This was the trick that Erik had employed to inveigle himself into the Vice President's entourage. There are obvious problems with this trick, namely that once discovered the people or animals whose brains have been temporarily fooled tend to overreact in a primitive fight or flight instinct.

Once in the car, the VP immediately turned to Erik and with what for the VP passed as a warm smile briefly embraced Erik by placing a fatherly hand on his shoulder. “Erik, good to see you. I must say you gave me a start there for a minute.” Despite the privacy screen being raised between the front section of the car and the rear, the Vice President was still concerned that their conversation may be overheard.

The other reason the Vice President had made the unusually warm and human act of hugging Erik was to be able to slip a thin envelope containing an electronic entry Key card into Erik’s jacket pocket.

It had been child’s play for the gifted tech entrepreneur Ethan Macdonald to gain access to the security codes for the warehouse facility belonging to the company that serviced and leased the President’s fleet of specially modified golf carts.

Indeed, the tech genius had gone one step further and identified from the company’s lightly protected servers, the serial numbers of the two particular golf carts that had been modified specifically to be able to travel at least 10 mph faster than the rest of the fleet.

Releasing themselves awkwardly from the embrace both men sat back in the plush leather upholstery of the Vice President’s personal protection vehicle and resumed what to any eavesdropper would be considered a normal conversation. “It’s wonderful to see you again Erik, tell me how your dear father the archbishop is? I do miss his sermons. He seems to speak from God to me with a directness that no-one else does?”

“Father is fine thankyou Mr Vice President. He hopes to come and visit Washington soon.” “Hmm I hope not too soon, I think I will be pretty busy in a couple of weeks as I am sure you have seen on the TV, the President will be visiting Mexico as a guest of the Mexican President and that will leave me assuming his responsibilities here for the week.”

“If he is planning to come that week, then maybe I could meet him back at the Church of the Pilgrims in two Sunday’s time, there is a special Service starting from midday. It really will be quite the event. It is the annual international congregation of the Puritan Church Federation. We will be inviting many guests from around the Globe."

The final piece of information that Erik had required for his upcoming mission was the confirmation of the time and date of his latest target's final day on this planet. Erik already knew the location. The Vice President embraced Erik once more then pressed the intercom button and asked the Secret Service agent in the front to bring the vehicle to a halt to allow his passenger to disembark.

As Erik stepped onto the sidewalk, the front passenger window of the limo was lowered and the lead Secret Service agent gave Erik a withering look. Erik simply smiled back at the stern-faced agent and went on his way.

The real beauty about the plan that was forming in Erik's mind was the fact that after the obvious forensic investigation had been completed, the finger of blame would point squarely at collusion between the UNCTC and the Russian government. Two organisations that thanks to several trending online memes emanating from both the west and the east, were already under suspicion for interfering at the highest levels in global political affairs.

It hadn't originally been part of the plan, but the specialist piece of hardware that Erik would need to successfully terminate his latest target was very rare indeed, and again thanks once again to Ethan Macdonald's tracking of all outgoing data from the CTC, they had managed to obtain the plans to the small shoe-box size EMP device used by the CTC in their little smart buggy.

From then on it hadn't been too difficult for a fellow society member Joseph Stilltmeyer, the Austrian, who was the head of the Tirol Privat Bank, to discretely but firmly request one of the small Austrian tech company's whose lines of credit were highly overextended with the bank to fabricate two of the E.M.P devices and ship them via a circuitous route to the port of Boston, aboard one of the Iron ore carrying ships from Brother Doug Macintyre's Northern Territory mining operation.

Erik glanced down at the dimly illuminated face of his tactical watch, 17 minutes, perfect he thought, right on schedule. The warehouse complex had always been the obvious weakness in the security of the most protected man in the world. Only after the insistence of the Secret Service had the company reluctantly installed a separate compound within the hangar for the President's fleet of golf carts.

The access card given to him by the Vice President a day ago was a clone of one of the technician's cards who worked at the Marshall Williams site. The technician's mind had been on things other than the security of his wallet whilst enjoying an early evening lap dance from a particularly enthusiastic hostess prior to going home to his wife. The only human security of the site after working hours was an hourly vehicle patrol made by two highly underpaid and very bored private security guards.

Installing the devices under the plastic battery cover had been relatively simple, merely a case of inserting the EMP in-between the final battery in the series of connected batteries and the output to the motor.

Due to the amount of power drain and limits to the battery life, caused by driving the car at its maximum speed a limiter switch had been installed next to the steering wheel and the buggy was only capable of accelerating past the regular speed if this switch was manually thrown by the driver.

This bit was essential to Erik's plan as he checked for a final time the accelerometer attached to the second of the two EMP devices. The accelerometer was designed to trigger the EMP device once the vehicle exceeded more than 30 m.p.h. Erik only hoped that none of the Secret Service agents felt like taking a joy-ride anytime between the day after tomorrow when the vehicles would be transported and loaded aboard one of the fleet of C130 USAF transport aircraft regularly used to transport the President's protective vehicles and security equipment on his overseas visits and when the President was due to play his much publicised game of golf with the Mexican President at the breath-taking Cabo San Lucas Country Club.

The real genius behind his plan, thought Erik as he calmly walked out of the front entrance of the Marshall William's Golf cart warehouse, baseball cap pulled tightly over his face, was that he was going to use the almost paranoid level of security that the Secret Service employed to protect their boss against them. In fact, the whole plan hinged on them reacting in a very specific and pre-planned way.

Chapter Seventeen

golf [noun]
Definition of golf
A game in which a player using special clubs attempts to sink a ball with as few strokes as possible into each of the 9 or 18 successive holes on a course.

Sitting roughly as far above the equator as South Africa sits below the equator, Erik had very quickly felt at home on the thin peninsular of land called Baja California Sur. The tip of the strip of land that stretched south from San Diego in the USA jutted unapologetically into the North Pacific Ocean. From its southernmost tip at Cabo San Lucas the slightly warmer waters of the Gulf of California were the only thing separating this part of Mexico from the western Sinaloan coast of the mainland.

If he was being honest with himself, insertion by parachute would not have been Erik's first choice to enter Mexican territory, however the remoteness of the location, specifically chosen to offer the US President as much protection as possible meant that approaching the peninsular by land or sea would attract too much unnecessary attention. There was also the small issue that one of America's immensely powerful destroyers and several US and Mexican Coastal Patrol boats would be effectively enforcing an exclusion zone around the tip of the peninsular.

A whole five days before the arrival of the US President the US Navy had been conducting enhanced patrols in conjunction with their Mexican counterparts and on an increasing daily basis more and more roadblocks were being established between the Aeropuerto Internacional de La Paz - Manuel Márquez de León, which lay around 170km north of Cabo San Lucas and the resort itself.

The roadblocks were manned by a mixture of Mexican Federal Police and Secret Service staff. The one thing that the proud Texan President Carlton P Simpson definitely wanted to avoid at all costs was any media shots of him driving through the Great US/Mexico Wall that his Presidency had been so adamant on building.

The small maritime task force would be led and coordinated by a US Navy Arleigh Burke destroyer whose sole mission would be to sweep the skies for any threats and unleash its deadly sea to air missiles to destroy any pilot foolish enough to disobey the no-fly zone.

Two US Coastguard patrol vessels and four Mexican patrol vessels completed the naval cordon in the waters. Together this substantial force was capable of interdicting or destroying any unwanted approach to the island by sea or air.

The main bulk of the President's security team and the President himself were set to arrive in Baja California in two days' time at the Manuel Márquez de León airport. In total three C130 Hercules aircraft, the President's own Air Force One and three Chinook helicopter gunships were going to land on Mexican soil.

Erik knew that as soon as the President approached the airspace over Baja California it would be closed off to all air traffic for the duration of his visit. This would effectively create an air exclusion zone to match the naval exclusion zone.

Bloemfontein was the last place Erik ever visited with his Uncle Rudy before he left South Africa. Erik had been a keen sports parachutist from the time he arrived in South Africa, the almost perfect weather allowed him to jump with his uncle nearly every weekend. The trip to Bloemfontein had been a special present for his 19th birthday.

Uncle Rudy had called in some favours from some of the instructional staff at the South African Army's Parachute training school and managed to secure Erik a place on the prestigious two-week High Altitude High Opening (HAHO) parachute course.

Typically, the jumps course was only attended by South African Special Forces personnel, but due to Uncle Rudy's legendary status within the South African Special Forces community and thanks also to a considerable donation from an unknown benefactor, Erik was able to take part in the course.

Four Days before Air Force One touched down in Baja California, Erik was being helped to stand in the buffeting wind that was tossing the light aircraft around. He struggled to drag the weight of his pack, that was fixed between his legs as he shuffled laboriously towards the aircraft's side cargo door.

Once the final detailed check of his equipment was complete, Erik placed his oxygen mask over his face, glanced down at his altimeter and registered the altitude at 29,000 feet then signalled with a raised thumb to the only other man in the back of the plane. Looking down briefly as he stepped over the threshold all Erik could see was the wide dark expanse of the Gulf of California beneath him.

Centering himself and preparing his body for the 20-second-long violent assault to his senses when he entered the freezing cold turbulent air stream, Erik glanced briefly heavenwards and allowed his body to tip forwards out of the small plane's side door.

Body stable, eyes fixed on his altimeter Erik tumbled earthwards, 18, 19, 20 seconds, he counted in his head. Reaching across his body he pulled the rip cord and after the usual unsettling feeling of appearing to be jerked upwards, Erik settled himself into the almost tranquil descent.

Except it wasn't any typical descent. Glancing down through the gloomy night sky all Erik could see was the brooding ocean beneath him. Somewhere, nearly 40 kilometres and almost 20 minutes' flying time away, was the southern tip of Baja California and Erik's entire focus now was on using his compass, GPS, and his wits to fly his highly manoeuvrable chute to the safety of the thin strip of land.

The King Air C90 B was one of the few light aircraft capable of flying at 30,000 feet and Erik knew very well that the crew of two, the only witnesses to his presence near Baja California, would be keen to get back to the Sinaloan coast as quickly as possible. Erik had judged the flight time back with a prevailing wind to be roughly 20 minutes and knew that that they would be keen to maintain their present altitude to save fuel for most of the return journey.

He had also estimated that they would begin their descent to the runway about 5 miles out from the coast. It was for this reason that he had set the altitude-sensitive detonators attached to the 1lb block of C4 that he had left in a holdall in the cargo section of the plane to detonate at an altitude of 20,000 feet.

He saw, then briefly heard, the violent flash far away in the distance as the small aircraft with its crew of two erupted into flames just five miles short of the coast. 'No loose ends' Erik thought to himself turning once more to focus on his precarious descent.

As an experienced parachutist Erik knew the perils of landing on an unknown and uncleared Drop Zone. Indeed, this had been his principle initial objection to inserting by parachute. To land unobserved would mean landing in the least populated area he could find. His extensive map and satellite photo recce had revealed the only safe option to be a wide dry riverbed roughly 12 km north of the Country club.

He had chosen a spot around half a mile south of a dusty vehicle track and now, using this track as a feature, he began to dump some of the air from his chute and allowed himself to spiral down towards his designated landing spot.

At the very last moment he released his Heavy Pack and allowed it to dangle on a tether 10 feet beneath his legs. Instinctively drawing his feet together and bending his knees slightly Erik flared hard on the highly manoeuvrable specialist parachute and braced for impact.

He felt the pack strike the ground first then less than a second later he lightly touched down. Even before the chute had completely collapsed Erik was busy hauling it into a tight bundle. He released his parachute harness and removed his oxygen mask. Bending, he heaved the heavy pack onto his back and wore the now useless parachute harness on his chest.

Clutching the bundle of silk and lines and with a bucketful of adrenalin coursing through his veins, he set off immediately at a fast trot. It was 11pm, perfect! He thought, he had 6 hours of darkness to cover the four miles to the point set one mile away overlooking the country club.

Under normal circumstances Erik would cover the four miles with a heavy pack in less than 90 minutes, however his need to be stealthy and the steep ravines and unforgiving cactus-ridden gullies were going to add considerable time to his journey to the place where he was effectively going to spend the next 5 days hidden from view.

Stopping briefly en-route to bury his parachute and oxygen cylinder Erik arrived 400 metres away from the spot he had chosen to be his hide by 2am. Erik was very fit, however it was his years of familiarity with jogging at a steady pace over rough scrubland that made such a journey seem almost effortless.

'Now the work begins' he thought to himself. From his prone position he observed the place where he was to set up his hide for nearly an hour. It wasn't that he had the luxury of so much time. The sun would begin to creep over the horizon in a little over 3 hours and he had to be hidden from view.

Amongst the preparation activities that Erik had undertaken for this particular mission, Erik had spent considerable time painting his equipment to match the hues of yellow, green and brown that defined the local area. He had painstakingly painted a sheet of light tarpaulin and cut and spray-painted camouflage netting to be used just in case.

However, his objective for tonight was to enter the hide location without leaving any trackable marks and completely disappear into the deep cave-like fissure in the rock. The entry point would be sealed for the night with his tarpaulin screen and the exterior foliage covering the entrance would stop any casual passers-by from spotting him.

The spot he had chosen, despite having line of sight to the northern most holes of the golf course which were situated nearly a mile from his location, was actually at least a mile and a half away from any useable tracks or roads.

Once secreted in the deep cleft, with the cover from view tarpaulin preventing any light to escape, Erik risked switching on his dim red night light and carefully unpacked and inspected the rest of his equipment from his pack. Much of the pack had been filled with enough water and food for the five days and plastic bags to collect any waste.

Surprisingly for a job like this Erik carried no obvious weapons. Confident in his plan, Erik had spent the remainder of his preparation time building and disassembling a small red remote control light aircraft. This also carried no weapons and was so ubiquitous that it could be purchased on nearly every continent in the world.

"Sculpted into rugged, cactus-covered foothills crisscrossed by canyon-like arroyos, the Desert Course at Cabo San Lucas is an upcountry stunner with an ocean view from every hole. Broad landing areas and large, undulating greens framed by rock outcrops characterize this well-balanced test revered for its outstanding mix of long and short holes."

The President was reading aloud to General Curtis Lee Hayward. The General sat reclined in one of the chairs surrounding the huge conference table on Air Force One and was relieved when Helen Broxton entered the partitioned area and suggested talking through the itinerary for the next few days.

Petulantly the President dropped the Golf magazine onto the table, making it clear to Helen and the General, just how much he had wanted to continue reading and talking about golf. Reluctantly he turned to Helen and beckoned her to sit down.

"Sir, Air Force One is due to land in 60 minutes. Your Secret Service advance team report that they have secured the airport and already begun transferring a lot of the equipment by road to the south." The President issued a bored nod of understanding.

Helen continued, not knowing if she would be able to maintain his interest levels long enough for the President to understand the detail of the complicated arrival plans. "On arrival and for the transfer, You, Sir, err, rather we, will be seen to get your protective vehicle and the convoy of decoy and support vehicles will set off with a Mexican Police and military escort to Cabo San Lucas."

Helen paused briefly to confirm that the President who along with the General had consumed generous amounts of champagne and whisky on the journey, was taking in what she was saying.

"After being observed entering your protective vehicle Sir, you will alight from the vehicle as the convoy passes through a security hangar. Only the Secret Service, the General and I are aware that you will not be travelling by road to Cabo San Lucas."

"One hour later Marine One with the two of the three Chinook escort gunships will fly you directly to San Lucas arriving there 40 minutes ahead of the convoy." With a faintly detectable slur to his words, the President murmured. "Won't El Presidente be pissed that we tricked him?" "Sir, President Vincente won't be aware." "Oh, really young lady and just how the heck are we going to avoid him seeing me NOT getting out of my car!?"

It was a fair question, although grammatically flawed and very condescending, thought Helen. "We are going to play our own little game of 3 card Monty Sir. You see everyone's attention at the reception in Cabo San Lucas will be on the vehicle that they saw you entering when you left the airport."

"However, as we approach your private enclosure at the club site, the other two decoy armoured cars will peel off as usual as if to park. Once inside our area, we will place you, who arrived 40 minutes before the convoy by helicopter into the car and drive you back round to the reception."

"In the meantime the lead car will be unloading the General and myself who will look as bemused as the invited guests will, at not finding you there." The President appeared to vaguely understand the plan and nodded his assent. "Sir, If I can speak openly for a moment?"

"The truth is that both Presidente Vincente and you know that this new cosier economic and political union between Mexico and the US is a marriage of convenience and the Secret Service are adamant that you cannot be allowed to undertake a 100 mile journey by car through hostile country."

"Thank you Helen, point taken, now remember I am relying on you to keep the President's wife occupied whilst I talk business with the President. I need a win on this one, God knows what will happen to my ratings at home if I come home empty handed."

For the briefest of moments, Helen looked on in pity at the dishevelled old Texan. The brief lapse into sympathy was quickly broken as she recalled just how little time and effort this man had put into running the country, allowing its competitors to steal victory after victory whilst all he ever bloody well thought about was Golf!

Erik hadn't forgotten just how insidious the cold could be in the desert at night. Strangely it was something that he didn't dislike, he actually sought it out. When back at home between jobs in Switzerland he would aften leave the confines of his chalet and deliberately trek deep into the mountains just to experience the discomfort of the chill night air and the hard rocky mountain floors beneath his body as he slept out in the open.

Erik's whole plan hinged on him flying a bright red toy model plane towards the President's party on the Golf Course. One problem he had to overcome was that he had to pre-position the aircraft so that it would appear to head towards the Presidential party from the West and not from his position in the Northeast.

Just before dawn Erik stealthily stalked out to of his hide, careful not to disturb the ground around him. He trekked up and over the opposing hill and found an ideal forward-facing slope to position the plane on. He knew he could leave the model plane's battery powered up for at least 12 hours, as long as it was not connected to the 35 MHz transmitter that he had left back at his hide.

After crouching to carefully place the plane on the ground, Erik methodically felt his way forward to ensure there were no stones or obstacles on the take-off path of the plane. In reality the plane only required about ten metres to get airborne, but Erik wasn't taking any chances.

Particularly, he thought as the take-off would be done blind and he would only get to see the plane in the air once it had cleared the hill opposite his hide and began descending down the dry riverbed towards the 13th hole of the Cabo San Lucas golf course. Leaving the plane unattended for several hours and attempting a blind take off were two of the riskier parts of the plan, that Erik would have preferred not to have had.

Erik had derived an unusual amount of pleasure from building the plane and had got even more fun as he practiced flying it. Unconsciously Erik was aware of himself stroking the wing of the plane in an intimate gesture as he prepared to walk back to his hide.

It was then, whilst recalling his fond memories of creating and flying his first model plane, a plane he was just about to watch get destroyed if his plan went well, that he heard the sound behind him.

Cursing inwardly at his lack of awareness and professionalism, Erik froze close to the ground and slowly turned his head to observe the intruder. The scrub goat, sometimes called the Spanish goat had been lazily picking on a few short tufts of grass and now stood stock still staring at Erik's darkened crouched form.

The two creatures crouched and held each other's gaze for several seconds. The goat detecting no threat from Erik had used the time to consider either munching further on the short, tufted grass directly in front of it or maybe moving on to what promised to be far more succulent leaves on the small young cactus a little farther off to the right.

Erik on the other hand, had worked through several different attack scenarios, each of which involved him killing the goat with either his bare hands or his small pocketknife.

After running through the scenarios and discounting the messy end result of each of them Erik decided that leaving the goat alive to hopefully wander off and leave his model plane in peace was a better option than slaughtering the beast and spilling blood on the ground. Purely because killing the goat would mean leaving himself with the job of hiding a rather large carcass from the goat's owner, or the inevitable local carrion birds that were sure to be drawn to the smell of fresh blood.

Despite being watered by an intricate sprinkler system, at some considerable expense, the golf course still revealed some signs of the inevitable desert creep at many of its northern-most holes. Indeed, in contrast to the southern and western holes that benefitted from the regular cool damp sea air that rolled in each morning from the amazing blue shimmering waters of the pacific, the holes in the northeast of the golf course were positively barren.

The 13th hole, the President had read in his guide, was just such an example with only thin greens surrounded by desert scrubland and a small green patch for the tees. This par 4, 415 yd hole would have to be played carefully he thought to himself, as he was met by his Secret Service agent and Golf Buggy driver for the day.

"Good morning Scott." "Morning Sir, it's a beautiful day for it Sir." "That it is Scott, that it is. Is everyone ready?" The question was completely unnecessary, the President knew. The rest of the players including the Mexican President and his wife had been waiting around for almost 40 minutes for the US President to arrive.

Super competitive as ever. The President had been on the driving range with a local caddy warming up and probing the young caddy for tips on the how to play the different holes and more importantly about the strengths and weaknesses of his Mexican counterpart's game. The man had been paid handsomely for his services.

The only other item of equipment left in Erik's pack was a pair of Steiner 6504 tactical binoculars, light and compact and extremely rugged, they were Erik's binocular of choice on a job like this. The 10 x 28 lenses would allow Erik to observe the Presidential party as they approached the 13th tee.

Still with his feet inside part of the protective cave, Erik had slowly inched forward and now lay with his torso flat on the desert floor shaded and camouflaged by the small piece of camouflage net he had spent so many hours preparing before he departed. Staring through his binos Erik could see the occasional flashes of light reflecting off the windscreens of the multitude of golf vehicles slowly making their way from fairway to green.

Pausing his observations briefly Erik felt for the reassuring feel of the hardened plastic casing of the toy aeroplane's remote control. He just prayed that the bloody goat he had encountered last night hadn't decided that his plane would make a better meal than the juicy cactus shoots it had been eyeing just before the pair had met.

Outwardly, and to anyone not familiar with the character of this US President he seemed genuinely concerned that he had kept everyone waiting. As such he was as ebullient, effusive and polite as only a man that had climbed the slippery slope to the top of American politics could pretend to be.

Knowing the President would arrive late, Helen and the General had arrived early to meet the President, his wife and the Mexican Foreign Secretary who had been brought along to make up the 4-ball group.

"President Vincente, and Sofia, isn't it?" President Carlton, P Simpson displayed not even the faintest hint of the bigotry and racism that had caused him to campaign principally on an anti-immigration ticket for the office for which he now held. Helen, standing slightly to one side, observed the President's demeanour and wondered to herself if she would ever know what the man thought of her.

Helen's svelte figure in light checked golfing pants and a well-tailored Polo shirt was juxtaposed in sharp contrast to Sofia, the Mexican President's wife. Where Helen was tall, yet not overly so, and moved with a grace and elegance only achieved through years of strict ballet training and yoga, Sofia, who was known to the Mexican people as 'Madre de la nación' had borne seven children yet this diminutive woman with large thighs and strong shoulders still retained a genuinely warm, kind and beautiful face thought Helen. The two women had gotten along immediately, both recognizing their individual subservient roles to two very powerful and narcissistic men.

President Vincente smiled graciously, yet guardedly, at the US President and glancing around at the assembled group clapped his hands and said. "Welcome Mr President to one of Mexico's many great golf courses. I will of course be hosting you today but that doesn't mean that I will let you beat me at golf!"

He laughed heartily at his own joke and was joined by his foreign minister. The US General who knew to his personal cost the price one had to pay if the 'boss' didn't win, also managed a slightly less hearty laugh and glanced nervously across at Helen.

Taking the look as her cue, Helen briefly laughed then said. "Well Gentlemen, Sofia and I have so many things to talk about, as I am sure, have you. We will let you get started and we will be along later."

The snipers positioned on the Club house roof and a nearby hillock, both radioed into their Boss to confirm that they had visual contact with the President and that the surrounding area was clear of any threat.

Scott, the President's senior agent, briefly responded to the message using his sleeve microphone before jumping into the Golf Buggy next to the President. Despite the course being closed to any other players there were still at least 20 golf carts on the course.

The pair of carts specifically assigned to the US President were easily distinguished by their strengthened canopies. The parabolic-shaped Kevlar and carbon fibre ballistic canopies had been retrofitted to the cart and were capable of stopping small arms fire from above. They wouldn't stop sustained heavy calibre fire for long, but would buy the Secret Service agents enough time to locate and respond to any threat.

General Curtis Lee Hayward eased himself with a groan into the seat behind the Secret Service agent and next to the President. "How's the head Mr President?" asked the General. It's been better, I knew we shouldn't have started on that Tequila last night. Say Scott, you go easy on that gas pedal today won't you. It wouldn't do for the most powerful man on the planet to be throwing his guts up now would it?" Signalling with a handwave and a smile to the Mexican President that belied his churning stomach and throbbing head, the President gestured for the convoy to depart.

The miniature convoy set off. At the front, as at the rear of the convoy, was a cart packed with four heavily armed Secret agents. Sandwiched between the two President's carts were two other modified carts. One carried the electronic countermeasures (ECM) The cart essentially created a bubble over the entire convoy that blocked or jammed any electronic signals within a 120-metre radius.

The device had been used extensively in conflict zones for years and prevented remote controlled detonation of Improvised Explosive Devices (IED) close to the convoy. The final golf cart had only a seat for the driver and a trauma doctor, with the back of the cart given over to two stretchers.

Glancing through his binoculars, from his vantage point high up in the hills Erik saw the lead convoy begin to leave the 12th hole and also took note of the smaller rear convoy protecting the Mexican President's wife and Helen Broxton who sat dutifully two holes behind the Presidents.

Reaching once more to his side, he powered up the remote controller and confirmed that it had a signal with the model plane. Now for the moment of truth he thought to himself. 'Let's hope that bloody goat wasn't too hungry after all!' The small camera mounted on the front of the remote control display flickered into life and to Erik's relief he could clearly see the image of the scrubby slope displayed on the miniature display housed in the remote control body.

Erik knew that the ECM bubble surrounding the President's convoy would disrupt the 35 MHz signal to the plane and that the light model aircraft would lose power some distance before it could get close to its target.

Pre-empting this Erik had been sure to buy what is known as a powered glider, essentially it was a large-winged lightweight model plane with a small engine, perfectly capable of continuing its flight path for several hundred metres with its motor switched off.

Naturally, Erik had rehearsed flying the plane and steering it with and without power and had again surprised himself at the pleasure he had derived in flying his new creation. He felt the unusual twinge of what could only pass for an emotional attachment, as he applied more power to the plane's throttle and watched as the small red toy plane bumped along the ground and swiftly took off.

He knew this would be a one-way flight. There was nothing more Erik could do now. He also knew as he banked the model glider easily around the back of the hill to begin its long low approach to the 13th tee that all he could hope for was that human nature and well-practiced protective drills prevailed and that the President's security team would act as they had been trained so rigorously to do.

"Damn fine shot President Vincente." Growled Carlton P Simpson. He knew it was what he was expected to say however, despite the best efforts of his Secret Service in inadvertently stopping balls rolling into water features and bunkers, the US President simply couldn't best his Mexican counterpart.

He knew why of course. Just before they were set to depart for the first tee, the Mexican President signalled for the convoy to wait. Carlton P Simpson had barely been able to contain his look of shock and anger, when the very man he had paid so well to give him some coaching on the course and tips about the Mexican President's game arrived, in a neatly pressed club caddy uniform and sat himself in the seat beside the Mexican President.

Erik watched intently as the bright red model plane slowly cut through the air on its easterly path seemingly coming from the ocean towards the Presidential party. Over the last two days ensconced in his tight cold lair, he had had a lot of time, to think about his target and his principle sins.

He knew to have been as successful as he had been in the oil industry that Greed must be vying for a place as his number one sin of the US President. However, after a lot of careful reflection, he decided that the President of the United States must have been destined to die this way in penance for his sin of Pride.

After his success in the oil business the wealthy Texan's excessive and arrogant belief in his own flawed abilities were what had convinced him to run for President and worse yet fail so completely in any attempt to apply himself to the job of running the most influential country in the world.

Well, he was certainly going to pay the price for his Pride now, thought Erik as he centred the joystick on the remote control and stopped tracking the model plane through the binoculars switching his attention instead, to the small black and white monitor on the controller's body.

The Secret Service has one primary function, namely, to keep the most powerful man in the world alive. To achieve this they follow a simple, tried and tested methodology, firstly they train their agents to be amongst the best at their job in the world. Secondly, prior to any event typically weeks of background threat assessments, vetting of personnel and practice take place.

Their reaction to a threat is based on two simple actions. Number one is to physically protect the President or remove him from danger as quickly as possible. The second and sometimes simultaneous action carried out by the extensive back-up teams of heavily armed men and snipers, is to destroy whoever or whatever is trying to kill their Principle, using overwhelming force.

Erik was counting on both of these reactions as the little red plane buzzed noisily seemingly out of nowhere towards the golfers. The President had been addressing his ball on the tee and was preparing to draw back his driver to strike the ball when one of the security men on the periphery of the group first heard, then saw the small noisy object buzzing like an angry wasp towards them.

Fearing a drone attack Scott Pearson, the Chief of Presidential security's first action was to be patched straight through to the

Captain of the Arleigh Burke destroyer which lay only a mile off the coast. This was one of those career-ending calls that the Captain of the destroyer had dreaded.

As soon as he replaced his comms handset onto the cradle on the bridge of the destroyer, and despite reassuring the agent that the ship had detected no airborne threat, the Captain of the powerful destroyer quickly scrambled his crew to their defensive action stations and looked immediately to his XO for reassurance that their ship hadn't been the one responsible for allowing a flying attack drone to threaten the President of the USA.

Back at the 13th Tee, the small plane could now clearly be seen for what it was, a child's toy. It was this positive recognition that Erik had counted on to confuse and delay the reaction of the security teams. Erik had used the strategy many times before and had even invented a name for it. He called it the 'What the Fuck !!! Moment.'

200 metres and closing estimated Erik. The first of the snipers had begun opening fire at the object. As a trained sniper himself, Erik knew very well that the shot would be almost impossible to make, and that the sniper was only engaging the small plane because he was expected to do so.

The heavy boom of the large calibre rounds echoed across the fairway and reverberated far off in the surrounding hills. Scott grabbed the President and bundled him into the specially modified golf cart. The General scrambling after the security agent, only just managing to launch himself into his seat, banging his head hard on the reinforced parabolic canopy as he did so. The Secret Service agent turned on the cart, flicked the motor's limiter switch and floored the accelerator pedal.

At 80 metres the jamming effect of the golf cart mounted ECM did its job, and the whining buzzing aircraft fell silent as the connection between the remote control and the tiny plane was severed. But the brave little toy plane didn't stop moving.

Instead, it glided silently and doggedly onwards towards its intended target. By now the little red aircraft held the attention of over 25 heavily armed and trained men. A hail of copper-coated lead rounds were hurtling towards the small red plane.

Yet still the fragile plane held its course. As the plane neared its target and the armed protective security men surrounding the President began to find their mark, Erik watched, fascinated as he observed the wing tips of the little plane twitch erratically each time the plane received a direct hit.

Disconcertingly for Erik, he also seemed to experience a brief stabbing pain somewhere in his chest each time the valiant little red plane twisted and jerked in the sky above the 13th tee.

It took a lot of focus and professionalism to tear his gaze away from the plane and focus back on the President whose cart was now in the process of accelerating towards its modified top speed of 35 mph. The cart almost took off as Scott cleared the raised teeing-off area at nearly full speed.

As the speedometer reached 30 mph the little golf buggy with its hardened parabolic-arced roof was sliding to maintain grip on the sandy track. Then it happened, or rather to the few people who were not focussed on the little red plane, that despite having one wing tip completely torn off and multiple holes in its fuselage still doggedly glided towards the 13th tee, nothing happened.

Helen and Sofia who had been waiting patiently to move on to the next hole, had stopped and were busy being bustled into their own vehicles for a fast evacuation. They watched on as the small golf buggy containing the President and General Hayward careered onto the gravel path then began skidding and accelerating down the dusty track. Then there appeared to be a huge jolt in the cart and all three men in the golf buggy seemed to jump momentarily out of their seats.

As the car rolled soundlessly to a stop the three men could still be seen to be moving, however it wasn't the natural urgent coordinated movement of men trying to flee danger, rather it was that of short spasmodic jerks. Violent at first but diminishing with every second. Helen didn't know it at the time, but she was witnessing the death of the American President.

What she was looking at was deeply disturbing and Sofia lay a reassuring hand on Helen's arm. The closest vehicle to the President's cart was that belonging to one of the Mexican President's protection team, the cart had originally been stationed at the end of the track between the green of the 12th hole and the teeing area of the 13th.

With no regard for their own safety and despite the men belonging to the American party and not the Mexican party, the cart raced forward to try and help the US President.

As they pulled up, weapons drawn the four Mexican agents slowly approached the cart. Just as they reached the cart the follow-up Secret Service vehicle crested the brow of the slope and saw the lifeless figure of the President, the General and their Secret Service Boss surrounded by three Mexicans armed with silenced sidearms.

Later, during questioning the three agents that began the shootout between the US and Mexican Presidential security teams simply said that they had reacted instinctively to what they had seen. After the little red plane had harmlessly crashed to the ground some 50 metres from the tee, and had not exploded or released any toxic gas, the Secret Service agents quickly realised that the plane had simply been the distraction.

On approaching the golf cart at speed, full of adrenalin after firing at the model aircraft they had simply opened fire on the four Mexicans surrounding the President's body in the belief that the whole thing had been set up by someone inside the Mexican President's security detail.

The contact with the Mexican agents was brief. Taken completely by surprise by the speeding golf cart and completely focussed on trying to rescue the US President, they were gunned down almost instantly. Only one agent managed to raise the alarm over his radio with his dying breath.

The result of the radio transmission to the remaining Mexican Security personnel was an eruption of gunfire as both security teams began targeting each other. In a surreal event, one of the US Secret Service agents managed to get close enough to the Mexican President to hold a pistol to his head.

Ironically, the Mexicans were forced into a Mexican stand off as their President, gun pressed tightly to his temple, gestured for his men to lower their guns. One brave Mexican agent thought he could take out the American, but as he quickly raised his compact sub-machine gun to fire, he was viciously cut down by a heavy sniper round from the distant Secret Service sniper still located on roof of the club house.

Once Erik had positively identified that the EMP had discharged its lethal electro-magnetic pulse, whose affect had been inadvertently magnified and focussed as it reflected off the parabolic reinforced canopy, he slowly and carefully crawled back inside his hide.

He knew from experience that with the amount of surveillance assets, including drones and helicopters in place and the series of roadblocks which precluded any movement out of the Cabo San Lucas area, it would be foolish of him to try and move. Instead, he would sit still in his hide and wait for the next 48 hours.

The extraction plan gave him a window of 72 hours to reach the giant iron ore carrying tanker belonging the Australian member of the Puritan society. The tanker was laid up just south of the port of La Paz in Baja California and would entail Erik making night hike of 20km to the coast where using his handheld GPS he would locate a stored cache of rebreather diving gear.

Under the cover of darkness, he would slowly swim on a compass bearing out to the tanker and be taken aboard by entering one of the tanker's service craft that had been lowered from the ship's decks to notionally pick up supplies whilst the ship was waiting to offload its cargo at the port of La Paz which lay just 5km up the coast.

During the planning stages of the mission, Erik had been obliged to watch a video of the EMP device being tested on two unwitting Bonobo monkeys. As the experiment ran its course a calm and detached voice, apparently the voice of the scientist conducting the experiment, talked the viewer through what was happening.

In a dispassionate voice he explained that the high-powered microwave energy that would be passed through the unwitting monkeys would disrupt any, and all chemical electric signalling in the two animals.

On low power this would result in disorientation, irrational mood swings, chest pains and severe headaches, but on full power one huge discharge of the 6 inline batteries of the type used in the golf cart would cause almost instant cardiac arrest and severe brain trauma.

The scientist concluded, almost triumphantly thought Erik, saying that all of this could be achieved with no outwards sign of harm to the target. The real beauty of the plan was that the phenomena known as Havana Syndrome, which had already successfully targeted hundreds of US Embassy and security staff for the past five years around the world was widely believed to be caused by a secret microwave-emitting weapon supposedly developed by the Russians.

Chapter Eighteen

ideology [noun]

Definition of ideology

A manner or the content of thinking characteristic of an individual, group, or culture.

Especially: A systematic body of concepts especially about human life or culture.

- *Political ideologies differ around the world.*

The Puritan Society didn't trust anybody else except themselves with access to their deepest secrets and future plans. It was for this reason that they had bucked the growing trend to use a server farm based in a foreign country such as Iceland or Estonia which could use its own national security laws to seize the data and information whenever they felt like it.

Instead, they had decided to physically protect their Server farm inside a secure compound hidden in a deep bunker in their Salem retreat, relying instead on Ethan's ingenious quantum encryption to encrypt the access to the source of the data and thus make it seemingly impossible to locate.

They hadn't however reckoned with the misogynistic and racist tendencies of Ethan himself, who's online gaming activities with Charu had unwittingly caused him to leak information that led to establishing the location of the server farm.

Having cautiously pieced together a probable scenario, that a cabal-like organisation with links to Puritanism was using the current global uproar to try and forge its own international alliance Maria and Charu needed evidence.

The message from Maria to her old Secret Service Boss requested that the Secret Service supported by the FBI seize the server farms and if they found any data referring to shipments of people, arms or anything else that seemed unusual they should send the info directly to the CTC. In return Maria had promised to share all of the circumstantial information that they had about the group's activities.

Unfortunately coming two days too late, the first act of the new President of the United States Charles Henderson, was to order the head of the FBI to return the servers taken from the facility in Salem. Not wishing to anger his new boss the FBI head did this immediately but not before a sizeable amount of data specifically about shipments had been transmitted to the CTC.

As an addendum to the report that Li had sent to the Secretary General of the UN outlining the CTC's view on China and Russia's strategic intent, Li had, after much pondering decided to include a short section, with a large caveat as to its accuracy, about the possible link between a western Protestant organisation and both possible terror attacks in Africa and maybe even extending as far as explaining the reason behind the sudden demise of several of Europe's most powerful leaders and the statistically unusually high amount of new European leaders that just happened to also be devout Protestants.

At the same time as Maria had reached out to the Secret Service and Li had sent his report to the UN Secretary General, Penny had used up the last of her credits with her former employer MI6, by asking someone she believed to be a friend, to discretely track a specific medium-sized 40,000-ton freighter.

She knew precious little about the ship other than that should be leaving the port of Durban and had scheduled stops at ports serving Mozambique Tanzania, Kenya and Uganda. Apart from approximate departure dates she only had a suggested name of an African mining company as the probable vessel's owner.

A late addition, because 'obviously' nobody could have foreseen the horrific events that ended with the murder of the President of the United States, to the formal electronic diary of the acting President of the United States was a private service of mourning and reflection, to be held at the Church of the Pilgrims in Washington. The formal State funeral of the late President was to be held in just over 2-week's time.

Coincidently, if one had been able to read the then Vice President's private diary, one would have observed that the Vice President already had an appointment pencilled in at the same church on the same day to be present at the annual international congregation of the Puritan Church Federation.

The Church only contained a very select and small congregation. The Service held by Archbishop De Vries was a short sombre event. The archbishop only briefly spoke about the former President and he seemed oddly to give more of his sermon over to the understanding of God's grace and how magnanimous he was in accepting all into his Kingdom, despite their past transgressions on earth.

After the conclusion of the unusually brief Sermon, a private communion had been organised in the church's crypt. Charles Laurel Henderson's Security team had long ago stopped wondering about their pious boss's affixation with the church and after a routine sweep of the sealed crypt buried deep underneath the main church, with only one entry and egress point they were content to allow their principle unescorted into the service with the other 12 invited congregation members, all of which who had undergone a voluntary sweep with a handheld metal detector before entering the Church.

Holding his pince nez deftly between the thumb and forefinger of his left hand and grasping the now President elect's hand firmly with his right hand. Sir David Simmingford-Bell had to crouch slightly in the dimly illuminated crypt of the old church as he drew his head forwards.

"Bloody well-done Charles old chap, many congratulations." The man looked back at the director of British Intelligence, known to all as 'C' he was one of the few men he actually admired, and for the first time in a very long time smiled. "Thank you Brother David, Thank you for everything you have done to get us this far."

The Head of British intelligence nodded briefly before adding. "Just to let you know those people at the UNCTC have been sniffing around our operation in Africa. They sent a back-channel request through to one of my team to track and follow the freighter we will be sending up the coast."

The President to be, raised an eyebrow and stiffened slightly. Noting the change in demeanour, C continued quickly. "Oh there's absolutely nothing to worry about old boy. I've intervened. I sent a missive this morning to the person in question explaining that we had no knowledge and couldn't locate any such vessel and reminding her that she is no longer part of our Service."

"Excellent, I knew I could rely on your steady hand brother. I feel the whole exercise may be a moot point anyway. In a couple of days once the journalists get their greedy little snouts into the technical information and the clear link it shows between the CTC and the Russians, that we are carelessly going to leak about the assault on our dear departed President, I doubt anybody will be queuing up to support the CTC, let alone take anything they say seriously."

The first use of the term 'Domino Effect' was attributed to Dwight D Eisenhower in 1954. He used the term to describe how the fall of Indochina, modern day Vietnam, would create an unstoppable ripple effect as one country after another fell under the influence of Communism.

Li, had assembled the entire CTC Staff based at the Singapore HQ and had been talking for over an hour without stopping. This in itself was unusual and pointed to just how angry, bewildered and frustrated he and his team had become with the sustained online Fake News discreditation operation being waged against the CTC.

"Today I believe we could accurately use the same Domino effect expression to describe the way country after country are deciding to join the Eastern Alliance." He paused to sip at his water.

As he did this, Matthias, for whom tact and diplomacy had never been high on his list of priorities, said "It also quite accurately describes the rate at which we are losing friends and support." A couple of the more cynically minded members of the team briefly laughed, but quickly stopped as they took in the stony-faced silence around them.

"Sorry, Matthias, did you have something to add?" Li glared pointedly at his long-time friend and de facto second in command. "Err, my apologies Li" Matthias rose, and after pulling his trousers up and smoothing down his crumpled shirt he spoke.

"Sorry, Li, we have all been under a lot of pressure over the last couple of weeks. I just wanted to lighten the mood for a moment." Li took a long and obvious intake of breath before he continued. "OK, just to make sure we are all on the same page I will once again outline our current position and define what we are going to try and do to survive it." Li now had everybody's fullest attention.

"As most of you already are aware, our former Australian colleague Walt Sanderson, decided he would leak sensitive CTC files to the Chinese. Admittedly they were blackmailing him over a rather large gambling debt that he had run up in Macau. These files have been used by the PLA cyber warfare units as deliberate propaganda tools to try and discredit and thus neutralise the influence of our organisation and more importantly to try and paint us as some sort of dark force at the centre of global politics."

"Charu's investigations have revealed the Deepfake Hologram of Matthias talking was re-rendered and distributed by the Chinese. Images of our holographic table laid out like a Go board which reportedly proved that we had a structured plan to fracture the current world order were being manipulated by hackers based in St Petersburg."

"Finally, as those of you who have been following the recent events involving the assassination of the US President will have seen social media posts showing our own invention the Drone buggy, which I believe some of you referred to as Snappy next to a Golf Buggy. Supposedly pointing to the fact that the EMP device that killed the US President was placed in the golf cart by us."

"It is true that the design is remarkably similar to our design, and as Charu can forensically prove, the files with the schematics to the buggy and therefore the EMP device were amongst those files uploaded by Mr Sanderson to the Chinese Government and their friends."

Li glanced quickly at his watch. "Philippe, could you take over please? I have a call with the Secretary General in two minutes." Philippe rose and stood before the assembled group. He looked over his shoulder to ensure that Li had left the room, then spoke.

"Guys before I get into our plan, I just thought I should share with you why Li is uptight at the moment. Every member of the EA has withdrawn its funding for the United Nations, the list grows by the day and as you can imagine the fight for resources is incredible at the moment. Add to that the fact that we are not currently flavour of the month, well, in short, Li's call with the Secretary General is to discuss our future as an organisation." Philippe, spoke as all good engineers do in a calm and precise way, however the words and sentiment were not lost on the assembled crowd.

"You are all well aware of what is happening in the world and the rate at which countries are deciding or being coerced into joining the Eastern Alliance?" The question was rhetorical but it gave Philippe a chance to glance around the room to ensure he had everyone's attention. "Remarkably, the recent events have presented us with an opportunity." Philippe was greeted by startled looks around the room. He twisted his own interactive ring on his finger and the team's interactive tabletop sprung to life with a scale relief map of Africa displayed on its surface.

Trapped between the two ossifying blocs of the Eastern Alliance and the much weaker and hastily cobbled together Western Alliance, Africa had now become the focus of the world's attention. Working down the eastern edge of the map five countries had been highlighted in red.

Philippe continued. "From the top then; Egypt, Ethiopia, Somalia, Uganda and Malawi have all already signed up for the EA. Our focus and that of the WA is to try and stop any more African countries joining the EA. Africa is essential to the survival of the Western Alliance. Oil, rare earths, precious metals and in time, it is hoped a lot of the world's calories will come from Africa."

With a weary look on his face, it was Matthias who raised his hand and interrupted. "So we are going to carve up Africa again are we? You see all those remarkably straight lines on that map over there? Well, that's what happened the last time the colonial powers tried to carve up Africa, genocide, apartheid, starvation, pollution, corruption, war and terrorism! This is the legacy of our interference in Africa!" Ruddy cheeked and slightly breathless after his outburst, Matthias glowered at the assembled group.

Philippe allowed him to vent and secretly wondered if his old friend had succumbed to the intense pressure they had all been under and begun drinking again. Or was he witnessing the intense rage that only a Professor of Anthropology such as Matthias, was capable of. A man who had dedicated his entire career to highlighting the plight of numerous indigenous groups that had been marginalised by larger more 'developed' and oppressive cultures and nations.

The genial giant Philippe, smiled a sincere and supportive smile at his old friend and began to speak again. "I couldn't agree more my friend. I would like to say that this time is different, but I guess history will be our judge." With Philippe's words echoing in their heads and following Matthias' outburst the mood in the room had become markedly more serious.

"I will keep this short as we have much to do. The framework for what will in time become the largest geoengineering project the world has ever witnessed is simple. This time the United Nations, which did not exist during colonial times, will be at the heart of the project. There will be no burdensome loans placed on the recipient countries. In fact, our aim is to build the resources and infrastructure using grants from major donor countries and global industrial companies."

"Err hold on a minute there Philippe." In her usual abrupt tone, it was Maria who had interrupted Philippe's presentation. Unruffled as ever Philippe responded. "Sorry Maria, do you have a question?" "Sure, so we are just coming out of a global pandemic, right? Interest rates are rocketing up and nearly every major country in the world is in debt up to its eyeballs after splashing so much cash on welfare programmes and vaccines. How in the hell are we now suddenly going to start donating billions to Africa?" A murmur of support rippled around the assembled group.

"Oh, that's easy Maria." If you didn't know Philippe, you would think he was being flippant or condescending. However, he was actually being perfectly serious. "You see, it's exactly because governments have had their wallets open for so long, pumping money into the economy, that the prospect of donating a couple of billion here and there now seems more achievable."

"Secondly, every major country in the world signed up to the Glasgow Climate Change goals, then promptly did nothing about it as they struggled to deal with the post-virus economic hangover and stalled industrial output. However, now with all that wasted time, the pressure to do something to slow down or reverse climate change is more intense than ever."

"If that is not enough of a motivator then consider all those huge conglomerates who have seen their potential market share slashed overnight as they, just like the individual countries have had to make hard decisions about which group they want to continue trading with. The recent formation EA means that keeping Africa, or as much of it as possible, aligned to the Western Alliance has become a matter of long-term survival for millions of Americans and Europeans."

This time it was Penny that spoke up. "Don't keep us in suspense Philippe what is this mega project you are talking about?" Matthias cut in before Philippe could respond. "You are not seriously talking about regreening the Sahara are you?" "Actually yes, Matthias. Would you like to explain the concept to the rest of the team?"

Still with a mildly sarcastic edge to his voice, Matthias stood and began to outline the project. "Every 15,000 years or so, believe it or not, the Sahara and Sahel region revert to a more temperate climate and the region actually evolves into a huge fertile belt capable of supporting large animals."

"Yes! It's hard to believe isn't it? But if you had been living anywhere in the northern part of Africa 11,000 years ago then you may have been eating mangoes, melons and coconuts for breakfast, picked from the lush vegetation near your village." by now the room had fallen completely silent.

"Since the late 1970s scientists, normally on the fringe of the mainstream, I might add, have been talking about grand schemes to stop the Sahara from spreading and even about reclaiming useable fertile land from the desert." The sarcastic edge to his voice had now disappeared, to be replaced by his more usual informative and beguiling style. Like nearly everyone in his profession Matthias grew in stature and passion once he realised that he had a group of people hooked onto what he had to say.

"But it has never been done, you see. I personally have large reservations as to whether it could ever be done. We know small-scale projects like this have been tried for a couple of decades before.

But a project of this scale!"

Matthias threw open his arms encompassing the shimmering surface of the holographic table in one broad sweep. "A project like this requires momentum and long-term investment on a scale that dwarves anything that mankind has so far achieved in our short and rather err, destructive history."

Picking up on the discrete nod from Philippe, Matthias sat back in his chair, still gazing fixedly at the table's surface. "Ok, well Matthias is correct about one point, the mega project is to regreen the Sahara. In time all 3.3 million square miles of it. Yeh that's right, 3.3 million square miles, that's about the size of Brazil for those of you struggling to get a grip on the scale."

In an effort to lighten the mood, after making a quick mental calculation, Charu cut in, "So for those of you who don't know how big Brazil is, it's approximately 400 times the size of Wales." Penny and Maria chuckled briefly, glancing at each other, Maria silently mouthed "How does she do that? We really need to get her a boyfriend. She has way too much time on her hands."

Philippe paused for it to sink in. "I understand Matthias' doubts, but things have moved on considerably since his flared-trouser wearing college days in the 1970s." This dig at Matthias, finally broke the last of the tension in the room and caused a small murmuring of laughter to peel around the room.

"No, seriously we have long-term data from a Chinese project that has been running for over 30 years, where they have been trying to build the Great Green Wall to stop the Kubuqi desert from encroaching any further eastwards. We also now have some really cool technology that has been tested and proven in the last couple of years. The only thing that we lacked until now was the will and funding to see such a project through."

"Yeh on that." It was Maria again. "You say to see it through. But it will take decades to achieve what you are saying and as I see it, we don't have decades. African countries are moving to the EA nearly every week."

"Fair point Maria. That's why we need to start now and why we need to start big. You see we don't need to finish the project to get the African countries on our side. Sorry let me rephrase that. It is of vital importance not just to the WA but to the survival of the planet that we successfully finish this project. We just don't need to finish it to get the remaining African nations on our side. What we need to do is enough with sufficient intent and commitment to show them that we are serious."

It was Andrei, ever the military thinker whose eyes lit up with understanding. "Seize the initiative, maintain momentum, and reinforce success." Cocking an eyebrow, Penny turned to Maria once more, "I thought you had been working on Andrei's social skills Maria?" Looking a little flushed Maria simply cocked her head in reply.

"Err well put Andrei, succinct as usual" with a slight smile curling around the edge of his mouth, Philippe continued. "First of all, we need project buy-in. We need to prove to the countries concerned that we can actually overcome all of the doubts you guys have raised so far. It sounds pretty farfetched. I know to be able to reclaim thousands of square miles of what has been, up until now, useless territory and turn it over to agricultural use or use it for renewable energy production."

Philippe who with Matthias' help had managed to rescue the livelihood of a group of Inuit villages in northern Canada now held a note of pride in his voice. "For the first time in their recorded histories, this project will enable these countries to be able to plan for the long-term. Reducing famine and drought, growing economies will for the first time seem achievable."

"I'm going to briefly pass you over to Charu who will give you the very broad bottom-line summary of the project and its tech then we will get started. Charu if you please?" Charu rose and swirled the dial on her ring transforming that relief map of Africa into a true 3D hologram.

"I will try and be brief because as you are all too well aware, time isn't exactly on our side. OK if we discount the countries already in red, then what we have left, the undecided nations are: Western Sahara, Morocco, Algeria, Tunisia, Libya, Eritrea, Sudan, Chad, Niger, Nigeria, Mali, Mauritania and not forgetting Senegal of course." A little red ball bounced clockwise around the map, briefly highlighting each country as Charu spoke.

"As we speak, representatives from our Namibia office who have been trialling most of the tech, are in discussions with government heads of these countries. In tandem the Ambassadors to the UN from these countries have been quietly called into a meeting with the Secretary General and Li, who are going through the political, social and economic aspects of the plan. Basically, they are outlining the proposed plan that I am laying out here."

Charu swished her hand once more and the western Atlantic coast from Senegal up to Morocco was inundated with clusters of floating wind turbines and what appeared to be small round saucer-shaped objects. Slowly but with increasing velocity thin tendrils creating a spider's web connecting the saucer-shaped objects wound themselves together and spread east to west and west to east in fine trails seemingly just under the surface of the fine Saharan sand.

"Obviously everything will be happening concurrently. Basically to achieve our ambitious goal of regreening the Sahara, we have a three element plan; generate energy from the sea; grow and terraform long rows of cave-like structures from the Saharan sand and build extensive renewable solar and wind generation plants. These plants will be capable of providing abundant energy not just for the local countries but also as an export product to Europe, serving both as a valuable reliable energy source for Europe as well as a useful income stream for the host countries."

"Along the West coast and matching this along the Red Sea coast hundreds of floating wind farms capable of creating green hydrogen through electrolysis will be positioned. Some of this energy will be transmitted ashore by High Tension cable and gifted to local communities, the rest will be transported as hydrogen and used to power the regreening project."

Maria raised her hand. "Just before you conjure up your next holographic spectacle, would someone mind telling me just what the hell green Hydrogen is?" Looking around the room Maria realised immediately that she was alone in not knowing what green hydrogen was.

A chorus of voices began babbling explanations at her. It was

Charu that saved her friend and brought order to the discussion. "Yeh basically, it's the good stuff, meaning all of the energy that is used to create the hydrogen comes directly from renewable sources. In this case from the adjacent wind turbines." "OK, got ya," replied a rather sheepish looking Maria.

Once more Charu raised her hand and this time slashed it down to the right. The dunes along the Sahel in the south and on the outer reaches of the Sahara, closest to the urban areas, in the north began to grow cave-like structures.

The growth spread like giant burrowing snakes, leaving ossified honeycombed trails behind them as they burrowed from West to East and East to West, forming a solid interconnected series of habitable tunnels and caves, formed out of the Saharan sand itself.

"This pattern will repeat itself every ten miles or so moving incrementally inwards towards the very centre of the desert. These weird honeycomb-like structures aren't actually built in the traditional sense. They are actually grown, believe it or not."

"We simply spray-form a special mixture of bacillus pasteurii, a bacterium with a very special property, namely that of microbially induced carbonate precipitation or MICP for short." Charu's voice lifted slightly as she excitedly explained the science behind the building technique.

"Basically, using pre-formed moulds that we bury in the sand, the well-fed bacteria are injected into the moulds and then they begin their magic. Within just 24 hours they begin to form a stable rigid crust as they interact with the sand and form calcium carbonate, or as we more commonly know it, limestone. After just one week the structures are robust and permanent."

"They will have a lot of complimentary uses. Being used to shelter pastoral animals from the harsh midday sun, they will also act as cultivation sites allowing for the planting of a wide variety of plants and grasses. In conjunction with the shade caused by the caves insulated by the surrounding sand, each plant in turn, will create and attract moisture from the air, thus helping to cool the local area." Charu paused briefly and noted the air of stunned silence in the room.

Clicking her fingers this time, Charu brought to life huge solar farms and wind turbine generation plants positioned in both the northern border of the Sahara in the centre of Morocco, Tunisia and Algeria, as well as throughout the semi-arid Sahel, that runs across the southern Saharan border.

"Recent research has shown that renewable solar and wind plants effectively reduce the local ambient temperature and attract moisture and humidity to the area." As she spoke Charu's latest incarnation of the North African map began to subtly morph chameleon-like from deep red to a slightly softer tone, reflecting the cooling effect of the solar and wind installations.

"In fact, simply by building and positioning them where you can see, we will be actively contributing to the cooling of the local area. Building these sites in the north and south will deliberately create a lot of much needed long-term employment across both regions as well as once they are completed, they will supply all of the energy needs for the host countries. It is hoped in the south that these energy networks can be developed to supply an uninterruptable energy supply to the very heart of Africa."

Charu was now speaking on auto-pilot, reeling off fact after fact from memory. "Initial conservative estimates reckon with a combined power output of around 3 terawatts of energy from these plants." Watching the thin tendrils representing a growing energy grid spread spider-like across north and central Africa created an exciting buzz around the room, a buzz of excited conversation slowly enveloped the room.

Matthias was heard to mumble "Bringing light to the dark heart of Africa." It was over 150 years ago that the famous explorer Henry, M Stanley, he of the 'Dr Livingstone I presume?' fame had coined the phrase the Dark Continent to describe the still sometimes lingering European view of Africa.

Raising her hand and in the final majestic stroke of her imaginary wand, Charu spun her ring one final time. "Nearly there," she said, trying to regain control of the room. As she spoke vast eucalyptus and palm forests interrupted by sweeping savannahs of tall grasses sprang up in neat clusters, forming dense green impenetrable barriers that slowly marched inwards towards the very heart of the desert.

"7.6 billion tons of atmospheric carbon annually. That's another conservative estimate of how much extra help we would get in achieving our climate goals if we pulled this off. These huge forests would be watered initially from our offshore reverse osmosis plants."

"The water, that's being pumped in the thin trails leading from the saucer-shaped reverse osmosis plants, would be transported through our cave system keeping it cool on its journey. Tiny amounts of the desalinated water would be released as a fine high pressure mist at specific intervals along its journey, in turn aiding the growth of the varied plants and vegetables being grown within the caves themselves."

"The huge forests will over time, form a natural barrier that will stop the spread of the Sahara and begin to anchor the soil and create a more nutrient dense soil." Once more the surrounding area lightened perceptibly as reflecting the expected local temperature drop in the area.

The atmosphere in the room by this point was electric. Laid out before them every member of the team could clearly see and now actually begin to believe in the chance that the greatest ever terraforming project ever undertaken might just actually be pulled off.

It was Maria, that once more brought everyone down to earth with a crashing bump. In her usual sardonic way she cut through the excited chatter. "Looks kinda expensive to me! Osmosis plants, renewable energy farms, green hydrogen, millions of hectares of trees, tunnels and caves out of thin air! Even if this was possible how the hell would we be able to pay for it?"

It was Philippe who once more rose to answer the question. "Believe it or not Maria, that's actually the relatively easy part. Countries and companies around the world see what is happening right now as a compound existential threat. Obviously, there's the Climate threat which our Domesday clock is currently measuring as less than a decade until we pass the tipping point. On top of that we have the now more urgent threat of the global community being cleaved in two. This we are measuring in months, not years."

Philippe had made his point. "Sovereign wealth funds, huge

private pension funds, national governments and the remaining large conglomerates were queuing up with tens of billions in investment funds, ready to throw at this effort."

"The Environmental, Social and Governance payback for investors coupled with the carbon offsetting opportunities, ..." Philippe now gave one of his famous wry smiles, "...Yes, not forgetting all of the new market opportunities are simply too big to be ignored. Our role is simple and depends to a degree on how the talk between the Secretary General and the African Ambassadors goes".

Penny spoke first. Hesitantly she said. "I hope I'm not speaking out of turn but it is a matter of record that many of these countries don't have the most, err, democratic of governments. How do we prevent all of this money just disappearing into the dark recesses of various Cayman Island bank accounts?"

Philippe gave Penny a lop-sided smile. "I share your concern Penny and sentient as usual you have struck the nail on the head. That is our job. The central governments are being offered money and technical help to build technical colleges to train their workforces to be able to build out the electricity and comms grids that this project will create. However,..."

Philippe paused briefly and scanned the room to ensure that he had everyone's attention, jabbing the table's surface with his thick finger as he spoke. "This project will deal directly with local communities and regions and not with the central governments." Now it was Andrei's turn to address the elephant in the room. Laconically he raised his hand. "Yes Andrei,"

"Da, what about the jihadis? Are we going to be dealing directly with them as well?" It was a very large elephant indeed. For years now successive US, French, African and British military missions had failed to stop the rise and spread of militant Islam in the Sahel region.

"Good point Andrei. Prescient as ever. The US the African Union and the UN have volunteered an unprecedented standing force of 50,000 troops and equipment for the first two years of the project, after that it is hoped, err rather expected, that the increase in economic activity and real hope for a more prosperous future for the young, disaffected men and women of the region, will cause people in the area to turn away from jihadist activity. The research that I have read, at least, is that for many of the militants waging Jihad is more of an economic activity rather than a spiritual or philosophical one."

In that instant, Li returned to the room, breathless, but smiling he raised a jubilant hand. "We did it! The Secretary General agreed to our involvement and to our plan and the best news is that all of the African Ambassadors seemed genuinely interested in the proposal and promised to get an answer back from their governments within the week." The room erupted into wild cheering, it was probably more an expression of the relief that everyone felt rather than genuine joy.

Looking momentarily slightly more serious Li called the room to order once more. "Just to temper your expectations we are still on probation and are basically acting as the silent partner in this. More importantly we will only get the proper green light in a week's time, however if I follow my hunch then I believe we should start getting things moving now."

Another cheer erupted around the room, the people began to disperse. "Matthias, Philippe. Shall we adjourn to our planning cell?" This was Li's all to obvious code for the two senior members of the CTC to join him for a much-needed smoke in the cube.

Without speaking, the three men began the process of quietly settling themselves into their seats inside the glass cube. To a casual observer it looked like some predetermined ritual. Over time each of the three chairs had moulded itself to the contours and most probably to the character of the three men. Once settled each man in turn began to go through the motions of his own individual smoking routine.

Philippe began as always by unrolling his immaculate set of tiny tools and carefully started to scratch and dig at his pipe bowl. Despite only ever keeping his cigarettes in his shirt breast pocket, Li searched his pockets, apparently at random, for his Marlborough cigarettes. Only Matthias changed his customary routine. Matthias was the only person in the room that smoked as a distraction rather than for the pleasure of the nicotine hit. Glancing briefly at the two other men he reached into his jacket pocket and withdrew three dull aluminium tubes.

"I've been saving these for just such an occasion. I figured if I was going to carry on convincing myself that I am a smoker I might as well find something I like to smoke!" A broad grin spread across his face as he handed the fat aluminium Monte Cristo cigar cases to his two friends. With a sideways glance Philippe asked. "So you like cigars do you?" "Don't know, but there's only one way to find out."

With a flourish he pulled an ebony cigar cutter out his left trouser pocket and a powerful butane lighter from his right pocket. Philippe usually had strong reservations about smoking anything but his pipe. However, the engineer in him was intrigued by the mechanism on the cigar cutter and the power of the butane lighter.

The three men resumed their contemplative silence, inhaling deeply on their cigars. 'This was different' thought Mathias examining the glowing end of his fragrant cigar. The usual dull fogging he got from smoking cigarettes had been replaced with a rich peppery and almost leathery smoky sensation in his brain.

He double-checked himself. Was he now smelling with his brain? I mean it wasn't the euphoric relaxing sensation he felt back when he had been a drinker, but it was interesting. Something worth exploring he thought to himself. Glancing around he noticed both Philippe and Li quietly nodding to themselves in appreciation of the fine cigars.

Out of habit, Maria glanced over at the smoking cube to see if she was being watched. 'Strange' she thought. The guys, each of which sat in silence, contemplating god knows what, appeared to be in some sort of trance. "Psst, Andrei, go and call Penny and Andrei over here, will you?"

Seconds later, walking slowly so as not to draw attention to themselves, Andrei, Maria and Penny took seats in a darkened corner of the CTC main office. The move hadn't gone completely unnoticed. Matthias the expert in reading body language, who was still laid back in his chair drawing deeply on his cigar with one eye half open had noticed the latent intent in their movement.

To no one in particular, he mumbled "It looks like the kids are planning something." Without opening his eyes, it was Li that responded. "If we don't know what they are planning we can't be held responsible right? Anyway, they are big enough and experienced enough not to cause too much trouble aren't they."

With the group trying their best to appear nonchalant Charu began to explain why she had called them both over. "Guys remember our secret cabal of religious zealots?" The remainder of the group exchanged a brief conspiratorial glance between themselves and let out a groan.

"Err, Hello Charu, Earth calling" It was Maria that, not so subtly vocalized what was on everyone's mind. "Charu, seriously, we have just been tasked with the biggest infrastructure project ever undertaken by humans on the planet and you are talking about conspiracy theories?"

A flicker of rage passed briefly over Charu's face. Briefly composing herself she attempted, in an unusually sarcastic tone, to explain herself again. "Yeh, err hello, obviously I understand what we have to do in Africa, but something has just come up that might just derail everything." Now she had their attention.

"You know that trace we put on the data from our mystery group up near Boston? Well after the seize and capture operation by the US Secret Service on their Server Farm, where, by the way, one agent was killed and three agents were seriously injured." The information about the Secret Service casualties was not lost on the group. Anybody willing to go to that extent and to be that well trained to protect a simple Server farm must really have something to hide.

"So, as I was saying, it seems the US government had a change of heart about sharing the data! However, before the data transfer was interrupted, we still managed to get a huge cache of info. I've sifted through it with the help of a couple of algorithms I wrote, and I think we have something. I mean if what I am reading is correct then we need to do something and we need to do it now!" This time it was Charu's closest friend Penny who interjected.

"Charu, you do remember that we are persona non grata right now, don't you? The only reason we are being allowed to participate in the Sahara project at all is because it is our idea and we control the tech." Charu nodded in assent and Penny continued. "We are officially under house arrest for all intents and purposes." "All the more reason why we have to be careful and keep this between ourselves." replied Charu.

"Remember the data spikes we spotted prior to each of the other African terror attacks. Well, I've just found the mother of all spikes.

This time though we have partial access to some of the actual files."

Charu's fingers seemed to blur as they swept efficiently over the keyboard. "I don't have it all but what I do have I don't like." "Don't keep us in suspense, what have you got." cut in Penny.

It was Andrei who reached across onto the desk by Charu's computer, quickly grabbing her mouse he steered it deftly onto a file folder called 'Debher' and double clicked. Surprised, Maria asked. "Hey Andrei, how did you know which file to open?" "Easy, Debher, is Hebrew for slaughter, disease, or death blow. It is usually used to express the biblical term pestilence. It's the only obvious file on her desktop."

"Well aren't you just the smart and mysterious one," muttered Maria in obvious admiration and wonderment. "You just keep on surprising me. Looking slightly sheepish Andrei explained that his grandma had been Jewish, and she had insisted on reading from the Tora in Hebrew to him as a child."

"Well we have the name of a freighter departing from Durban in three days' time. We have its itinerary, it's a pretty tight one expecting to steam up the coast of Africa and arrive in Mombasa in just two weeks, apparently stopping at 3-4 different ports on the way. We even have a satellite photo of the vessel and from this picture it looks like some serious work has been done on it."

It was Penny, who had spent many years analysing satellite imagery in MI6 that noticed the incongruity first. "It's well done. Very well done indeed. Look here." she used the mouse to trace out a square platform that despite being painted to match the colour of the containers could just be made out. It looked like it they had welded nine containers together and placed a thin steel platform on top.

"Helicopter landing pad." confirmed Andrei. "But why indeed would a medium sized tanker like that need a helicopter landing pad, especially one so big. From the size of it, you could probably land a big double-bladed Chinook on that thing."

It was Maria that spoke next putting all of the pieces together. "So, what do we have: An organisation who we believe…" She stressed the word believe. "Who we believe has form on no less than 6 different occasions if we include the European attacks. They are incredibly well organized and funded and a list of names we have who seem to be connected by trusteeships on various charitable boards is like a who's who of men in power."

The group were nodding in agreement. Charu went next. "My take is that we have near enough actionable intelligence. We have a timescale and locations, plus a target – the ship. From the files I have decrypted we also have probable cause to believe that this next attack is going to be on a far larger scale than before and from the snippets of data that I could rescue I keep finding reoccurring references to bio labs, pestilence and target vectors."

Penny finally spoke. "Look, this is just a theory OK, but going by the recent 'unusual' deaths in Europe of key politicians and their replacement by random of apparently devout Protestant candidates, I think this African attack is aiming to do the very same thing. Namely put preferred candidates in power."

"The difference, and probably the reason for the increased scale of this attack is that Africa is still very much tribally organised. Simply getting rid of one candidate from a political party won't achieve the effect they want. He will simply be replaced by the next most senior from the tribe or clan. I think they are trying to wipe out whole elite political groups, with, from what we have managed to piece together, some serious bioweapons."

Charu glanced between the faces that were peering at her monitor bank. "So" they all turned to focus on her. "So what do we do about it?" "We should take it to Li and then let him deal with it, maybe alert the Intelligence Services?" As usual Andrei cut in with typical logicality and bluntness.

"By the time the right agency has received the info and thought about what to do, it will be too late, we have three days, maybe four max before god knows how many hundreds or thousands of people start dying. Secondly, you have all seen the names on the list of people we think are involved. If that is to be believed then your Head of MI6 and the Vice President are mixed up in this, not counting some of the most influential men on all 5 continents. There's no chance we could let anybody else know about this without them finding out."

"President" Maria corrected. "Sorry?" "He was the Vice

President he is now the President of the USA." Penny was the last to speak. "We are going to be in deep, deep shit if we are wrong on this one. If what you say about the list of important people behind this is true, it would explain the shitty letter and lack of cooperation I got from MI6. But Andrei is right we need to act. You know how Li and Matthias like to divide our group between the thinkers and the Doers? Well, I think it's about time the Doers started doing."

Charu slumped slightly in her chair. Maria gave her a light punch on the shoulder. "Don't you think you got away with it. After what Andrei told me about how you reacted in India, you are now officially a member of the Doers club!"

Charu smiled a nervous smile back at Maria. They all stared momentarily at each other, then Andrei said. "Act now and ask for forgiveness later?" They all nodded in agreement. "OK, listen we have not got a lot of time. Our mission is simple to stop any of the cargo on board the ship from getting to its targets. Agreed?"

They all nodded in assent. "So, if I could suggest the following: Me and Maria will be out on the ground, I would like Penny to act as our local control in theatre and Charu to coordinate everything from here. With this Sahara project gearing up we have the perfect opportunity to get to Africa, we can call it a probable site recce for the offshore wind turbines in the Red Sea. Let's meet up at our place tonight to confirm tasks and actions?" There was a slight hesitant pause before the group all nodded in agreement.

The group tried their best to drift casually away from Charu's desk as if nothing particular had just been discussed. Philippe had enjoyed the cigar and even found pleasure in extinguishing the final embers as he ground the stub methodically into the steel ashtray. "It really does look like the kids are up to something." he said to his two colleagues as he stared out over the main office space.

"I just hope whatever they are planning, they are discreet about it and it goes to plan." It was indicative of Li, that at the very point in his life and career where he was on the verge of losing everything he had worked for, he was still able to have the trust in his team to do the right thing without questioning them.

Chapter Nineteen

pestilence [noun]

Definition of pestilence

A contagious or infectious epidemic disease that is virulent and devastating.

- *Through fire, famine, and pestilence some people always profit.*

The teapot, according to its owner, had not been washed since its first use over 75 years ago. It wasn't necessarily a beautiful pot. It seemed to be slightly out of proportion, its thick cylindrical body appeared a little too industrial for a family tea pot. The brass handle was affixed through two porcelain eyelets on the top of the pot and the spout was a thick bulbous adjunct to the delicately painted blue and white body of the vessel. The painted scene on the pot, was equally unremarkable, depicting two peacocks rising over a field with a small wooden house in the background. The brush strokes were fine indeed, it was just that the scene was uninspiring.

Zhang had been staring at the pot of tea for a good five minutes, not sure where else he should look. President Zhao Leji had called Zhang to his private residence and insisted that he came alone. After being admitted by the President's security team the two men had been left in an ornate study together for what to Zhang at least, felt like an eternity.

The President stood, back erect, gazing out of the window at the garden below. The pocket in his smartly tailored Mao Suit bulged slightly through the weight of its contents. In his hands the President held four polished red Go pebbles, that he nonchalantly clinked together in time with his thoughts.

To the President, indeed to most of the majority Han population, the whole world was simply divided into two groups. Han or Laowai, (foreigner). This firm belief was reflected in the intricately carved Go board that sat on the table next to the imposing yet ugly tea pot. As in the CTC the Chairman of the Standing Committee of the Communist Party of the People's Republic of China, had overlaid a detailed and intricate world map onto the board's surface.

The disposition of the counters on the finely crafted mahogany board reflected this man's view of power and influence in the world. There were no neutral countries, as there were on the CTC board, there were only black counters placed as holders over the Western Alliance and neutral states.

Black being an unlucky colour for the Han, representing evil, cruelty and destruction had been an obvious choice as a counterpoise to the shimmering red counters with the two symbols 中国 inlaid in fine gold leaf. The characters Zhōngguó meaning China, in this instance represented Chinese and therefore Han dominance wherever they had been placed.

US forces had been stationed in the south of the Korean peninsula since the Soviet and US forces agreed on a line of demarcation after the Japanese surrender at the end of the Second World war. The recent expulsion of all US troops from Korea, served to grossly deplete American influence and military capability in the area and at the same time it piled further pressure on Japan.

In line with the overall Chinese strategy, this effectively cut Japan off from any real strategic or logistic support by the Western Alliance, except via very expensive, vulnerable and slow shipments from Northern Australia.

Only now did the Chinese President Zhao Leji, turn to his Zhang his protégé. 'At last.' thought Zhang, who still had no clue why he had been summoned and didn't know if that was a good or bad sign.

Still gently clinking the 4 polished red Go counters as he spoke, the President neared the table. "Can I offer you some tea Zhang?" The question was rhetorical Zhang knew. Bowing his head in acquiescence he waited whilst the older man knelt at the low table to enact the intricate process of serving the tea.

Eventually, with the soothing aroma of Jasmine being carried by the steamy vapour wafting from the hot teacups, Zhao Leji spoke again. As he did so, Zhang once more caught a brief glimpse of his older mentor's maniacal and somewhat childish smile.

"Excellent work…" Zhang's shoulders slumped slightly, and he quietly exhaled the breath he had been unknowingly holding in. 'Thank the ancestors for that!' he thought to himself. As the Chairman continued to speak, he placed one of the red Go pebbles onto the board neatly covering both Koreas.

"Your diplomacy in resolving the Korea problem has not gone unnoticed Zhang. You have been praised publicly by the Standing Committee itself. Now that we have united Korea it has removed the final lingering remnants of American Imperial occupation from the Asian mainland. Not to mention the access it has granted us to Korean technological innovation."

"Thank you, Zhao Leji, and I thank the Party for my recognition. I hope you are happy with my arrangements for the North's dear Leader." The faintest hint of a sarcastic smile played at the edges of Zhang's mouth as he uttered the word 'dear'.

"Removing Kim from Korea, and granting him asylum in China has brought the stability we need on the Peninsular. Now we can continue to further isolate. Japan." The older Chinese lowered his porcelain teacup to the table and nodded in agreement.

Zhang took this as a sign that he should continue his briefing. "It was actually not that difficult really. Given a choice between national reunification and joining the Eastern Union, which essentially meant keeping the peace with its two biggest geographical neighbours or remaining indeterminately separated from the north and being forced into a closer union with its historical enemy Japan due to its membership of the Western Union, it wasn't really a contest.

The real deal clincher in my opinion had been the offer of asylum for their Dear Leader. We have given him a valley in Wuzhou as far south and as far away from North Korea as possible." "Excellent" encouraged the Chairman. "If I may Zhao Leji? How are the plans in the Straits of Hormuz progressing?" "I am glad you asked."

The older man peered closely at his watch to check the time. "In just under one hour, I along with the Iranian President and the leaders of Iraq, Bahrain and Qatar will hold a news conference in the Zǐjìnchéng. Yes, Zhang this will be the first official Chinese government announcement from the Forbidden City since 1912."

Zhang knew that the Mao suit that the Chairman was wearing today was no coincidence. After all wasn't a figure like Mao the closest thing to an all-powerful Emperor that Communism would allow. Of course, Zhang had known about the upcoming announcement. Feigning surprise he looked back at the older Chinese over the rim of his nearly empty teacup.

Sandwiched between Russian-controlled Syria to the north, Iran to the East and a still hostile Saudi Arabia to the south, getting Iraq to agree to join the Eastern Alliance had been a relatively simple task. Most of the work had been going on since the withdrawal of US forces from Iraq. The Iranians had been very busy, buying, bullying and convincing most of the majority fellow Iraqi Shi'ites to vote for their preferred candidates in the last three elections.

The decision by both Shia dominated Bahrain and Qatar didn't serve to alter the geopolitical map to any great extent. However, the hurried and deeply embarrassing departure of US Navy's 5th Fleet based in Bahrain had been another stick in the eye for the West, with it came the departure of the much smaller but equally strategically important UK Naval base.

The withdrawal of the 5th Fleet had been a close-run thing with the new US President being on the verge of quite literally drawing a line in the sand and deciding to stand and fight. However, if they did remain then they would technically be occupying Bahrain whose King had officially served notice on the Fleet to leave.

Beijing had seen how close they had come to conflict over Bahrain and decided on another tactic for Saudi Arabia. Instead of trying to sway the government they instead fomented insurrection and civil disobedience. Uprisings had begun in the mainly Shi'ite Eastern Province of Saudi Arabia, which had almost brought Saudi Arabia's oil production to a standstill.

The decisions of Iraq, Bahrain and Qatar to join the EA had, in one fell swoop almost completely removed US influence from the Straits of Hormuz and placed even more strain on the world's available gas and oil supplies.

Glancing once more at his watch the Chinese President said. "I would like you Zhang, to introduce us to the TV audience. It is only fair that you share in the glory after all of your hard work. I have taken the liberty of obtaining a decent suit for you. You may get changed in my bathroom."

'Share in the glory and be the patsy to take the blame if it all goes wrong' thought Zhang to himself, as he produced his most radiant smile and stood to head towards the bathroom. "It would be my honour Zhao Leji." As Zhang began to walk towards the bathroom, he watched the older man as he carefully picked up the black Go counters that had been covering, Iraq, Bahrain and Qatar and placed the remaining three red Go counters in their place.

It seemed that the western world at least had simply decided that the best way to deal with the persistent strains of Covid that continued to mutate and spread despite the exorbitant quantities of treasure expended on vaccine roll-outs and almost total so called herd immunity was by choosing not to acknowledge it anymore and carry on life as normal.

The parts of the world worst affected by this strategy were, as usual, the developing world where, forced between the choices of starving or being evicted. They reluctantly returned to their overcrowded workspaces to work for much less than any western minimal wage simply to keep up with the very important developed countries citizens' demands for an ongoing supply of throwaway fashion and electronic items.

The obvious knock-on effect of this return to crowded work places and packed public transport systems was that many more adults and children in Africa, Asia and South America were still succumbing to the mutating virus. As global travel began to resume, driven by the need to satiate the inalienable human right of rich westerners to wear their throwaway fashion items and show off their disposable electronics whilst enjoying a holiday in the sun, the virus continued to linger, mutate and migrate from country to country.

Even so, the developed north, continued with its policy of ignoring the virus, based on the simple statistics that people weren't dying from the virus in large quantities anymore because most of the vulnerable had already succumbed in the earlier waves and they now had access to a plethora of new drugs that vastly increased survival rates for the few already vaccinated individuals that became seriously ill with the virus.

The only help that most of Africa was receiving to combat the increasingly deadly new variants of the disease came from charitable foundations and the grindingly bureaucratic and infuriatingly slow Global Vaccine for All campaign. During the early planning stages, the Puritan society had given very strong consideration to employing vaccinations as the delivery method for their deadly modified SARS virus.

However, due to a number of factors such as the traceability of medicinal batch numbers and more importantly the continued reluctance by many of the African elites to take the vaccine following the repeated false claims of malicious side effects, the Puritan society had settled on impregnating thousands of masks with a 3D Gel lattice containing the dormant virus.

Only the moist vapour from the breath of the mask's user would reactivate the dormant virus and allow it to innocuously seep deep into the lungs of the wearer. With chosen loyal successors already primed and waiting to seize power, the deaths of the current government incumbents of Mozambique, Tanzania, Kenya and Uganda like so many recent deaths around the world would simply be recorded as further tragic statistics of the recent pandemic.

Order would quickly be restored in the countries and the new governments would roll out very effective economic Universal Income for all reforms, initially subsidised by Puritan Society funds. The short-term cost for a couple of years of subsidy would be high, in the tens of billions, but it would pale into insignificance at the long-term wealth, power and influence that would flow from these countries in the future, as they, with the help of efficient Puritan inspired governance, developed into major world food exporters and consumers of manufactured products.

The elegant modern apartment block had been designed as an architectural fusion between man and nature. The steel cladding which had intricate floral designs cut into it had been allowed to rust in the ever humid and salty Singaporean air. This allowed the building to 'relax'. The geometric cubes seemed to be stacked upon each other in an almost ad-hoc manner, with each cube offset by several degrees from its neighbour. The effect was of a tall helical spiral with three prominent crenelated grooves running from the street below, up to the 30th floor over 90 metres above the pavement.

Each of the gigantic ornately designed rusted steel cubes held within it a complete modern 3-bed apartment. The whole effect was made complete by three giant yellow Meranti trees that had been planted and trained to grow in the grooves left by the gaps between the rusting steel cubes. As the now mature trees spiralled skywards it was difficult for the casual observer to establish if the building was supporting the trees or vice versa.

The smell of Maria's world-famous Chili Con Carne greeted Charu and Penny as they arrived at Maria and Andrei's apartment. Charu who hadn't yet visited the new apartment nearly tripped over the kit bags packed in the hallway. "Say, you guys planning on going somewhere?" she asked innocently. "Oh you know Andrei has invited me for a special weekend treat in Africa." replied Maria from the kitchen. "Hey guys that's not fair. There's no way I am going to play gooseberry between you two lovebirds all weekend in Africa." piped in Penny.

Andrei exited the bedroom, pulling a very tight T shirt over his lithe muscular shoulders. Penny's eyes lingered a fraction too long. Noticing the attention, Andrei smiled as he walked towards the two women. Speaking directly to Penny he said. "Don't worry Penny, I have plans to make up a foursome with a mystery guest for you!" "You intrigue me Andrei, pray tell more." purred Penny in reply, only realising afterwards that she had just been speaking to his still uncovered tightly muscled abdomen and not to his face.

"Ok you guys, dinner's ready." yelled Maria "Come through to the balcony." Following Andrei, Penny and Charu strolled through the huge open-plan dining / living area with its floor to ceiling windows and walked out onto the balcony. "Shitty view huh." muttered Charu as she gazed out to the horizon. The iconic Marina Bay hotel rose resplendent before them, hinting at the open ocean that lay beyond.

The food tasted even more delicious than it smelled, and they were all on their second serving before Andrei began to outline the detail of the plan that he and Maria had spent most of the previous day discussing. "So the limitations are that we obviously need to stop the first shipment getting to its targets in Maputo, Mozambique. That doesn't give us too much time, but it is manageable." Charu had already done the speed time distance calculation in her head and said, "Manageable if we use the company jet. How do we do that without alerting Li?"

This time Maria spoke, after hurriedly swallowing a rather hot mouthful of chili. "Simple, I have spoken to Guenther, Fabio and Christi. They say we can file a flight plan to Egypt, as planned, to notionally check out the siting of the hydro power turbines and because of the hell that has broken out in India, he is more than justified he says in avoiding India and flying due west from Singapore directly to the lower eastern coast of Africa. From there he will simply ask for permission to land and refuel at Maputo, where he coincidently might encounter a little bit of engine trouble and need a couple of days for the repairs."

"Ingenious," said Penny, wiping the last of the chili from her lips and reaching for her wine glass. Andrei continued to outline the plan. "So, Maria and I both believe that we simply don't have the manpower or equipment to seize the boat at sea and figure that it will probably be least protected when the cargo has been handed over and is being driven back to the Charity HQ just southwest of Belo Horizonte."

"In short, we land 24 hours ahead of the boat's arrival. This gives us time to identify the vehicle these Puritan creeps will be using and possible pick-up routes. We will prepare a decoy vehicle and intercept the delivery when it gets out of Maputo and the people transporting it begin to relax. We have one aim that is to seize the cargo and destroy it but we must keep some samples to be analysed. Once we can positively show that the shipment contains hazardous cargo an anonymous message will be sent to the port and police authorities of every port from Maputo to Mombasa along the coast."

"As we discussed Maria and I will do the snatch, Penny will be driving a decoy vehicle." Penny spluttered slightly mid-gulp on her Chardonnay. "I will." "Err yes, we haven't spoken about this but this cargo will for sure be tracked electronically. As soon as they see that it hasn't arrived where they expected it, then someone or something will come looking." "And what are you going to be doing whilst I'm being hunted by lunatic monks?"

"Well, firstly it won't just be you being chased by lunatic monks." Andrei grinned. "It will be you and Vihaan, Charu's cousin. We need another good pair of hands on this job to prepare for the snatch and to carry out the escape. Secondly, Maria and I will be watching your back."

"Sorry," cut in Penny. "If I have followed the plan correctly, you and Maria will be covering my escape whilst sitting in a vehicle with one of the most dangerous bioweapon cargoes imaginable?" "Hey, nobody said it was a perfect plan." Said Maria.

"And you are happy with this Charu?" questioned Penny. "I wouldn't say happy, but I know my cousin and he is a good person to have around in a crisis." Charu then switched her gaze to Maria. "And what will I be doing whilst you guys are playing hide the bioweapon in Mozambique?"

"Good question." replied Andrei. "You are going to be tracking the ship's progress and keeping us updated. We also need to know when the cargo is going to be unloaded and if they plan to use that improvised flight deck for a helicopter. That could really complicate our plans if they plan to fly the cargo all the way to its ultimate destination."

Charu, who had been scanning a map of the east coast of Africa on her tablet spoke. "Looking at the ship's aggressive schedule, my guess is that they will use the helicopter to bring the cargo ashore, that way the ship can keep moving up the coast and the use of the helicopter gets them around any unusually curious customs officials."

"But I don't think they will fly the cargo all the way. It is too risky if they fly too far south or inland whilst the ship continues to sail full steam in the opposite direction, they may not make it back to the ship."

"Good point Charu, I would also need you to discretely track down a level 4 bio lab as close to our location as possible and convince them to quietly test the samples. If we manage to get hold of them that is." "Oh, is that all? A level 4 bio lab in rural Africa!"

Andrei grinned, knowing fully how difficult the task was, not only to find a lab but to be able to get them on side discretely would be a big ask. "Finally, it will be you sending anonymous alerts to the African coastguards, port authorities and police forces." We have five days max between the ship leaving Maputo and it arriving at its next scheduled port of Dar es Salaam in Tanzania. It must not reach the port and be allowed to unload its cargo." A brief silence fell around the table as each of the four CTC members grappled with the threat and risk of their forthcoming mission.

Chapter Twenty

virus [noun]

Definition of virus

A disease or illness caused by a virus.

Especially: the causative agent of an infectious disease.

- *There are many different strains of flu virus.*

The first heavy drops of tropical rain struck the jet's windscreen and exploded, momentarily distorting Guenther's view. These huge water-laden amorphous globules that accelerated groundward from the pitch-black sky had always fascinated Guenther Kramer. The crew had meticulously planned their flight over the Indian Ocean to land just before the regular seasonal daily rainstorm.

It had been a close-run thing, accompanied by the chorus of the deep rumbling thunder and the spit and crack of electrical discharge that always presages such storms, the thick water-laden cumulus nimbus clouds were building rapidly, billowing outwards and upwards, becoming darker and more sinister by the minute.

Although such electric storms brought a daily respite from the intense humidity for the people, plants and animals below, they were certainly to be avoided at all costs when flying a small aircraft and more particularly when trying to bring that same small aircraft safely back down to earth.

Completing the last of his rundown checklist Guenther glanced over at his co-pilot Fabio, flicking the switch on the internal intercom as he did so. The intensity of the rain had picked up considerably and he found he had to shout to be heard over the sound of the raging tempest outside. "Guys, I've got bad news." Fabio noticed the grin broaden on his friend's face as he continued with his announcement. "We've got a couple of concerning engine warning lights flashing here, once we have refuelled, I think we will need to wait for the engines to have a thorough check over. This might take a couple of days depending on how quickly we can get an engineer over. Again, I'm sorry, but if you follow Christi, she will take you through immigration and get you settled into a hotel for a couple of nights."

The immigration formalities at the private terminal of the Aeroporto Internacional de Maputo Mavalane were cursory. In full knowledge of the 'unexpected' engine troubles they would have on arrival, Christi had already completed most of the advance bureaucracy before their journey had even begun. The team had travelled light, Penny, Maria, Vihaan, and Andrei stepped out of the plane's small side door into searingly bright sunshine.

The rich smells of earth and grass battled with the sunshine to overwhelm their senses. The tropical storm had stopped as quickly as it had begun. The only evidence of its presence was the quickly drying puddles on the flat tiled rooves of the nearby terminal buildings and the glistening sheen on the encroaching vegetation.

They worked together to remove the large hardened plastic case from the aircraft's small hold. The case was approximately as large as two family-sized normal suitcases. It was bulky but unusually light for its size. The main reason for its light weight was the amount of laser cut foam padding that had been carefully installed to protect the 30 miniature carbon-fibre drones that had been carefully packed inside.

The customs inspector had been patiently waiting by the side of the aircraft for the group to remove its cargo. His wait hadn't been in vain. It took him a good couple of seconds to stop staring as first Penny then Maria bent over to grab the handles of the large black case, their short khaki skirts riding higher up their pale white thighs as they did so.

He actually fumbled and dropped his clipboard when Christi strode around the back of the aircraft to offer him the flight manifest. The tall blonde Norwegian who also acted as the Team's patrol medic, close protection officer as well as general fixer, was one of those women who once seen was never forgotten.

She wore tight cargo pants, and a faded green strapped top that fell just short of her belly button, revealing her peerless rippling stomach as she extended the manifest to present it to the Customs Officer.

The poor man did not know what to do with his eyes. He hurriedly and very briefly cast an eye over the manifest and without daring to lift his head asked if he could look inside the black transport case. Maria and Penny could barely contain their smirks as they watched the poor Customs Officer straining to keep his eyes from drifting down away from Christi's eyes towards her body.

Switching effortlessly to Portuguese, to further ingratiate herself with the Customs Official, Christi explained why they were all staring at a box of the most advanced drone swarm in the world.

"So, you see Sir, we are keen botanists and we plan to take some cool aerial shots of the Banhine National Park for the documentary we are making." Even Andrei found himself staring, he had never seen Christi acting coquettishly before. He could certainly see the attraction and he felt for the poor guy.

Maria's punch to his shoulder, which was a little heavier than what could be described as a playful punch, broke Andrei from his gaze. "Err, sorry, Christi are we good to go?" Andrei was keen to get clear of the airport they only had a little over 24 hours until they estimated that the cargo would be offloaded at the port and there was much to do to get ready.

Petrus Hambuda's, father had been one of the thousands of emigrees fleeing the Angolan Civil War who had eventually settled in Namibia. Petrus himself who had been working for the last five years at the Namibian Regional tech hub of the CTC had been a particularly bright student as a child, quickly adding German and English to his knowledge of Portuguese, he found he not only had a flair for languages but also for science and engineering.

Arms folded and with a broad smile on his sun-burnished face, he pushed himself clear of the rented Toyota pick-up truck that he had been leaning against and hurried over to hug Penny and Maria. "My Goodness me, how long has it been. You two look amazing." The girls were equally glad to see Petrus and showered him with kisses and hugs.

Eventually, releasing himself from their embrace, he turned to face Andrei. He had only encountered Andrei once, back in Namibia, when they were testing out the small six-wheeled electric buggy affectionately called Snappy. There, out in the bush and semi-arid desert land of Namibia, Andrei had raced the buggy through the desert and high up into the upper reaches of the Brandberg mountains.

Indeed, it was Petrus who had retrofitted the little Buggy with the EMP device that had saved Andrei, Vihaan, and Charu's life in Kashmir. "Andrei my old friend, how are you?" said Petrus, grinning from ear to ear as he reached out his hand to shake Andrei's offered hand. "I'm great and I wanted to thank you for your work on the Buggy, it really got us out of a scrape in Kashmir."

Petrus affected a serious look "You mean the Buggy that you completely destroyed, after all my years of hard work?" Andrei was momentarily taken aback, until Petrus' broad grin returned itself to its customary position.

"Sir, are you the man who developed Snappy?" This time it was Vihaan who spoke. "I am and you don't have to call me sir. You must be Charu's cousin Vihaan. Charu tells me you are a fine engineer yourself. How is your leg coming along?"

Tapping his thigh gently with his fist, Vihaan replied. "Not quite as good as new but getting there." "Good to hear, please let's get inside the car before it rains again."

For the sake of discretion and expediency Charu had called ahead and asked that Petrus give some local support to the new arrivals. Petrus had already spent a couple of days in-country casually observing the daily routine of the Puritan missionaries, identifying their vehicles and routes and getting a fix on their main compound.

In addition, he had already checked out several car hire firms. He had yet to conclude his most important task. Tomorrow whilst the team prepared themselves for the operation, he would visit the National Institute of Health in Maputo, where coincidentally a German university with funding from the UN had established a next generation Genomic analysis and sequencing for SARS CoV-2.

If Petrus could work his magic, it would be this site that would be able to deliver the result of the bio pathogen that they presumed was a modified SARS virus within eight hours. This short timescale would give the CTC team just enough time to get the warnings and alerts circulated before the ship that was at this moment heading northwards, managed to disgorge any more of its deadly cargo and inflict untold misery and death on innocent families.

With his usual efficiency Petrus had done more than the team had asked. As he and Vihaan finished the preparation of the second of the two rented white land cruisers, they stood back to admire their handiwork. Petrus, who had been observing the Puritan missionaries for the last couple of days had just finished helping Vihaan to apply black transfers made from thick parcel tape onto the doors and roof of the two vehicles.

The missionary's logo certainly was a mixed metaphor. In principle it could be seen as simple tall black cross with the narrow horizontal bar placed slightly higher than usual and being slightly shorter than usual. The effect of the size and placement of the cross' horizontal bar coupled with the finely tapered end at the base of the cross was unmistakably that of a large broad sword pointing down towards earth.

It had been easy enough to create using the tape and after slinging a couple of cargo nets into the back of the vehicles and tying down the box containing the drones into the back of the lead vehicle both men moved indoors.

The shipment was expected to be transferred tomorrow at some time and the team had decided to keep a low profile until they set out to intercept the cargo. Yet again Petrus had thought of everything. He had rented a small bungalow with a lock up garage on the west of the town, just on the western side of the river Matola. The bungalow sat equidistant between the port of Maputo and the Puritan missionary camp which lay just ten kilometres to the southwest, just past the small but vibrant town of Belo Horizonte.

The rest of the team had, had time to shower, change and check through their equipment. Penny had just finished setting up her lap top communication gear and checking in with Charu back in Singapore. Petrus who was the only team member that was allowed out of the bungalow, staggered back from the compound's exterior wrought iron gate overladen with plastic bags and polystyrene containers brimming with hot, spicy take away food.

Maria opened the door and stepped back to allow the smiling Petrus to enter with the food. The rest of the team who had been sat around the dining table discussing the latest update from Charu and reviewing the satellite photos of the cargo ship all looked up and stared at the beaming Petrus. “I hope someone likes Afro-Portuguese fusion food?” He exclaimed. The flurry of movement that followed this statement was answer enough.

As Andrei hurriedly cleared the photos and laptop from the table Penny and Vihaan stood to help Petrus with the bags of food. “Bloody hell that smells good Petrus.” said Penny as she peeled the last of the lids form the containers. With each of the team armed with a simple wooden bowl and a spoon they dug in heartily to the food.

“Come on Petrus don’t keep us in suspense, what are we eating? I see shrimp, chicken and beans and what’s that yellow gooey stuff?” asked Maria. It wasn’t what Petrus explained, it was rather how he explained it, that marked him out as a serious Foody.

Using very precise movements of his small sun-burned hands, Petrus began to gesticulate as he animatedly explained what they were about to eat. “This perfumed aroma that you can all smell wafting up from Penny’s bowl is made from probably the most succulent giant locally caught shrimp you will ever find. They are seared on a charcoal grill, then marinaded and slowly cooked in coconut milk, local spices and the legendary Mozambiquan fiery Peri Peri sauce. This dish alone is truly worth travelling to Mozambique for.” Penny’s eyes rolled upwards in pure delight as she bit into one of the juicy seared shrimps dripping in the deliciously hot sauce.

“Over there, the chicken that Andrei is piling onto his plate. That’s called Galinha Asada. It is a whole roast chicken, basted in a marinade of herbs, butter and of course Peri Peri sauce, then shredded before serving. Andrei try the Xima, use it to pick up the chicken like a spoon.”

“Try the what?” spluttered Andrei through a mouthful of shredded chicken. “Xima, it’s the stodgy looking cornflour porridge in the small pots, but don’t let its looks put you off. This is eaten with every meal here in Mozambique, it's great for soaking up the juices and because it is really thick you break a bit off and can pick it up and use it like an edible spoon."

Vihaan was busy spooning the thick black bean casserole into his bowl. "I've no idea what this is, but it smells awesome." he said dipping the spoon back into the pot to try and fish out more or the chunks of pork and chorizo sausage.

"That my friend is Feijoada. It is another staple food here and also in Brazil. The slow cooked black beans are spiced with pepper and salt, onion and garlic. Then the bacon, chorizo, pork sausage and beef chunks are added with just a little tomato sauce. The secret is in cooking the beans really slow." His mouth full of sausage and beans Vihaan simply nodded in agreement.

It wasn't until every last morsel of shrimp, piece of tender shredded chicken and mouthful of delicious Feijoada had been eaten that Andrei brought thc group's attention back to the next day's events.

Spreading a scale map of the Maputo area out on the tabletop Andrei began to speak "OK guys, I'll keep this short." Using the end of one of the plastic spoons they had been eating with, he jabbed at a dusty unpaved car park that sat immediately on the far side of the main bridge out of town that crossed the river Matola.

The group had all been quite jetlagged as they were driven from the aircraft to the safe house and it was left to Petrus to nervously point out the tiny, yet obvious flaw in the plan. "Err Andrei, sorry to be picky. You know that your rendezvous point is on the opposite side of the road to the direction the cargo will be coming from, don't you?" Andrei looked again at the map, tilting his head quizzically he wrinkled his forehead into a tight frown. He couldn't see Petrus' point.

Cutting in quickly to avoid any further embarrassment, Petrus added. "Mozambique is one of the err 76 countries in the world that drive on the left-hand side of the road, just like we do back in Namibia." "Ahh" Looking sheepishly at the group, a slightly red-faced Andrei continued "OK, sorry about that."

Shifting the end of the spoon to the other side of the road, he said "Well it's not quite as good as the other side but it should do so this is where we will wait for the package. Once we intercept it Penny and Vihaan will drive directly north with the cargo strapped down in the back of their pickup and Maria and I will follow some way behind and act as overwatch in case, or maybe I should say, when, these lunatics realise their precious cargo has been taken."

This last remark seemed to jolt Vihaan awake. "Sorry Andrei. You really think they will come after us?" "Not sure Vihaan, we will have to head north anyway where the population is sparce once we get the package. We don't know exactly what it is yet and we don't want to take any risks. The problem is that it will keep us exposed out on the roads for longer than I would like."

Still visibly unsettled Vihaan nodded in agreement. Andrei continued "Once we are sure that we are in the clear, we will take a sample, destroy the rest of the shipment and get the sample up to the test lab where, hopefully, our good friend Petrus has arranged for a quick and unobtrusive analysis."

Petrus picked up quickly on the cue. I am speaking to a colleague tomorrow who, err how do you say "fingers clicked" Maria stifled a snigger. "I think it's "Crossed", Petrus, fingers crossed." Petrus' smiling countenance didn't waver for a second.

Penny, who had spent the last three years developing her skills in reading people's micro gestures with Matthias, often wondered about Petrus. The guy was simply so nice, she believed that purely because he was so nice he simply didn't see or perceive malice, or schadenfreude even when it was levelled however obliquely against him.

"Thanks Maria. Yes, fingers crossed he will meet me at the lab after-hours tomorrow and we can get the analysis done overnight when the facility is quiet." It was Penny that spoke finally. "Thanks Petrus, you've been amazing. Personally, I'm not exactly thrilled at the prospect of driving around Mozambique with a flatbed full of bioweapons whilst being chased by pissed off Monks. But if they do try anything Vihaan. You just keep driving and I will make them regret they ever thought about messing with us."

With that Penny lightly tapped the Glock pistol which was sat on the edge of the table next to her. Andrei grinned and gave Vihaan a reassuring smile. "Don't worry Vihaan, buddy. I have a lot of confidence in Penny's ability to defend herself. I've seen her first hand on the judo mat. And if, even she can't cope then rest assured Maria and I won't be far behind with our own little box of tricks." With this he glanced over at the large hardened plastic case containing the drones that was stowed by the front door.

"Thanks Andrei," said Penny appreciatively. "Oh, I nearly forgot. The latest update from Charu is that the boat will be passing Maputo at around midday tomorrow, local time. Based on Charu's calculations, and let's face it who is going to argue with Charu's calculations?"

A collective snigger rippled from the group. "Yeh, so anyway. She is still calculating that the cargo will be brought ashore by helicopter, picked up near the port and then we know that the bridge where we will be waiting is the only bridge the vehicles can take for these guys to get their cargo back to their base."

It was Maria that commented. "There's an awful lot of ifs in the whole plan guys. But it's the best we have to go on I'm afraid." Petrus nodded sagely, then added. "I agree with Maria, but I got to say, if I had to rely on the hunches and calculations of anybody it would be Vihaan's cousin Charu." With that they raised their glasses and toasted Charu.

"Well, I don't know about you guys, but I've had a pretty full day. I'm going to turn in for the night." "Sounds like a good idea Petrus," said Andrei nodding in agreement. He turned to Maria and she stepped closer, placed her arm around his waist and kissed him lightly on the cheek. "We have a big day tomorrow. Let's get some sleep." She said staring up into his eyes. Penny looked across at Vihaan with raised eyebrows. "I guess I'll take this couch and you can have that one." she said pointing to the other couch in the corner of the room.

It was hot, a lot hotter than any of them had expected and surprisingly difficult thought Penny to 'pretend' to be broken down by the side of the dusty road for over an hour. Petrus, diligent as ever, had volunteered to position himself on the far-side of the bridge to be able to identify the Puritan missionaries' vehicle as it crossed and recrossed the bridge. It was 10am as Petrus radioed into the team's temporary base that one Puritan Hilux with four occupants had crossed the bridge heading in the direction of the Port.

Roughly one hour later Charu had messaged Penny to say that according to the Automatic Identification System, installed on every large container ship of this type, the vessel was steaming north at 25 knots and would be passing Maputo harbour in one hour. Of course, they would have no way to track the helicopter, but they already knew the ship wouldn't be stopping and that any helicopter pilot worth his salt would want to make a journey over the sea as short as possible.

A relatively strong northerly wind blowing down the east African coast would slow the helo even more as it flew to catch back up with the fast-moving freighter. These facts when considered together meant that the team had a window of about 90 minutes in which they believed the missionaries would attempt their pickup.

One of the team's Hilux vehicles masquerading with its temporary livery as a Puritan vehicle had been hidden a block away, whilst the vehicle which Penny and Vihaan had been assigned had been positioned by the roadside in full view of anyone crossing the bridge from the port.

The unfortunate fact that racism abounds in nearly every society had been used to good effect. For the last hour Vihaan had been leant over the engine compartment of the Hilux pretending to fix a problem with the engine. In that time not one local passer-by had attempted to offer assistance.

The bet the team were making was that by placing Penny under the hood of the large white Toyota wearing tight khaki shorts and with her auburn hair flowing in the wind, that the passing Missionary vehicle would stop to render assistance, especially as they would presume the vehicle to be one of their own.

"I have them in sight" Erik was stood in the back of the large Chinook helicopter he was wearing a rigger's harness that secured him to the inside bulkhead of the helicopter but allowed him free movement around the inside of the aircraft. He had been observing the Landing Zone (LZ), through one of the round bulbous side windows of the long double-bladed helicopter.

He had identified the waiting vehicle which had been parked just west of the port on a patch of scrubland that ran down to the muddy waters of the Maputo delta. The ground team had done a good job, as asked, they had set up a clear landing zone, marked the area with a T shape and popped a red smoke canister after sighting the helo for the pilot to be able to judge the wind.

Erik now moved back down the helo to give the precious cargo one final inspection. Checking that the pallet containing the masks was secure he remotely activated the tracking beacon which had been affixed to the inside of the hardened waterproof carbon-fibre case that held the masks, He signalled using two short presses of his helicopter intercom that the pilot should begin to descend towards its target.

Erik hadn't actually been told that he was required to accompany each package, however he wanted to observe at least this, the first exchange, and ensure it went smoothly. Once loaded into the Hilux the relatively lightweight pallet containing 1,000 specially designed masks would be the responsibility of the heavily-armed four man ground team. Two of which carried assault rifles, with the driver and front seat passenger also carrying sidearms.

After having to switch their waiting point to the opposite side of the road, Maria and Andrei had secreted themselves behind a nearby skip, just metres to the side of the broken-down Toyota. As the heat and humidity rose, they were beginning to regret their choice of hiding place.

It was all Maria could do to stop herself from retching as the pungent odours of rancid garbage threatened to overwhelm her. Crossly she glanced across at Andrei, who from his position had a clear line of site over the bridge. "I don't know how you can stand the smell An…" Andrei raised a hand to cut her off. "Listen." he commanded.

Maria strained and at first she could hear nothing but the sound of passing traffic. Andrei looked at her and without speaking swirled his index finger in the air, mimicking the action of a helicopter's blades. Then he pointed with an outstretched hand to the south-east of their position. It was then that Maria could hear the faint, but unmistakeable whoomph, whoomph, sound of the two bladed chinook helicopter.

The winding water of the broad delta acted as a perfect sound board for the helicopter's blades and even though the pair were sat nearly a kilometre away the sound was unmistakeable. Andrei touched his earpiece and whispered to Penny, "the helo is landing, give it five, then switch with Vihaan and try and act like a helpless beautiful damsel needing help from her knight in shining armour won't you."

Penny smiled to herself, "Roger." "Remember keep Vihaan safely inside the truck until we have dealt with the four targets. They will be armed, but they will be unsuspecting as well. Just do as we planned and practiced. Play dumb, allow them to get close to you then stick them in the neck with the syringe. Maria and I will deal with the two carrying heavier weapons riding in the back of the truck."

"Gotya, replied Penny." It was now as she removed the caps on the two syringes she had been given, each containing a strong sedative that Penny began to feel edgy. Signalling to Vihaan that he should get back in the vehicle she stepped outside. As she stepped down from the running board of the truck, her legs nearly buckled underneath her.

'Come on girl get it together, you've got this' she spoke silently to herself. Behind the rank smelling rubbish skip which as the day got hotter had begun to writhe, with the movement of the vermin that burrowed and scavenged for scraps within its depths, Maria and Andrei prepared themselves to take out the incoming vehicle's passengers.

Still strapped into his harness, Erik depressed the large red button hanging on a cable to lower the back doors of the helicopter. Even before the ramp had hit the floor the four men jumped into the back of the helicopter. Once inside, they were greeted by Erik holding a Minimi 5.56 machine gun steadily into his shoulder.

The 200 round magazine bag fitted to the weapon would make short work of the four fragile bodies stood in front of it. All four men surprised by Erik and more than a little angry, slowly raised their hands as Erik pointed a scanner at each in turn.

The scanner read a code from a chip embedded in the neck of each of the puritan missionaries. Once satisfied that these were the correct men, Erik relaxed and simply said "Hi" All four men visibly relaxed and one of them even laughed. "Shit, I thought you were going to waste us for a minute there."

Coldly and without blinking, Erik replied. "I would if you hadn't checked out OK. Take the box, it's light it will only need two of you to lift it. But be careful. You cannot damage the integrity of the box. If any moisture gets in there, you will not live to regret it."

"He was a cheery bastard, wasn't he?" muttered the driver to his colleague in the rear of the Hilux as they drove away. "Who is that guy?" Replied the man in the back. "No idea, but somebody high up trusts him, so I ain't asking any questions." The Box containing the virus-laden masks had been strapped to the flatbed with a cargo net, but considering what the cargo was, the driver wasn't going to take any chances as he carefully drove the vehicle off the hard rutted mud track and back onto the smoother road.

Petrus' normally melodic voice seemed strained as he spoke into his microphone. "The vehicle is approaching the bridge Andrei. They have the cargo in the rear and there appear to be four personnel in the vehicle." "Thanks Petrus, we're ready at our end." "Get yourself up to the Biolab and pray we arrive with the package intact."

Unfortunately for Penny, her lithe legs and auburn hair had been too attractive a proposition for at least one passing motorist, who, began quite quickly to show more than a professional interest in helping her fix her broken down truck.

Although Penny was more than capable of defending herself and incapacitating this unwanted attention, it was down to Vihaan who strode irately out of the passenger side of the vehicle and exploded into a violent rage at the passer-by who he perceived to be molesting his wife. The man quickly slunk back into his vehicle and hurriedly drove off, with Vihaan chasing him some way down the road.

Penny's radio squelched in her ear. "Get Vihaan back here now, the target vehicle is halfway across the bridge. They will smell a rat if they spot Vihaan outside the vehicle, and they definitely won't stop and help."

Vihaan slammed the passenger door shut and sat breathing heavily and perspiring as, glancing in the rear-view mirror he watched as the Puritan vehicle with its hazardous cargo carefully drove over the pothole-filled bridge towards them.

The radio bleeped twice in everyone's ear. The signal to go had been given. Maria and Andrei slowly crawled through the muddy pools of fetid water that had accumulated at the side of the skip until they were just feet from the rear of the puritan Hilux that had pulled over to offer help to what they believed was one of their own vehicles.

"You guys stay here," said the driver to the two heavily armed men in the back of the cab. "John," he said turning to the passenger. "You come with me and let's see if we can help this poor lady out."

With her head hidden by the vehicle's bonnet Penny had begun to sweat. She breathed deeply trying to calm herself and relax her mind for what was about to happen. She held one hand with her thumb on the syringe's plunger covering her right temple, her long auburn hair fell over her hand and completely masked the syringe. The other hand, holding its own syringe, was stuck deep into the recesses of the engine well.

"Say are you new around he....?" The first of the two Puritan's didn't get to finish his sentence as the syringe in Penny's right hand darted out in a blur from behind her hair and expertly found its mark in the driver's neck. Seeing his partner choke and seize his throat the passenger instinctively reached to draw his pistol from his hip holster. Fully committed now, Penny's movements became instinctive.

Instead of stepping back as the Puritan guard had expected, Penny stepped forward and quickly closed the gap between them, her left hand shot out and covered the gunman's hand that was trying to recover his pistol, simultaneously her right arm punched forward and the sharp needle tip found its mark with enough force to bury itself deep into the man's neck.

Both of the Puritan guards in the back of the Hilux cab turned to look at each other as they noticed the first of their colleagues slump to the floor. The larger of the two nodded to his colleague and was just a fraction ahead of him as they both reached for the door handles and burst out of the vehicle.

Like a cat Andrei sprang up from the ground and delivered a straight punch to the larger man's solar plexus as he tried to stand. The man slumped back towards the ground and Andrei quickly slid the needle into his neck and looked across at Maria.

Maria had been less fortunate than Andrei, having had to circle around the back of the vehicle her opponent was already clear of the vehicle and was preparing to place the butt of his rifle into his shoulder when he spotted Maria's shadow creeping around the vehicle.

Turning swiftly and expertly, he levelled his rifle directly at Maria who was still crouched on the floor. "Freeze Bitch." he screamed at her. It was to be the last thing he remembered doing as Maria deftly swept out a leg and viciously struck her opponent in the side of his knee. He screamed as his leg buckled and he collapsed onto one knee.

Now down at the same height as Maria, his face barely inches from Maria's and unable to bring the long barrel of his rifle to bear, he drew his left arm back to strike Maria in the face. Maria's years of combat training with the Secret Service had taught her how to predict and easily evade such a move.

Both now kneeling on the muddy floor and unable to pivot their bodies, it was Maria that took the advantage, as the assailant's huge fist began to accelerate forward from its cocked position, she abruptly drove her forehead straight forward covering the few inches that separated them in a fraction of a second and struck the big man squarely on the bridge of his nose.

Blood sprayed from the man's crumpled nose and immediately began pouring down his face, as he reared back in shock, Maria lifted herself to a kneeling crouch and seizing the big man's chin by his beard, she viciously drove his head sideways slamming it against the side of the car door with enough force to dent the tough metal panel.

The man was still dazed as Maria began to inject him with the sedative. "Better safe than sorry my friend." She muttered to herself as she squeezed the plunger. "Err, if you are quite finished Maria?" It was Andrei, who had watched the whole incident from barely three metres away. "Hey, how long have you been there?" "Long enough to know that you didn't need any help." Andrei replied with a broad smile on his face.

By the time Maria had stood up and wiped most of the mud off her shirt, both Penny and Vihaan were by her side. "What took you so long Maria?" Penny said with a broad smile on her face.

Maria glanced back at Penny, "old beardy here wanted to dance, so we danced!" Finally, Vihaan spoke. "Penny, please remind me, if Maria ever asks me to dance. I must say no."

The group all laughed then Andrei took charge. "OK guys, the clock is ticking. We need to transfer that box to Penny's vehicle and you and Vihaan need to head north as quickly and carefully as you can to the point we marked as our RV." "Sure thing Andrei" said Vihaan as he turned and gingerly approached the hardened plastic container.

"But what if they have a tracking device fitted to the cargo?" "They probably do. It's what I would do. The problem is, we just can't risk opening that box in a crowded place like this to check. We don't know what type of agent or delivery system we are dealing with here and we only want to try and open the box once and do it properly. With luck. Petrus will be waiting in his Hazmat suit and respirator for us at the RV point."

Maria and Andrei waited several minutes before setting off after Penny and Vihaan. Despite having the AC cranked up to full, perspiration streamed down Vihaan's face and his shirt clung to his chest. He was sat bolt upright in the driver's seat, staring fixedly out of the front windshield. "Vihaan, you must try and relax." said Penny "We've got over 70km to travel on these roads until we get to Moamba."

"I'm trying Penny, but just knowing that I am sitting just one metre away from an unknown and unstable bioweapon is making me kind of edgy you know." "I get that but if you relax you will…Watch out!" Vihaan wrenched the wheel violently to the left to avoid the cow that had just wandered onto the road in front of them.

"Err, as I was saying, if you relax a little and turn your head from time to time to look sideways and use your mirrors, we might manage to get to the bio lab in Moamba in one piece and without turning any wildlife into hamburgers!"

With great effort he forced himself to breathe deeply and forcibly lower his shoulders and relaxed back into the vehicle's seat. Sheepishly he turned to face Penny, "Sorry, I got this. What is the plan when we arrive in Moamba?" "At this rate we will be there by

5pm and I am hoping Petrus will be waiting for us all suited and booted in full Hazmat gear, then we can distance ourselves from that thing behind us."

As they left the suburb of Boane behind them, they passed by a Mozambiquan military camp on the outskirts of town, its tin-roofed barrack blocks shimmered in the mid-afternoon sun and luckily for Penny and Vihaan there was no sign of movement around the camp entrance. The road now began to gently curve northwards cutting its path through the red earth and rock. The pick-up left a trail of red dust in its wake as they once again tried to settle into a comfortable speed on the heavily rutted road.

It was Vihaan that was first to comment, "I know we have dirty rivers in India Penny, but just look at the colour of that water over there." The route northwards ran parallel to a narrow meandering river, the dull grey water churned past them as they headed northwards. "You would have to pay me a lot of money to swim in that, never mind drink from it." said Penny.

Vihaan approached a small bend in the road and slowed as they carefully took the corner an enormous opencast copper mine came into view. Laying between the road and the river, the gouged and rutted earth cut like a scar through the otherwise lush and verdant landscape. "I guess we now know why the water is so dirty" said Penny half to herself.

Just then the radio squawked in her ear. "Guys, we just caught sight of you rounding the corner, we are about 700m behind you following your dust trail. The coast looks clear for now." "Roger that Andrei, we are just admiring man's awesome efforts to destroy and pollute the environment up here. My ETA is still 1700hrs." Penny released the PTT button and glanced back towards the river.

"Wow, Vihaan, look at the river now." What previously had been a dull grey sludgy lifeless channel of water had now transformed into a lively bubbling emerald green river that cascaded and meandered its way through the stark red earthen channel. "Wow what a difference. It's incredible" exclaimed Vihaan as he swiftly turned his attention back to the road.

"Say, Penny, I can't see Andrei's headlights anymore in my rear-view mirror." Penny glanced over her shoulder as she pushed the radio to talk. 700 metres further back, Maria jumped quickly out of the back of their vehicle and released the latch on the hardened drone case, strapped to the back of the vehicle's flatbed.

After giving a quick visual check to the three neat rows, each containing 10 mini drones tightly nestled in its own section of laser cut foam, she quickly reached into the box and grabbed the drones' remote controller.

As she slammed the passenger door shut Andrei punched the accelerator hard with his foot and slew the truck back onto the road. Pushing the PTT button on her radio Maria answered Penny. "Penny, we have company. We just stopped to prepare our counter measures. We are catching back up now. You have a chinook helicopter heading from the east vectoring onto your vehicle. They have picked up the tracking device and are using it to hunt you down."

Vihaan's face instantly drained of colour. "We have a helicopter hunting us while we sit in a truck full of the black death or God knows which virus?" Calmly and efficiently, Penny turned in her seat and glanced out of the rear window, pulling her Glock pistol free from its holster as she did so. "Andrei, I read you loud and clear, just hurry up and close the distance. I don't see my little 9mm pea shooter being too effective against the sort of firepower they may have inside that thing, do you?"

"Vihaan, we are still all good, try and relax and continue driving, as of yet, nothing has changed." "Do you think we will make it there before the helo arrives?" "Honestly? No, that thing will be moving at nearly 300kmh, and we are doing what? 60?" "OK you are not helping to relax me here Penny." "Sorry, Vihaan but it gets worse I am afraid."

Vihaan just turned and stared blankly at Penny momentarily. "They will probably land on the road in front of us. The downdraft from the twin rotors will kick up a ton of dust and you won't see anything. If you don't stop immediately and get too close to the helo, then the power of the rotors will flip us over."

"Freaking hell Penny, couldn't you try even a little white lie just for me." "Sorry Vihaan, it sounds bad, because it is bad, but we have a surprise that they don't know about."

Penny's voice was drowned out as the huge helicopter made its first pass low overhead, the vehicle rocked wildly from left to right and Vihaan struggled to keep it on the road. "Shit Penny what do we do?" "Just keep driving until they force us to stop."

As the huge green hulking frame of the helicopter passed slowly overhead both Penny and Vihaan peered silently into the rear door. Like a huge mouth it gaped at them, hidden in its dark recesses Penny could just make out a small human shape, swaying with the movement of the helicopter.

Penny was trying to work out how anybody could stand upright in a helicopter moving at such speed. Just then the sunlight flashed off the pintle mounting embedded in the base of the open door. Then all was clear. The small human shape was sat cross-legged and appeared to be tethered by some sort of strap. His hands were clasped in front of him onto the two-handed grip of a very heavy machine gun, which right now was trained directly at them.

500 metres further back, Andrei veered his vehicle sharply off the hardened road surface and Maria cried out in pain as her head hit the vehicles roof. "Fuck me Andrei, you are going to pay for that." Andrei, smirked as he swerved the vehicle hard to the right again and joined one of the myriad of smaller mining tracks that ran parallel to the main road.

Maria was fully focussed on powering up the drone remote control. Andrei gunned the engine harder, and the little Toyota land cruiser sped forwards through the dense brushland past Penny's vehicle until it was just out of the line of sight of the helicopter.

"Now Maria, release the drones." shouted Andrei. Each of the identical mini drones sat in its own individual bay within the container. Securely coiled in a neat ring around the body of each drone was a thick plastic strip looking more like a thick strip of liquorice, than the deadly strip of dark grey plastic explosive that it was.

Each explosive strip was attached to the drone by an electric detonator that could be activated and fired from the control set. Beneath each of the foam cut outs sat a small propellent charge that fired the cluster of 30 drones high into the air, giving them an initial inertia and allowing the drones time to power-up and communicate with each other like a swarm.

Now that Maria's vehicle had come to a halt and stopped its violent bouncing, she could finally view the camera screen on the controller, she had divided the drones into three mini swarms of ten drones. This was the interesting part for Maria. From now on the artificial intelligence in the drones would have as much control and decision-making capability as Maria herself.

Having pre-determined the drone groupings, the last thing that Maria did was to command the drones onto specific attack vectors, then reluctantly she stopped fingering the joystick and sat back and watched the screen intently.

Having completed her targeting sequence, Maria glanced up briefly to find Andrei leant hard over the bonnet of the Hilux, his muscles strained as he adjusted the rifle's sling and pulled the weapon firmly into his shoulder.

"Brake, Vihaan break!" Penny shouted as the huge aircraft swooped once more overhead then flared violently pointing its nose abruptly upwards towards the sky before beginning descent eventually landing and settling onto its haunches like a huge preying mantis.

As usual in such situations, Erik's mind was in another state entirely. He was recalling a time in South Africa, he was sat on a rocky ledge high in the Drakensberg mountains on a cold winter afternoon with his Uncle. They had been hunting a magnificent old Nubian ibex for several days and now they found themselves finally sat staring down at the animal, who, in its nearly exhausted state had stopped running and had now turned to stare up at its tormenters.

Bringing himself back to the present, Erik tightened his grip on the 50 calibre machine gun and began applying just enough pressure to the twin triggers. At the same time the first futile rounds from Penny's pistol began to ping off the aircraft's fuselage. The effect of Eric's opening burst however was far more dramatic. Deliberately aiming just to the right of the vehicle, he let loose with a vicious four round burst, walking the heavy barrel of the gun towards the target as he fired.

The thunderous noise and intense vibration as the heavy depleted uranium rounds ploughed into the hard red earth around the vehicle was totally debilitating, both Penny and Vihaan shrunk down into the footwell of the vehicle and began to pray.

The final round struck the front driver's side wheel, which detonated with terrific force almost crushing the front wing of the car as the heavy rounds ploughed through the wheel and thumped into the engine block. The pressure wave felt by Penny and Vihaan was as if they had been physically punched in the chest.

Both Penny and Vihaan now crouched deep in the recesses of the vehicle's footwell, Vihaan's hand slid instinctively over towards Penny and grasped hers. "Are you hit Vihaan?" "I don't think so." Penny could hear the tremors of fear in his tight high-pitched response.

"Good, sit still, keep your head down and let's hope Maria and Andrei are close by." As she finished speaking, she popped her head up and fired once more emptying the final 6 rounds of the pistol's magazine at the open back door of the helicopter.

Smiling, Erik looked out of the helicopter's gaping doorway and viewed his prey. Through the red dust that swirled around the vehicle, he could just make out two small human forms, hunched tightly into their seats, frozen like rabbits in a car's headlights, He unclipped from his harness, released the heavy machine gun and shouldered his Minimi light machine gun.

'Time to finish this' he thought to himself as he prepared to leave the helicopter. Just as he reached to swipe off his headset, a burst of muffled chat came through the earpiece. Reluctantly he replaced the headset and pressing the Pressel switch, asked for the message to be repeated.

"Alpha 1, this is the pilot. We have a problem here. We have ten unidentified drones at 12 O' clock, in formation heading towards our cockpit. We need to evade. Over." Powerful as the twin engine turboshaft helicopter was, it had no defensive or offensive weaponry at the front. Its only chances of escape was to get airborne and use its limited agility to avoid the drones.

The pilot immediately dismissed this as an option after weighing up the chances of his 50,000 lbs aircraft against the tiny swarm of highly manoeuvrable mini drones in front of him. He could, he thought, release his anti-missile chaff flares, but that would only work if the drones were heat seeking. Just as he came to his decision Erik shouted over the intercom. Spin the helicopter round and I will shoot them.

Maria was watching the whole event on the small LCD display on the drone's control box. Powerless to intervene in the drones' attack, she just hoped that her initial programming of the target vectoring was a good enough plan to at least get Penny and Vihaan away from the maniac who had been ripping chunks out of their vehicle with his 50 cal.

Peering through his sniper scope, Andrei followed the helicopter's reaction to the drone threat approaching the cockpit. "They are turning to engage the first group of drones. I don't think they have spotted the others yet." "Roger that," replied Maria, still staring fixedly at the tiny LCD screen.

Her initial input had defined the groupings and instructed one group to attack the front windscreen of the helicopter, the tiny explosive charges carried by each drone, probably weren't powerful enough to damage the windscreen, particularly in such an open space where the blast would quickly dissipate, however it had been planned as a diversionary attack.

Simultaneously she had programmed the other two groups of ten drones to attack the heat source pouring out of the twin Lycoming T55 turboshaft engines, mounted aft on either side of the rear pylon.

The only instruction she had given these two groups of drones was to approach from above and from either side, exactly how the drones would achieve her instructions and how they would react to the evasion measures of the helicopter was all down to Charu's complex algorithm.

In lab tests she had 'virtually' trained the drone swarms using machine learning to act out thousands of different scenarios based around 20 pre-programmable attack solutions. Following a series of basic rules, the complex interaction between the drones was now in full evidence as the three distinct miniature swarms danced and wheeled their intricate choreography in the sky above their heads.

Pushing the send button on her handset once more Maria spoke. "Guys, sit tight, Andrei is observing and ready to engage if necessary. The drones are airborne now and I'm afraid we have to leave it up to the robots. I guess we will see just how good that cousin of yours is with this computer stuff now won't we Vihaan."

Squashed down in the recesses of the foot well of the Hilux, Vihaan glanced over at Penny. Penny, thought she saw a flicker of a smile pass over his pale face. Hoping she sounded more confident than she felt, she said "It's going to be OK Vihaan," Penny whispered to him. "If Charu programmed those things, then nobody can beat us."

Just then the whole sky seemed to erupt with a deafening boom. Penny risked a glance over the dashboard and out of the cracked front window. The helicopter had lifted slightly from the ground and was rotating. The man in the back was being shaken about violently as he sprayed huge quantities of copper tipped lead rounds into the air at the ten loitering minidrones. The nearest drone was struck, detonating the plastic explosive as the bullet impacted with its plastic casing.

Frustratedly, after expending 200 rounds in less than a minute, Erik only had one confirmed kill. The tiny black drones were deceptively agile and continuously kept changing their formation to try and minimise their chance of being hit. It didn't help that he was being flung around in the back of the helicopter like a rag doll, as the pilot tried increasingly violent manoeuvres to avoid the drones.

Erik had begun to replace the 200 round ammunition bag on his Minimi when a new idea occurred to him. He had detected a pattern to the drones behaviour. When they were fired upon, they formed an extended line stretching back away from the threat. Effectively making as small a target as possible. Once the drones perceived the threat to have gone away, they moved back into a cluster formation. Eric waited and prepared two hand grenades.

"Alpha 1, this is the pilot. We have to get out of here, if one of those things detonates by my windscreen we could be killed." Erik's voice was cold and detached, he hated fools that panicked as soon as things got hot. "Hold your position. I repeat hold your position. I want those drones a little closer." "Alpha 1, are you…." Eric didn't hear the rest of the blustering pilot's message as he ripped off the headset and crawled forward towards the edge of the helicopter's loading ramp.

'Closer, closer my little friends'. The drones reformed into their cluster and in what, if it were a human or animal would be described as a stealthy approach, they buzzed slowly closer to the open door of the chinook from just below the helicopter. In turn, the red arming pre-detonation lights illuminated on each of the remaining drones as they began to rise up to the level of the helicopter's large ramp.

In one fluid and well-practiced movement Erik released the fly off levers on the two grenades, calmly waited for a count of four seconds with one of the heavy fragmentation grenades in the palm of each hand, then he released both grenades and allowed them to roll, then drop, off the large metal ramp.

Erik crawled quickly backwards as the outer metal casing of the ramp absorbed the tiny shards of fragmentation released by the grenades. The initial dull crump of the grenade was joined by a much brighter and louder percussion sound as the ten drones detonated leaving only tiny plastic and carbon fibre fragments to tumble and spiral earthwards.

"He's destroyed the first set of drones Maria," Peering through his sight, Andrei had witnessed Eric's remarkably calm and dangerous move with the hand grenades. "This guy has some balls, I'll give him that." Maria clicked the arm button for the remaining two sets of drones then spoke into her microphone. "We have him just where we want him. The first set of drones was a decoy. Something to occupy his attention whilst the other two groups get closer to him."

"I have set the explosives to detonate as close as possible to the major heat sources on the helicopter. Each group is targeting one of the two engines and exhaust manifolds." "Well, whatever they are doing, they need to do it fast Maria." shouted Penny into her mic. "That thing is turning round again and beginning to lower back to the ground. I'm not looking forward to round two of acting as his target." "Roger that, Penny, sit tight and get as low as you can, the action is about to start."

Andrei glanced back through his scope as the first of the drones entered directly into the exhaust manifold of the lefthand engine and detonated, another drone was chopped out of the sky by the heavy rotor blade before it got close. “We scored a hit guys, lefthand engine is on fire.” Penny squeezed Vihaan’s hand hard and in the cramped recesses of the Hilux she could now see him grinning from ear to ear.

Erik was in the action of standing after successfully destroying the first ten drones when the huge helicopter lurched suddenly sidewards, He had unclipped from his harness to throw the grenades and was flung violently like a tiny doll against the helicopter’s fuselage.

The force of the jolt hurled Erik headfirst against thc heavy aluminium cast of the bulwark. His unconscious body slumped to the floor of the aircraft and lay perilously close to the tail ramp, as he lay prone and unmoving on the hard metal ramp of the helos tail lift. The wind soon began to snatch his lifeless form and slowly dragged Erik towards the edge.

The pilot reacted to the loss of power in the port engine by increasing power in the starboard engine and flipping the helicopter strongly back to the right. Erik would never know this, but it was this final manoeuvre that saved him from falling unconscious from the erratically moving aircraft.

Unable, anymore to raise Erik on the intercom and battling to keep the helicopter airborne, the pilot made the decision to disengage from this mad assault and head at full speed to the cargo ship which had the whole time been cruising northwards at 30 knots per hour. As the wounded helicopter limped forwards and regained a modicum of stability, the pilots who were unaware of Erik’s predicament, began to plot their course and calculate their journey back to the ship.

“Skipper, we have a leak in the port fuel tank, I’m going to try and pump to the starboard tank. I calculate we have 45 minutes of flying time at this rate of fuel loss. How far is it to the ship, do we have their position yet?” The pilot who was struggling to keep the helicopter flying in a straight line against the strong north westerly wind, repeated his call to the cargo ship. “I got their position, they are sailing north at 25 knots, if this wind slackens a little we may just make it. But we need to be prepared to ditch in the sea.”

“The captain is reluctant to stop the ship, in these rough seas.

He said he will slow to 20 knots for us to catch up." Pressing the lever to retract the tail lift and prepare the helicopter for a maritime landing the co-pilot looked across at his old friend. "This is going to be interesting my friend. I hope you brought your swimming trunks."

Just then a red light began flashing on his display. The final drone strike had fallen short of its intended target but it had managed to detonate on the tail ramp next to the hydraulic ram, that was used to raise and lower the tail ramp.

"Skip. We got trouble. We can't raise the ramp. We've lost pressure I guess we've lost the hydraulic fluid in the piston. If we do ditch in the sea, then we are not going to be afloat for very long." The captain shrugged his shoulders in a resigned manner and said. "What about that idiot in the back that got us into this mess. Is he still on board?"

Briefly unstrapping and stepping back, the co-pilot spotted Erik's body laying motionless on the bed of the helicopter. "He's out cold and I for one don't have the time or inclination to see to him. He can wait until we land if we ever do land that is."

Efficient as ever Andrei had folded and packed his rifle and scope back into the soft case and was back in the car with Maria bouncing their way back towards the main road where Vihaan and Penny were stood inspecting the damage to their vehicle and more importantly checking if any stray rounds had penetrated the deadly cargo.

"OK guys, good news and bad news." Penny stood hand on her hips, and idly kicking the flat front tyre. "The cargo is intact, thank God, but this pile of junk isn't going anywhere, we need to transfer the box to your vehicle and hightail it out of here."

Maria was already releasing the cargo straps, as Andrei spoke. "I've just got through to Petrus, He's keeping our contact at the bio-hazard centre occupied. I think we'll be good but we need to get their as quickly as we can. They only have a window of an hour after the main day shift leave before they seriously begin to lock down the facility for the night. Our guys need to be in there before that."

As he finished speaking, he reached for the driver's door handle to get in. "No way." Maria said pushing past him to get into the driver's seat. "After the way you bounced me down all those roads back there, it's about time you got a taste of your own medicine." That said she sunk her foot hard down on the accelerator and the whole group were forced back in their seats as Maria slewed and skidded her way back onto the main road. Vihaan turned to glance across at Penny. "I think we may have been safer where we were!" Penny laughed loudly, relieved that the terrifying experience was over.

The pilot and co-pilot had been forced to compromise deciding to spend as much time as possible travelling northwards over the land had meant that now they had to break free of the relative safety that the land afforded them. As they sighted the huge estuary at Beira the helicopter began to precariously limp out over the Mozambiquan coast heading almost directly eastwards towards the container ship.

They first sighted the ship which had been slowly lumbering through the roiling waves in the large channel between Mozambique and Madagascar. Although the sun was behind them and beginning to slowly sink in the western sky, the visibility had deteriorated to the point that the ship was no longer visible by sight alone and the pair of pilots were now flying blind into the intense tropical storm using their instruments alone to find an 80ft by 80ft metal structure that was the only place where the helicopter would be able to land in an area of over 100 square miles.

The co-pilot glanced once more at his cluster of gauges then over at his old friend and captain. The captain knew the reason for the look and stoically nodded his head in agreement. The Chinook had been listing slightly to port and had only slowly been able to crab its way forward due to the wrecked port engine and the huge drag the damaged tail door was creating.

"I am going to radio the ship and tell them to continue at full speed. This aircraft can't make good enough speed against that North Westerly to catch the ship. I will try and raise the Madagascan Coastguard and tell them of our course direction and speed. God willing someone will get to us."

"Roger that," replied the pilot, who checked the zips on his immersion suit one more time, then altered his heading to fly as low and fast as possible towards Toliara on the southwest tip of Madagascar.

As the afternoon squall began to dissipate behind them, the pristine sands of Toliara gradually came into sight far in the distance. The frothy waves that licked and curled over the sharp edges of the offshore reefs became clearer and clearer as the helicopter approached.

"You know we might just do this" declared the pilot. As he spoke a temperature warning light began to flash on the display. "Our starboard engine is nearly cooked. If we can only make it across that line of reefs then we can ditch there in that tidal pool and we will be safe."

As he uttered these final words of hope, the plastic explosive wrapped around the final minidrone that had been chopped by the propellor before falling into the starboard engine cowling, finally reached its critical temperature and exploded.

The aircraft was barely 20 feet above the roiling sea when it was spun violently around the axis of its front rotor blades and the rear of the craft plunged down towards the cruel sea below. The violent rotation had taken the pilot by surprise and both he and the co-pilot were pinned to their seats by the violent centrifugal force like crash test dummies, able only to watch and witness as the rear of the fuselage began to rip open like a tin can as the aircraft was flung along the line of sharp reef crowns.

Later crash investigators and local divers would comment that nobody could have prevented the crash and certainly nobody would have been able to survive the sucking force of the water that flooded the entire fuselage in minutes as the plane scraped and ground its way down the side of the reef to be trapped on the shallow ocean floor for eternity.

It was therefore an equal shock to both Erik and the German couple who were sunning themselves on the small private beach to see a black-clad man raise himself up ghost-like out of the surf and stagger onto the shore. Still dazed and in shock, Erik walked determinedly straight past the gawping German tourists and quickly disappeared from sight into the mangrove forest that lay just beyond the beach.

The violent rotation that had spun the helicopter on its axis had had another effect. It had managed to fling Erik's unconscious body straight out of the rear door and over the reef into the calmer tidal pool beyond. The shock of the impact with the water had woken Erik quickly orientating himself to his situation he struck out with weak but even strokes towards the shore.

Three people, it was impossible to say with any certitude if they were male or female inside their heavily over pressurised bio-hazard suits were waiting to meet the team when they finally arrived in Moamba. As usual Petrus' smile radiated from behind his mask and visor as he strode forwards to greet the team.

Excitedly, he gestured for them to stand clear of the vehicle as the three-man bio team stepped forward with a large bio sample hazard container of their own. Without touching the hardened plastic box, they attached retractable rods to the container and carefully lifted into from the bed of the truck and placed it into the biohazard container. With the pressing of a button the lid sealed tight and the container was locked safely into the pressurised container.

Petrus had continued walking, guiding the team away from the container and to a small door at the side of the main complex. Penny stepped forward to reach for the door handle and Petrus raised a hand in alarm. Speaking through his mask, he motioned for them to enter the room but not to touch anything.

"Guys I am really sorry, but we have to do this. The sample is safe, and we will get it tested and destroy the rest in the incinerator. I will inform CTC HQ when we have confirmed what it is. But for you guys, I am afraid, this next part is a little bit delicate."

"Technically you have to be quarantined and that starts with you all having to remove your clothes in this chamber here, then step through into the next room where you will be cleaned and disinfected. After that you will all be given clean clothes in the final room. Then, I am afraid you will have to wait in their quarantine facility here for 48 hours together whilst we confirm that nobody is contagious."

Surprisingly it was Penny who was the first to begin to remove her clothes. Cheekily she winked at Vihaan, who had begun shuffling towards the corner of the room. "Say Vihaan are you going to scrub my back or shall do you first?"

Chapter Twenty One

restructure [verb]

Definition of restructure

To change the makeup, organization, or pattern of.

- *Is this the time for a massive restructure?*

Despite formally being proclaimed as the new President of the United States, Charles Laurel Henderson still hadn't bothered to move from the Vice President's official residence to live full-time in the White House, and he was using the opportunity this afforded him. Unlike calls made from the Oval Office, calls made from this residence weren't automatically recorded, logged and archived for posterity, later to be pored over by academics and lawyers. Reclining back in his wingback chair and staring out over the grounds of the Observatory, the President listened intently to what Sir David Simmingford-Bell had to say.

"Well Mr President we can now confirm the worst is true. The cargo was intercepted in Mozambique and has somehow been analysed. High level alerts have been sent out across the continent. Unfortunately, our ship was also later seized and impounded" "Don't worry Brother David, it's only a ship. Did they manage to dump the cargo before being captured?"

In a more sombre tone, Sir David steeled himself before delivering the final piece of bad news. "Yes, no trace was left onboard the ship, however there is even more bad news I am afraid. It is believed that all three of our personnel who were in the helicopter that was attacked may have drowned. Recovery work is still ongoing in Madagascar, but up until now they have only found the Pilot and Co-pilot's bodies. We believe Erik was in the back at the time and his body may have been flung far from the aircraft on impact."

What Sir David saw on the video screen unsettled him and caused him to pause fractionally. On hearing that Erik, the son of the President's oldest friend and a martyr to the Puritan cause was probably dead, Sir David noticed only the most incidental of interruptions in the new President's visage, a momentary creasing of his eyebrows and a brief diminishing of his usual maniacal gaze were the only signs that betrayed the merest hint of emotion from the President.

Pausing briefly before continuing Sir David considered what to say next. "Well Brother Charles, the good news is that whoever did intercept our cargo, and we are still not sure who it was, they wanted to remain discreet. We have been checking media feeds about the incident and my agency and our GCHQ have only found a couple of column inches in a short piece in the Kenyan Daily Post about the seizing and impounding of the ship." the President nodded and began to speak.

"Brother David, I think we can relax I don't think we will hear anymore about our failed attempt. We need to focus on the positives and move forward accordingly. The situation is turning in our favour, due to the threat from the EA and our err, few successful interventions in Europe, we have now stopped Europe from fracturing further and have firmly brought the centre of gravity of the EU back towards France. As a bonus we now have more political control over Europe and the UK than ever before."

"I have a meeting this morning and shortly afterwards I will be making a public announcement. I would like you to support me in encouraging the UK government and your cyber guys at GCHQ to follow us on this one and bring yourselves under our umbrella as it were. We have wasted too much time over the last twenty years fighting a foolish War on Terror when we really should have been focussing on the War on Cyber."

Helen Broxton, the National Security Advisor and sole US survivor of the Golf Course massacre had been the only member of staff that newly inaugurated President Charles Laurel Henderson had retained. Like the former President, the supercilious General Hayward who was in the golf cart at the time the EMP was detonated lay in a vegetative state in a private nursing home with no prospect of ever regaining any semblance of normal cognitive functioning. The fawning and ineffectual Chuck Lewis, who's idea it had been in the first place to travel to Mexico and play golf had been the first to go, along with the former Press secretary John Linton.

It was ten minutes to nine in the morning and Helen had learned the hard way that if the President said their meeting would be at 9am, then you weren't expected to enter the Oval office until 9am, not a moment earlier, not a moment later. Currently Helen found herself at the front of a queue of people waiting to enter the Oval Office. The new President operated much differently than the last one she thought to herself. The man appeared to never rest. He was usually at his desk by 6am sharp and didn't leave the office until past nine in the evening on any normal weekday.

Initially, it had come as a huge relief to work for a President that actually drove the agenda, however recently Helen had begun to have some concerns. She looked briefly over her shoulder and glanced down the line at the waiting crowd. It was like the who's who of tech billionaires. Helen smiled inwardly as glancing once more at the group of entrepreneurs, noting that to a man, and yes they were all men, they were all wearing suits and ties.

Wait, was that Ethan Macdonald she could see loitering by the cooler and chatting up one of the female staffers? Wow, even the mighty and powerful Ethan Macdonald had to wait in line for the President.

She wondered to herself, if their looks of discomfort came from being forced to wear a tie, or with the ultimatum they had just been 'encouraged' to sign up to, that would fundamentally reshape their companies' ideology, business model and most importantly their bottom line.

Much of the detail about exactly what had taken place at the San Cabo golf course in Mexico had been quietly hushed up. However, the now infamous video purporting to show the former President and the ex-Chief of the Army hurling insults at the Mexican President had now been proven by the NSA to be a Deep-Fake.

The popular rhetoric amongst all of the talking heads on the weekly news programmes had drawn the same obvious conclusion that Deepfakes, interference in US elections and online newsfeed manipulation by the Chinese government were quite reasonably to be considered as acts of information war against the US and these same talking heads had been calling out the new President to defend America against this manipulation.

After the murder of US President in Mexico, the US had instinctively placed itself on an informal war footing. The new President, who was well-known on both sides of the aisle had worked swiftly to use this new state of alarm to his advantage and make both the state of emergency and his own tenure more permanent and legal.

He had actually managed to unify the famously fractious US political divide, temporarily at least, to focus the country's efforts on what he called the greatest threat, both internal and external to US security since Pearl Harbour.

This had meant invoking the Defense Production Act and through the clever manipulation of the War Powers Resolution, an act originally designed to limit the power of the US President to unilaterally declare war, President Charles Laurel Henderson had managed to convince Congress to declare war on cyber criminality.

The Bill had been passed unanimously and was more commonly referred to as the Fake News Bill. More importantly, at the same time, using the argument that until the US was confident that no external power could interfere in domestic elections then the new President, President Charles Laurel Henderson would remain in office until it was deemed safe to hold elections free from interference by outside States.

At five minutes to nine exactly the new President strolled past the collected mass of Silicon Valley's finest minds, looked on imperiously as the Head of the NSA and CIA parted way subserviently to allow him to pass unimpeded through the door and into the Oval Office. The President, sat into his deep leather chair behind the ornately carved Resolute desk, leant back, closed his eyes, smiled and inhaled deeply.

If, or rather when, this meeting went as he planned he would become the most powerful person in US history, maybe even the world. With a start he sat forward abruptly in his chair and fixed his steely gaze on the trio of portraits on the wall opposite him. There in front of him Jefferson, Washington and Lincoln stared back at him, in, what to the President's mind at least, they seemed to be smiling back at him with mute admiration. "Enter!" he bellowed, standing stiffly to welcome the group as they filed docile like lambs to the slaughter, into his office.

Helen had been feeling more and more uncomfortable over the past few weeks. As the National Security Advisor, she had been extremely busy coordinating the US reaction to the announcement of the formation of the EA and dealing with the effects of the President's murder. It was like trying to herd cats, she had been heard to say in several of her recent vents of frustration and anger.

Space and Cyber had been officially accepted as defence domains by the USA for several years now, but only token efforts and funding had gone into establishing true defensive capabilities and virtually nothing had gone into creating any offensive capabilities. Helen was a libertarian at heart and as a non-elected official, she had worked for both Republican and Democratic Presidents. The step she was about to make now went against everything she believed in.

The new President had promised the US people at his swearing-in ceremony that he would do everything in his power to restore democracy and in a subtle twist to Elmer Davis' famous words, he boldly proclaimed that he would make America 'once more the land of the free by being the home of the brave'.

This meeting and the subsequent announcement was to be the President's flagship policy and strategy against the Eastern Alliance and would ensure his re-election by the American people. It would also quite deliberately serve a far darker purpose.

The President began the meeting by introducing the new head of the NSA, Mitch Downey. A relative outsider to Washington, Mitch had been a long-time friend of the President from Boston and was known to be extremely conservative and very religious.

Somebody who needed less of an introduction, a Silicon Valley legend and wild child turned good, was Ethan Macdonald. Pointing over at Ethan, the President said. "I'll let our newly appointed Special Envoy for Cyber Security take you through the proposal. I am sure he can speak your language better than I can."

"Thank you, Mr President," Ethan stood as he spoke and turned to survey the collected group of entrepreneurs and government security specialists. "$13.7 billion, $600 billion, $10 billion." He paused briefly and glanced around the room. He had no notes, no charts or screen, as with many such talented people with an off the charts IQ, he could simply engage an audience and speak to them.

"$13.7 billion is lost each year to ransomware attacks on the US, most of these attacks come from either Russia or China. $600 billion is lost in Intellectual Property theft, the bulk of this going to China. $10 billion dollars per year is what I have calculated the US will need to find in order to fund the Great Atlantic Firewall and finally and irrevocably begin the Balkanisation of the internet."

The tech guys, began to look even more uncomfortable, some reflexively reached to loosen their ties. "Under the Defense Production Act, the President is using his authority to ask, or maybe I should say, instruct your companies, to work in the interests of the US government and against the interests of foreign powers. As of today, we will be asking the entire tech sector to comply with the following."

To a silent room, Ethan then read out a long list of conditions that the companies would have to comply with. Notable amongst the conditions were that all servers and data storage had to be moved to US soil and that the NSA would be allowed access to data in the interests of national security to ensure no foreign incursions into the new balkanised US internet.

Chad Vogler, founder of the popular Zapp App, that essentially acted as a portal for everything allowing online payments, social media accounts and food and shopping delivery all to be accessible through one account was the first to stand and vent the frustrations that nearly everyone in the room was feeling.

"That's bullshit Ethan. You've been out of the game for too long, you don't know what you are talking about. You can't make demands like this!" "Actually Chad, we can. You see from this point forward your company will either sit on our side of the Firewall or the Chinese side. You make the choice." Chad physically recoiled as the force and implication of Ethan's threat struck him like a punch to the nose.

Ethan noted the effect of his words and seized the opportunity. "Oh and by the way, I have kept my hand in since I left the Valley. My new quantum encryption will be used to secure the Firewall and to create safe data access between the government and all the companies inside the Firewall." Firmly put back in his chair Chad sat back down and like a scolded child stared broodily down at the floor for the rest of the meeting.

Not even Helen knew the dark depths to which the President intended to exploit the new bill. Only three people in the room new the full depth and ramifications of the new Fake News Bill. Those people were the President, Ethan Macdonald and the newest Brother to join the Puritan Society: Mitch Downey the freshly appointed head of the NSA.

As part of the verification program that each company who wanted to operate within the Great Atlantic Firewall would have to undergo, a very small and classified section within the NSA, in coordination with Ethan was going to scoop vast volumes of data and begin to establish lists by subject category.

The subjects, according to the President in a secret memo, were lists of those people deemed to be a threat to the moral fibre and being of US Democracy. Amongst these categories were Pro-abortionists, Muslims, people with Chinese or Russian heritage and LGBTQ activists.

delta [noun]

Definition of delta

A nearly flat plain of alluvial deposit between diverging branches of the mouth of a river.

Mathematics:The incremental change in a variable.

- *The Mississippi delta.*

The sludgy brown and green waters of the Lagos lagoon whose interminable flow between the Gulf of Guinea and the endless series of creeks and estuarine waterways would, under normal circumstances, ensure a richly diverse and well sedimented coastal front teeming with life.

However, this was Nigeria after all, as well as transporting tons of mineral rich sediment and depositing it into the sea, the waterways that seeped insidiously out of the Lagos Lagoon and into the Gulf of Guinea also dragged with them untreated sewage, dirty tar-like crude oil and piles of discarded plastic.

The lights had been dimmed in the COBRA Room as the Prime Minister the Foreign Secretary, the Head of MI6 and the Chief of the General Staff watched the helicopter live-feed of the highly polluted effluent-rich water oozing out onto the beaches and Nigerian shoreline. “It’s bloody disgusting. If you ask me the Russkies are welcome to it.” The Foreign Secretary verbose as ever was only articulating what most in the room were thinking.

It was at the very moment the Foreign Secretary turned from the screen to rearrange some of his papers that the helicopter panned back from the Nigerian coastline and revealed the whole picture. Removing his spectacles and dropping them in surprise onto the highly polished conference table, it was the Chief of the Defence Staff who spoke next.

“No, that simply can’t be. It’s one of those fake thingamajigs.” Still without spectacles and apparently unaware of anyone else in the room he stepped right up to the screen and started to almost physically caress the three long matt-black objects.

Displayed on the screen in front of them, standing sentinel in front of the capital of Nigeria were the three largest submarines ever built by any nation on earth. Designated K-329 by the Russian Navy. NATO knew of course that the Russians had been trying to develop such a vessel but according to current intelligence work they had barely begun on the first in class, the Belgorod.

Satellite reconnaissance by the NSA and GCHQ clearly showed it still laying half-finished in its St Petersburg shipyard. Extensive delays due to the crippling tech transfer sanctions imposed by the West and the supply chain disruptions caused by the previous year’s pandemic were the reason for supposed non-completion.

Quietly in the background, Sir David Simmingford-Bell, whose hawklike presence unnerved so many of the other attendees hissed into his mobile phone. "I want every single photo of the Belgorod re-examined and a report on my desk by the time I get back from this meeting."

The head of satellite imagery, who at the time was stepping up to the 5th Tee at the very exclusive St George's Hill Golf Club, should have known better, when he sought to mollify his boss. Certainly C, however I don't see the rush, old Ivan was only halfway through building the bloody thing the last time I looked. "

"Really," whispered Sir David into the phone's microphone, then dropping his voice several tones he rasped, "then why the bloody hell am I sat here watching a live feed of three of the dammed beasts floating outside the port of Lagos?" He finished the call by slamming his phone back down hard onto the desk. The conversation hadn't gone unnoticed by the PM or General Sir Rupert, who was still etching his long bony fingers around the silhouettes of the boats on the large screen.

Ebullient as ever and always keen to see a glass half full, the PM tried to break the silence. "General you look like you have seen a ghost. Surely, we have all seen Russian submarines before?" It was the Foreign Secretary, who was more inclined to the glass half empty school of thought, that rose, walked to the screen and physically turned the by now pale General from the screen to face the remainder of the meeting.

"Rupert, out with it man, out with it." Recovering himself the General spoke in clipped tones even as he spoke, he was withdrawing his mobile from his pocket. "PM, gentlemen, I see three immediate problems, firstly, none of our seafloor sensor arrays, surface ships or submarines picked up any sign of these boats transiting to the area on our screens. Which leads me to believe that their active sonar is as good as my tech whizz's fear it might be."

It is a little-known fact that many areas of the planet's ocean contain deep floating buoys and strings of acoustically sensitive arrays with the sole purpose of tracking the passage of unfriendly nations' submarines.

"'Secondly, I see three boats on our screen and common sense would tell us that you would not leave three such valuable assets as those simply floating in close formation so close to the shore. As I recall the Russians always intended to build four of this class. My suspicions are that the fourth boat has also been completed and is lurking somewhere out there on overwatch."

"Finally, and most disturbingly, as with everything we are witnessing today, it awaits confirmation by our specialists, but if, and just if, the Russians have successfully developed their new missile for this class of submarine, then NATO, at least to my knowledge has no effective counter against it. Now PM, Gentlemen, if you could excuse me for just a moment."

Removing the Foreign Secretary's hand from the sleeve of his Service Dress jacket the General began to dial. The PM cut in, "Err General is there something we are missing?" The General replied even as he was putting the phone to his ear. Turning back to stare briefly at the group around the table. "Only that one of our subservice nuclear deterrents, a Vanguard class nuclear submarine which may or may not be carrying Trident nuclear missiles, may or may not currently be operating off or near to the West coast of Africa."

Russia had been quietly pursuing its own more subtle and vastly more strategic expansionist strategy for nearly a decade now. Far away from the kinetic and destructive assaults on Lithuania and Ukraine, Russia had been quietly rebuilding its alliances and relationships with the post-Cold War African leaders. Some five years earlier work had begun on the first of a series of military bases in the Central African Republic and Egypt, more recently Uganda had supported the building of a Russian Air Base and Malawi had allowed the Russians to build a further military base on the shore of Lake Malawi.

Now, with the formation of the EA and with Sudan, Somalia, Eritrea, Ethiopia, Mozambique and Madagascar joining the other African states, all were keen to receive the latest Russian Air Defence systems and advanced aircraft.

It therefore made sense, reflected Viktor Voronin as he gazed out from his perch high up on the massive conning tower of the Belgorod, that he, the President of the Russian Federation should be the one to oversee the signing the Eastern Alliance accession papers and not his useful but nevertheless overbearing and increasingly arrogant Chinese partner.

It was a bleak and depressing sight indeed he thought to himself as he stared at the turgid waters of the Nigerian estuary. Constructing the new oil terminal and building out the pipeline infrastructure would be a very lucrative contract indeed for his government and once this Russian infrastructure support reorganised and streamlined the Nigerian oil production capability, then the EA would have an alternative source of fossil fuels to help with the industrialisation of Africa.

Some of the money so gratefully received from the Chinese for the land sale in Siberia had already been put to great effect. It had allowed the Russian admiralty to accelerate the building of their K-329 program and its newest potent nuclear-powered underwater Poseidon torpedo.

A weapon, unique in the history of weapons. It was capable of targeting and laying radioactive waste to any target in a radius of up to 500km. Better yet, the torpedo travelled along the sea floor and its launch was all but undetectable to hostile observers.

However, for the Russian President his country's greatest achievement had been to build the submarine in complete secrecy and to conduct the most successful Maskirovka deception the world had ever witnessed. His long-time friend and closest confident Grigori Grigorovic Popov, the Head of Russia's Intelligence agency the FSB had personally overseen the deception operation.

A complete mock-up of the building works had been built at the St Petersburg dockyards where according to media sources leaked by his own agency the nearly 190 metre long nuclear powered and nuclear torpedo-capable submarines were to be built.

This fake dockyard which the President knew was observed each day by passing US National Reconnaissance Office satellites received regular deliveries of raw materials, had its own inevitable social media post leaks and even a much publicized strike by the workers who complained of poor and unsafe conditions during the recent pandemic.

What the western observers failed to notice was that seven time zones further east and over ten thousand kilometres away, work was forging ahead at a furious pace on the concealed construction of not one but four of the giant submarines simultaneously. These were the sister ships to the Belgorod, the Novosibirsk, Omsk and Yekaterinburg and all of them now sat sentinel in full view of the world off the west coast of Africa.

The embarrassment that this action alone would cause western intelligence agencies and the fear it would strike into the minds and hearts of Western Alliance militaries had been worth the price, reflected Viktor Voronin as he scaled the final few rungs of the internal ladder leading out of the large cupola and into the bright African sunshine that illuminated the glistening superstructure of the submarine.

The now famous Sinews of Peace speech delivered on March 5 1946, by Winston Churchill at Westminster College Fulton Missouri, was delivered just six months after the formation of the United Nations and more importantly, it was made in a new world order, where to the western world at least, the USA had grown to an unassailable position of political and economic dominance over all of the former European Empires that now lay shattered and crumbling after six long years of war.

It was also the speech in which the famous British orator declared that in respect to Europe "From Stettin in the Baltic, to Trieste in the Adriatic, an iron curtain has descended across the continent," a point in history from which the Soviet Union had also begun measuring the official beginning of the Cold War.

Timing was everything and it hadn't taken too long for the Russian and Chinese cyber units to piece together what this current, somewhat weaker, and reactive US government was about to declare. For Russian President Victor Voronin it was simply a media opportunity that could not be missed.

Deliberately mis-citing Britain's most bellicose and popular wartime leader, Victor Voronin held a brief press interview from the enormous conning tower of the Belgorod. He exclaimed, whilst peering imperiously skyward directly into the news helicopter's camera lens, that with much sorrow 'a Digital curtain has descended between continents'.

Incidentally, it also hadn't taken long for the soon to be balkanised social media platforms to produce Deepfakes and memes of the Russian President dressed in Churchill's famous black Homburg hat, clutching a fat cigar to his mouth with his right hand and displaying the reverse of the famous Churchillian peace sign with his left hand. Assembled on the bridge of the conning tower around the Russian President were the Presidents of the latest ten African countries who had elected to join the Eastern Alliance.

empire [noun]

Definition of empire

A major political unit having a territory of great extent, or a number of territories or peoples under a single sovereign authority.

- *The days of the Empire are long gone.*

Zhang, no stranger to symbolism himself, was dumbstruck when he was handed a red embossed formal invitation card to meet with the Chairman of the Standing Committee of the Chinese Committee Party inside the Forbidden City.

Exiting his office in the Great Hall of the People, he found the official limousine which was waiting for him on the edge of Tiananmen Square. Red pennants marking this car out as no less than the Chairman's own car, swirled and fluttered as the driver processed at a glacially ceremonial pace through the deserted streets past the Monument to the People's Heroes.

The short 15-minute drive on roads cleared specifically to allow his vehicle unimpeded access felt to Zhang like he was being transported back in time. Leaving behind the edifices and temples that had been built or in some cases, redesignated to glorifying the brutal Communist struggle of the 20th Century, Zhang found himself wondering what the old man had planned. Was he about to unveil a new display in the Palace Museum? Or did China's new President have other more sinister plans in store for Zhang?

Inside the Forbidden City, the vehicle slowly drew to a halt in front of the huge Pagoda that is the Palace Museum. The sheer scale of the Forbidden City and this building in particular, never ceased to awe and at the same time intimidate Zhang.

Unusual, Zhang thought, where were all the tourists visiting the museum. The museum was one of the most visited sites in the country by local and foreign tourists alike. It was a place where many came to marvel and learn about how mighty the Chinese Empire had actually been.

Four plain clothes State Security Officials met Zhang's car and quickly formed a box around him effectively herded Zhang up the vast stone stairway towards the main entrance. It was a hot day and despite an intensely dry mouth, Zhang had begun to perspire as the security detail hurried his approach to the entrance.

Zhang was a political survivor and none of his well-placed group of informers and moles had reported anything unusual to him. 'Was this how it was, when you fell out of favour?' he thought to himself as he neared the top step. By now rivulets of sweat were flowing freely down his back inside his shirt. Was this to be the last time he saw the sun and smelled the polluted Beijing air?

Zhang slowed his pace as much as possible and peering backwards over his shoulder and glimpsed up at the shining sun that cast its light and warmth over the huge square below. He stumbled slightly and reluctantly turned his head away from the glowing orb to focus on the last few stairs.

The four-man box steered Zhang to the threshold of the main entrance then, as in a perfectly executed drill movement the lead agent stepped smartly to one side and Zhang was propelled by his own momentum into the Grand Entrance.

The contrast of the darkened entrance with the bright warm sunshine outside temporarily discombobulated Zhang and he rubbed his eyes quickly to try and restore his vision. As he did this, he heard a slow hand clap from over his right shoulder. The clap was accompanied by a child-like sniggering that seemed vaguely familiar.

"Your face Zhang." sniggered the older man's voice. "Priceless. You looked like you were going to cry and wet your pants!" This time the high-pitched sniggering voice was accompanied by a maniacal laugh.

"Chairman. Is that you Chairman?" Straining to adjust his vision, Zhang could just about make out the thin reedy shape of the Chairman of the Standing Committee of the Chinese Committee Party, dressed in his formal Mau suit and beaming from ear to ear.

"I am sorry my old friend, I just couldn't help myself. I wanted you to be the first to see the fruits of our labours." 'Had the Chairman finally gone mad', thought Zhang to himself as the Chairman led them through the now practically bare entrance hall.

Zhang knew from previous visits that this area would on any normal day, be teeming with tourists poring over the trove of treasures to be found within. The Chairman stepped aside to reveal two solid gold Chinese characters on prominent display. They stood four feet tall and had been mounted on intricately carved Jade pedestals.

The two characters 先手 represented Sente the ultimate strategy in the game of Go. The characters shimmered and almost appeared to glow with their own luminescence catching and reflecting every small ray of light that shone towards them.

The Chairman gave his protégé just the briefest of moments to admire the characters before striding off briskly towards a side door. "Come now Zhang, we have work to do, let's begin with some tea in my office, shall we?" 'Your office?' thought Zhang.

There hadn't been a functioning government office in the Forbidden City since end of the Qing Empire which had collapsed during the Chinese Revolution in 1912. Dumbfounded and completely lost for words Zhang followed on behind Zhao, zigzagging their way through the labyrinthine maze of corridors until they reached two large wood-panelled doors which swung silently open as Zhao approached them.

The office was a complete replica of the Chairman's old office in the Hall of the People, thought Zhang, even noticing the ugly teapot that was sat next to the low ornately carved table. Over by the window, which had one of the most magnificent views in China,

Zhang watched Zhao as he stood.

His boss' posture was now erect, observed Zhang. He carried no trace of his usual hunched demeanour. The Chairman was staring fixedly out across the courtyard towards the magnificent Gate of Heavenly Peace. In his hands he clutched a fist full of highly polished red Go counters.

The only disturbance to this very Chinese scene in front of him emanated from the wall-mounted television that beamed silent images of the Russian President sat in his giant submarine off the coast of Africa. The aromatic flavours of the spiced green tea were percolating through the air and ever so slowly beginning to calm Zhang down.

Zhao moved sideways from the window and stood in front of the beautifully carved Go board with its red and black polished pebbles neatly arranged on its surface. Removing the first of the ten red pebbles from the pocket of his Mao jacket, Zhao beckoned for Zhang to approach the board.

He began by tracing his bony nicotine-stained finger around the contour of the African continent which formed part of the world map that had been etched into the Go board. He then proceeded to punctuate each of his sentences with the sound of a hard polished red pebble clicking neatly into its position on the Go board.

"500 years of unbroken Imperial rule." clink, "Our century of humiliation." clink, "Extortion and addiction by the British." clink, "Subjugation and rape by the Japanese." clink, "Misery and famine fighting the Nationalists." clink, "Communist doctrine with Chinese characteristics triumphs" clink, Zhao continued, now seemingly oblivious to his guest's presence, releasing each shiny red pebble in turn and allowing it to drop lightly but audibly onto the African map etched into the Go Board.

"And finally, The Eastern Alliance, our new era, a new Chinese Empire." clink. After the final pebble had ceased spinning on the board, the Chairman turned, strode across the room and knelt opposite Zhang. 'Did Zhao believe himself to be a new Chinese Emperor? Had the old man finally gone insane?'

As had become customary for their meetings, Zhao lifted the

heavy brass handled teapot and poured tea for them both. Taking the offered cup in two hands, Zhang bowed slightly and settled back on the low divan.

Despite the fact that it had been Zhang who had done most of the work and conceived many of the most important plans, Zhang knew that this was lecture time, the time when his boss, probably the most powerful man the world has ever seen, lectured Zhang on what it meant to be in his position. 'Oh well' he thought as he took the first slurp of his scolding hot tea.

"Let me tell you what it means to have achieved Sente my old friend. Sente simply means that China, or rather the EA has put the WA in a reactive position. For the first time in centuries, the East will be dictating the game to the West."

Zhao jabbed a triumphal finger upwards as he spat out the word West. "We didn't get here by chance though. Only through choosing the right strategies at the right time and sticking with them for many years did we manage to achieve this great position of power." 'Here we go, thought Zhang, this is where he teaches me how to play Go.'

"For over ten years, we have used our One Belt One Road project to achieve our strategy of Connection. Joining up our Asian neighbours and extending trade and communication routes across the globe. Through the expansion of our South China Sea island complex and our alliance of military ports and bases around the world we have achieved the strategy of Cut, putting thousands of miles of ocean between the Western Alliance major members." This strategy, for which Zhang himself had been the architect had been particularly brilliant he thought as he tried a second time to take another slurp of his scolding tea.

Gesticulating wildly with his free hand at nothing in particular, Zhao said. "Imagine the amount of territory that is now effectively under Chinese economic or political control?" The question was rhetorical, and Zhang knew when to keep his mouth shut. Keeping a concentrated and what he hoped looked like an interested gaze firmly on the Chairman, Zhang focused on his tea once more.

"And where we couldn't achieve our aims by diplomatic or economic means. We used the strategy of limited invasion, our limited military operations in Lithuania, Ukraine and Kashmir have created the effective land bridges that we need to secure our Eastern Alliance."

Zhang nodded and smiled obsequiously at the new Emperor. Summoning his most respectful tone he spoke. "A truly masterful strategy Chairman. You have completed the work of a hundred years. The Party is honoured to have you serving us."

Over the lip of his teacup, Zhang noticed Zhao smiling back at him with as ever just the faintest hint of cruelty to his demeanour. "Our work is not quite complete." Zhao stressed and elongated the word quite. "We still have to complete our Cut strategy. Physically and geographically, we have cut up the WA, and thanks to that fool of a US President we now have a Great Atlantic Firewall creating a virtual divide between our cultures. Now all that remains is the final economic cut."

cut [verb]

Definition of cut

To penetrate with or as if with a sharp-edged instrument or object.

Especially:To divide with, or as if with, a sharp-edged instrument.

- *To cut a rope.*

6,000 kilometres away to the south, another Chinese man was updating his own Go Board. Reluctantly Li removed ten more of the grey digital placeholder pebbles and replaced them with new white ones representing yet more African territory that had just signed up to the Eastern Alliance.

Sat in his baggy cardigan, cigarette in one hand and stylus in the other, Li had been updating the Go Board on his tablet with each update immediately captured and displayed on the series of large displays around the CTC.

"I think we are just about there." It was Philippe who had been scraping hard at his pipe bowl whilst Li updated the board who answered. "Where is there, Li?" Now Matthias awoke from his smoke induced slumber. "The bottom Philippe, the bottom."

Li nodded. "I don't think it can get much worse than this. The EA is now dominant and they have very cleverly followed a consistent multi-decade strategy to get where they want to be. They don't actually need anymore land or resources and they know full well that it is going to take years if not decades for the WA to align internally, come up with of a suitable strategy to regain the upper hand and begin to execute it."

"Anyway, as I said I think we are just about at the lowest point." Li quickly filled in the blanks on his tablet. A much battered and bruised India, soon to be the world's most populous nation and a democratic one at that, after its recent crushing defeat and loss of Kashmir, had reluctantly agreed to join the WA, breaking its long history of being a non-aligned state. historic enmity with Pakistan and recent violent history of Kashmir annexation and border disputes with China had finally managed to convince the Hindu Nationalist government to reluctantly choose sides.

"Here look at this." Li showed his tablet to Matthias and Philippe. "Tanzania, Kenya, the rest of littoral states from Zimbabwe, down to South Africa, then up the west coast through Namibia, Angola and Gabon, with the exception of Africa's largest economy Nigeria, all of the North African states excluding Egypt and Sudan." "That's quite a collection and when you add India, it isn't looking too bad is it?"

Philippe was always polite, precise and optimistic thought Li, He couldn't say the same for Matthias. "Most of those countries on the map struggle to generate enough electricity for people to light their homes, never mind build any sort of industry. Many of them also struggle to feed their own populations. They have been reliant on loans and aid for years and now...." Li cut Matthias off.

"Yes, yes, yes, I know all that. It is exactly our challenge now to somehow make the best of what we have. That means after years of promising and failing to 'level up' and share global wealth, we only have one more chance to get it right. If these countries aren't adding benefit to the WA in three to four years' time then I agree Matthias, things look bad, very bad indeed." Philippe stood abruptly, stretched his broad shoulders, stowed his pipe in his pocket and finally spoke. "Well, what are we waiting for The Sahara won't green itself you know."

"Philippe." Li caught the big man's shirt sleeve and bade him wait. "Before we go out there, I just want to let you both know what the Secretary General and I decided regarding our team of Doers and their recent trip to Africa on our private jet." Matthias glanced up at Li, interested to hear what Li had said to the other team members.

"Go on Li tell us, what did you say when you had them in your office?" For once Li looked indecisive. "Well, what can you say to a group of people who took the initiative and saved potentially hundreds of lives and stopped political chaos breaking out in Africa?" "Yeh when you put it like that." said Philippe. Li spoke "They know we are disappointed that they didn't trust us enough to tell us of their plan, but also because of our black name at the moment, their excuse was that they didn't want the operation associated with the CTC if it went wrong."

Both men nodded in agreement. "And the people behind the attempt, this Puritan Society. There are some seriously big names and powerful people on the lists that Charu showed me." Philippe was scrolling through a list of known Puritan members on his tablet and pointing out several key people.

With a weary and resigned look on his face, Li said. "You've heard the expression 'too big to fail' haven't you? Well, the Secretary General thinks that with the precarious position the WA is in at the moment, that these people are simply too systematically important to try and remove." Matthias and Philippe glanced at each other, eyebrows raised.

"Anyway, until we get this new firewall in place. Do you think anybody is going to believe us of all people. Remember we are the CTC, the very same organisation about whom memes were recently circulating purportedly showing us plotting the downfall of Europe. What do you think the response will be if we release this information about a Secret Cabal, a group of the world's most powerful men, assassinating European politicians and trying to kill off many of East Africa's leading political families. Events by the way for which not one shred of evidence exists outside the stolen data that Charu managed to get from the US. What do you think will be said, huh? Remember it is only a couple of months ago that we ourselves were being accused of being a secretive and manipulative cabal plotting the disintegration of Europe."

Chapter Twenty Two

tariff [noun]

Definition of tariff

A schedule of duties imposed by a government on imported, or in some countries, exported goods.

- *America decided to raise tariffs on Chinese aluminium.*

Tensions had been rising for several weeks now around the real elephant in the room. Throughout the maelstrom of historic announcements about territorial divisions and new regional groupings, nobody had been speaking, at least not openly, about the true economic effects this global decoupling was bound to bring with it.

The term domino effect tends to indicate lots of small equally sized actions happening quickly one after another. Up to this point, this may have been a fair description of recent geopolitical events. The long-prophesized political and economic fracturing of the European Union, then the even longer- talked about annexation of strategic land corridors by the Russian Federation.

For analysts and think tanks alike that focussed solely on China's One Belt One Road Initiative, the slow and deliberation agglomeration of political, economic and technological power being ceded to China through its system of development loans and the infrastructure projects it delivered to its near and not so near neighbours could only ever have one outcome.

The problem with forecasting major geopolitical moves is always one of timing. Under Deng Xiaoping, China's guiding philosophy was 'Hide your Strength, bide your time'. The new Chairman, Zhao, would argue that China had been forced to adopt a new strategy not because it was powerful enough or even willing to take on a world leadership role, but rather because the US was sticking dogmatically to a strategy of clinging on to the status quo, as hurriedly thrashed out at the end of the Second World War.

A status quo that had left the US very much the dominant, political, military, and economic centre of the world. In Zhao's opinion, China certainly was now ready to resume a more dominant regional power role after its century of humiliation and the many disasters that had befallen its population during the rise of Communism.

It seemed however that although the US had turned its energies and focus inwards for the past ten years, it was still trying through every prejudicial means possible short of war, to limit China's own regional expansion.

The relative scale of the two countries' population was most definitely in China's favour and although China still lagged just behind the US in several key areas, its rate of growth and development and more importantly, its scale of growth and development, quite simply couldn't be matched by the US. Added to this China wasn't wasting billions of dollars per year on trying to police the entire world with multiple Carrier Fleets stationed around the world.

In Chairman Zhao's mind and according to his Chief Aid Zhang, the West was resorting to gunboat diplomacy once more, however this time unlike Commodore Perry's famous intimidation of the Japanese or the British Gunboat Diplomacy of the Opium Wars, they wouldn't find it quite so easy to sail into an Asian harbour and demand easy trading terms or special Government concessions.

The first Coup de Main had come when Chairman Zhao had taken over the floor of the UN General Assembly and announced the formation of the Eastern Alliance. The geopolitical effects and fallout of this one act, were on a scale with the building of the Berlin Wall and the formation of the Warsaw Pact.

The second Coup de Main, came when China, having consolidated its EA membership, took the fiscal policy step of announcing that tariffs would be levelled against the import of any good or service that was already being manufactured to a sufficient quality and standard within the newly formed Eastern Alliance.

Hotly on the heels of this move came the joint Russian / Chinese declaration that the Eastern Alliance would be seizing the physical and Intellectual Property assets of all western companies based in their territories and that these companies had two months to remove their employees from the Eastern Alliance territories.

As part of this insulating strategy, in one of the most bizarre scenes ever observed, a team of Russian oil engineers onboard a huge salvage ship sailed to within a hundred metres of the 12 nautical miles that are the internationally accepted limit of a nation's territorial sovereignty. And off the coast of northern Germany in the cold Baltic Sea, they began physically ripping up and dismantling the recently built Nordstream 2 Pipeline in order to begin recycling the steel pipes for future projects along the Silk Route.

Western nations and NATO in particular, still cognizant of the sight of three enormous Russian submarines appearing out of nowhere off the coast of Africa were reluctant to do anything more than submit formal complaints to the respective governments.

debt [noun]

Definition of debt

Something owed.

Especially: a state of being under obligation to pay or repay someone or something in return for something given.

- *Shrinking economies mean falling tax revenues and increased debt.*

However, it took a further month for the final coup de grâce to be acted out. It was an action that has been the subject of so much academic research and debate for at least the last 30 years. Could another country establish a financial banking and payment transfer system that would be completely outside of the USA's control and influence?

The answer was delivered like a dagger to the heart, on what later came to be known as Black Sunday. At exactly 5pm New York time, as the Global Foreign Currency Exchange Markets reopened for the week, the National Bank of China began selling its foreign currency holdings denominated in US dollars.

They bought Roubles and Renminbi and transferred the resulting currency into the account of the Eastern Alliance Investment Bank. The strategy was never designed with the sole purpose of realising a good price for the over 3 trillion dollars China held in dollar reserves, rather it was aimed at creating a catastrophic drop in the value of the dollar, to demonstrate China's commitment to a complete economic decoupling and strengthen the value of the Rouble and Renminbi in the process.

Most importantly for the other members of the EA, it would provide sufficient liquidity to the newly formed Eastern Alliance Investment Bank to inspire confidence amongst its EA members.

As with all things done by the Eastern Alliance it had been very well coordinated. Zhang was enjoying one of his very few weekend breaks from Beijing. As he had long promised himself, he had taken one of his junior secretaries to the Party's own exclusive beach resort on Hainan Island.

5pm in New York would mean 5am on Hainan Island. Zhang's main preoccupation at that moment as his lithe young secretary slowly allowed her silk sarong to slide from her pale smooth body, was whether to stay up all night with this heavenly creature or whether to wake up early and enjoy feasting on the dual delights of his passive and very willing secretary and the forthcoming US currency collapse.

'Hmm, problems, problems.' he thought to himself, 'I'm not getting any younger you know'. With that thought he gulped back the last of his amphetamine-laced tea and decided he would try and do both.

5pm in New York was exactly midnight in Moscow. President Mikhail Mikhailovich Voronin had decided to enjoy a glass or two of vodka with his oldest friend whilst watching the US FX market meltdown, before moving onto a softer more sensual dessert. These evenings had started to become a regular event thought Grigori Popov as he deftly cut the wax seal on yet another bottle of the President's Vodka.

He wasn't sure what he was looking forward to most. Watching the final death blows being dealt to Russia's long-time enemy or the dessert course of Katarina and Tatiana who were waiting next door and if he had understood the President correctly, they had a new friend with them tonight, Kira, she was meant to be quite the disciplinarian and both men were looking forward to playing with her.

Just to the North-West of Bryant Square a stone's throw away from Times Square sits a billboard-sized electric sign. It is fastened several tens of feet above the pavement onto the side of the Bank of America main building known as One Bryant Park.

It was first installed in 1989 and ran at almost $3 trillion dollars, roughly 50% of US GDP at the time. As the camera feeds began at 5pm on that auspicious Sunday afternoon the clock stood at over 31 trillion which is roughly equal to 125% of US GDP.

Simultaneously on Hainan Island and in the Kremlin expectant eyes focussed on their trading terminals and on the live feed of the US debt clock. As the markets opened the Chinese immediately began flooding the market with sell orders for their dollar holdings. For the first hour the market seemed to be absorbing much of these sales and the dollar had only lost a little of its value, however there had been a noticeable increase in the value of the Renminbi and Rouble as the demand increased for the currency.

The Chinese strategy had always been to inflict the maximum political and reputational pain on the US. They knew that such trading systems had automatic brakes built into them and that is exactly what they were counting on.

Their aim was to inflict a death by a thousand cuts on the US economy. They were quite happy and committed to continue selling vast quantities of dollars every time the market reopened. Each time the Americans were forced to cease trading would be another bitter humiliation for them.

What happened after an hour of hard selling surprised both the Chinese and Russians. The US Federal Reserve Bank had stepped in to stop the dollar price collapsing and decided to buy-up the US dollars flooding the market. Essentially adding minute by minute to the already huge public debt.

Zhang, who had been dutifully woken in a most stimulating way by his young assistant simply couldn't control himself any longer as the debt clock began spiralling ever faster upwards, the figures, like Zhang's own vision began blurring as he climaxed. Breathing heavily, he reopened his eyes to find the secretary smiling back up at him and a blank billboard where the debt clock had been.

Grigori and Misha had unconsciously been synchronising their drinking, increasing the speed with which they downed their vodka shots in lock-step with the increase in speed of the climbing US debt clock. Tossing his head back to finish another glass Grigori glanced back at the screen, he had been standing at the time whilst reaching once more for the chilled vodka bottle when he stumbled slightly.

Rubbing his eyes and balancing himself on the side of the ornate table he took a second glance at the debt clock. "Misha" "Err, what?" Grigori gave Misha a not too soft kick. "Misha, it worked!!" They've switched the clock off. Both men jumped to their feet and embraced each other warmly. The Russian President held his old comrade's ruddy face between his hands and kissed both cheeks hard. "Now Grigori Grigorovic Popov, now we go and have some fun, yes?"

To say that President Charles Laurel Henderson the 47th President of the United States and the de facto leader of the hastily cobbled together Western Alliance was having a bad week would be a gross understatement. His whole day recently seemed taken up with bitter fights with the Treasury and leaders of the House of Representatives about the Eastern Alliance's unanimous decision to remove themselves completely from the international banking system.

Not only had this been a slap in the face for American leadership and credibility, it had also in one fell swoop, removed the effects of any of the money-withholding sanctions that the US had long placed on countries like, China, Russia, North Korea and Iran.

Several of the Hawks in the Treasury Department had spoken about what would happen if China did the unthinkable and tried to sink the US dollar and the President had made the surprise, but as it came to pass, most inciteful decision that his government would override the usual safety brakes that would automatically kick in if the dollar started to sell of too quickly.

Charles Laurence Henderson wanted the plaster to be pulled

off quickly and to take all the pain at once, rather than suffer the ignominy of death by a thousand cuts as the market was repeatedly opened and then forced to close over several weeks. He had instructed the treasury to buy-up US dollars just as quick as they came onto the market.

The effect he knew would mean a crippling economic blow to the US' pre-eminent economic position. It would mean an immediate increase of ten percent in the US National Debt in a day. But he personally couldn't be blamed, could he? He had only just reluctantly become President.

The President knew that limiting the humiliation and reputational damage, was more important than any short-term economic pain. Nothing worse could be done and now he would use the situation to his own political advantage. The harsh economic times that everyday Americans would face for the foreseeable future would allow his administration to 'reset' the country's values.

He would move America away from its rampant consumerism and get its people to focus on higher values such as a commitment to a strong and, simple faith and a reminder of what good religious Americans can achieve when they are faced with adversity. The President cast his gaze one more time at the portraits of Jefferson, Washington and Lincoln as he rose to leave the Oval Office for the night. 'One day' he mused. 'One day, maybe long into the future, a President will find himself looking up for inspiration in this very office and find himself staring at four portraits of the most important Presidents in US history.' He allowed himself a brief smile as he tried to envisage how his portrait would look next to the three greats.

Epilogue

> ## Simulation [noun]
> **Definition of simulation**
> The imitative representation of the functioning of one system or process by means of the functioning of another.
> - *The scientists developed one model to simulate a full year of the globe's climate change.*

With a worried look on his drawn and tired face, the UN Secretary General gave the order for the exercise to stop at 1700 hours exactly. The CTC team had been running the World Event Scenarios Exercise non-stop for the past 72 hours.

the Combined Arms Staff Trainer (CAST) belonging to the Singapore Defence Force's Training Doctrine Command, looked from the outside like any other shiny corrugated-rooved hangar on the Pasir Laba Army Camp.

As dusk began its insidious creep over the Singaporean Peninsular and the light began to fade, a stream of weary delegates was being disgorged from the CAST building. Among the tired and dishevelled delegates were Ambassadors, Industry Leaders, Government Scientific Advisors and University Professors.

The CAST system, or Virtual Command Simulation Suite in Singapore, is based on the type that western militaries use to test their senior commanders. Innocuous to the outside observer, the inside of such buildings is filled with large planning cells, briefing areas, communication suites and networked systems.

Its accompanying Combined Arms Tactical Trainer (CATT) resembles a series of connected hi-tech shipping containers. Inside each of which are a complete set of controls for different fighting systems.

Charu Usmani, the CTC's technical wizard had developed her own series of complex systems' algorithms. Using these algorithms and with an exercise scenario set up by the CTC's Danish head of anthropology, Matthias Peterson, she had programmed the equipment's suite of virtual applications to act out probable future events, in real-time.

The decision-tree matrix had been based on the decisions made after consulting the group of professional delegates that had been gathered at the request of the UN Secretary General no less. The CTC team had been acting as umpires and adjudicators, each advising on their own personal areas of expertise.

Li Qiang Wu, a man recently made stateless by the Chinese government and the popular Head of the CTC had chosen the exercise start point. Unfortunately, it could have been one of a whole series of threats to global stability such as climate change, mass migration or pandemics.

However, Li wanted a very concrete and localised starting point and also one which had not, up to the time of writing the exercise, actually happened. He selected the potential Russian annexation of Lithuania as the exercise start point.

Charu with the advice of some of the world's foremost experts had programmed a baseline set of scenarios into her complex system's model. The scenarios were basically the extrapolation of current long-term trends that were likely to occur if nothing was done about them.

These scenarios included critical debt default in the EU, the effect on global trade of the Chinese One Belt One Road Project, increased desertification, and the rise of pro-christian militant groups.

Using a relatively simple series of 'What if' and 'Then' rules, her AI program then gamed the flow of events. Critical to the flow of events and to the unforecastable outcome was the interaction of the 'real-time' expert decision makers who had been assembled to 'play the game'.

In the warm Singapore twilight, Mathias, the anthropologist, offered Li, the former diplomat, and Philippe, the larger-than-life Canadian Engineer, a celebratory cigar. Each man, tired to the point of exhaustion, silently peeled the foil covering off the rich Cuban cigars and began gratefully inhaling their first nicotine hit for 72 hours.

The three men sat on the decking of a shaded porch of a nearby building, watching the equally exhausted delegates file out of the huge warehouse-like building and onto the queue of waiting air-conditioned buses.

As the sun began to cast long shadows over the scene, Li glanced across at the other two men, in what he referred to as his 'Thinking Team'. Peering closely at each in turn, he knew they were all wondering the same thing. Could it really all go so wrong so quickly? Would it really spiral so quickly into another bipolar world? And most importantly could their team the Centre for Technology and Culture really be able to deliver on its technology promises so efficiently?

Finally, it was Matthias that spoke. "Well at least we have identified the emerging battlegrounds for the UN Secretary General. I think I will call them the three A's." Without turning his head, Li stole a sideways glance at Matthias. Philippe spoke next. He and Matthias had long been able to read each other's thoughts and communicate without talking.

"Let me guess Matthias? Africa, important as the world's new breadbasket and renewable energy hub?" Through the haze of cigar smoke, Matthias nodded once. "Australia, as one of the only other sources of rare earth metals outside of China and Russia?" Again, Matthias made the briefest of head inclinations.

"And finally, if I am not wrong, the Arctic? The closest point of intersection between Northern Asia, Russia, Northern Europe and North America, abundant in oil and gas and soon, thanks to global warming to be a major freight and container shipping route, saving thousands of miles and many days travelling time off any intercontinental trade?"

Li struggled to his feet and turned and faced his colleagues. "Well, are you two just going to sit there and smoke, or are you going to help me do something about our little three-A problem.

About the Author

Douglas Blackburn, a British author, brings a wealth of diverse experiences to his writing. Having lived and worked extensively across Europe and the Middle East, he possesses a deep understanding of various cultures. With a background in the British Military, he honed his linguistic skills as an Arab linguist and is also fluent in German. Furthermore, Douglas holds an MSc in International Security, enriching his academic knowledge.

In his writing, Douglas Blackburn seamlessly integrates his academic expertise in International Security with the insights gained from his real-life encounters in foreign lands. This book, the second in a series, presents a captivating narrative that explores a potential sequence of events. While the storyline holds plausibility, it serves as just one among countless possibilities in our rapidly deglobalizing world.

Printed in Poland
by Amazon Fulfillment
Poland Sp. z o.o., Wrocław

33092061R00233